SACRIFICIAL PRINCESS AND THE King of Beasts

8

Yu Tomofuji

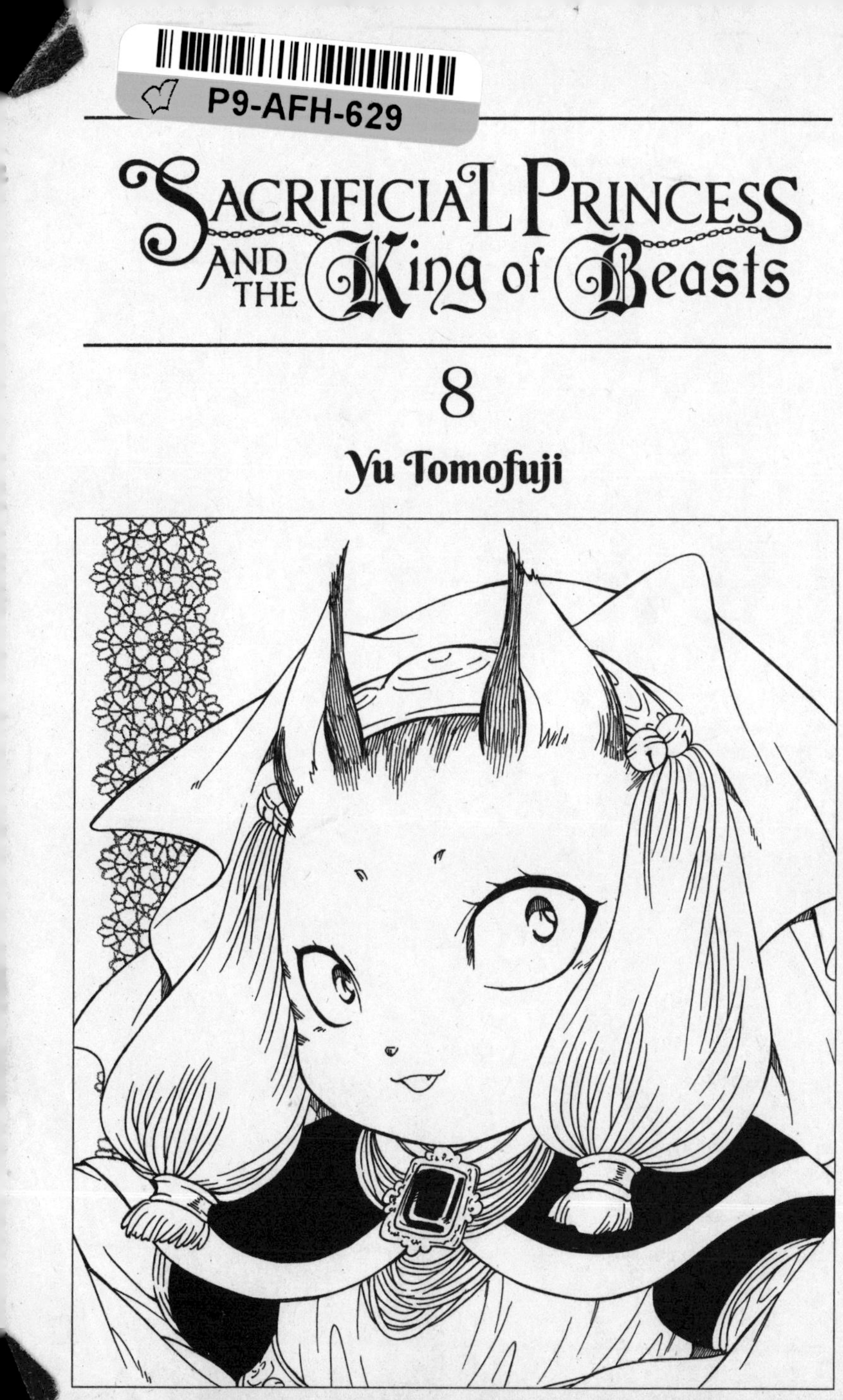

SACRIFICIAL PRINCESS AND THE King of Beasts

8

c o n t e n t s

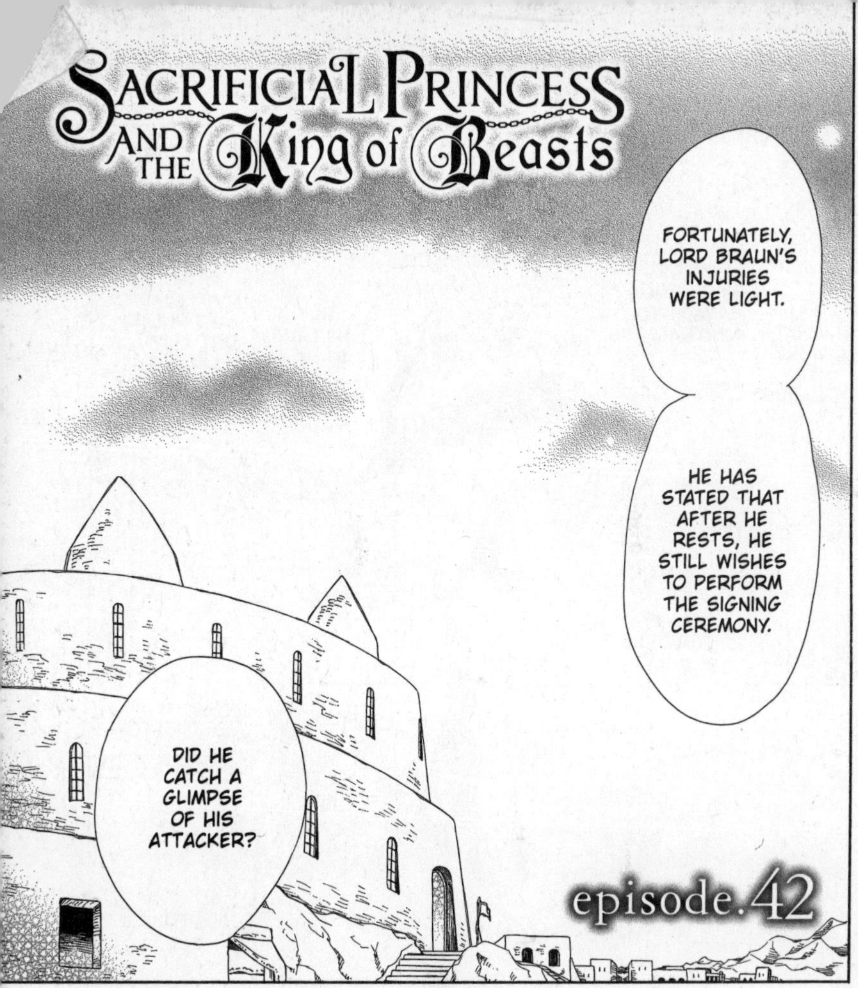
SACRIFICIAL PRINCESS AND THE King of Beasts
FORTUNATELY, LORD BRAUN'S INJURIES WERE LIGHT.
HE HAS STATED THAT AFTER HE RESTS, HE STILL WISHES TO PERFORM THE SIGNING CEREMONY.
DID HE CATCH A GLIMPSE OF HIS ATTACKER?
episode.42

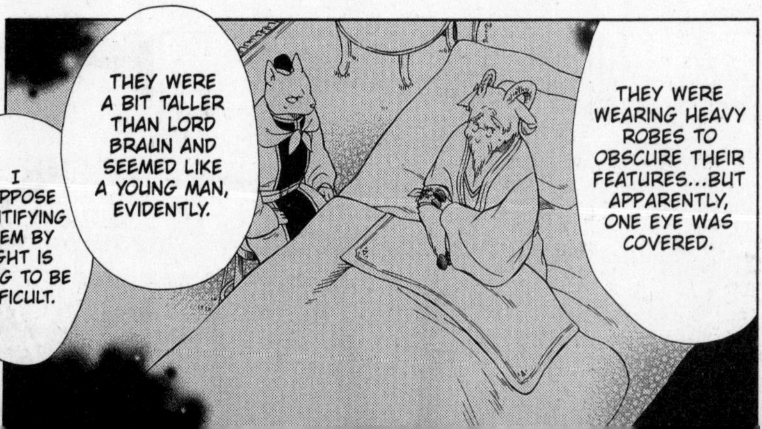
THEY WERE WEARING HEAVY ROBES TO OBSCURE THEIR FEATURES...BUT APPARENTLY, ONE EYE WAS COVERED.
THEY WERE A BIT TALLER THAN LORD BRAUN AND SEEMED LIKE A YOUNG MAN, EVIDENTLY.
I SUPPOSE IDENTIFYING THEM BY SIGHT IS GOING TO BE DIFFICULT.

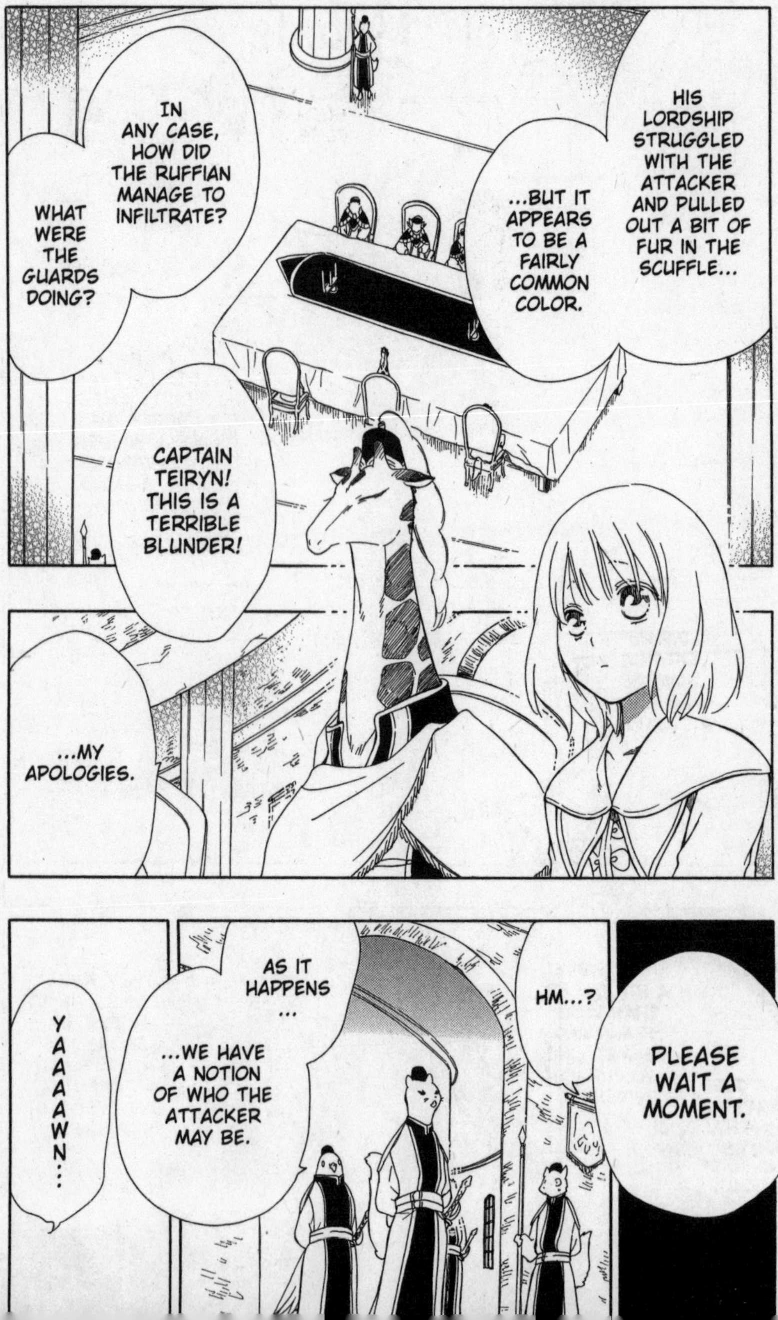
HIS LORDSHIP STRUGGLED WITH THE ATTACKER AND PULLED OUT A BIT OF FUR IN THE SCUFFLE...
...BUT IT APPEARS TO BE A FAIRLY COMMON COLOR.
IN ANY CASE, HOW DID THE RUFFIAN MANAGE TO INFILTRATE?
WHAT WERE THE GUARDS DOING?
CAPTAIN TEIRYN! THIS IS A TERRIBLE BLUNDER!
...MY APOLOGIES.
PLEASE WAIT A MOMENT.
HM...?
AS IT HAPPENS...
...WE HAVE A NOTION OF WHO THE ATTACKER MAY BE.
YAAAAAWN...

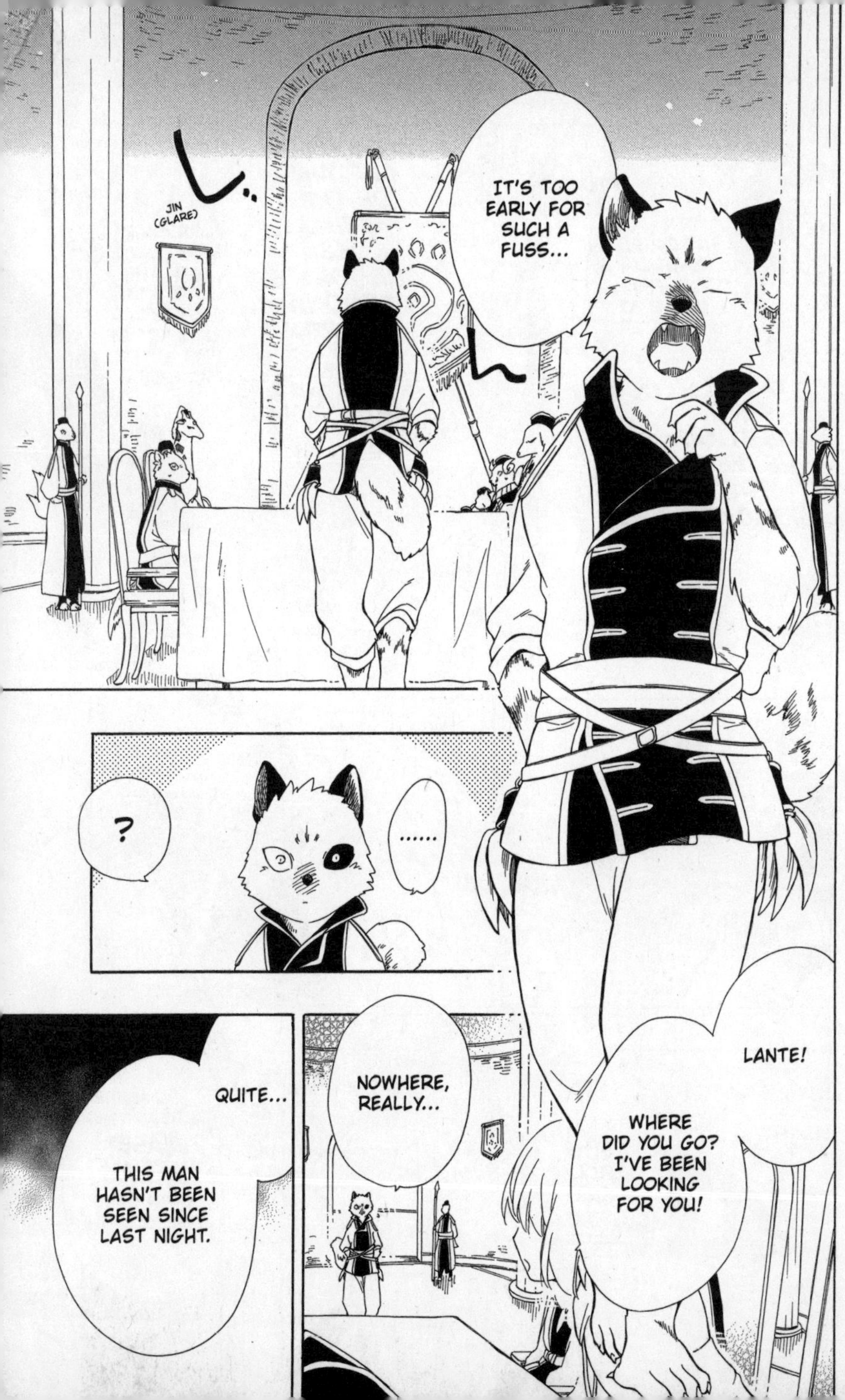
IT'S TOO EARLY FOR SUCH A FUSS...
JIN (GLARE)
......
?
LANTE!
WHERE DID YOU GO? I'VE BEEN LOOKING FOR YOU!
NOWHERE, REALLY...
QUITE...
THIS MAN HASN'T BEEN SEEN SINCE LAST NIGHT.

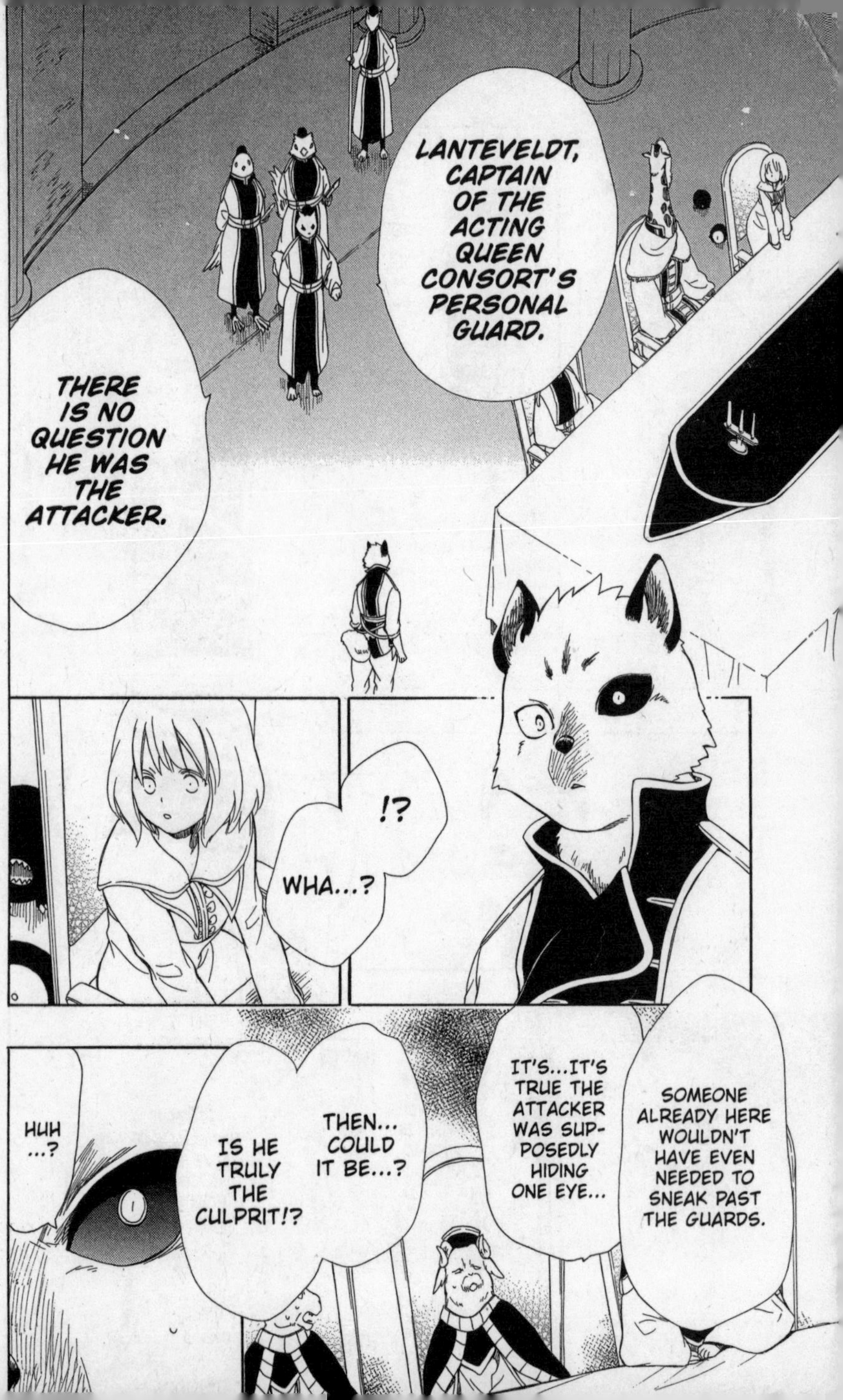
LANTEVELDT, CAPTAIN OF THE ACTING QUEEN CONSORT'S PERSONAL GUARD.
THERE IS NO QUESTION HE WAS THE ATTACKER.
!?
WHA...?
SOMEONE ALREADY HERE WOULDN'T HAVE EVEN NEEDED TO SNEAK PAST THE GUARDS.
IT'S...IT'S TRUE THE ATTACKER WAS SUP-POSEDLY HIDING ONE EYE...
THEN... COULD IT BE...?
IS HE TRULY THE CULPRIT!?
HUH ...?

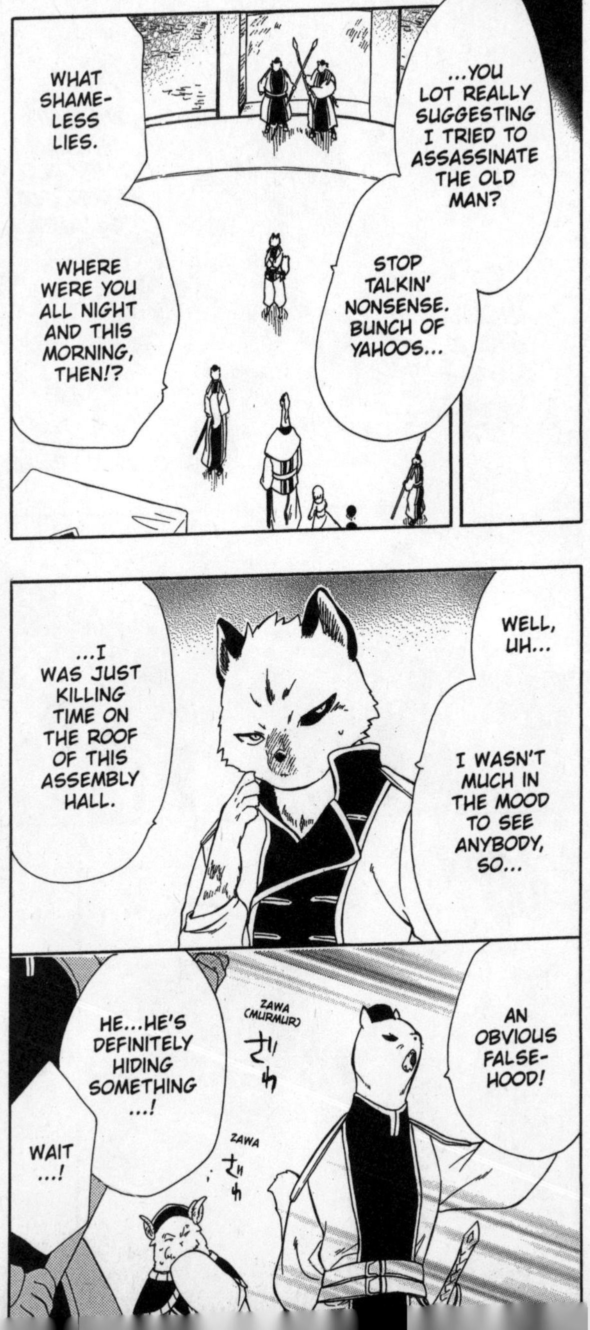
...YOU LOT REALLY SUGGESTING I TRIED TO ASSASSINATE THE OLD MAN?
STOP TALKIN' NONSENSE. BUNCH OF YAHOOS...
WHAT SHAMELESS LIES.
WHERE WERE YOU ALL NIGHT AND THIS MORNING, THEN!?
WELL, UH...
I WASN'T MUCH IN THE MOOD TO SEE ANYBODY, SO...
...I WAS JUST KILLING TIME ON THE ROOF OF THIS ASSEMBLY HALL.
AN OBVIOUS FALSEHOOD!
ZAWA (MURMUR)
ZAWA
HE...HE'S DEFINITELY HIDING SOMETHING...!
WAIT...!

SACRIFICIAL PRINCESS & THE KING OF BEASTS...

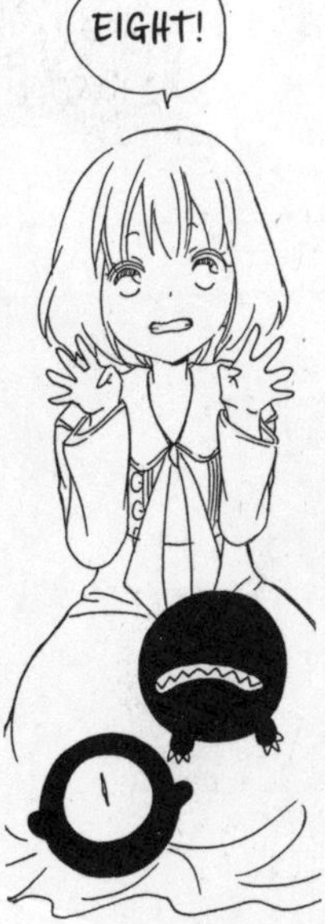
EIGHT!

...STARTS HERE!

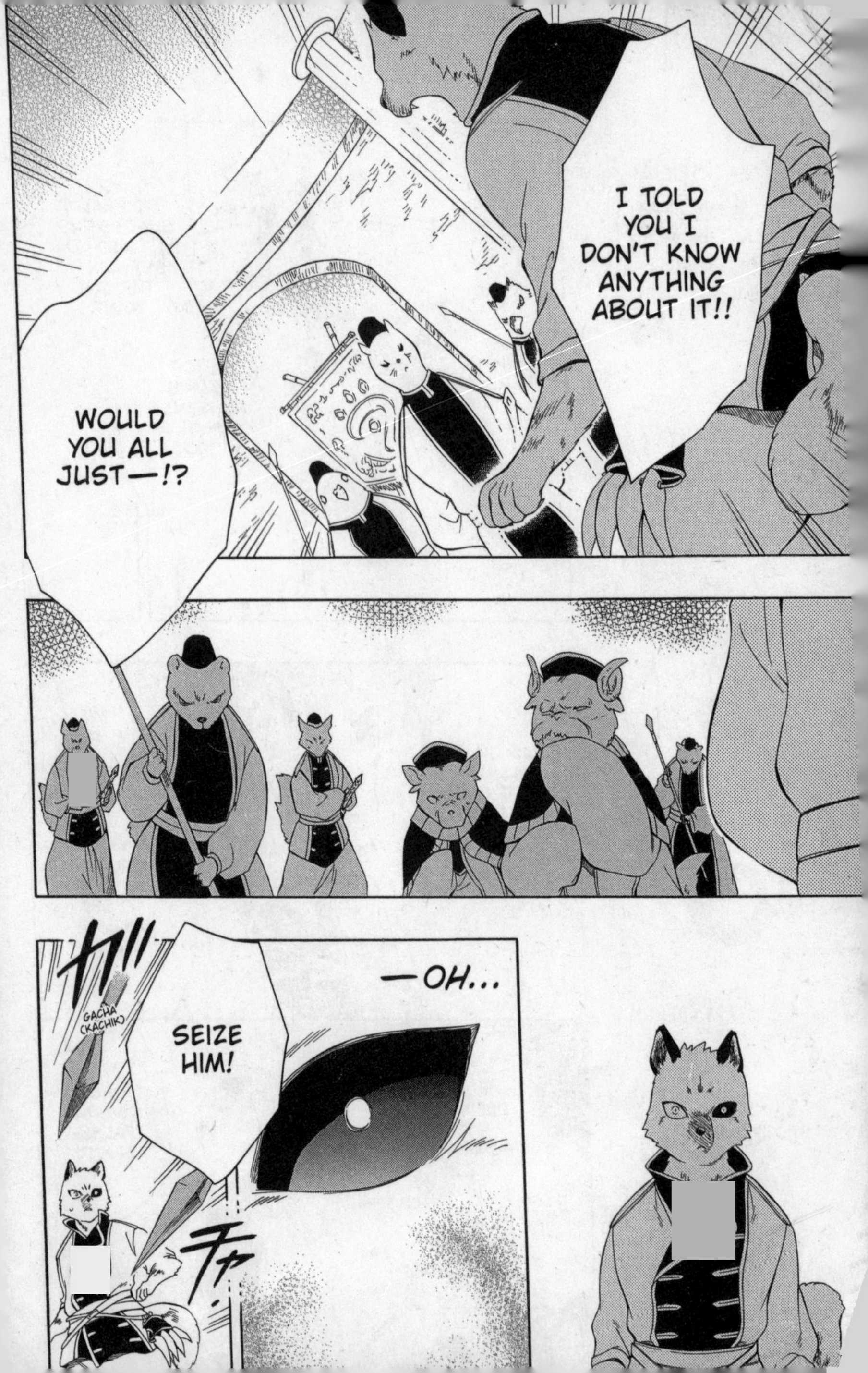
I TOLD YOU I DON'T KNOW ANYTHING ABOUT IT!!
WOULD YOU ALL JUST—!?
—OH...
SEIZE HIM!
ガ
GACHA (KACHIK)
チャ

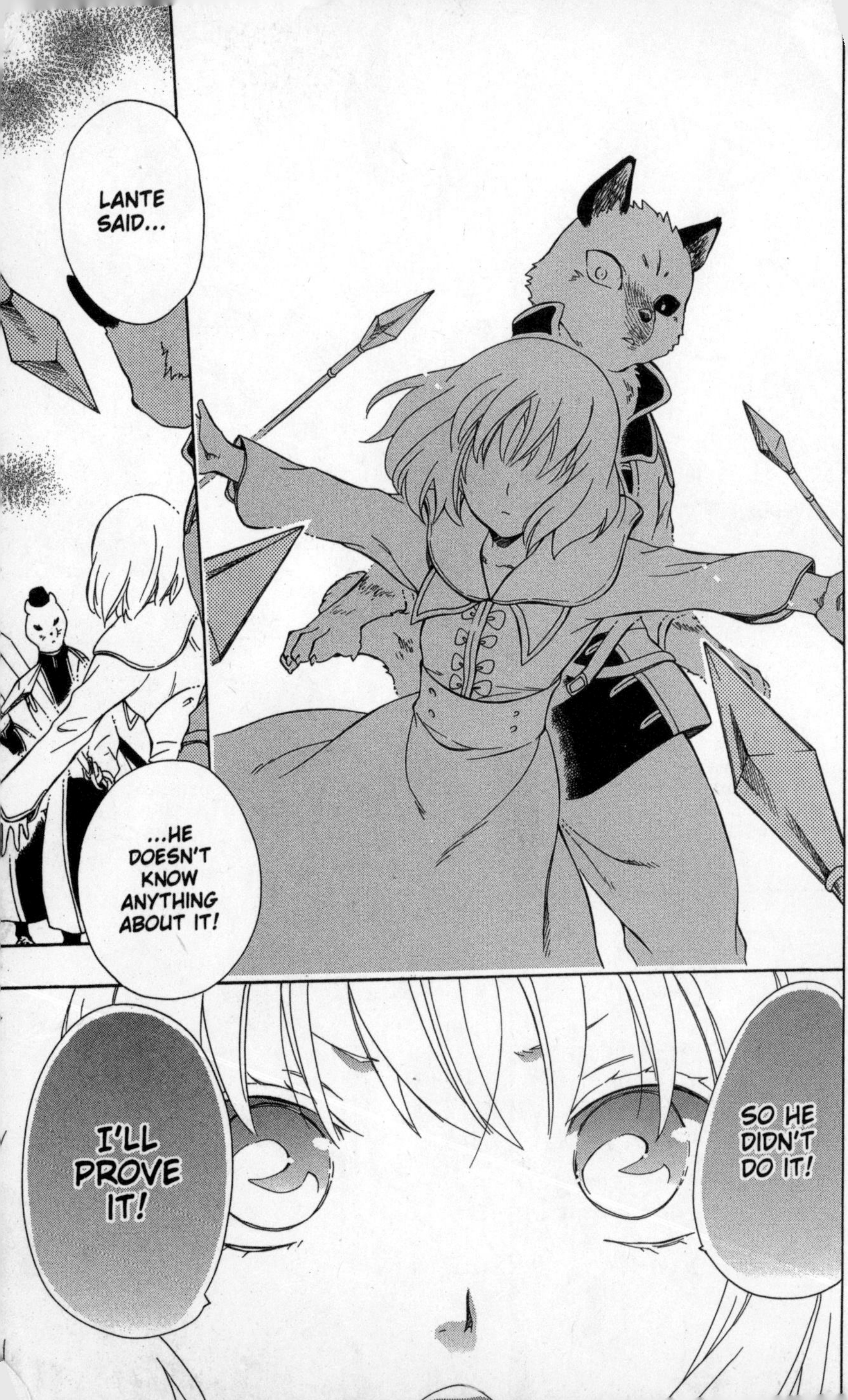
LANTE SAID...
...HE DOESN'T KNOW ANYTHING ABOUT IT!
SO HE DIDN'T DO IT!
I'LL PROVE IT!

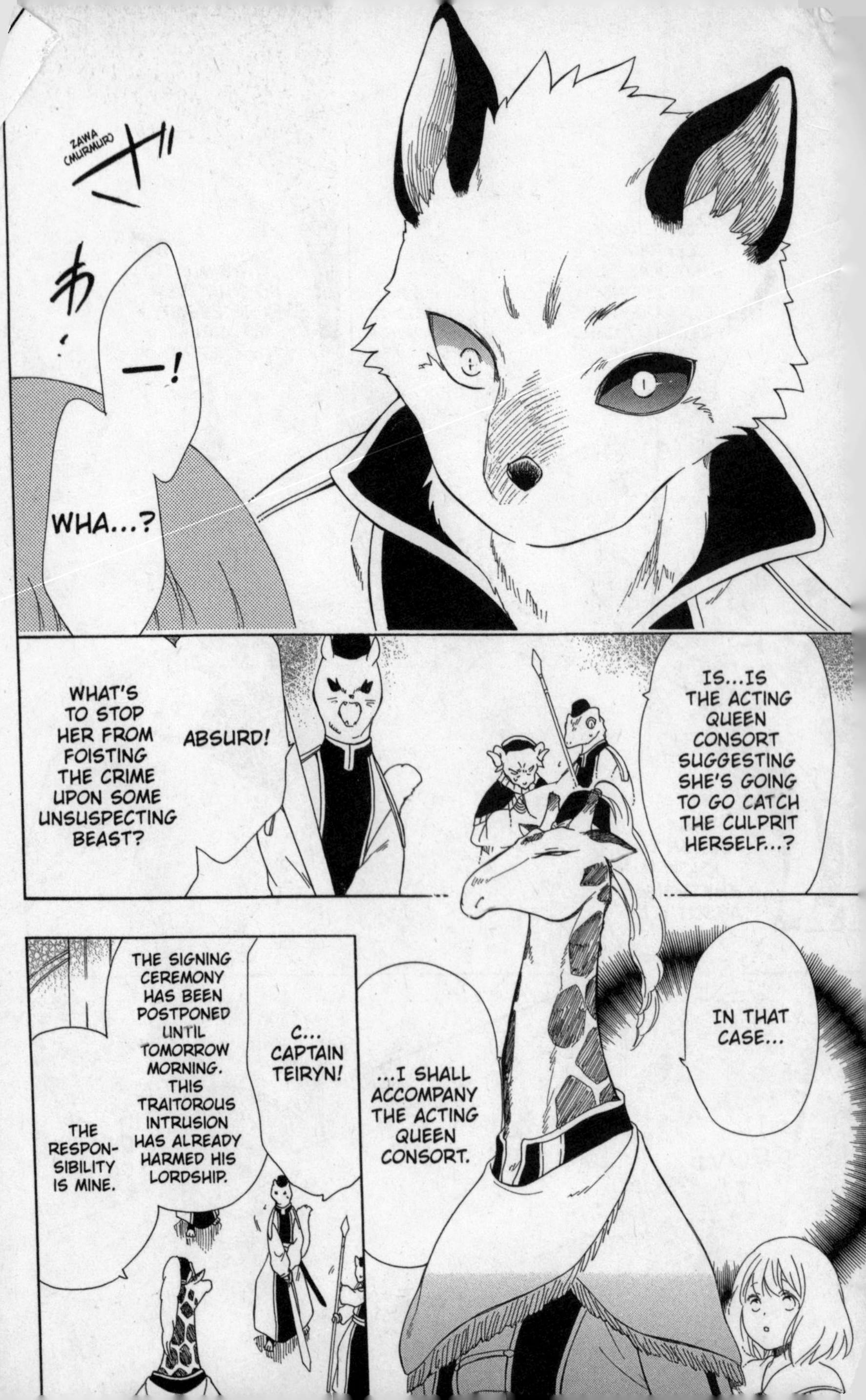
ZAWA (MURMUR)
WHA...?
IS...IS THE ACTING QUEEN CONSORT SUGGESTING SHE'S GOING TO GO CATCH THE CULPRIT HERSELF...?
ABSURD!
WHAT'S TO STOP HER FROM FOISTING THE CRIME UPON SOME UNSUSPECTING BEAST?
IN THAT CASE...
...I SHALL ACCOMPANY THE ACTING QUEEN CONSORT.
C... CAPTAIN TEIRYN!
THE SIGNING CEREMONY HAS BEEN POSTPONED UNTIL TOMORROW MORNING. THIS TRAITOROUS INTRUSION HAS ALREADY HARMED HIS LORDSHIP.
THE RESPON-SIBILITY IS MINE.

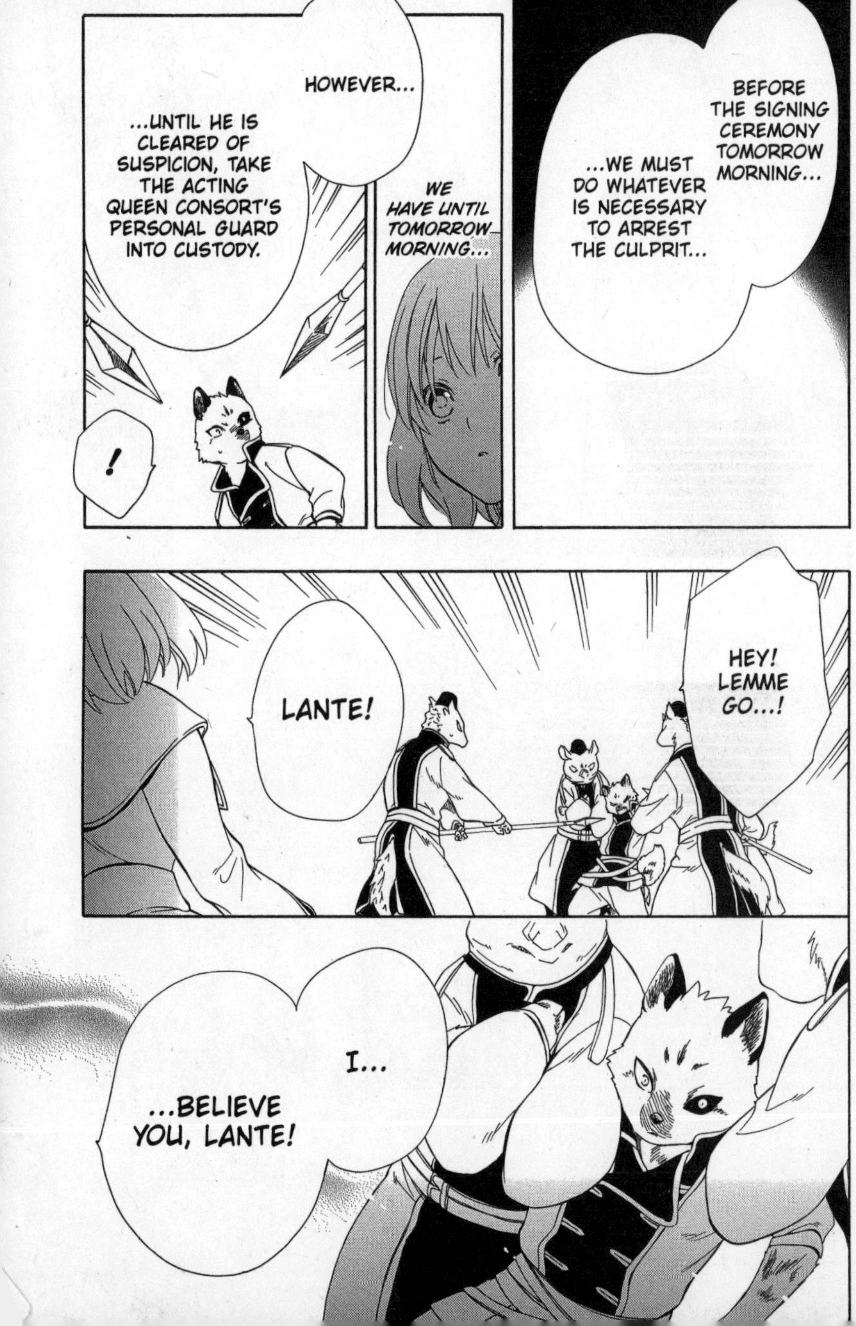
BEFORE THE SIGNING CEREMONY TOMORROW MORNING...
...WE MUST DO WHATEVER IS NECESSARY TO ARREST THE CULPRIT...
WE HAVE UNTIL TOMORROW MORNING...
HOWEVER...
...UNTIL HE IS CLEARED OF SUSPICION, TAKE THE ACTING QUEEN CONSORT'S PERSONAL GUARD INTO CUSTODY.
!
HEY! LEMME GO...!
LANTE!
I...
...BELIEVE YOU, LANTE!

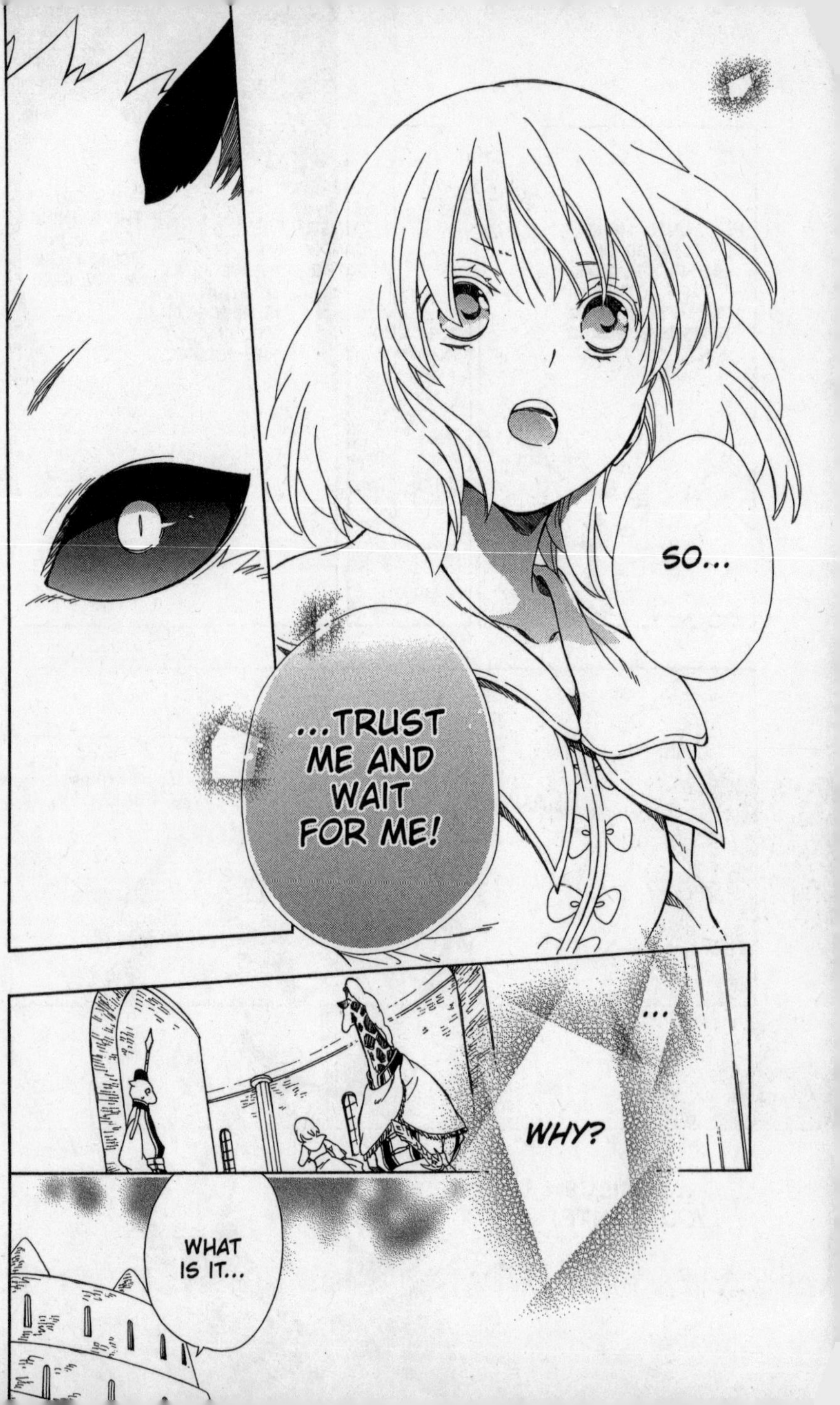
SO...
...TRUST ME AND WAIT FOR ME!
...
WHY?
WHAT IS IT...

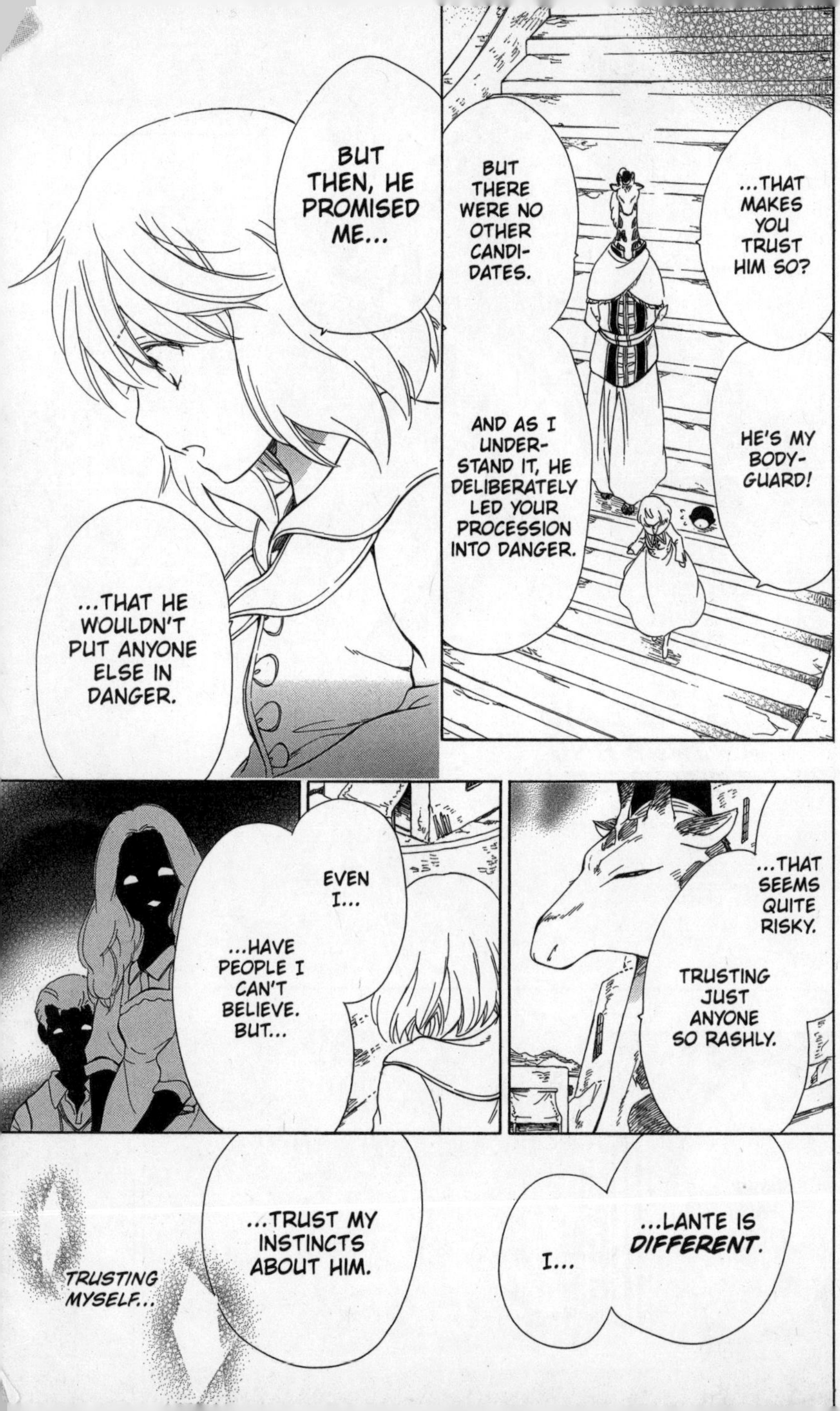
...THAT MAKES YOU TRUST HIM SO?
BUT THERE WERE NO OTHER CANDIDATES.
HE'S MY BODYGUARD!
AND AS I UNDERSTAND IT, HE DELIBERATELY LED YOUR PROCESSION INTO DANGER.
BUT THEN, HE PROMISED ME...
...THAT HE WOULDN'T PUT ANYONE ELSE IN DANGER.
...THAT SEEMS QUITE RISKY.
TRUSTING JUST ANYONE SO RASHLY.
EVEN I...
...HAVE PEOPLE I CAN'T BELIEVE. BUT...
I...
...LANTE IS *DIFFERENT*.
...TRUST MY INSTINCTS ABOUT HIM.
TRUSTING MYSELF...

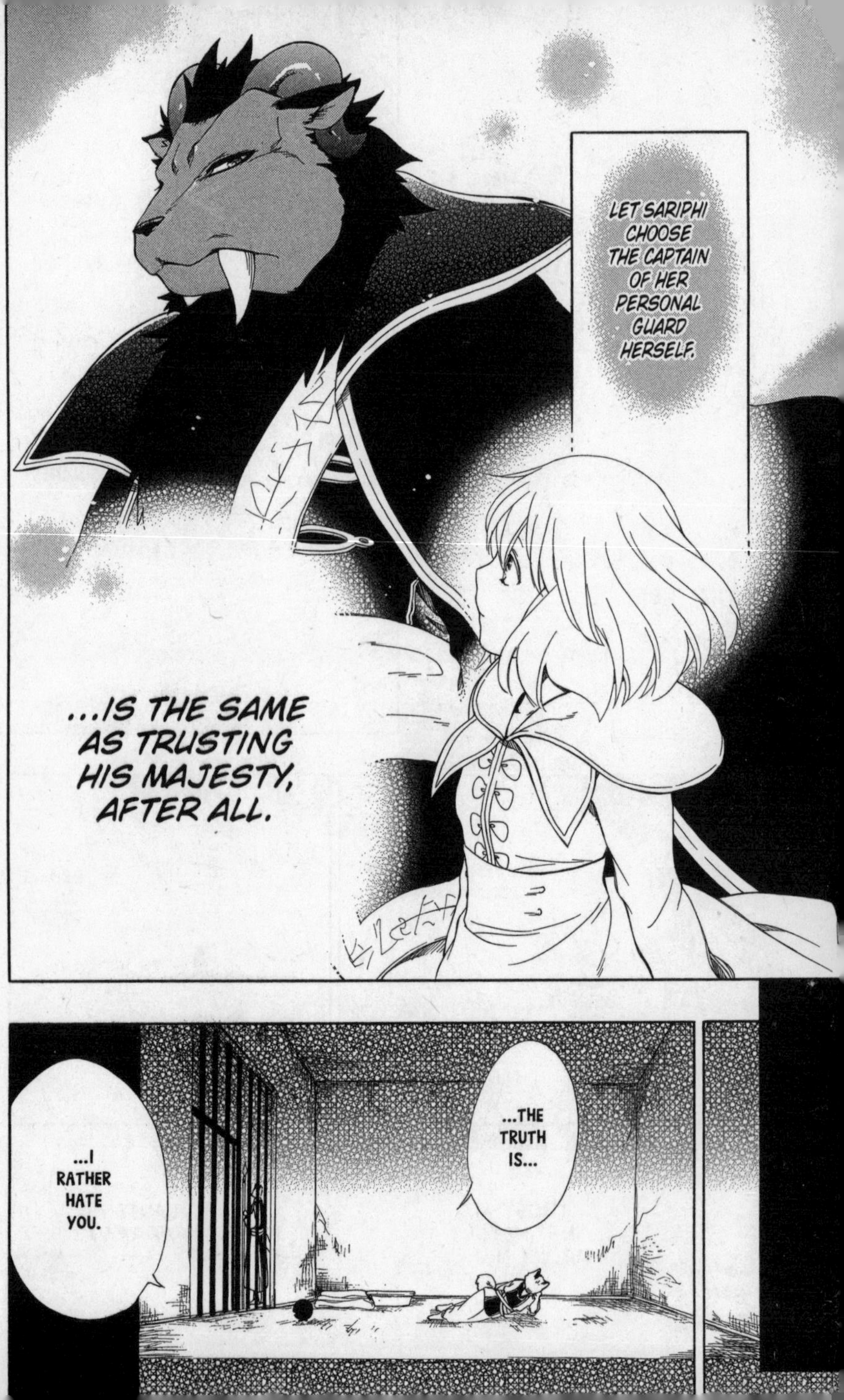
LET SARIPHI CHOOSE THE CAPTAIN OF HER PERSONAL GUARD HERSELF.
...IS THE SAME AS TRUSTING HIS MAJESTY, AFTER ALL.
...THE TRUTH IS...
...I RATHER HATE YOU.

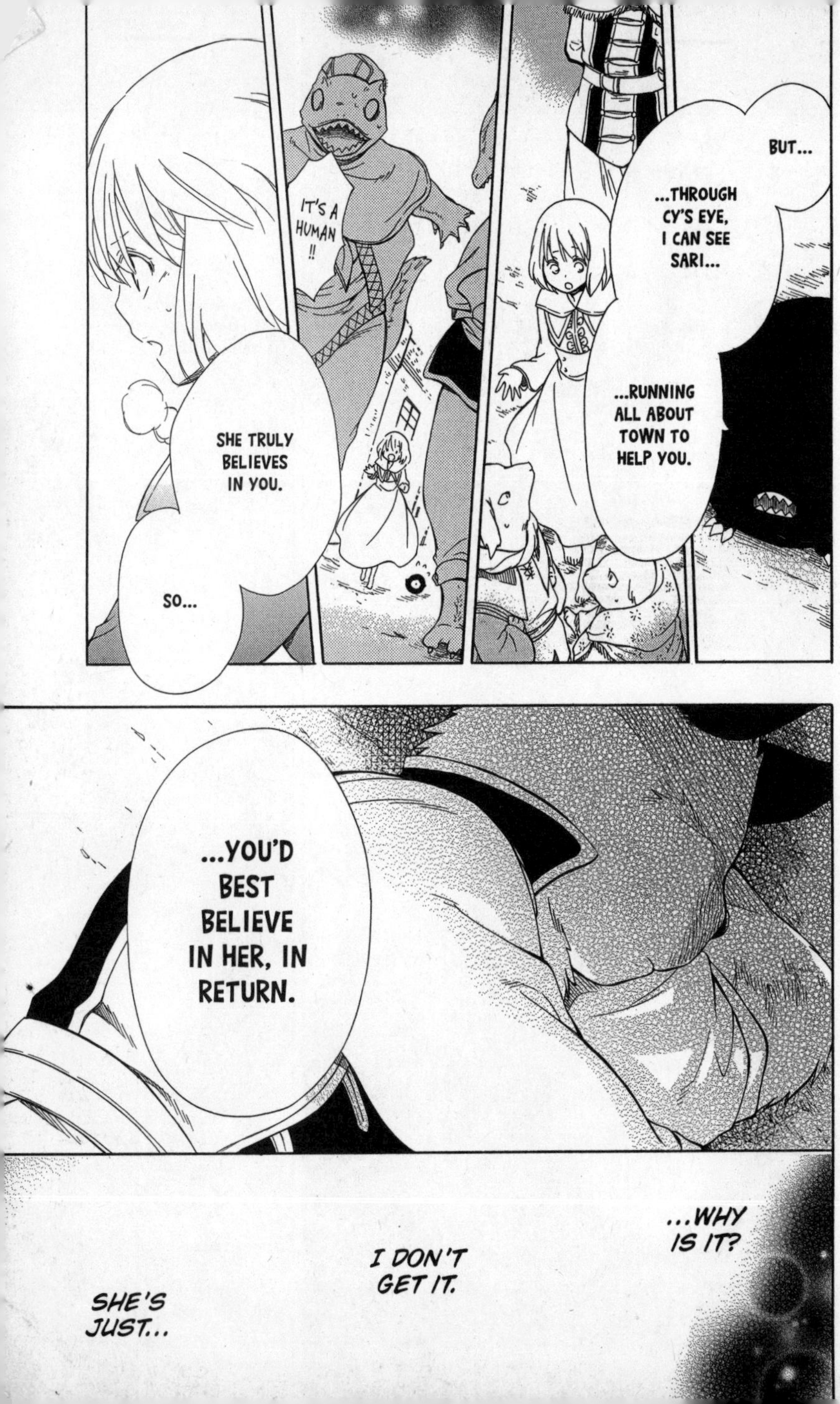
BUT...
...THROUGH CY'S EYE, I CAN SEE SARI...
...RUNNING ALL ABOUT TOWN TO HELP YOU.
IT'S A HUMAN!!
SHE TRULY BELIEVES IN YOU.
SO...
...YOU'D BEST BELIEVE IN HER, IN RETURN.
...WHY IS IT?
I DON'T GET IT.
SHE'S JUST...

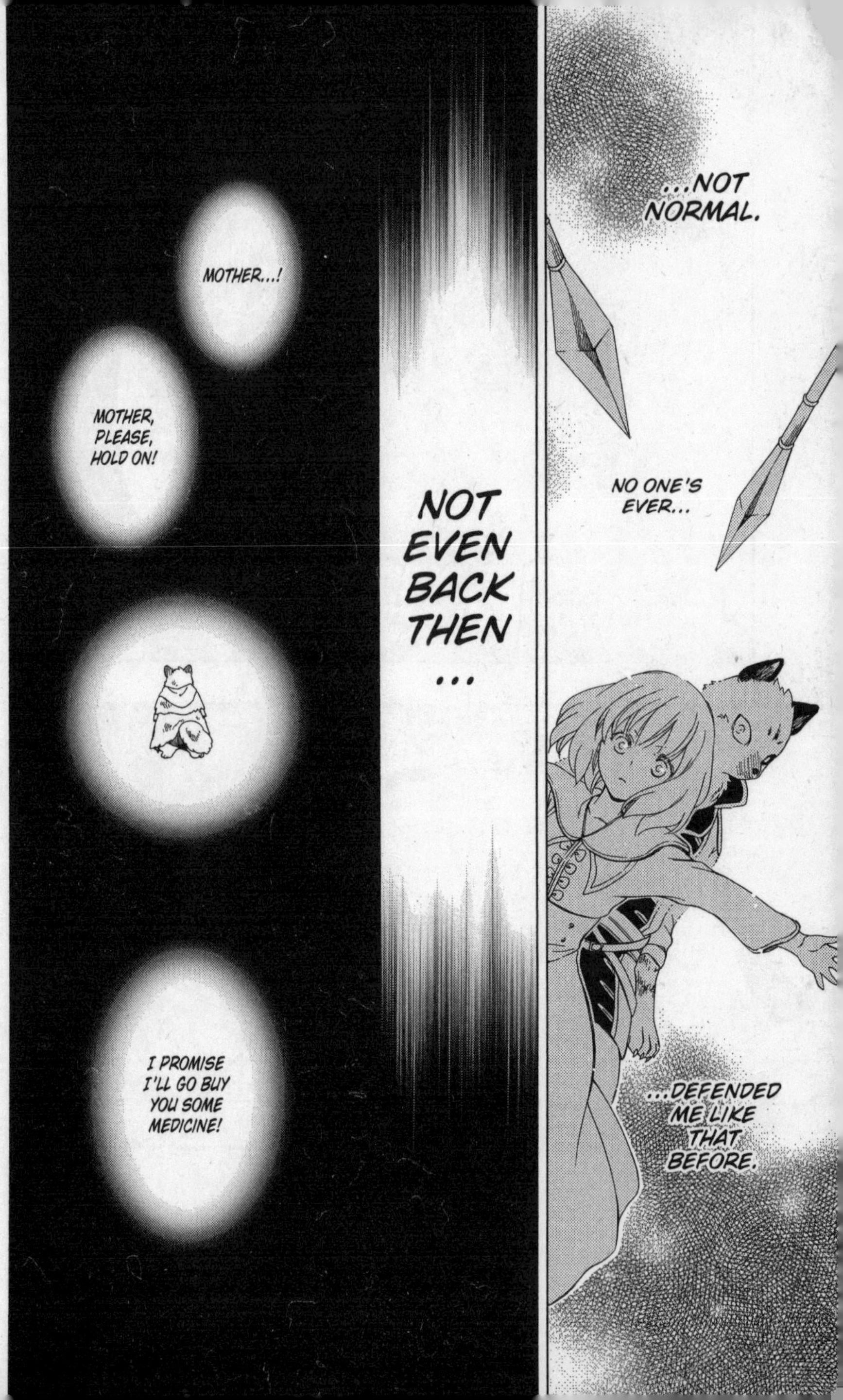
...NOT NORMAL.
NO ONE'S EVER...
...DEFENDED ME LIKE THAT BEFORE.
NOT EVEN BACK THEN...
MOTHER...!
MOTHER, PLEASE, HOLD ON!
I PROMISE I'LL GO BUY YOU SOME MEDICINE!

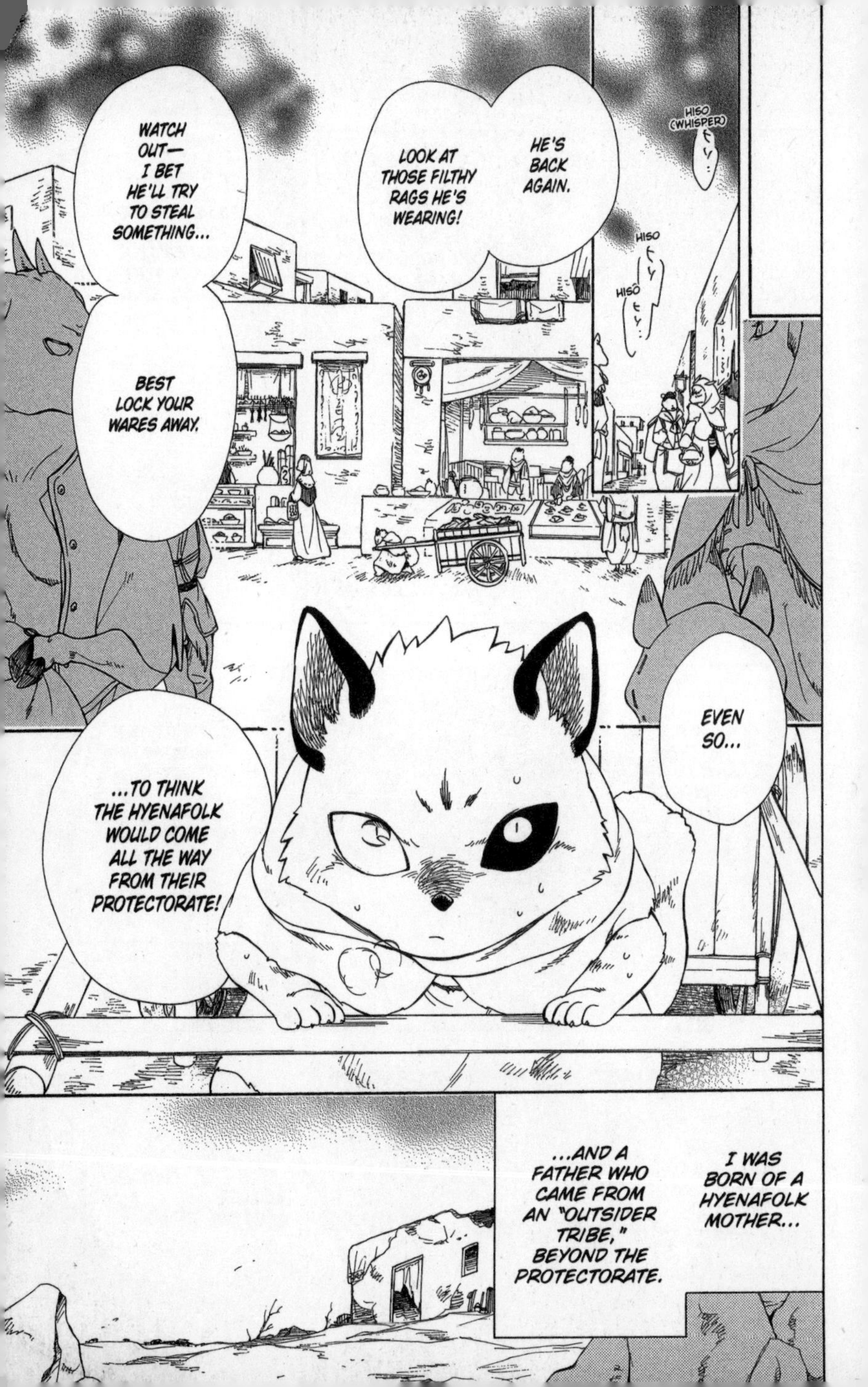
HISO (WHISPER) ヒソ…
HISO ヒソ
HISO ヒソ…
HE'S BACK AGAIN.
LOOK AT THOSE FILTHY RAGS HE'S WEARING!
WATCH OUT— I BET HE'LL TRY TO STEAL SOMETHING...
BEST LOCK YOUR WARES AWAY.
EVEN SO...
...TO THINK THE HYENAFOLK WOULD COME ALL THE WAY FROM THEIR PROTECTORATE!
I WAS BORN OF A HYENAFOLK MOTHER...
...AND A FATHER WHO CAME FROM AN "OUTSIDER TRIBE," BEYOND THE PROTECTORATE.

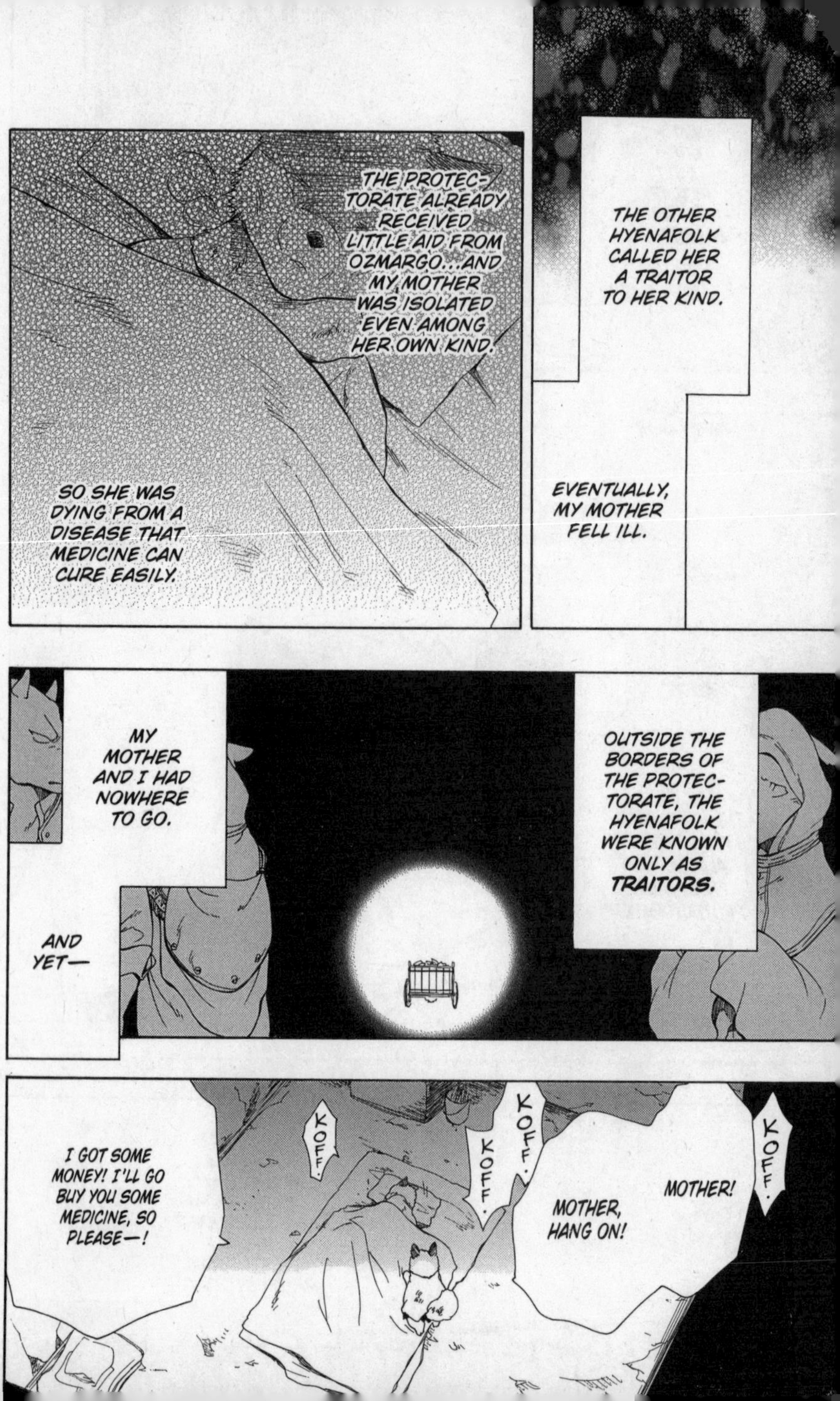
THE OTHER HYENAFOLK CALLED HER A TRAITOR TO HER KIND.
EVENTUALLY, MY MOTHER FELL ILL.
THE PROTEC-TORATE ALREADY RECEIVED LITTLE AID FROM OZMARGO...AND MY MOTHER WAS ISOLATED EVEN AMONG HER OWN KIND.
SO SHE WAS DYING FROM A DISEASE THAT MEDICINE CAN CURE EASILY.
OUTSIDE THE BORDERS OF THE PROTEC-TORATE, THE HYENAFOLK WERE KNOWN ONLY AS **TRAITORS.**
MY MOTHER AND I HAD NOWHERE TO GO.
AND YET—
KOFF.
MOTHER!
MOTHER, HANG ON!
KOFF.
KOFF.
KOFF.
I GOT SOME MONEY! I'LL GO BUY YOU SOME MEDICINE, SO PLEASE—!

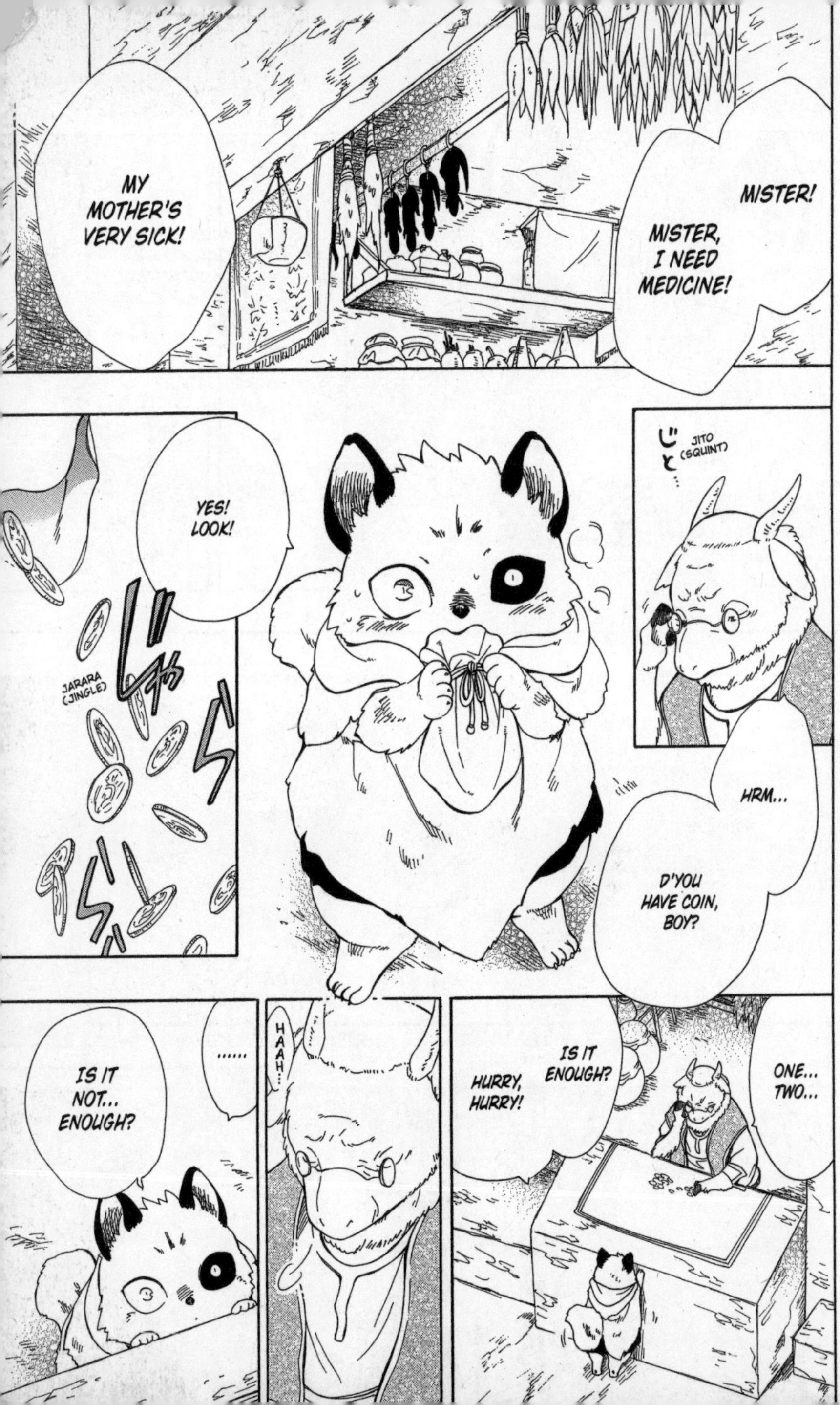

MISTER!
MISTER, I NEED MEDICINE!
MY MOTHER'S VERY SICK!
じと…
JITO (SQUINT)
HRM...
D'YOU HAVE COIN, BOY?
YES! LOOK!
JARARA (JINGLE)
ONE... TWO...
IS IT ENOUGH?
HURRY, HURRY!
HAAH...
......
IS IT NOT... ENOUGH?

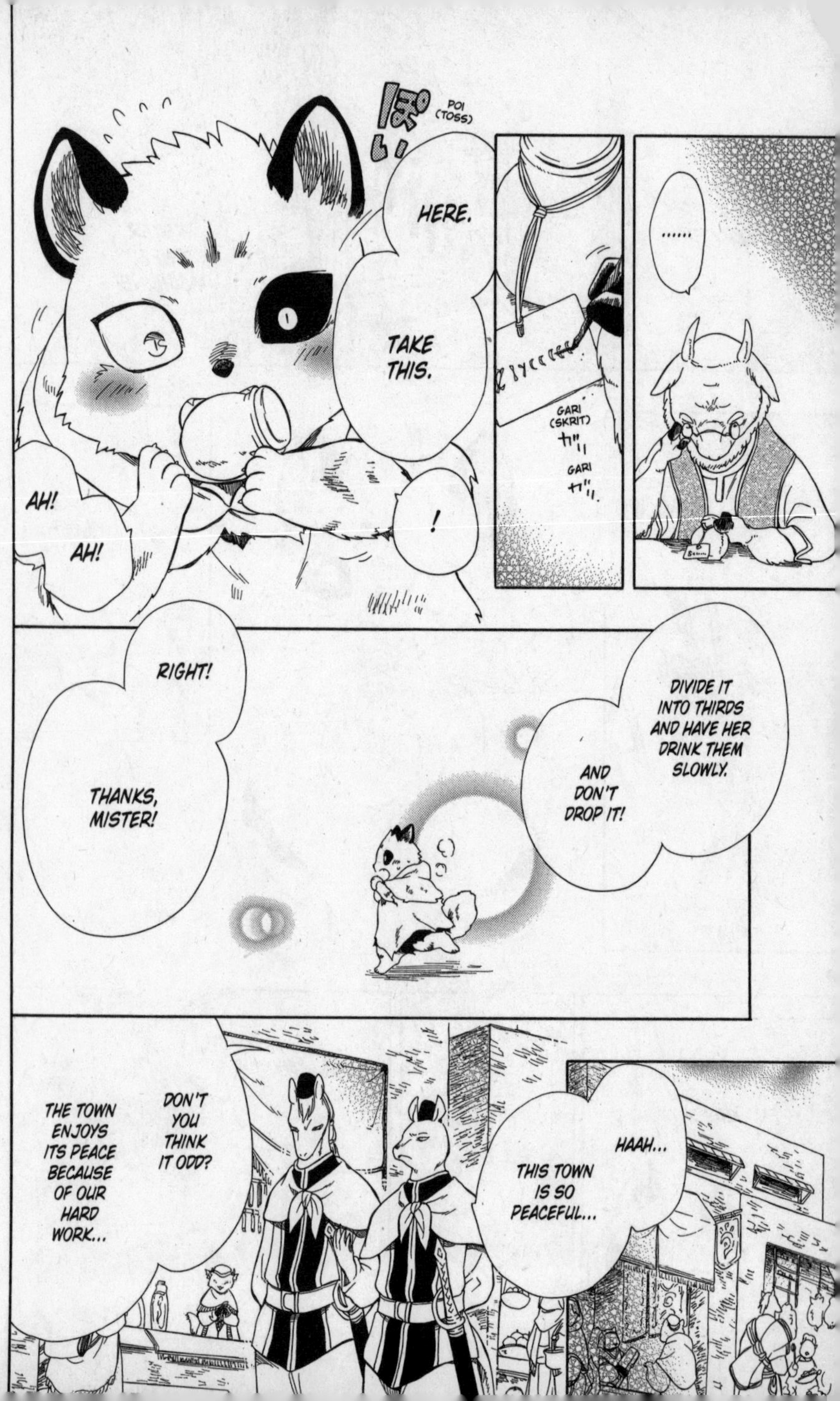
......
GARI (SKRIT)
ガリ
GARI
ガリ
ぽい
POI (TOSS)
HERE.
TAKE THIS.
!
AH!
AH!
DIVIDE IT INTO THIRDS AND HAVE HER DRINK THEM SLOWLY.
AND DON'T DROP IT!
RIGHT!
THANKS, MISTER!
HAAH...
THIS TOWN IS SO PEACEFUL...
DON'T YOU THINK IT ODD?
THE TOWN ENJOYS ITS PEACE BECAUSE OF OUR HARD WORK...

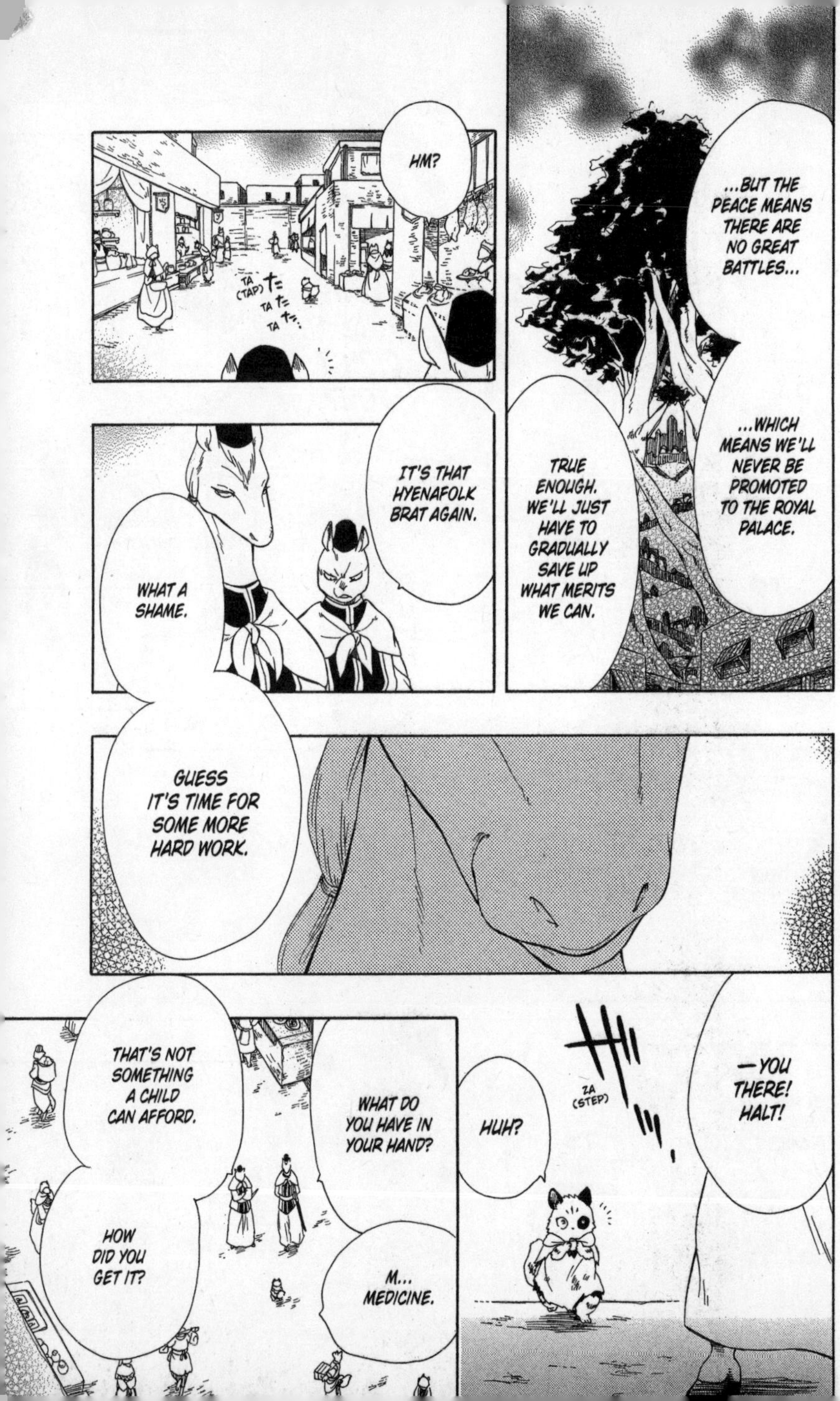
...BUT THE PEACE MEANS THERE ARE NO GREAT BATTLES...
...WHICH MEANS WE'LL NEVER BE PROMOTED TO THE ROYAL PALACE.
TRUE ENOUGH. WE'LL JUST HAVE TO GRADUALLY SAVE UP WHAT MERITS WE CAN.
HM?
TA (TAP)
TA
TA
IT'S THAT HYENAFOLK BRAT AGAIN.
WHAT A SHAME.
GUESS IT'S TIME FOR SOME MORE HARD WORK.
—YOU THERE! HALT!
ZA (STEP)
HUH?
WHAT DO YOU HAVE IN YOUR HAND?
M... MEDICINE.
THAT'S NOT SOMETHING A CHILD CAN AFFORD.
HOW DID YOU GET IT?

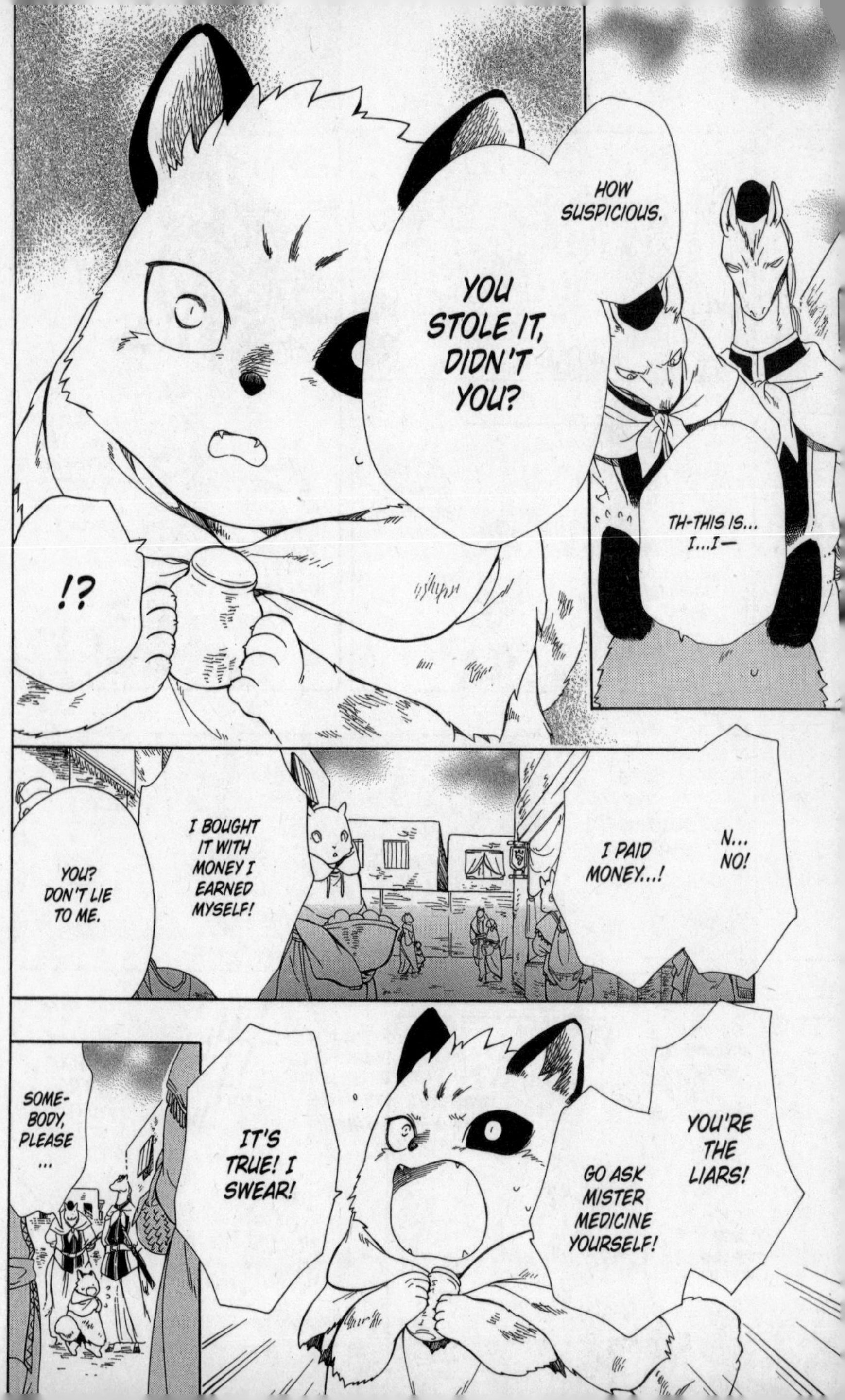
HOW SUSPICIOUS.
YOU STOLE IT, DIDN'T YOU?
TH-THIS IS... I...I—
!?
N... NO!
I PAID MONEY...!
I BOUGHT IT WITH MONEY I EARNED MYSELF!
YOU? DON'T LIE TO ME.
YOU'RE THE LIARS!
GO ASK MISTER MEDICINE YOURSELF!
IT'S TRUE! I SWEAR!
SOME-BODY, PLEASE ...

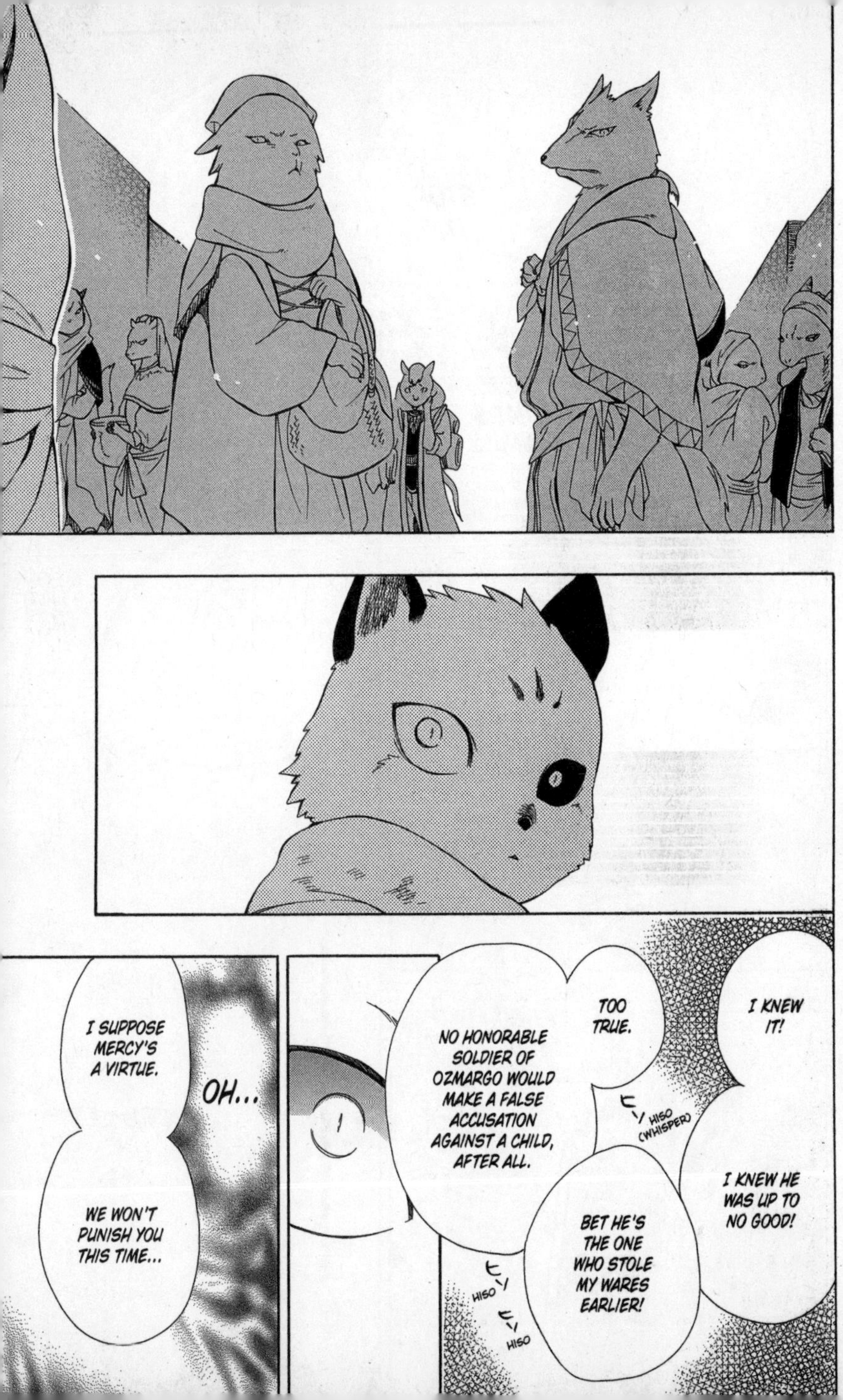
I KNEW IT!
I KNEW HE WAS UP TO NO GOOD!
TOO TRUE.
ヒソ HISO (WHISPER)
NO HONORABLE SOLDIER OF OZMARGO WOULD MAKE A FALSE ACCUSATION AGAINST A CHILD, AFTER ALL.
BET HE'S THE ONE WHO STOLE MY WARES EARLIER!
ヒソ HISO
ヒソ HISO
I SUPPOSE MERCY'S A VIRTUE.
OH...
WE WON'T PUNISH YOU THIS TIME...

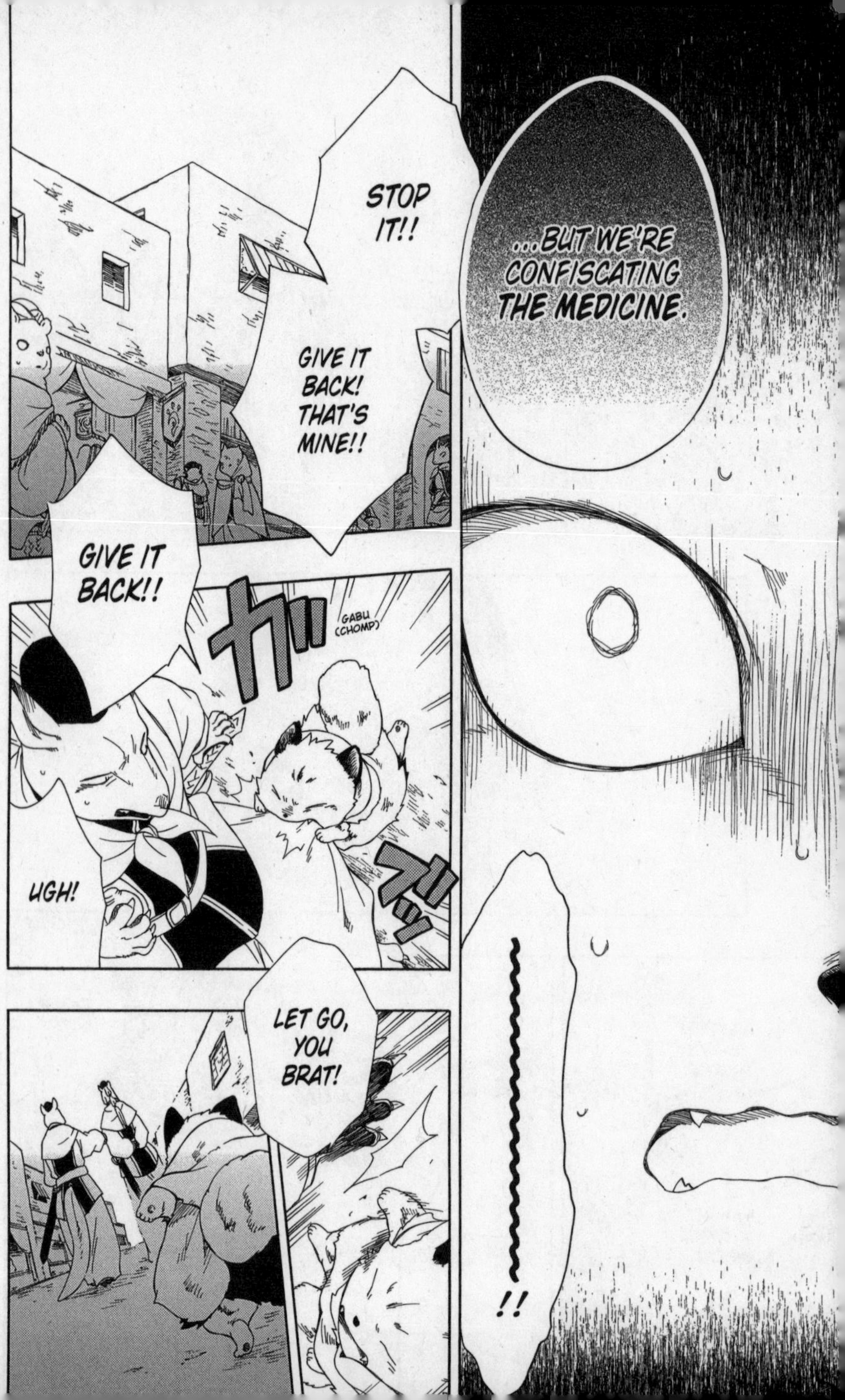
...BUT WE'RE CONFISCATING THE MEDICINE.
!!
STOP IT!!
GIVE IT BACK! THAT'S MINE!!
GIVE IT BACK!!
GABU (CHOMP)
UGH!
LET GO, YOU BRAT!

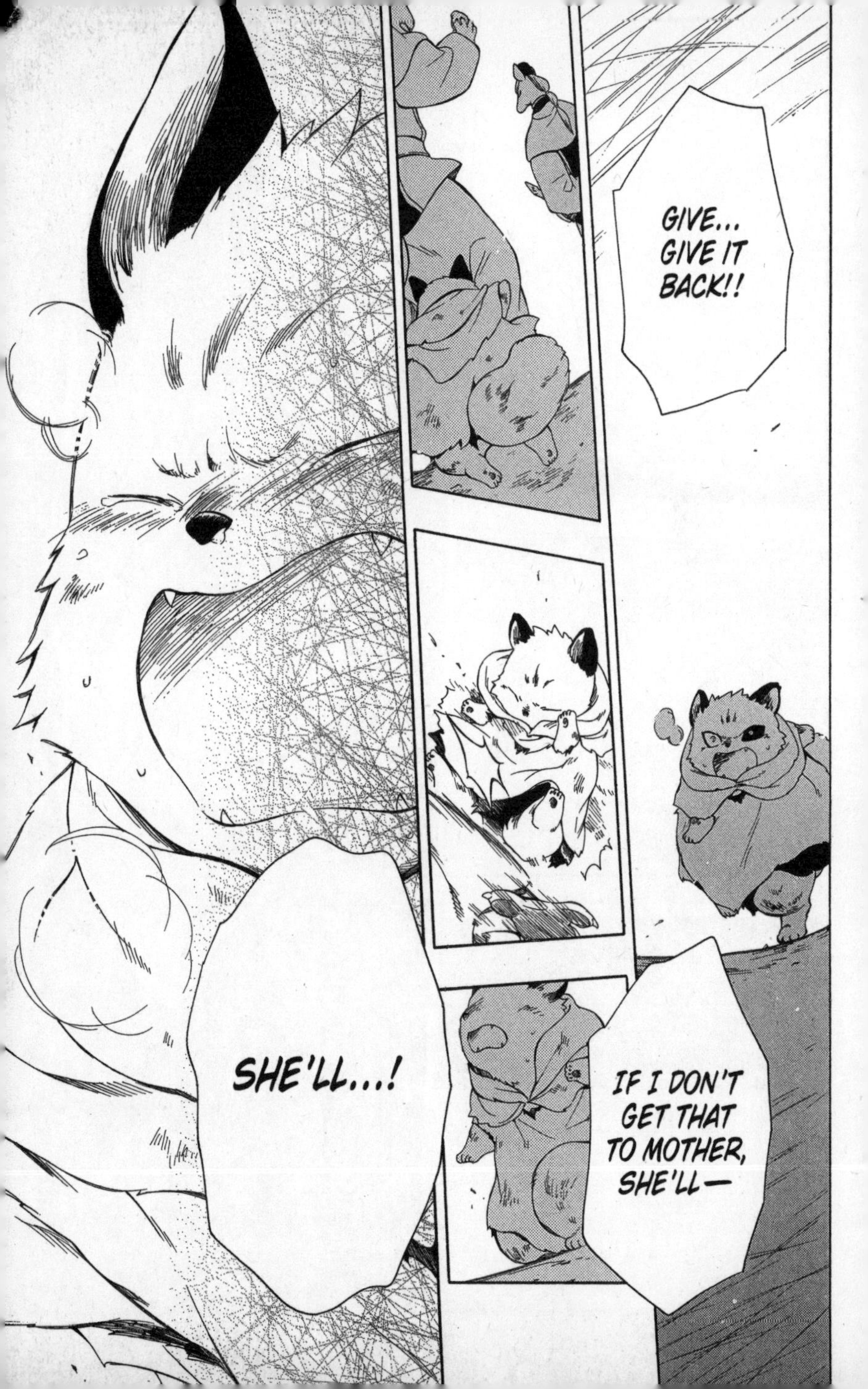
GIVE... GIVE IT BACK!!
IF I DON'T GET THAT TO MOTHER, SHE'LL—
SHE'LL...!

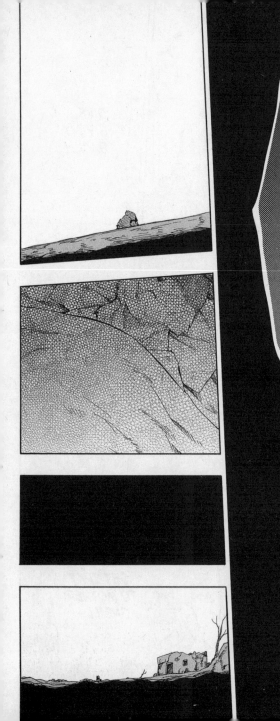

SHE'LL
DIE...!!

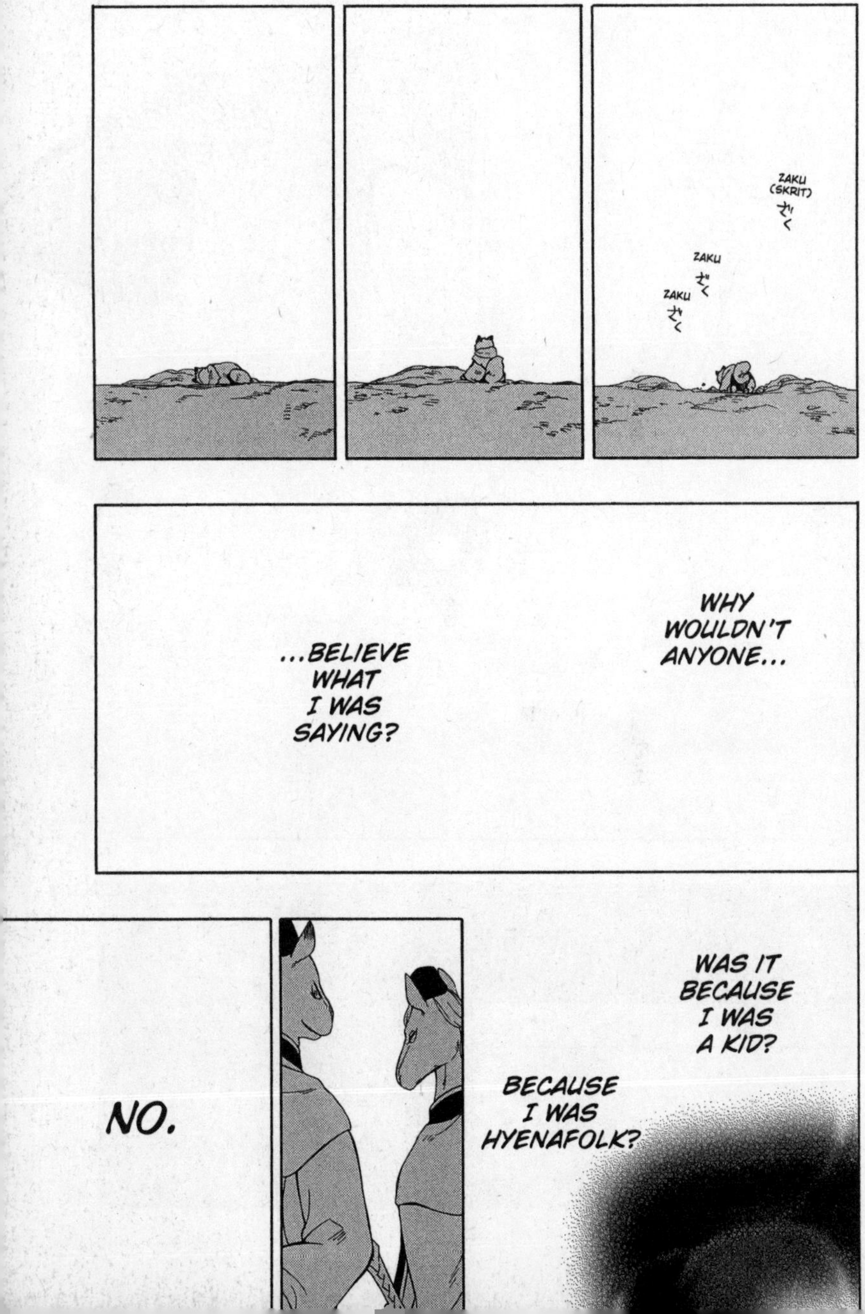
ZAKU (SKRIT)
ざく
ZAKU
ざく
ZAKU
ざく
WHY WOULDN'T ANYONE...
...BELIEVE WHAT I WAS SAYING?
WAS IT BECAUSE I WAS A KID?
BECAUSE I WAS HYENAFOLK?
NO.

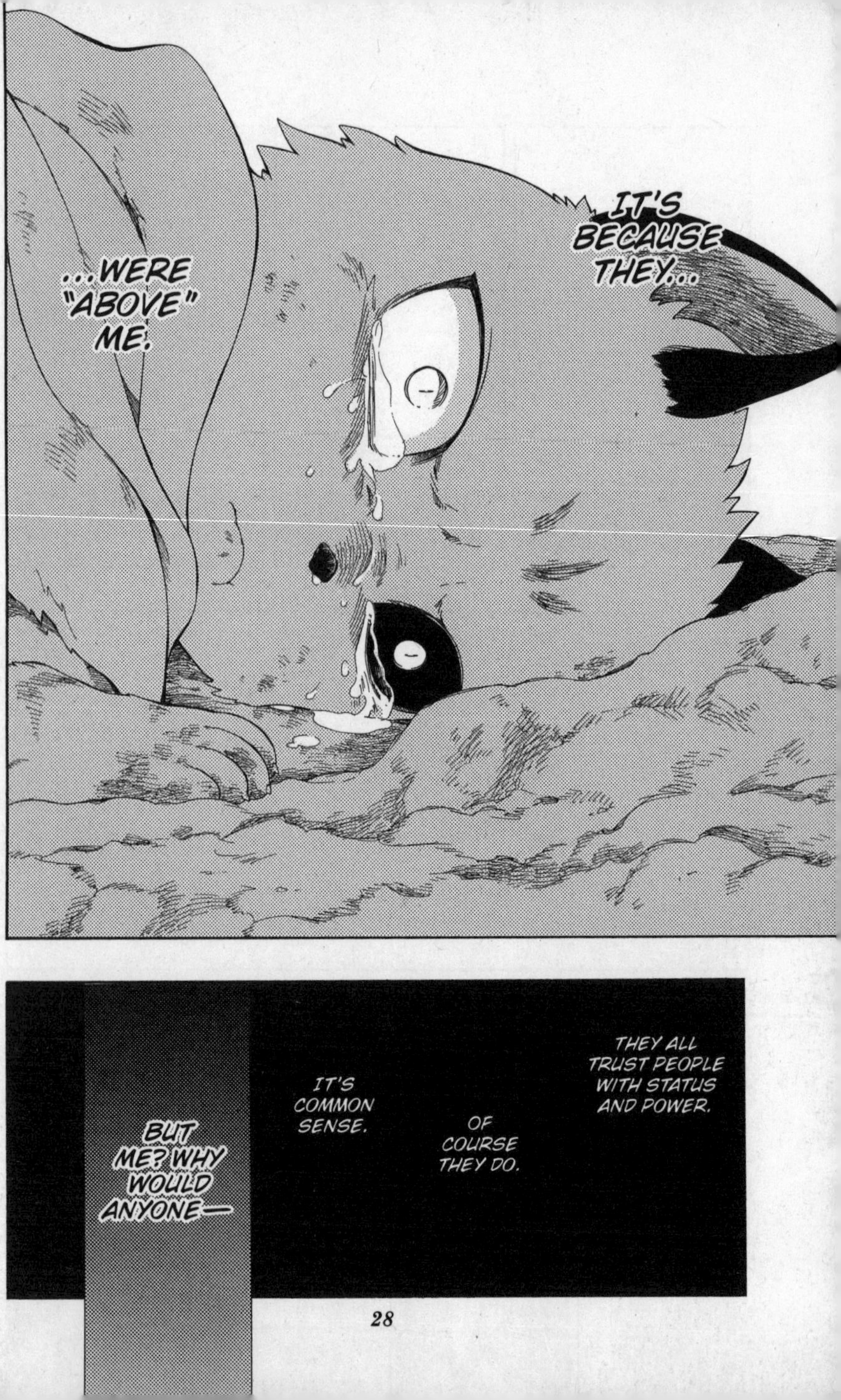
IT'S BECAUSE THEY...
...WERE "ABOVE" ME.
THEY ALL TRUST PEOPLE WITH STATUS AND POWER.
OF COURSE THEY DO.
IT'S COMMON SENSE.
BUT ME? WHY WOULD ANYONE—

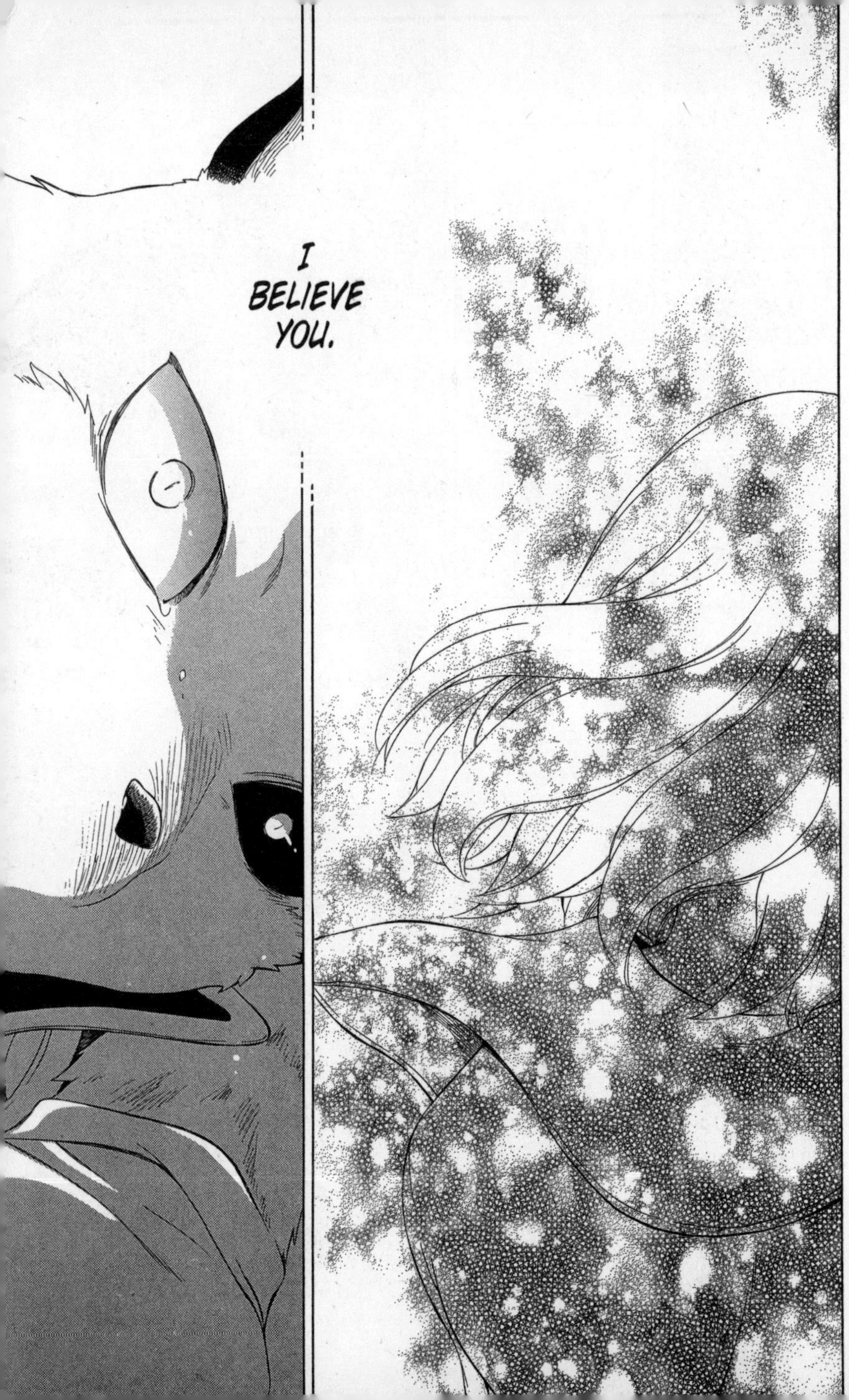
I BELIEVE YOU.

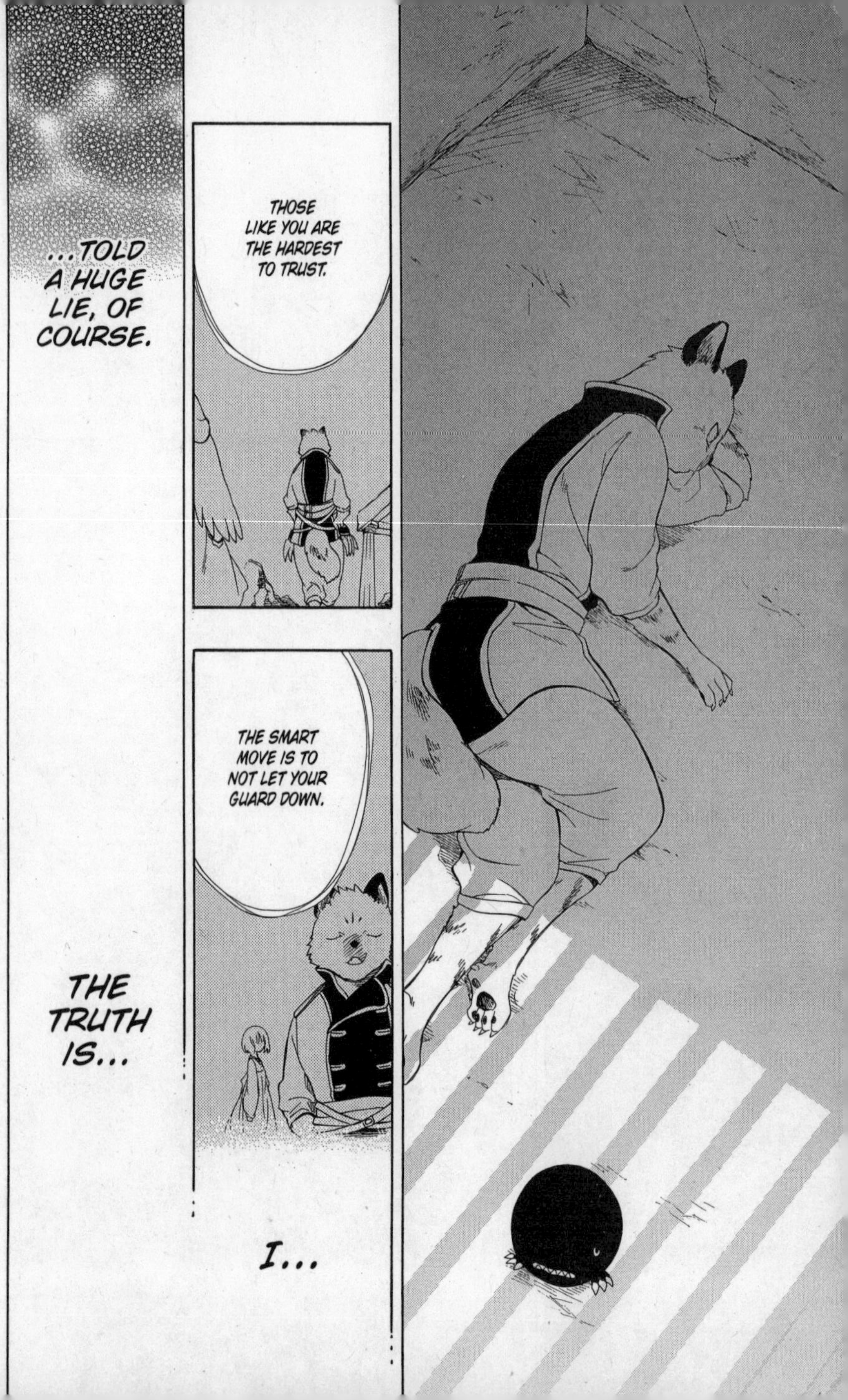
THOSE LIKE YOU ARE THE HARDEST TO TRUST.
THE SMART MOVE IS TO NOT LET YOUR GUARD DOWN.
I...
...TOLD A HUGE LIE, OF COURSE.
THE TRUTH IS...

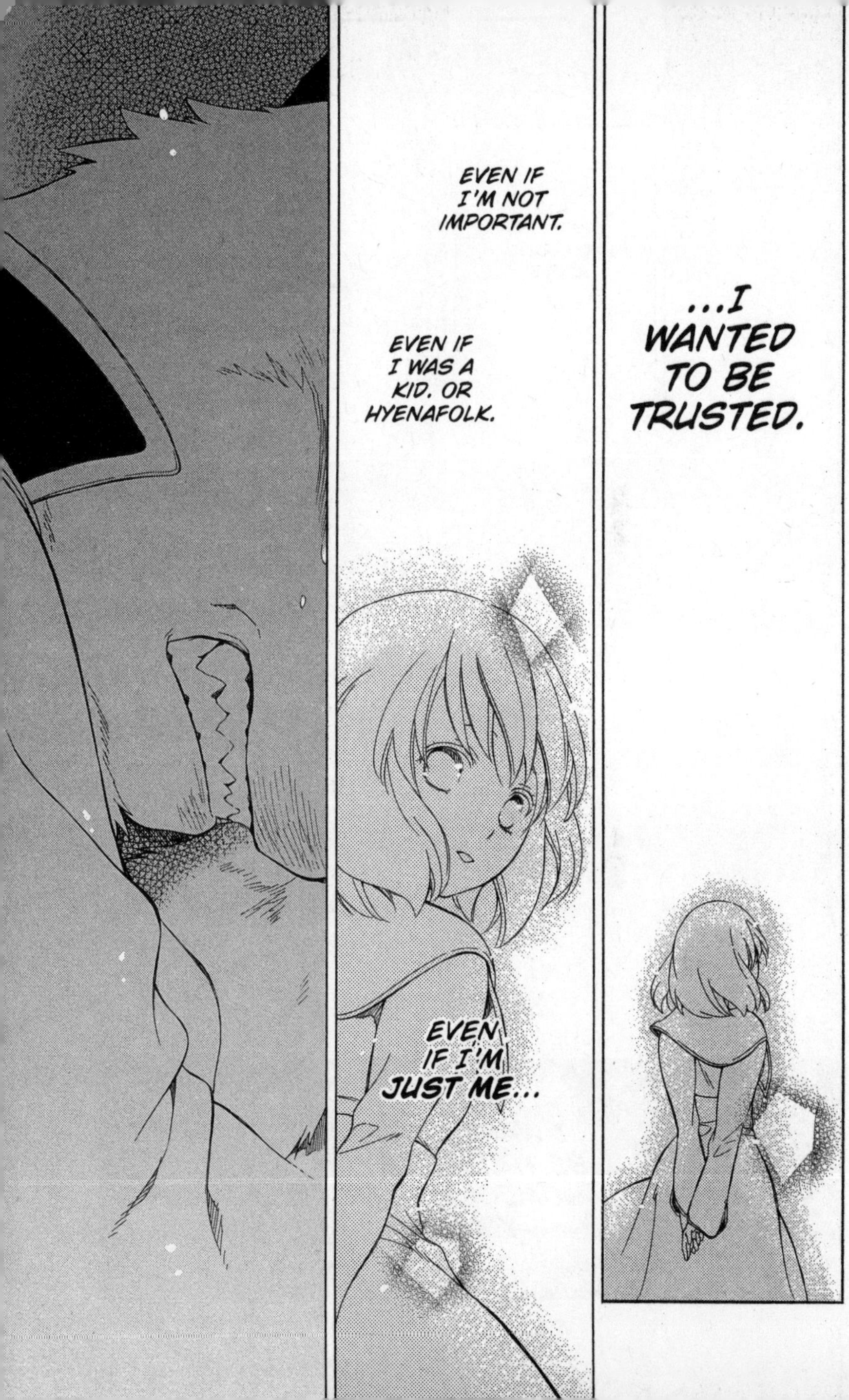
EVEN IF I'M NOT IMPORTANT.
EVEN IF I WAS A KID. OR HYENAFOLK.
EVEN IF I'M JUST ME...
...I WANTED TO BE TRUSTED.

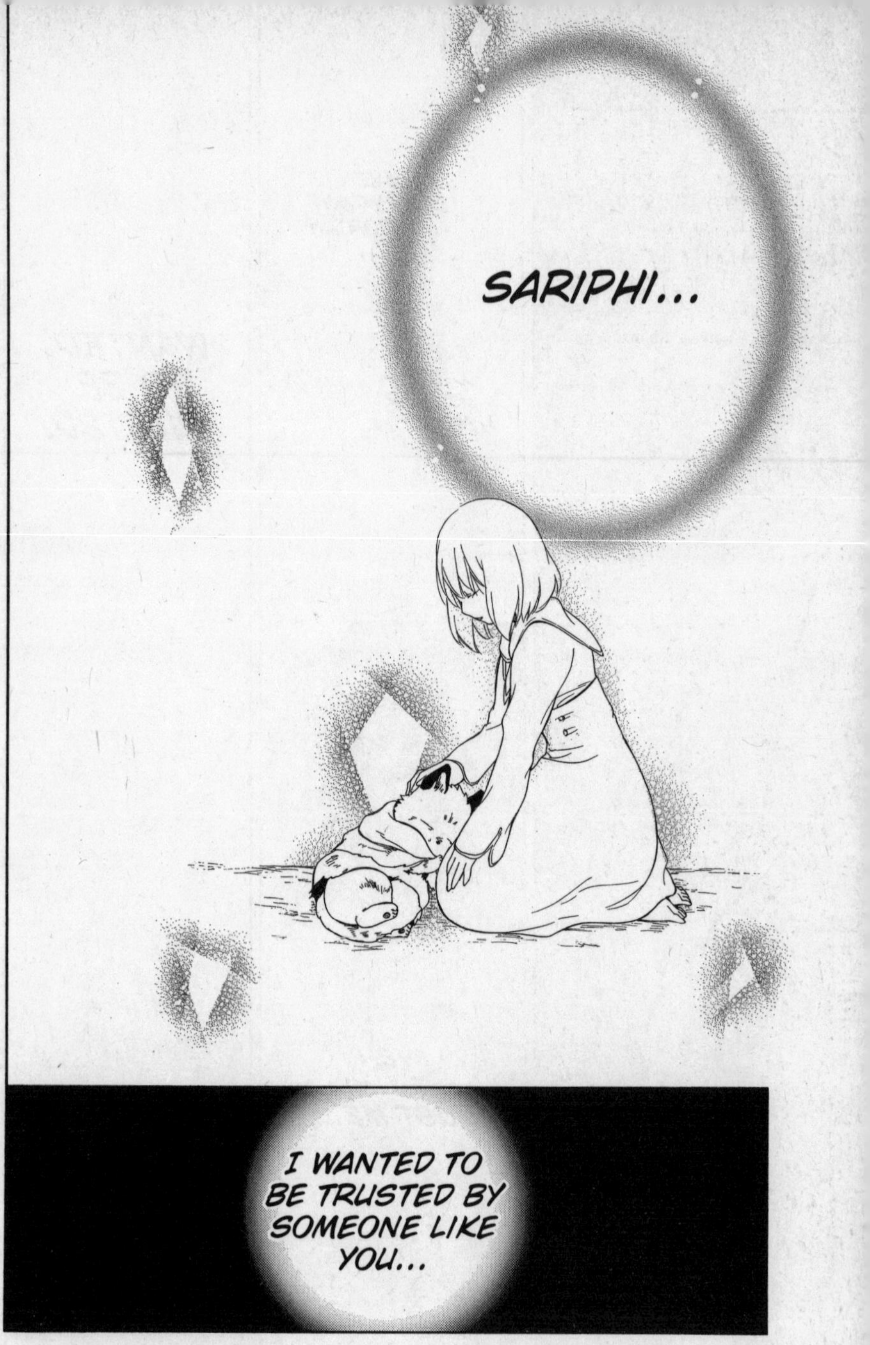
SARIPHI...
I WANTED TO BE TRUSTED BY SOMEONE LIKE YOU...

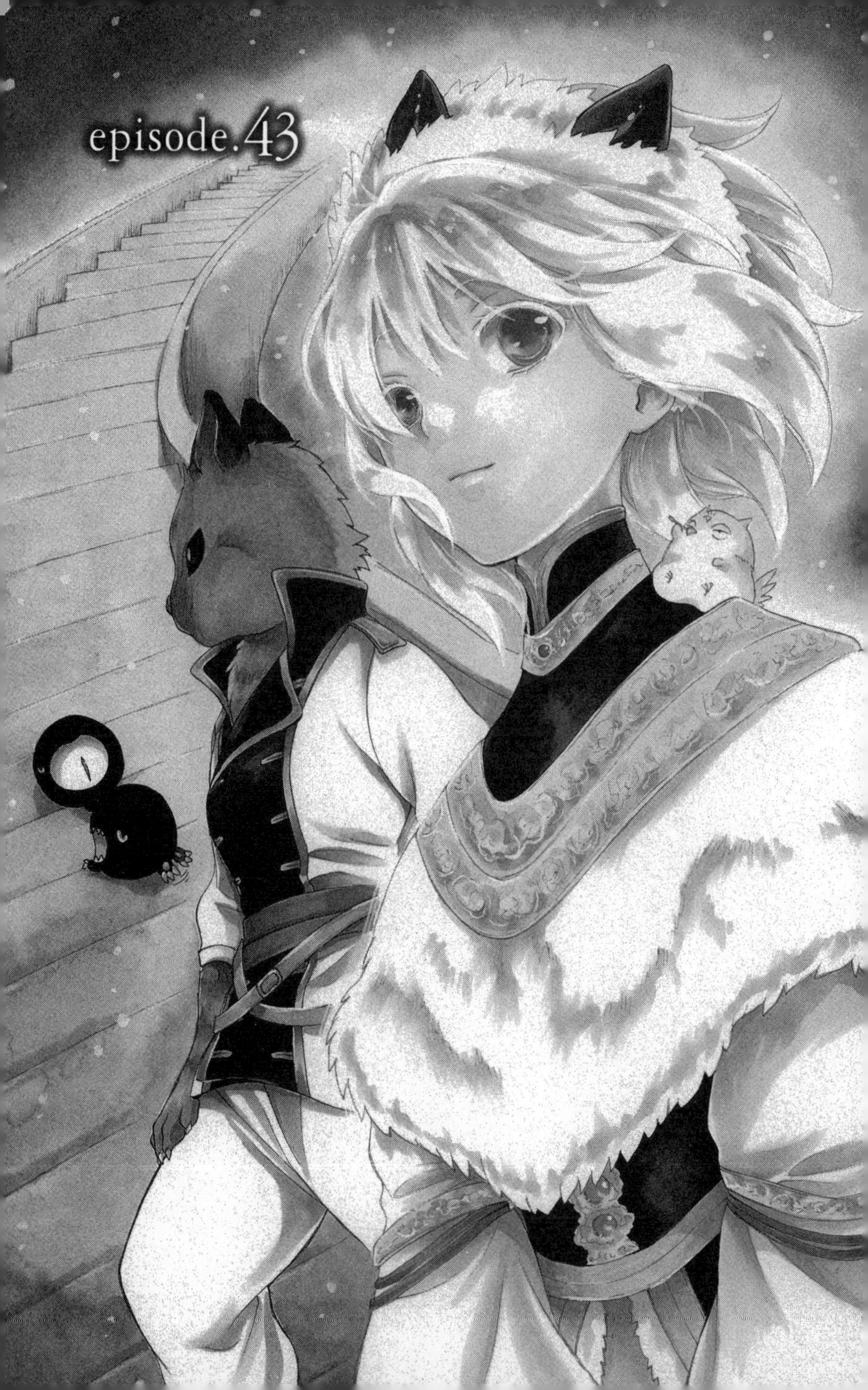
episode.43

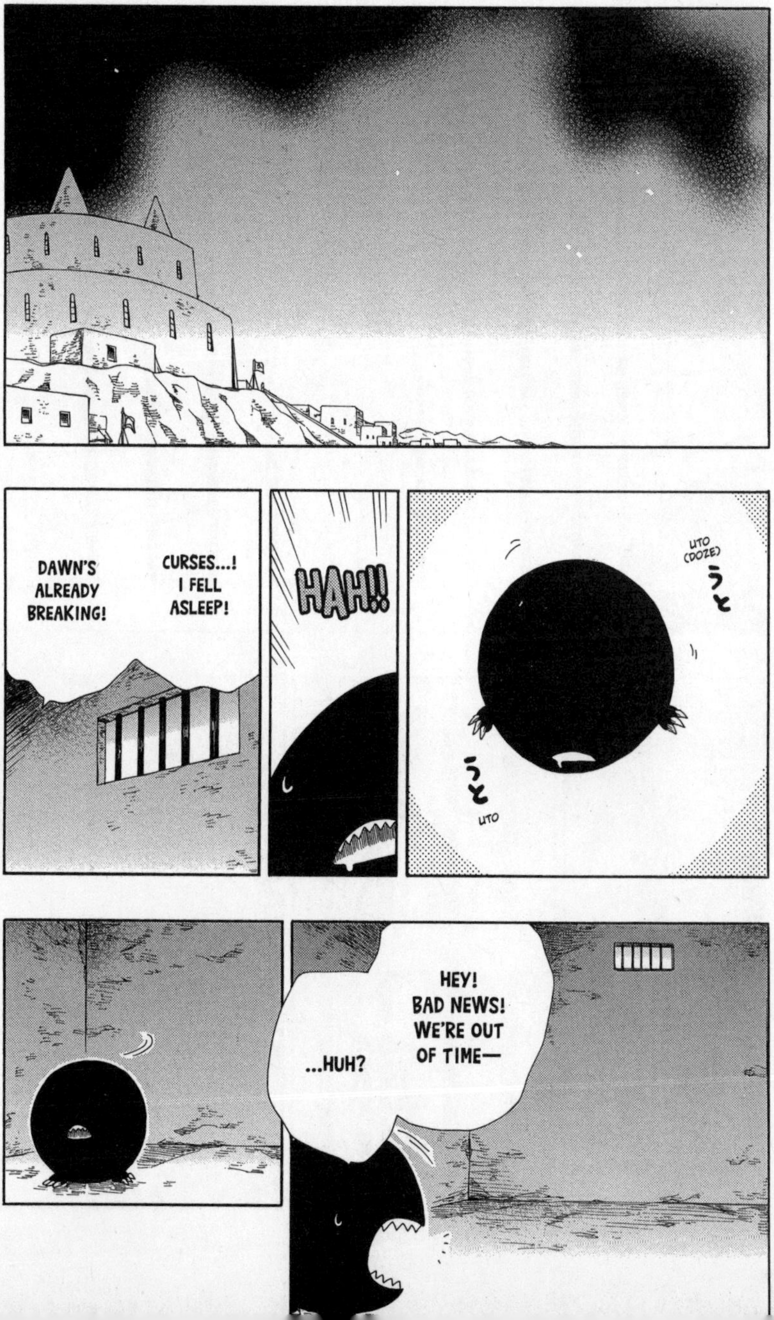
うと
UTO (DOZE)
うと
UTO
HAH!!
CURSES...! I FELL ASLEEP!
DAWN'S ALREADY BREAKING!
HEY! BAD NEWS! WE'RE OUT OF TIME—
...HUH?

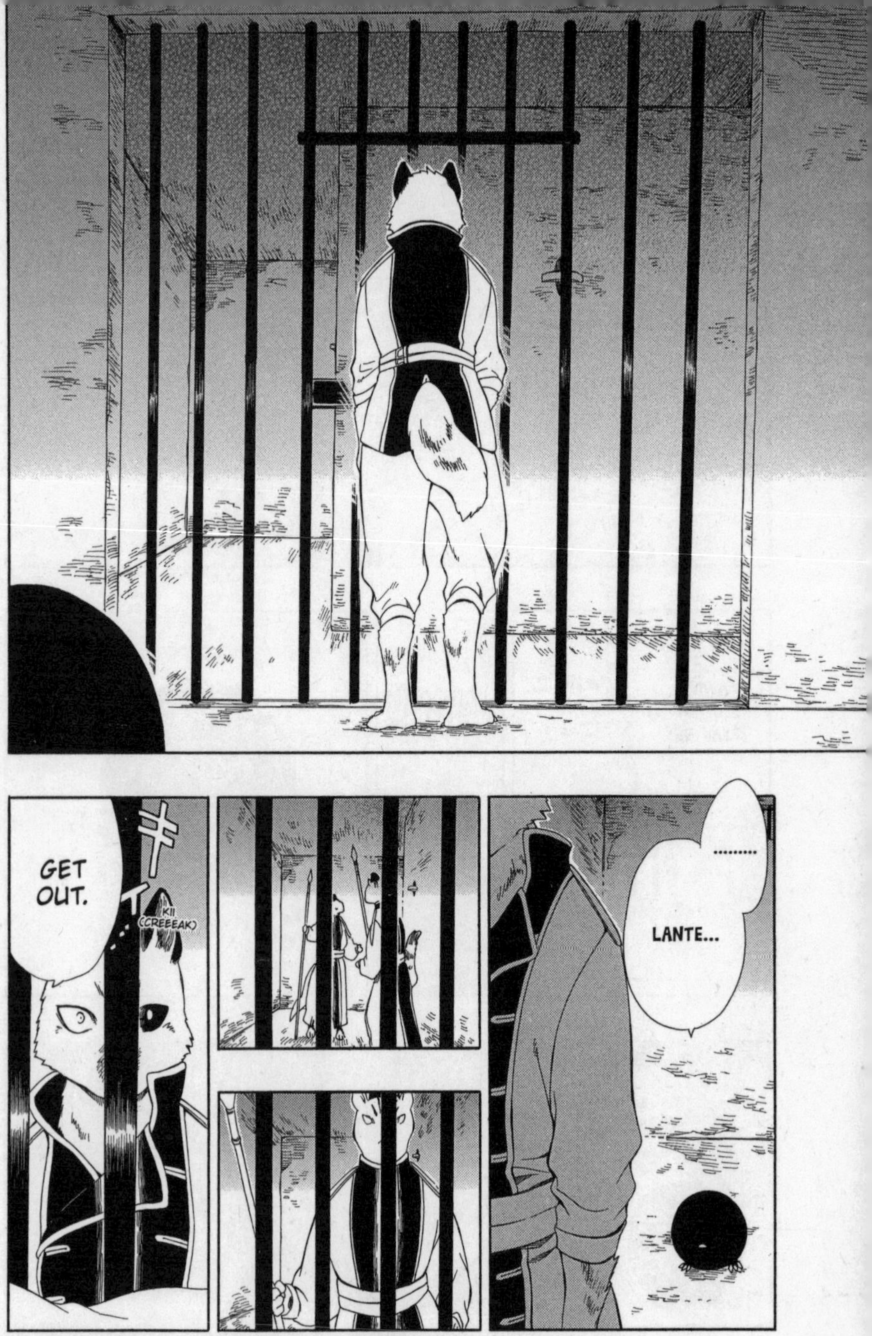

....
LANTE...
GET OUT.
KII (CREEEAK)

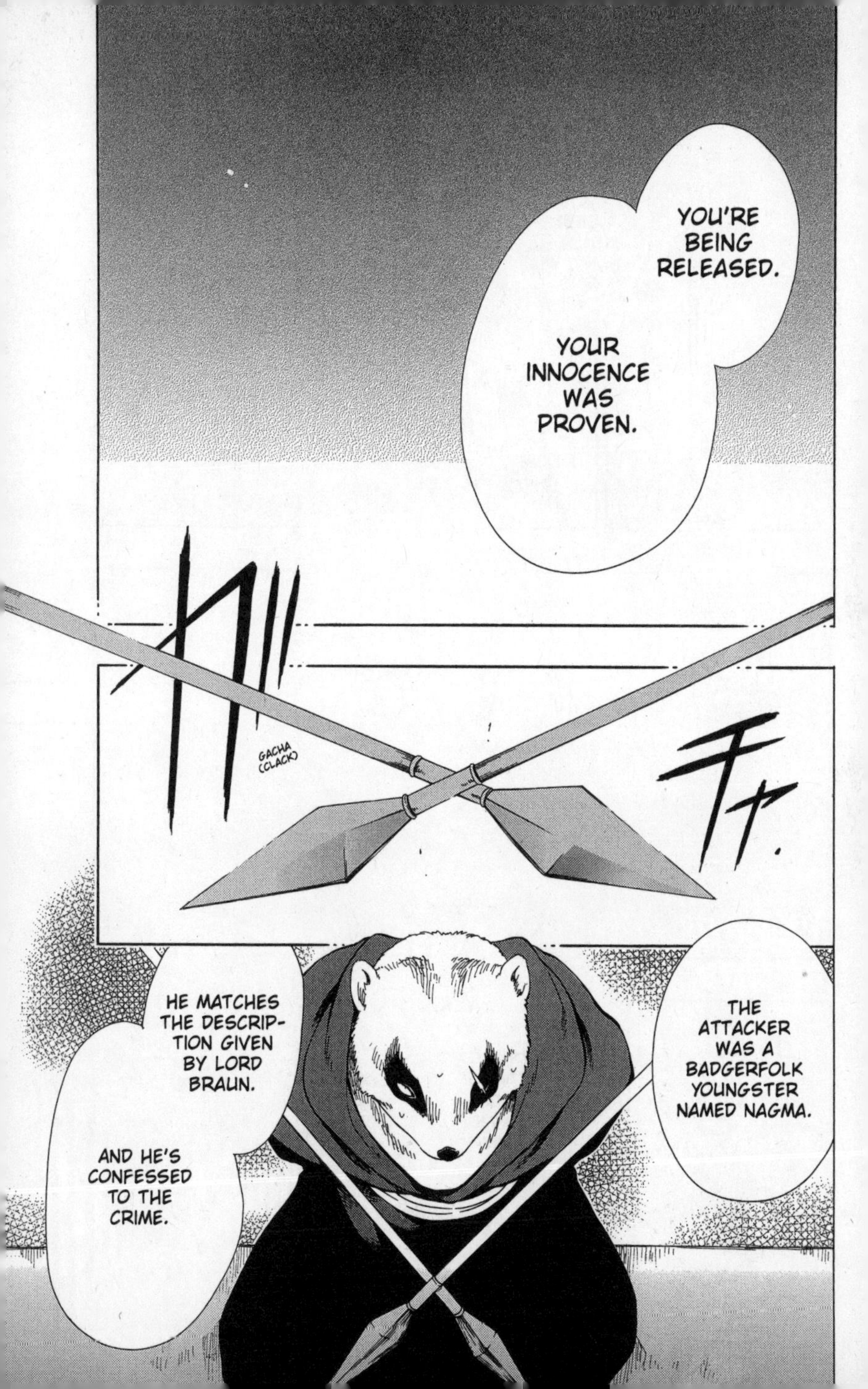
YOU'RE BEING RELEASED.
YOUR INNOCENCE WAS PROVEN.
GACHA (CLACK)
THE ATTACKER WAS A BADGERFOLK YOUNGSTER NAMED NAGMA.
HE MATCHES THE DESCRIP-TION GIVEN BY LORD BRAUN.
AND HE'S CONFESSED TO THE CRIME.

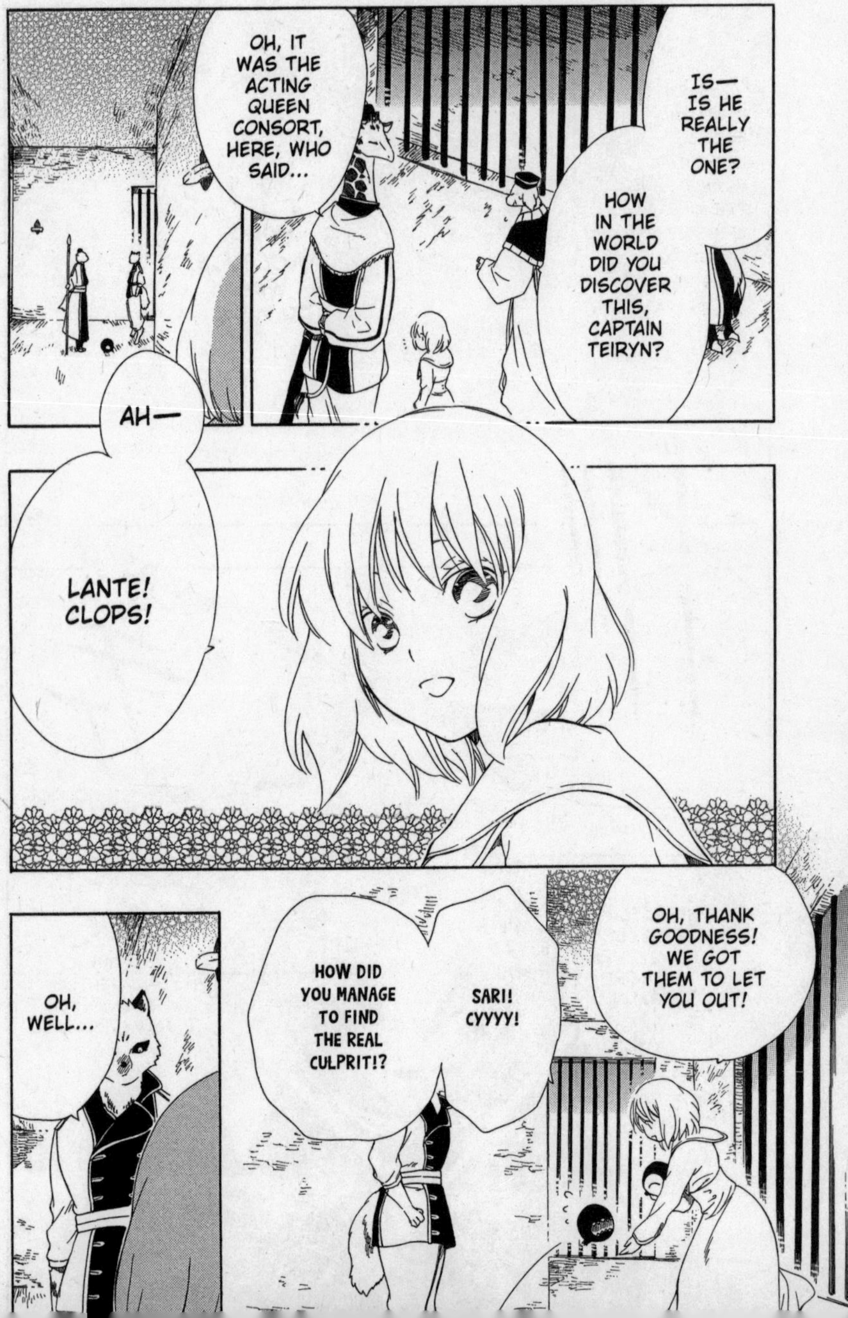
IS— IS HE REALLY THE ONE?
HOW IN THE WORLD DID YOU DISCOVER THIS, CAPTAIN TEIRYN?
OH, IT WAS THE ACTING QUEEN CONSORT, HERE, WHO SAID...
AH—
LANTE! CLOPS!
OH, THANK GOODNESS! WE GOT THEM TO LET YOU OUT!
SARI! CYYYY!
HOW DID YOU MANAGE TO FIND THE REAL CULPRIT!?
OH, WELL...

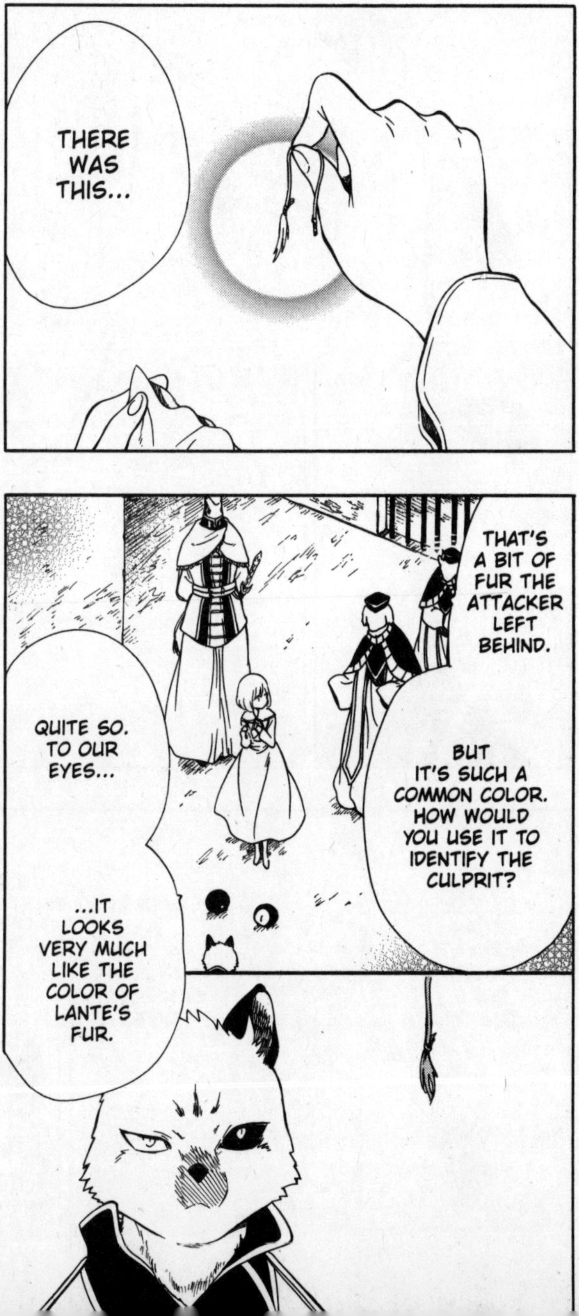
THERE WAS THIS...
THAT'S A BIT OF FUR THE ATTACKER LEFT BEHIND.
BUT IT'S SUCH A COMMON COLOR. HOW WOULD YOU USE IT TO IDENTIFY THE CULPRIT?
QUITE SO. TO OUR EYES...
...IT LOOKS VERY MUCH LIKE THE COLOR OF LANTE'S FUR.

NOW THEN, HERE'S *SACRIFICIAL PRINCESS AND THE KING OF BEASTS*, VOLUME 8! GOSH, WHAT TO DO? I FEEL LIKE I END UP SAYING THE SAME THING EVERY VOLUME, BUT REALLY, THANK YOU ALL SO MUCH. I'M DOING THE BEST I CAN. I HAVE SO MANY PLOTS I STILL WANT TO EXPLORE, SO I REALLY HOPE I CAN KEEP GOING FOR JUST A LITTLE BIT LONGER, AND I HOPE YOU'LL STICK WITH ME. LET'S DO THIS!

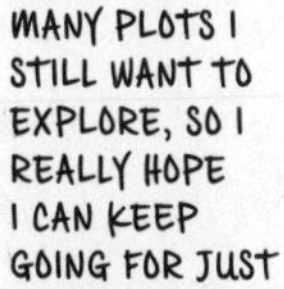
YO. !

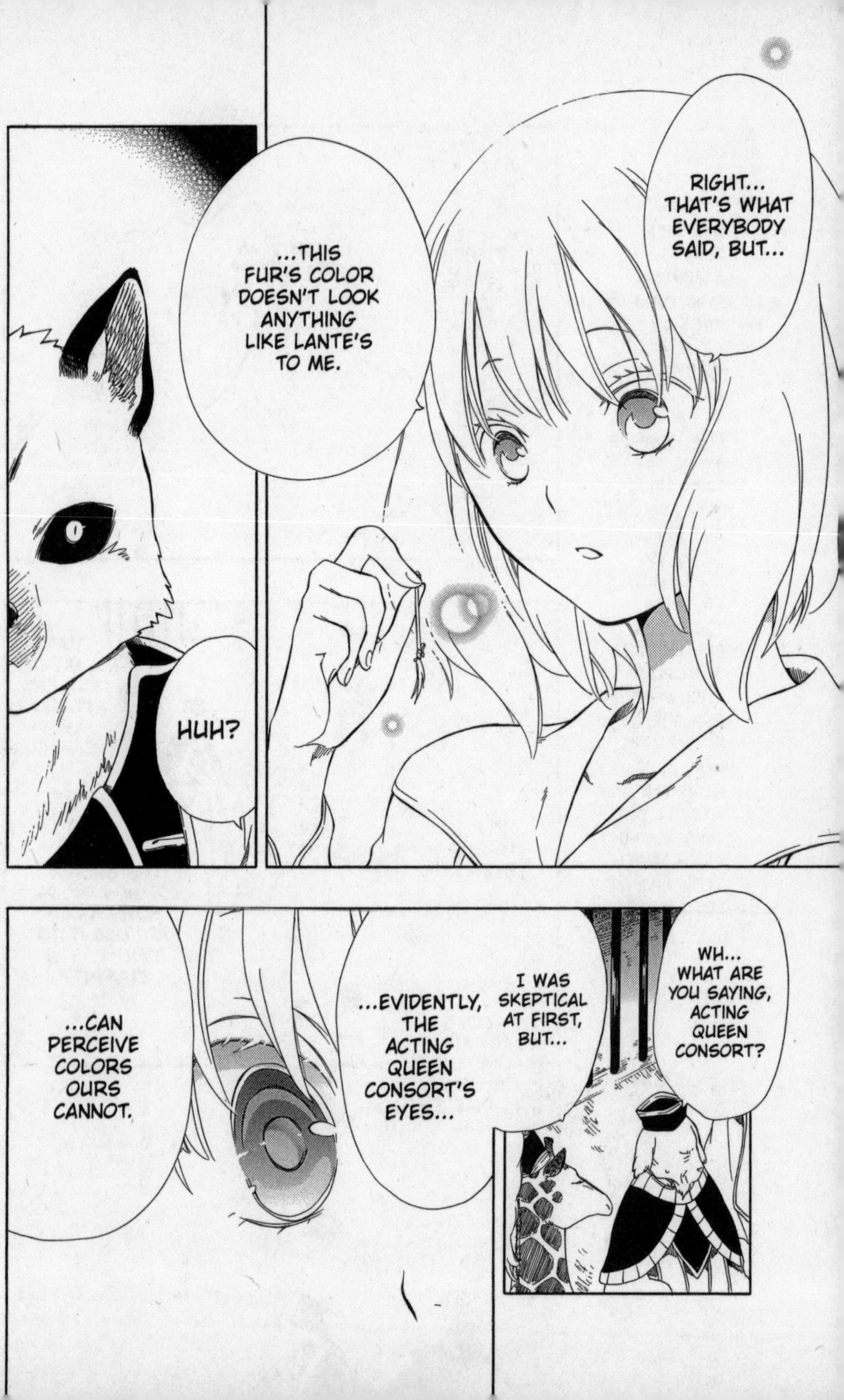
RIGHT... THAT'S WHAT EVERYBODY SAID, BUT...
...THIS FUR'S COLOR DOESN'T LOOK ANYTHING LIKE LANTE'S TO ME.
HUH?
WH... WHAT ARE YOU SAYING, ACTING QUEEN CONSORT?
I WAS SKEPTICAL AT FIRST, BUT...
...EVIDENTLY, THE ACTING QUEEN CONSORT'S EYES...
...CAN PERCEIVE COLORS OURS CANNOT.

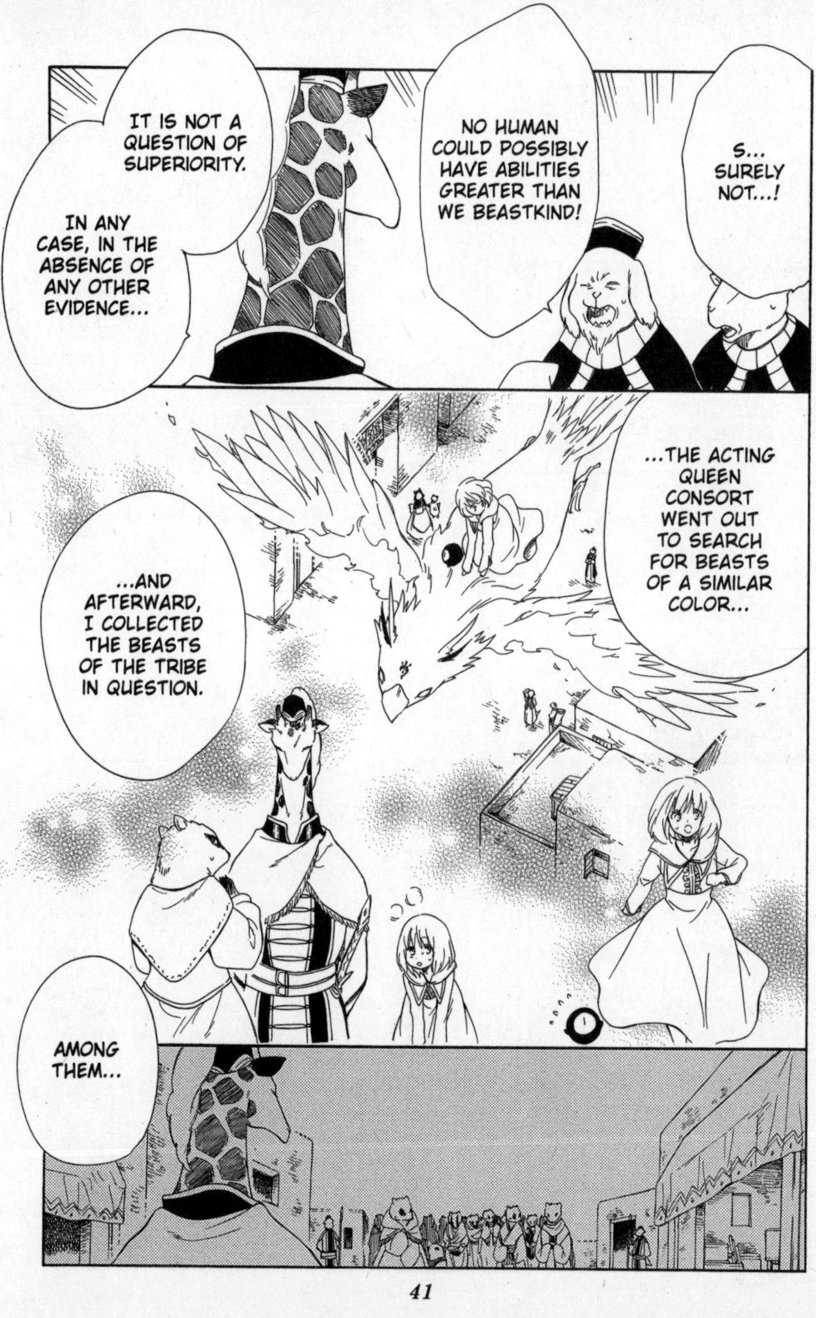
S... SURELY NOT...!
NO HUMAN COULD POSSIBLY HAVE ABILITIES GREATER THAN WE BEASTKIND!
IT IS NOT A QUESTION OF SUPERIORITY.
IN ANY CASE, IN THE ABSENCE OF ANY OTHER EVIDENCE...
...THE ACTING QUEEN CONSORT WENT OUT TO SEARCH FOR BEASTS OF A SIMILAR COLOR...
...AND AFTERWARD, I COLLECTED THE BEASTS OF THE TRIBE IN QUESTION.
AMONG THEM...

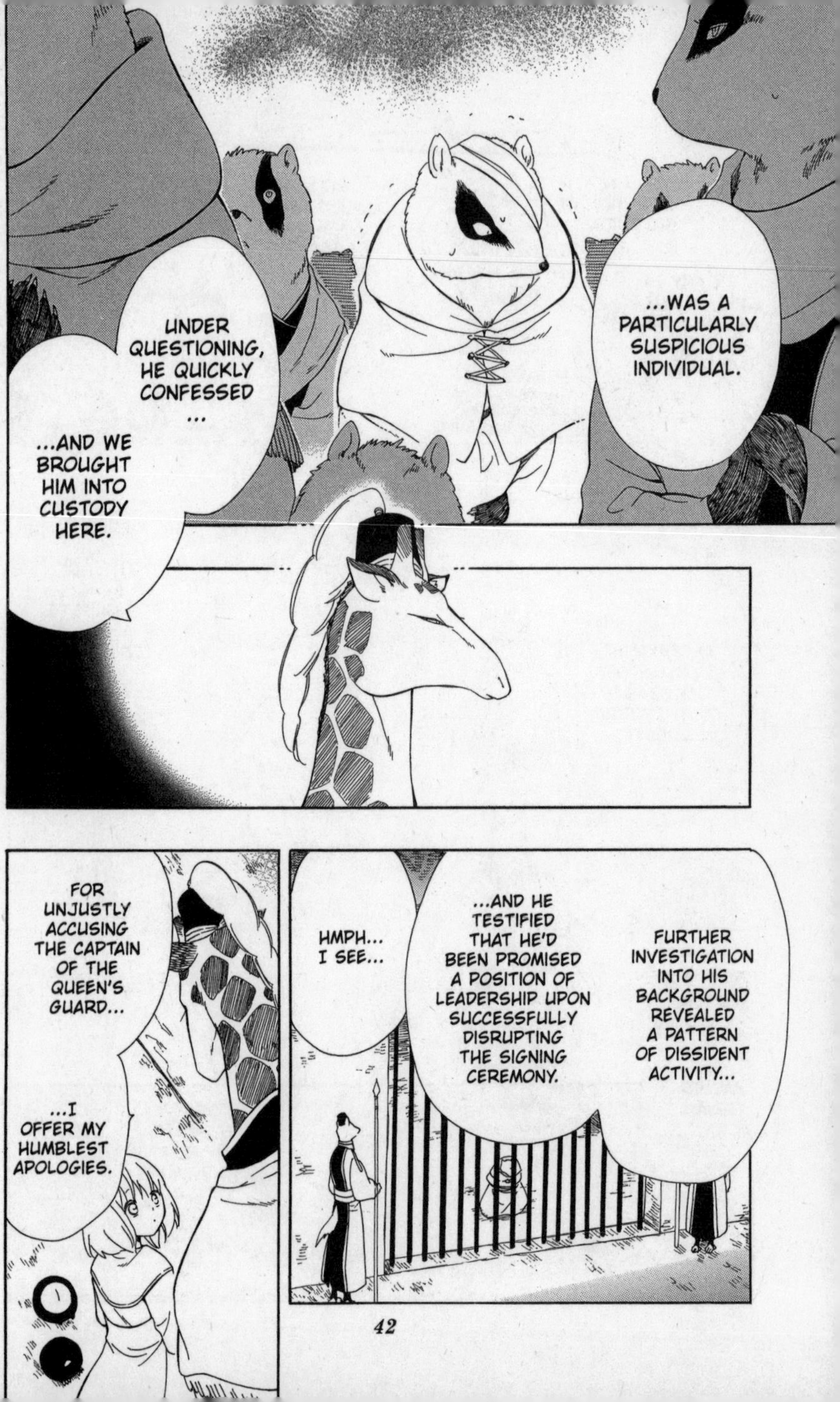
...WAS A PARTICULARLY SUSPICIOUS INDIVIDUAL.
UNDER QUESTIONING, HE QUICKLY CONFESSED...
...AND WE BROUGHT HIM INTO CUSTODY HERE.
FURTHER INVESTIGATION INTO HIS BACKGROUND REVEALED A PATTERN OF DISSIDENT ACTIVITY...
...AND HE TESTIFIED THAT HE'D BEEN PROMISED A POSITION OF LEADERSHIP UPON SUCCESSFULLY DISRUPTING THE SIGNING CEREMONY.
HMPH... I SEE...
FOR UNJUSTLY ACCUSING THE CAPTAIN OF THE QUEEN'S GUARD...
...I OFFER MY HUMBLEST APOLOGIES.

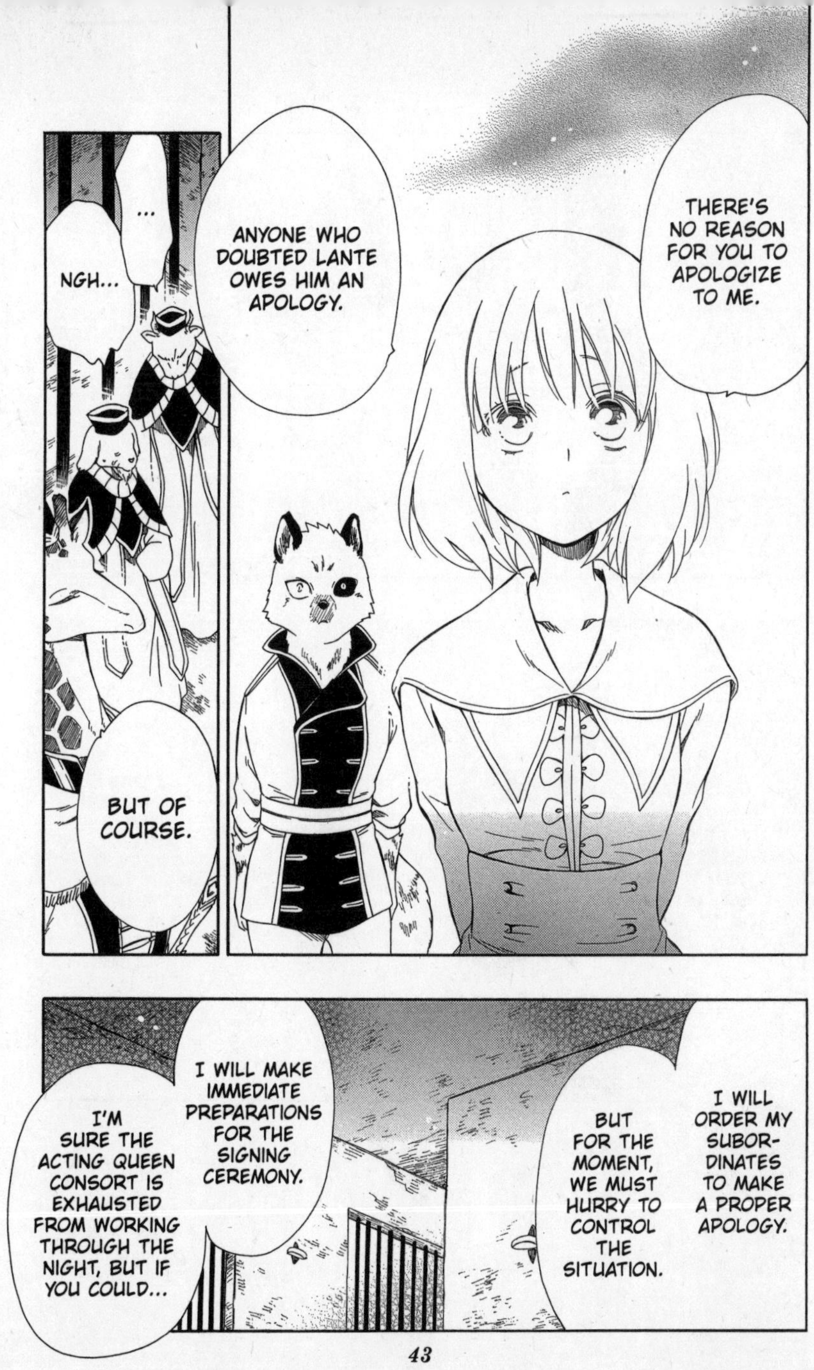
THERE'S NO REASON FOR YOU TO APOLOGIZE TO ME.
ANYONE WHO DOUBTED LANTE OWES HIM AN APOLOGY.
...
NGH...
BUT OF COURSE.
I WILL ORDER MY SUBOR-DINATES TO MAKE A PROPER APOLOGY.
BUT FOR THE MOMENT, WE MUST HURRY TO CONTROL THE SITUATION.
I WILL MAKE IMMEDIATE PREPARATIONS FOR THE SIGNING CEREMONY.
I'M SURE THE ACTING QUEEN CONSORT IS EXHAUSTED FROM WORKING THROUGH THE NIGHT, BUT IF YOU COULD...

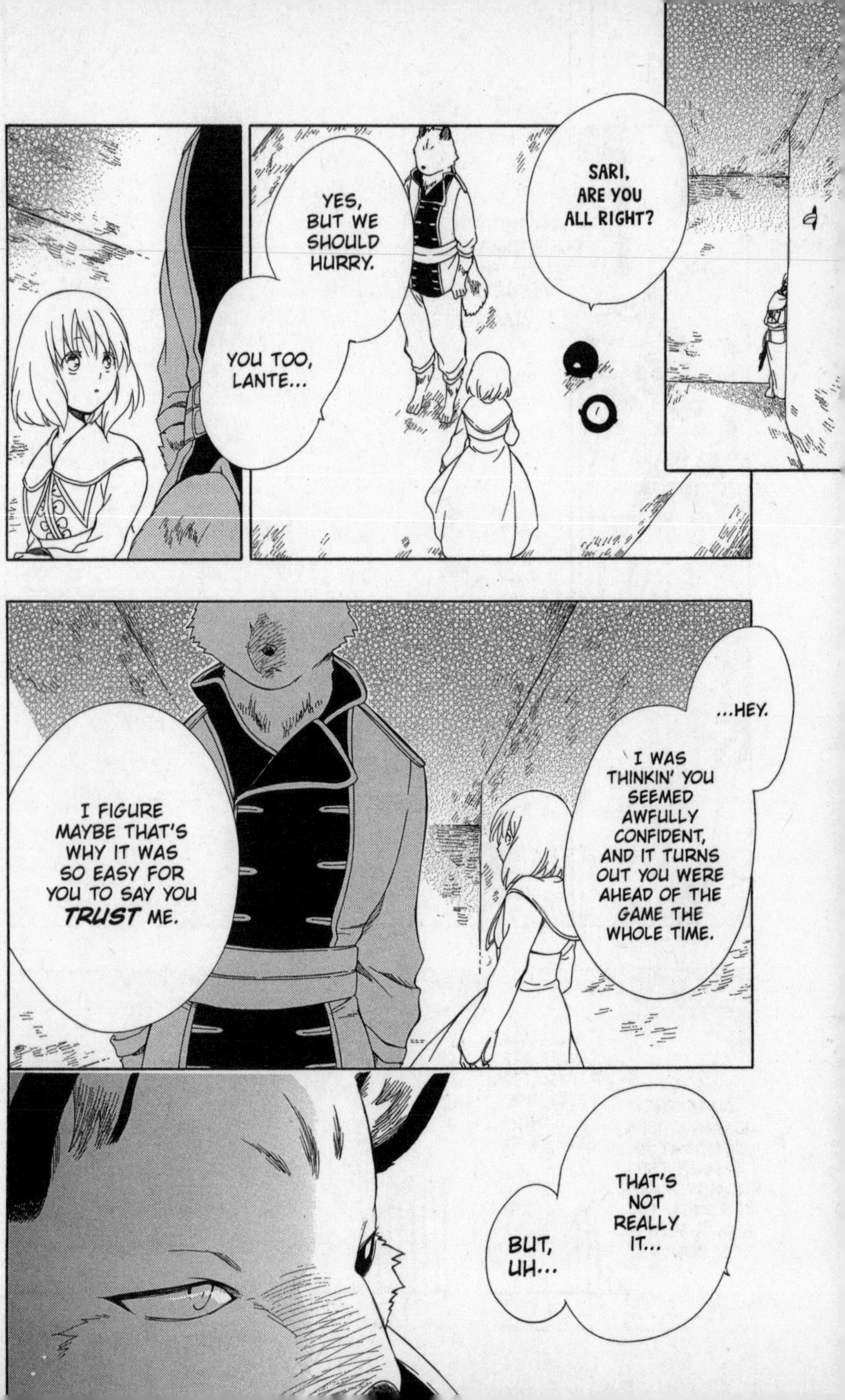
SARI, ARE YOU ALL RIGHT?
YES, BUT WE SHOULD HURRY.
YOU TOO, LANTE...
...HEY.
I WAS THINKIN' YOU SEEMED AWFULLY CONFIDENT, AND IT TURNS OUT YOU WERE AHEAD OF THE GAME THE WHOLE TIME.
I FIGURE MAYBE THAT'S WHY IT WAS SO EASY FOR YOU TO SAY YOU TRUST ME.
THAT'S NOT REALLY IT...
BUT, UH...

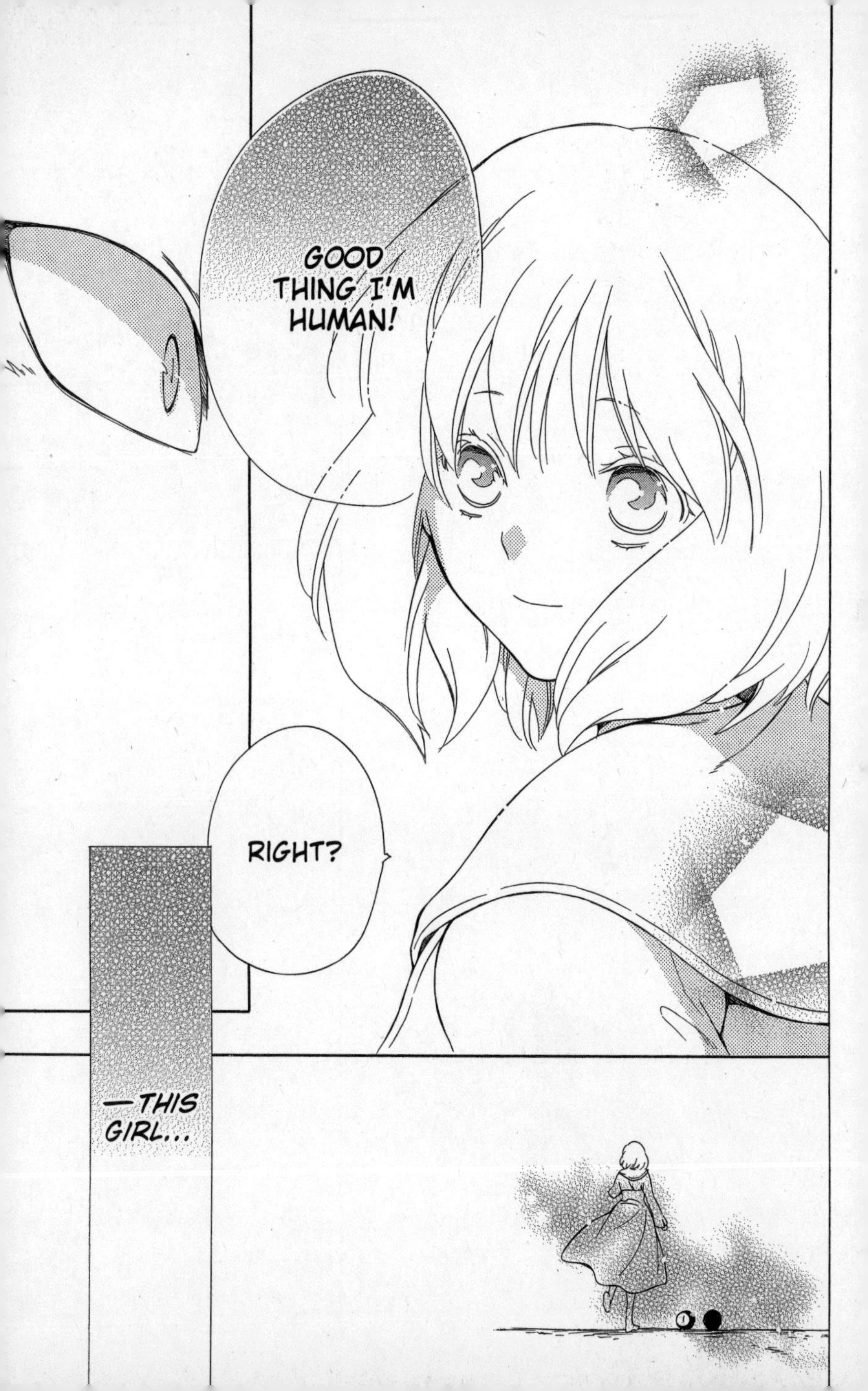
GOOD THING I'M HUMAN!
RIGHT?
—THIS GIRL...

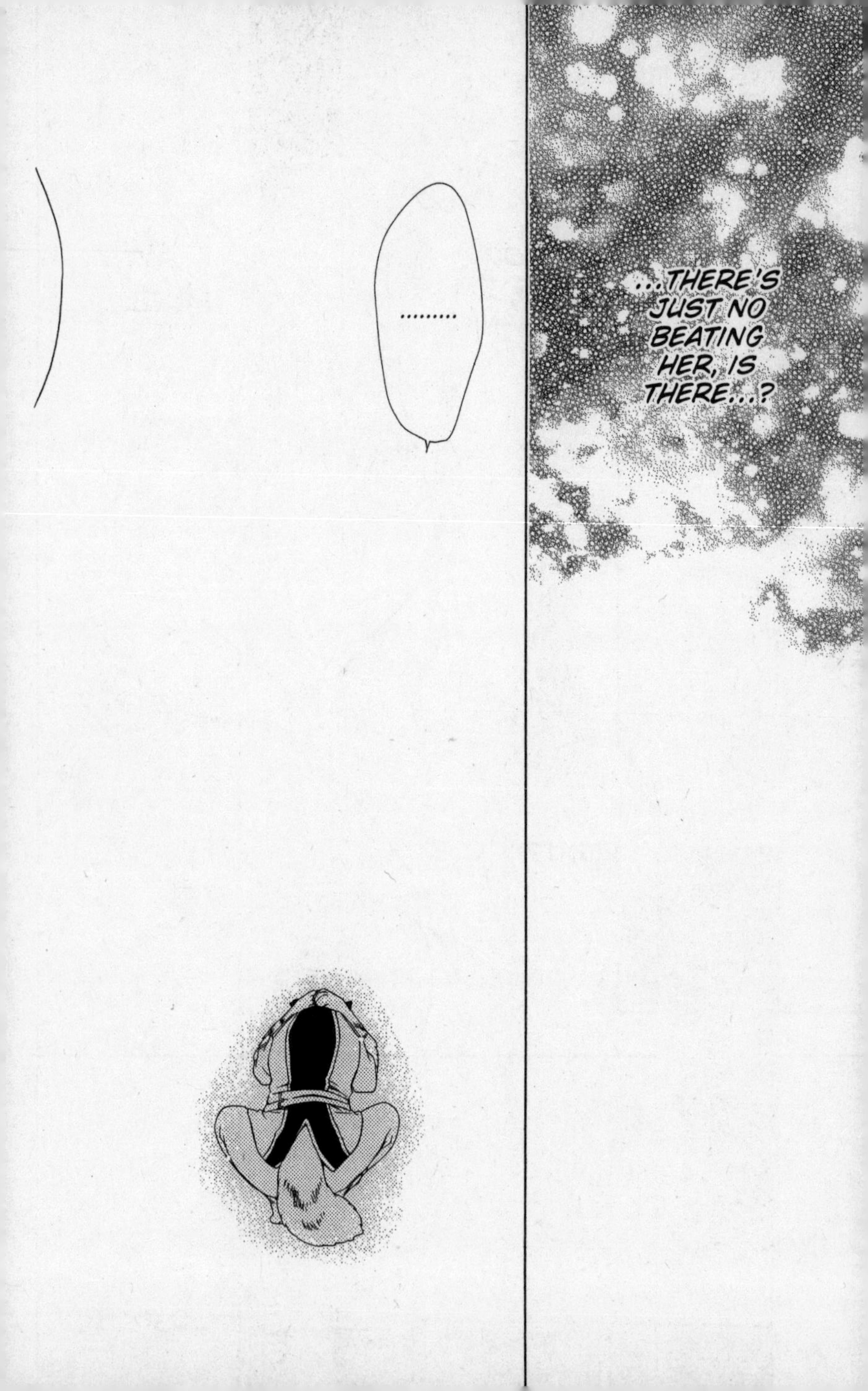
...THERE'S JUST NO BEATING HER, IS THERE...?
....

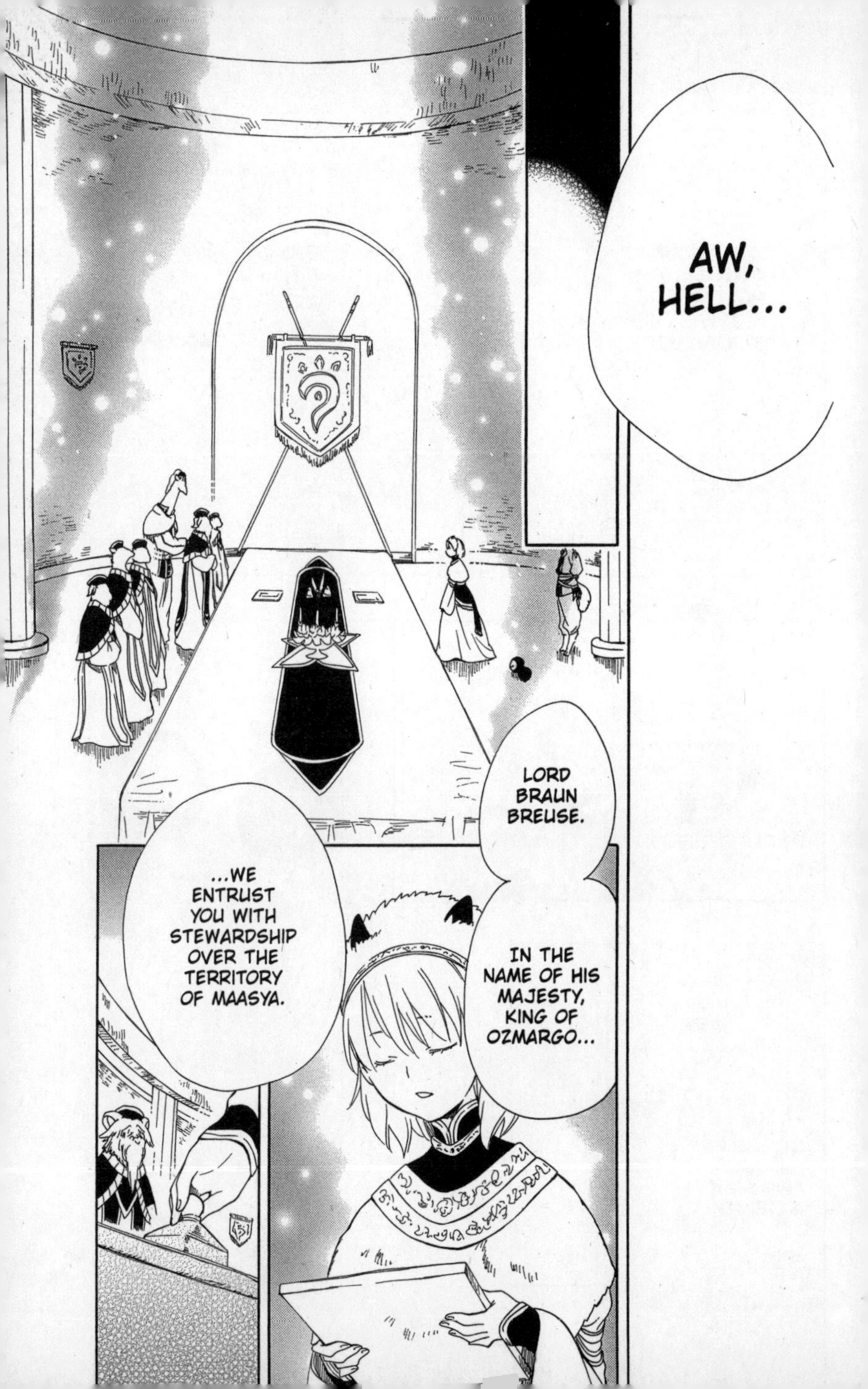
AW, HELL...
LORD BRAUN BREUSE.
IN THE NAME OF HIS MAJESTY, KING OF OZMARGO...
...WE ENTRUST YOU WITH STEWARDSHIP OVER THE TERRITORY OF MAASYA.

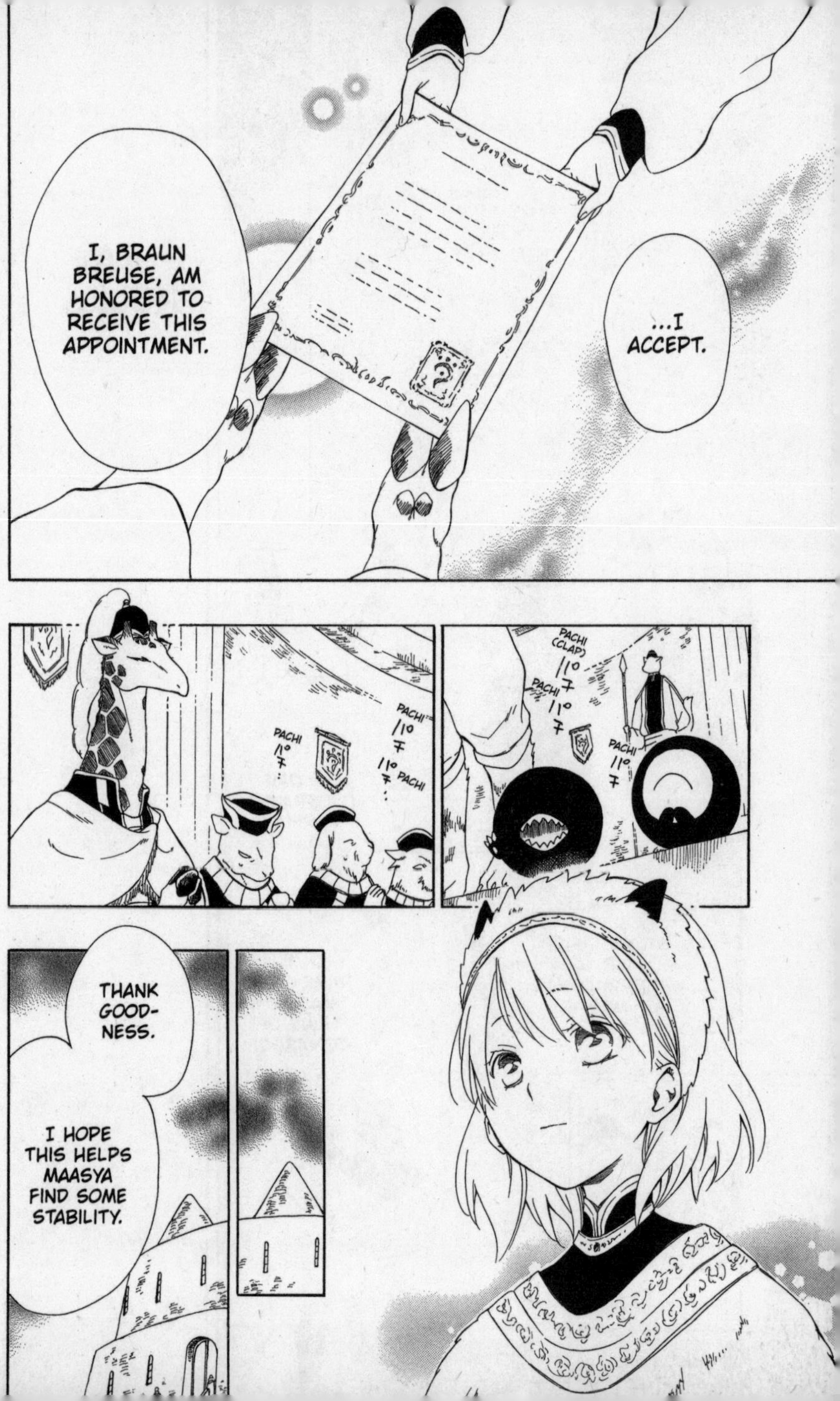
...I ACCEPT.
I, BRAUN BREUSE, AM HONORED TO RECEIVE THIS APPOINTMENT.
PACHI (CLAP)
PACHI
PACHI
PACHI
PACHI
PACHI
THANK GOOD-NESS.
I HOPE THIS HELPS MAASYA FIND SOME STABILITY.

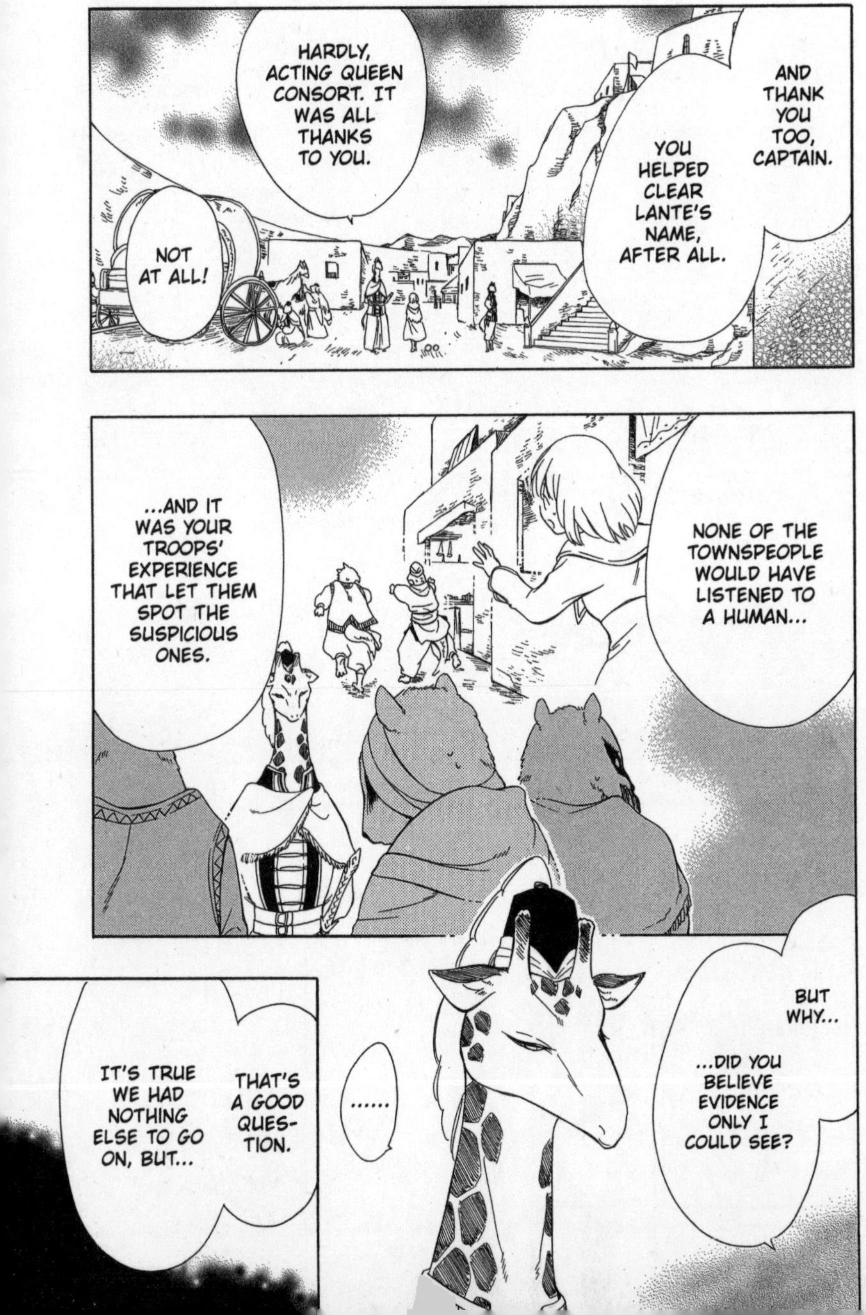
AND THANK YOU TOO, CAPTAIN.
YOU HELPED CLEAR LANTE'S NAME, AFTER ALL.
HARDLY, ACTING QUEEN CONSORT. IT WAS ALL THANKS TO YOU.
NOT AT ALL!
NONE OF THE TOWNSPEOPLE WOULD HAVE LISTENED TO A HUMAN...
...AND IT WAS YOUR TROOPS' EXPERIENCE THAT LET THEM SPOT THE SUSPICIOUS ONES.
BUT WHY...
...DID YOU BELIEVE EVIDENCE ONLY I COULD SEE?
......
THAT'S A GOOD QUES-TION.
IT'S TRUE WE HAD NOTHING ELSE TO GO ON, BUT...

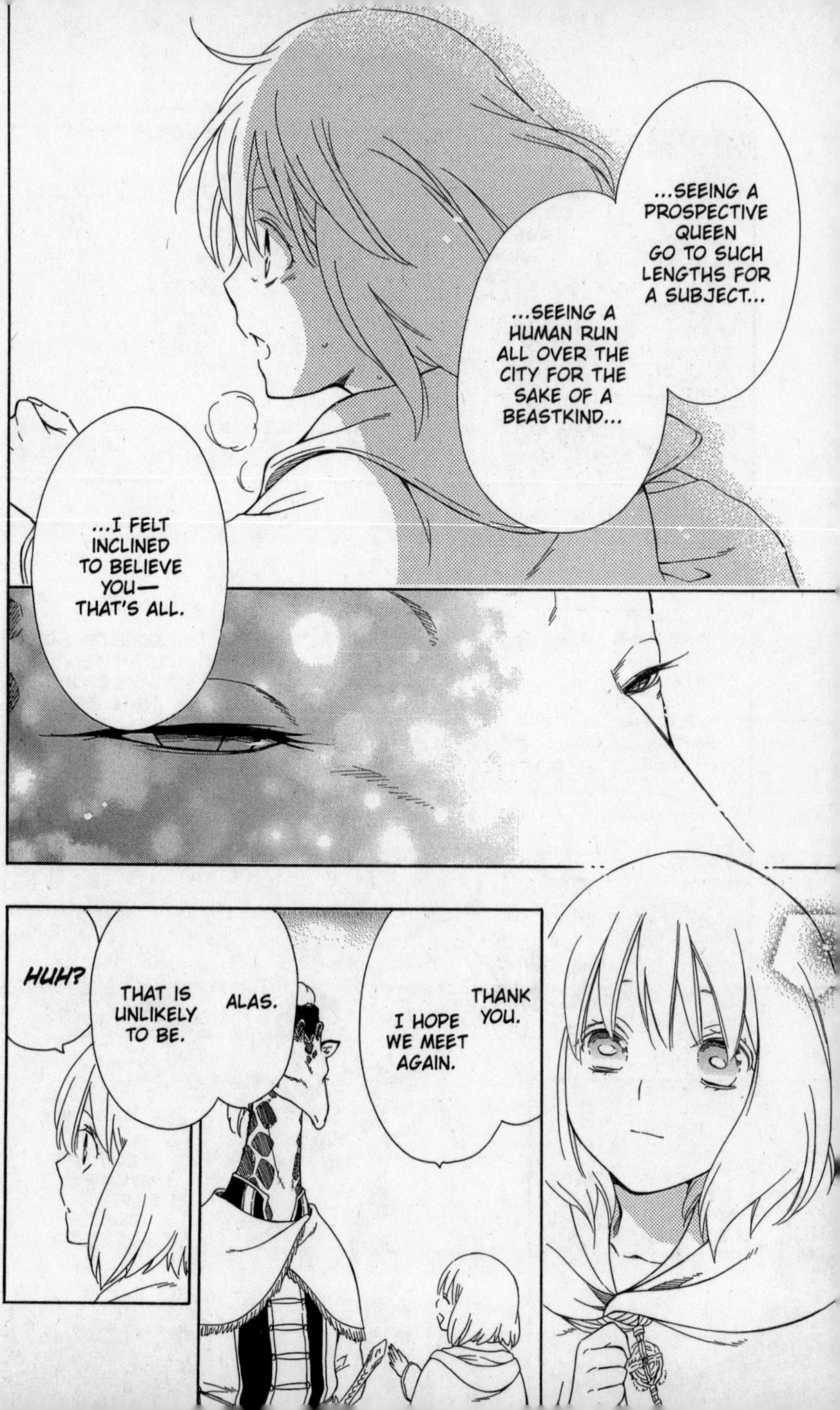
...SEEING A PROSPECTIVE QUEEN GO TO SUCH LENGTHS FOR A SUBJECT...
...SEEING A HUMAN RUN ALL OVER THE CITY FOR THE SAKE OF A BEASTKIND...
...I FELT INCLINED TO BELIEVE YOU—THAT'S ALL.
THANK YOU.
I HOPE WE MEET AGAIN.
ALAS.
THAT IS UNLIKELY TO BE.
HUH?

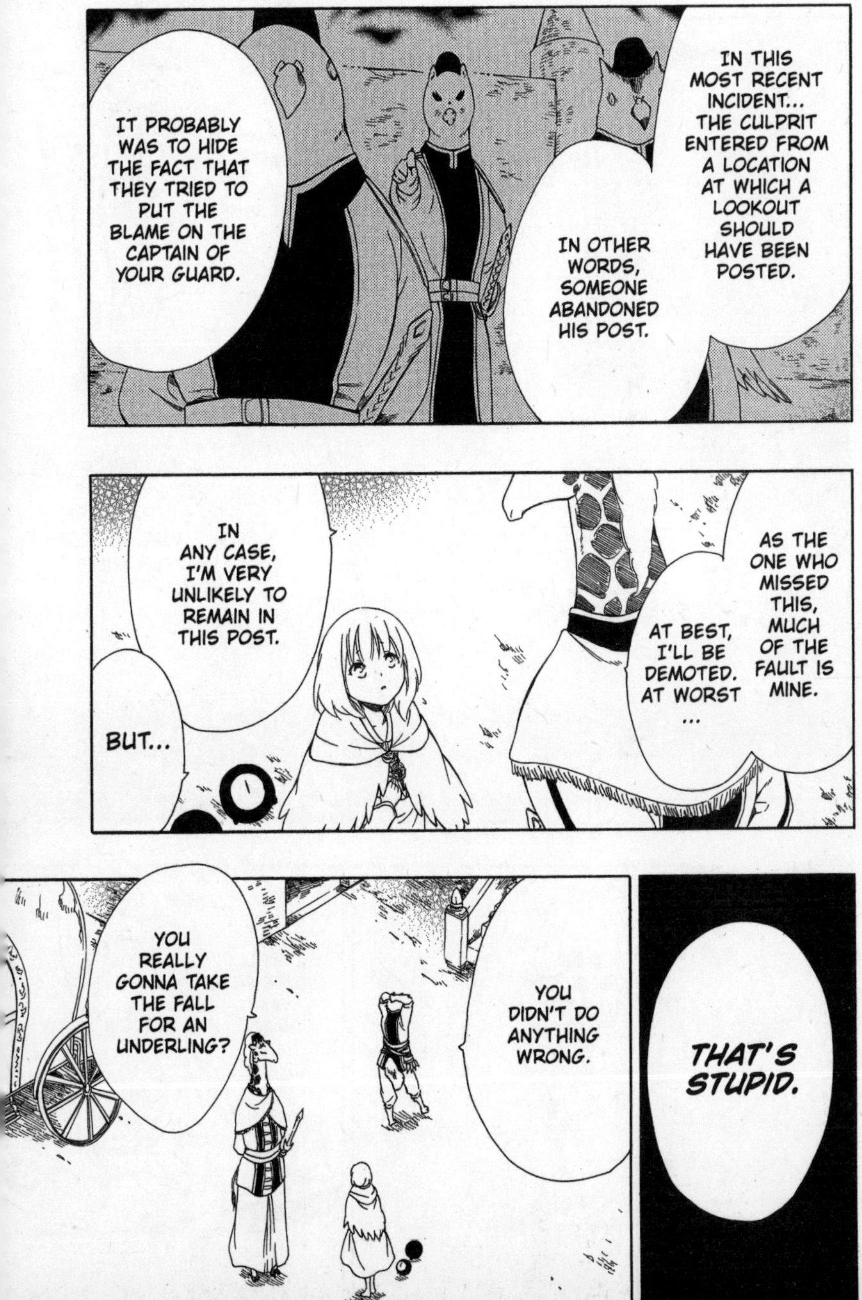
IN THIS MOST RECENT INCIDENT... THE CULPRIT ENTERED FROM A LOCATION AT WHICH A LOOKOUT SHOULD HAVE BEEN POSTED.
IN OTHER WORDS, SOMEONE ABANDONED HIS POST.
IT PROBABLY WAS TO HIDE THE FACT THAT THEY TRIED TO PUT THE BLAME ON THE CAPTAIN OF YOUR GUARD.
AS THE ONE WHO MISSED THIS, MUCH OF THE FAULT IS MINE.
AT BEST, I'LL BE DEMOTED. AT WORST ...
IN ANY CASE, I'M VERY UNLIKELY TO REMAIN IN THIS POST.
BUT...
THAT'S STUPID.
YOU DIDN'T DO ANYTHING WRONG.
YOU REALLY GONNA TAKE THE FALL FOR AN UNDERLING?

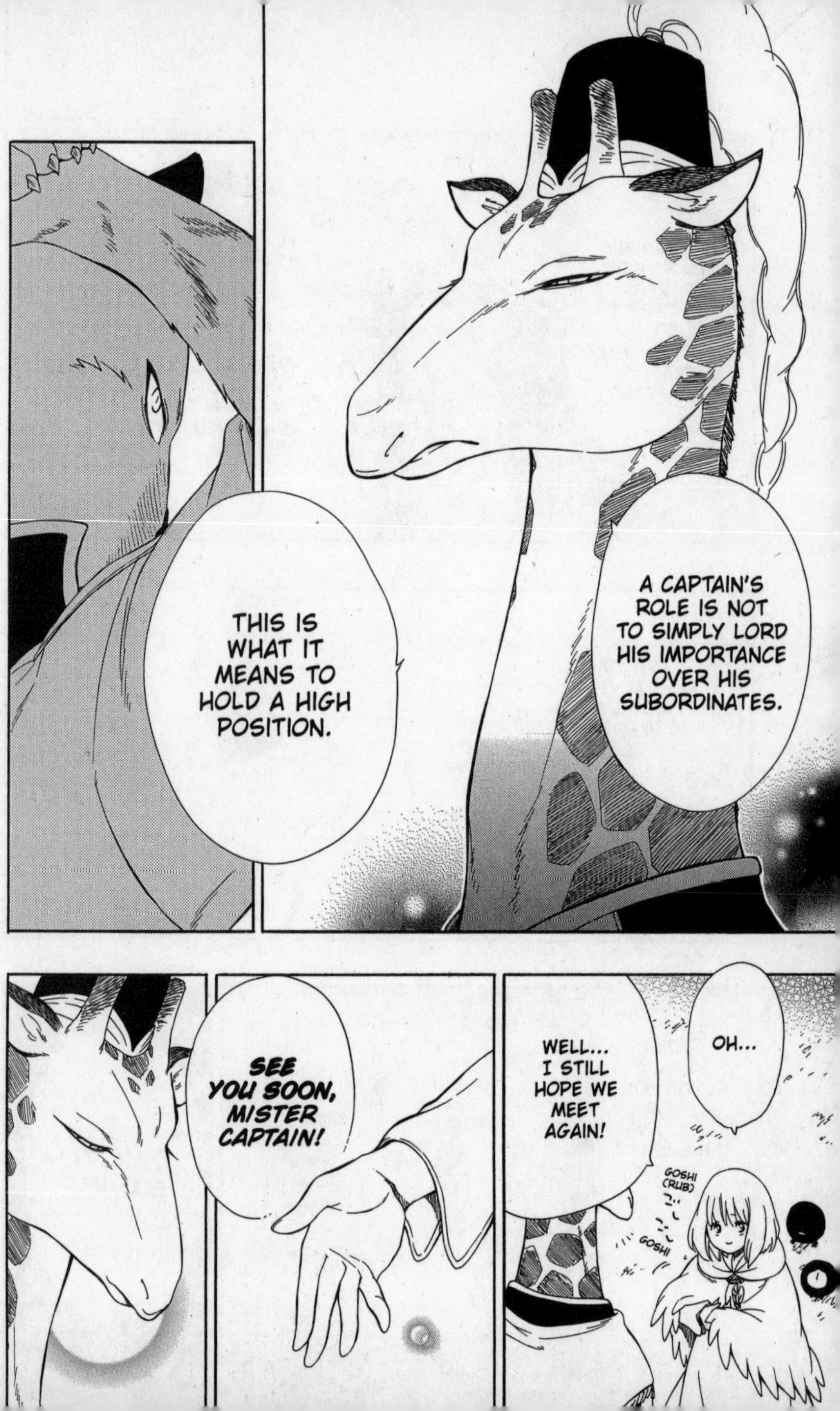
A CAPTAIN'S ROLE IS NOT TO SIMPLY LORD HIS IMPORTANCE OVER HIS SUBORDINATES.
THIS IS WHAT IT MEANS TO HOLD A HIGH POSITION.
OH...
WELL... I STILL HOPE WE MEET AGAIN!
GOSHI (RUB)
GOSHI
SEE YOU SOON, MISTER CAPTAIN!

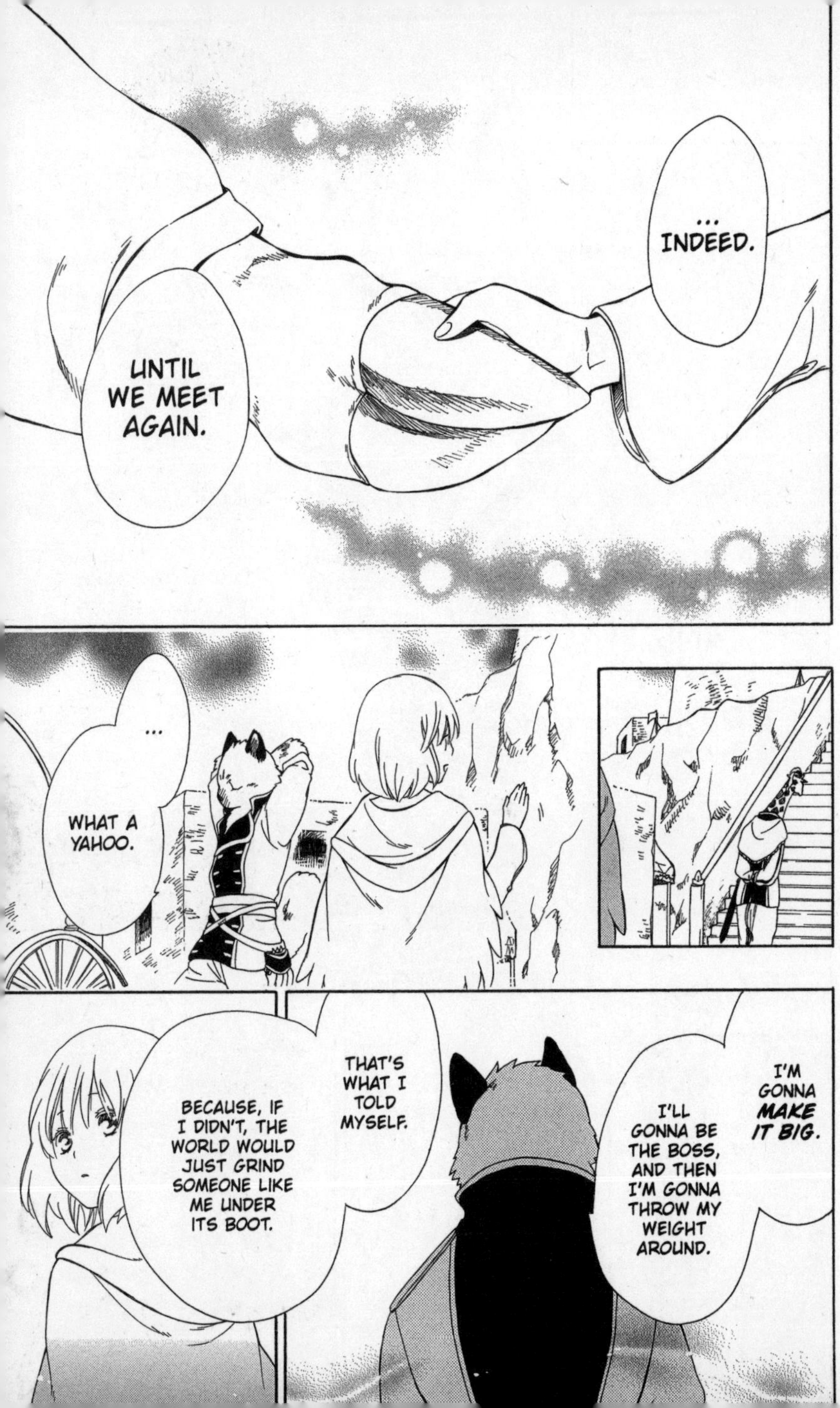
... INDEED.
UNTIL WE MEET AGAIN.
... WHAT A YAHOO.
I'M GONNA *MAKE IT BIG*.
I'LL GONNA BE THE BOSS, AND THEN I'M GONNA THROW MY WEIGHT AROUND.
THAT'S WHAT I TOLD MYSELF.
BECAUSE, IF I DIDN'T, THE WORLD WOULD JUST GRIND SOMEONE LIKE ME UNDER ITS BOOT.

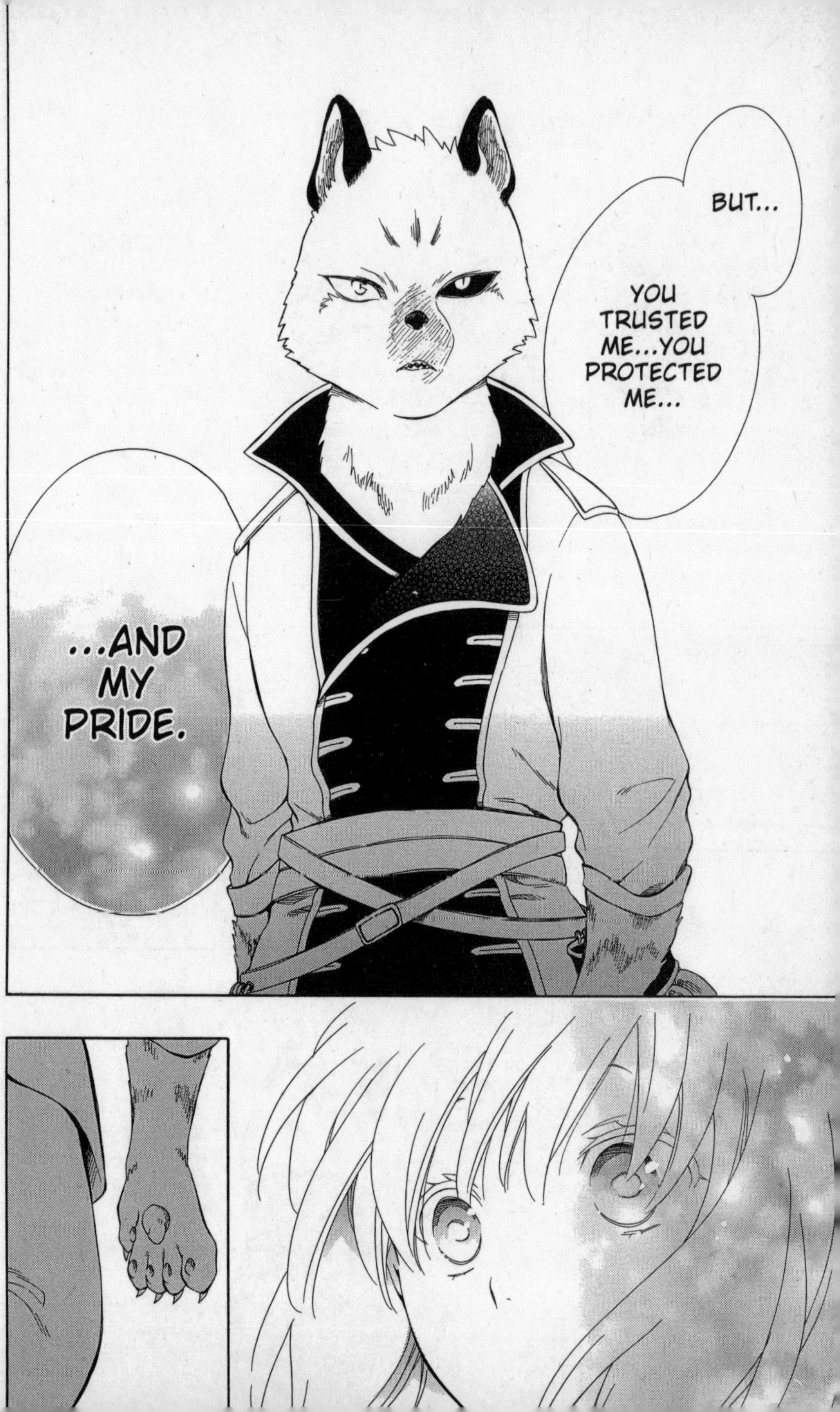
BUT...
YOU TRUSTED ME...YOU PROTECTED ME...
...AND MY PRIDE.

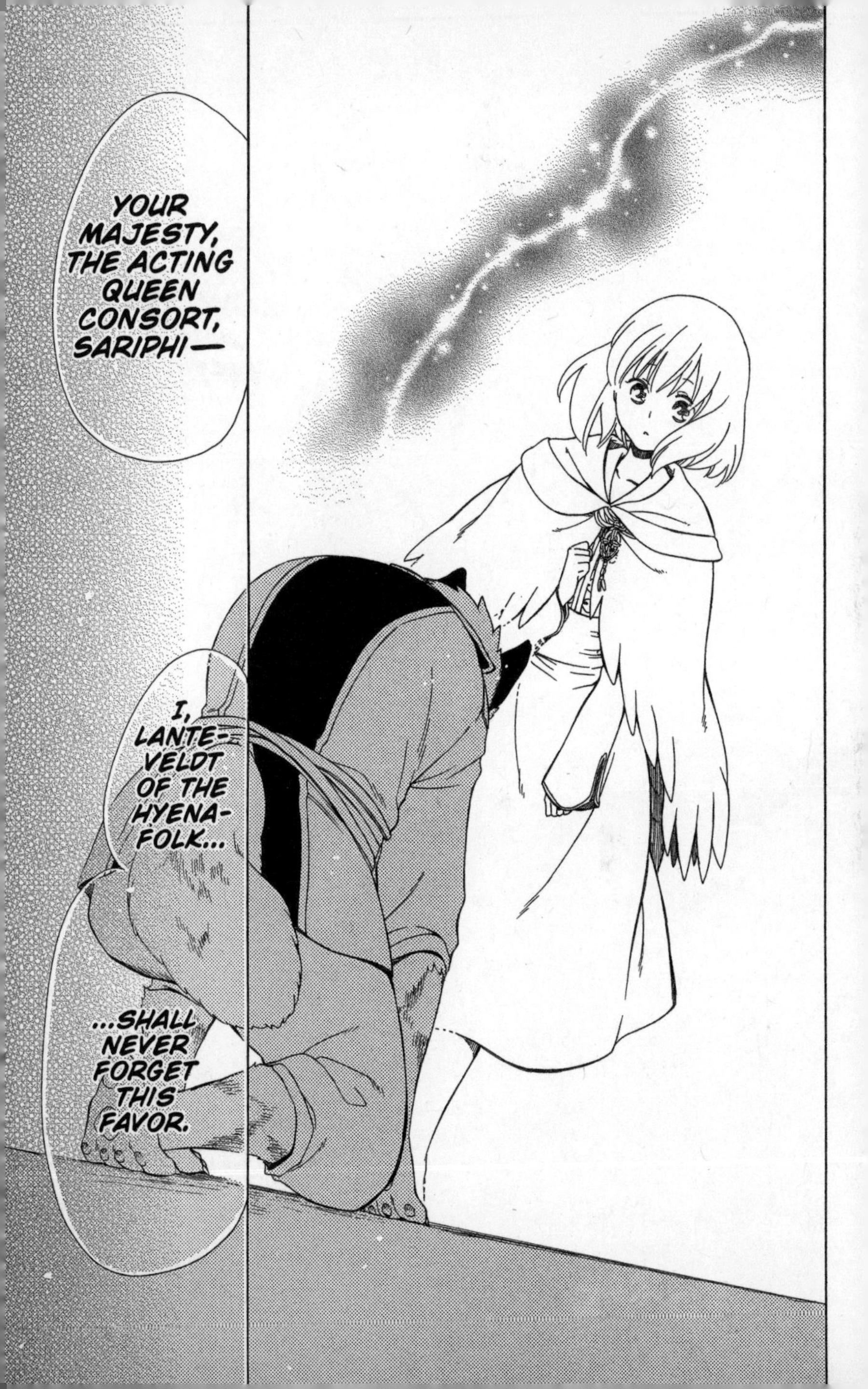
YOUR MAJESTY, THE ACTING QUEEN CONSORT, SARIPHI—
I, LANTE-VELDT OF THE HYENA-FOLK...
...SHALL NEVER FORGET THIS FAVOR.

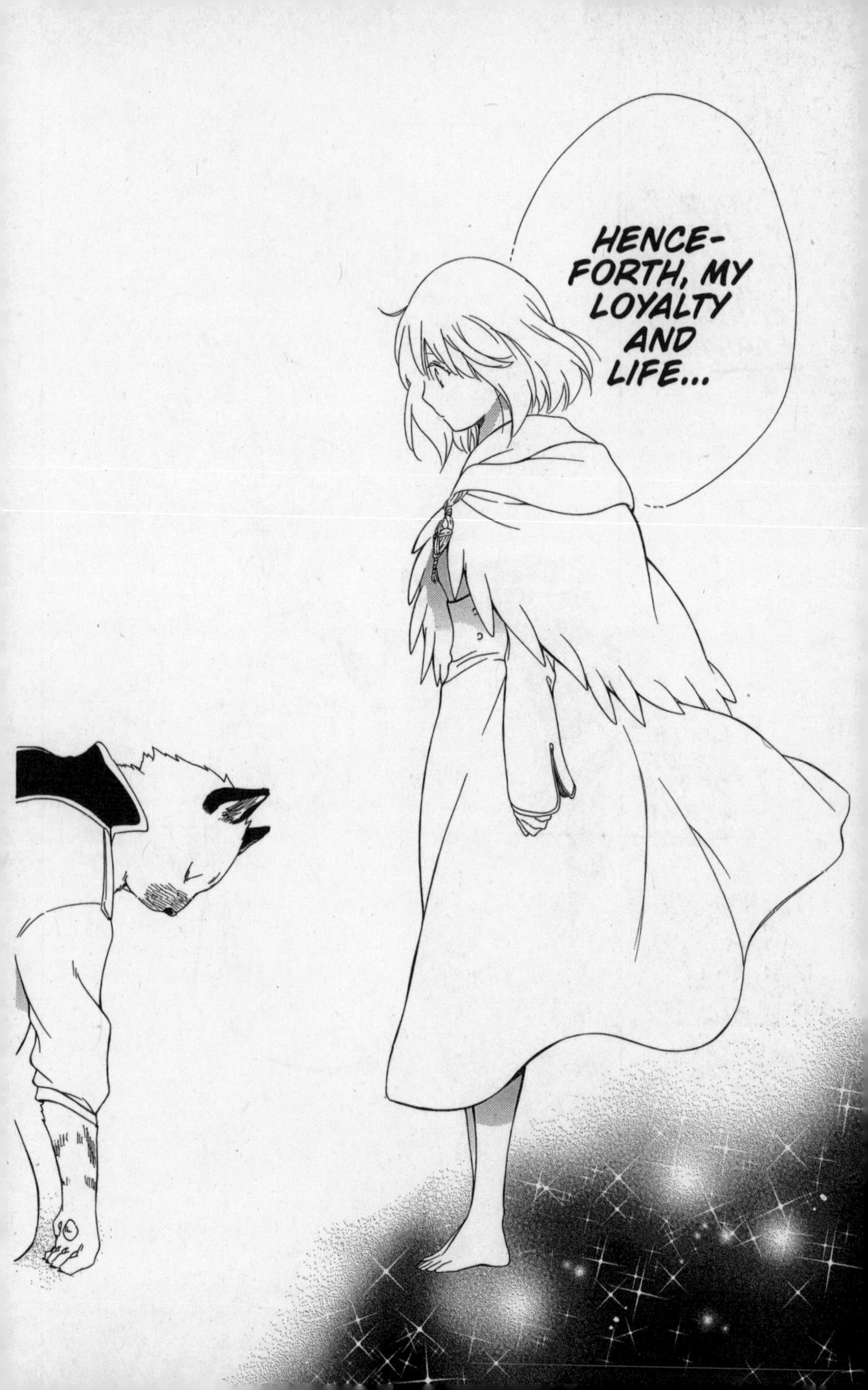
HENCE-FORTH, MY LOYALTY AND LIFE...

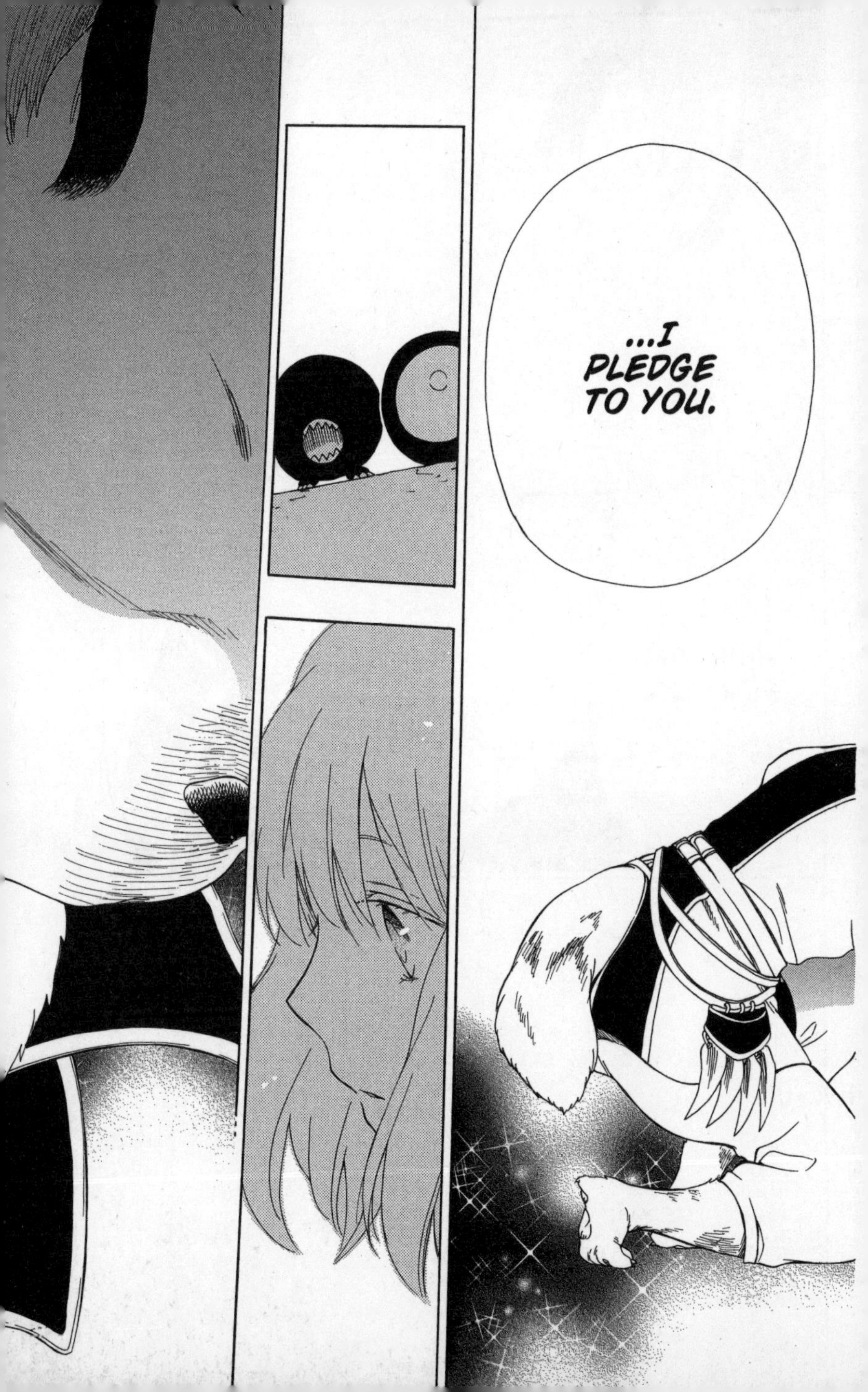
...I PLEDGE TO YOU.

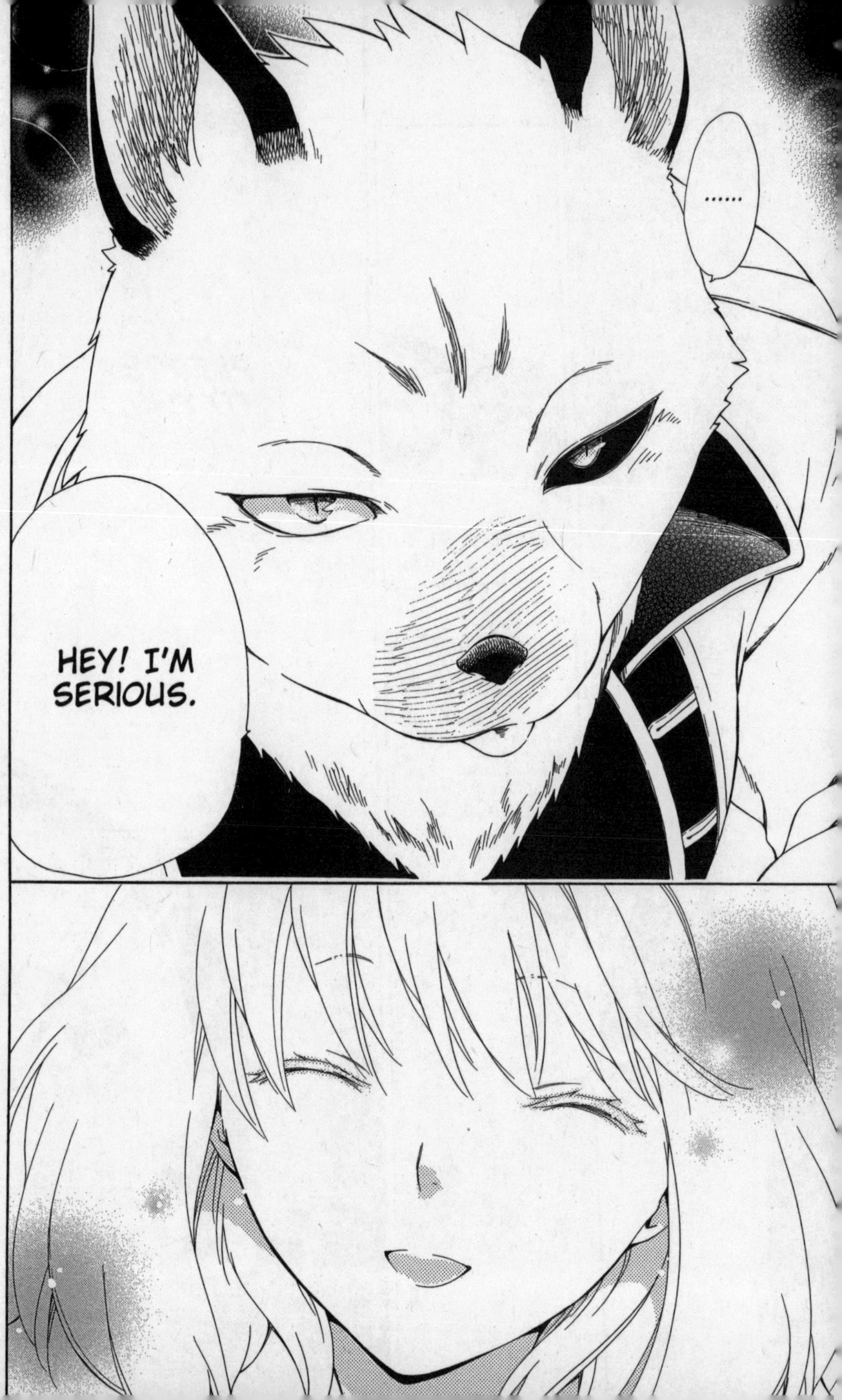
......
HEY! I'M SERIOUS.

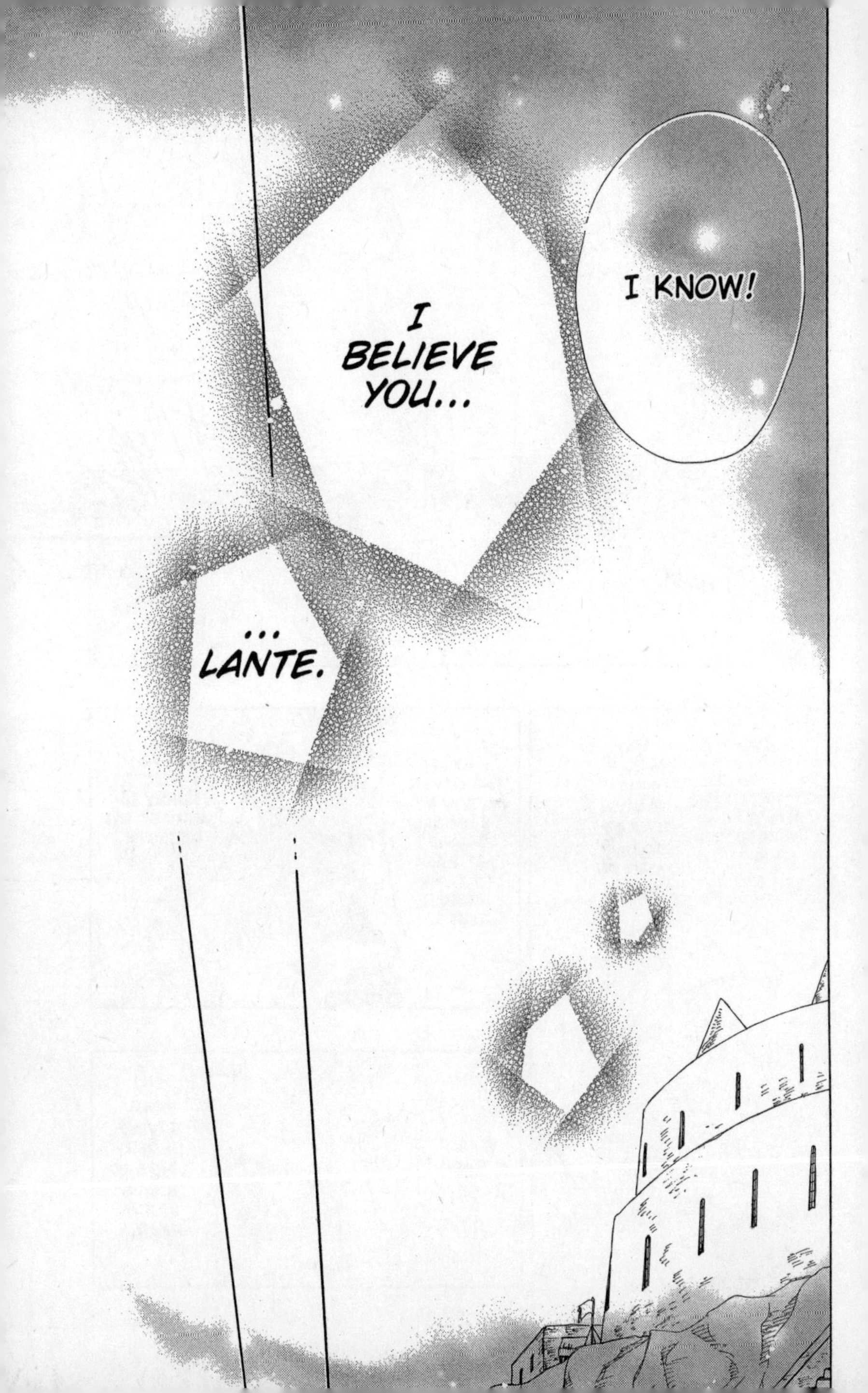
I KNOW!
I BELIEVE YOU...
...LANTE.

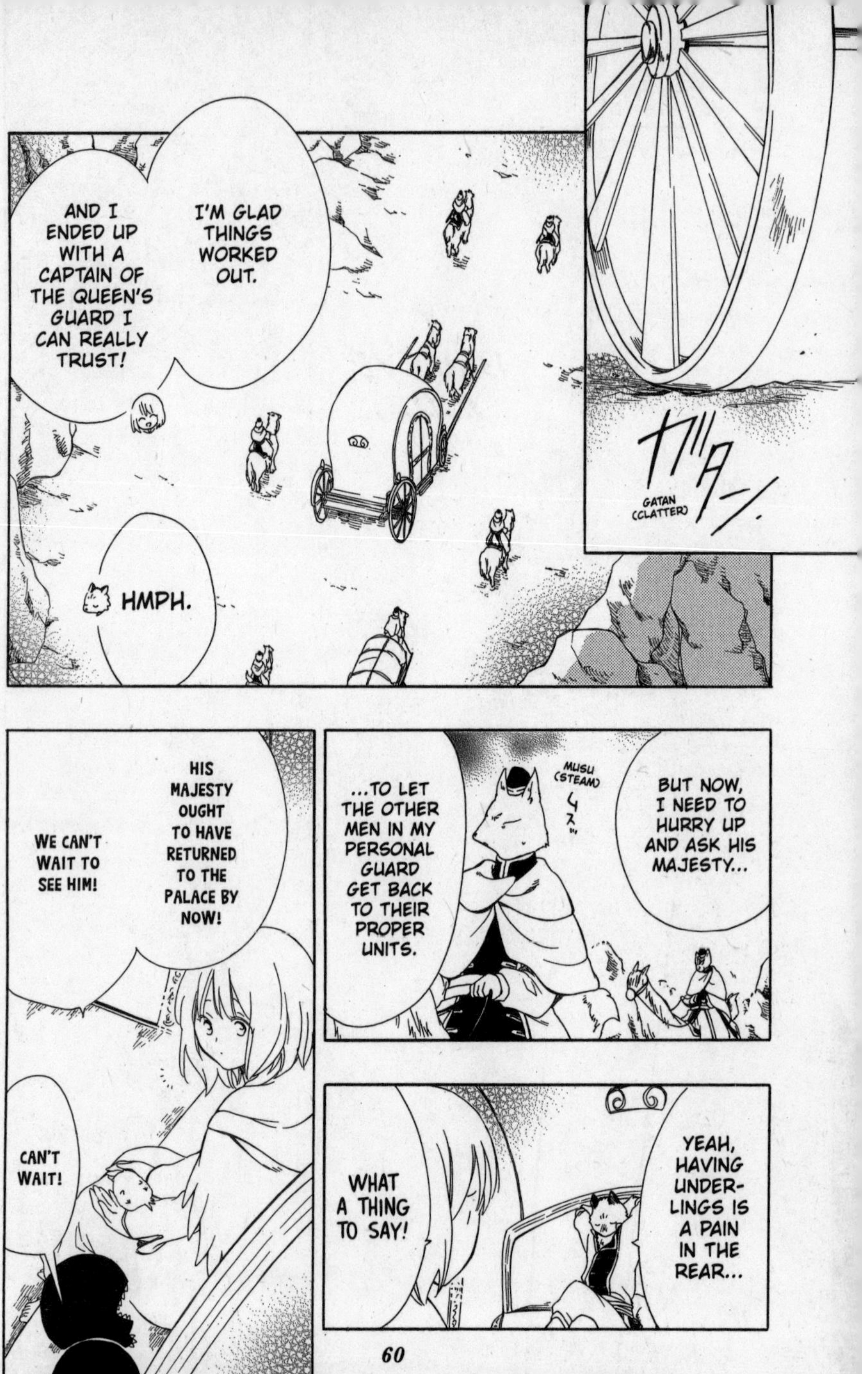
GATAN (CLATTER)
I'M GLAD THINGS WORKED OUT.
AND I ENDED UP WITH A CAPTAIN OF THE QUEEN'S GUARD I CAN REALLY TRUST!
HMPH.
BUT NOW, I NEED TO HURRY UP AND ASK HIS MAJESTY...
MUSU (STEAM)
...TO LET THE OTHER MEN IN MY PERSONAL GUARD GET BACK TO THEIR PROPER UNITS.
YEAH, HAVING UNDER-LINGS IS A PAIN IN THE REAR...
WHAT A THING TO SAY!
HIS MAJESTY OUGHT TO HAVE RETURNED TO THE PALACE BY NOW!
WE CAN'T WAIT TO SEE HIM!
CAN'T WAIT!

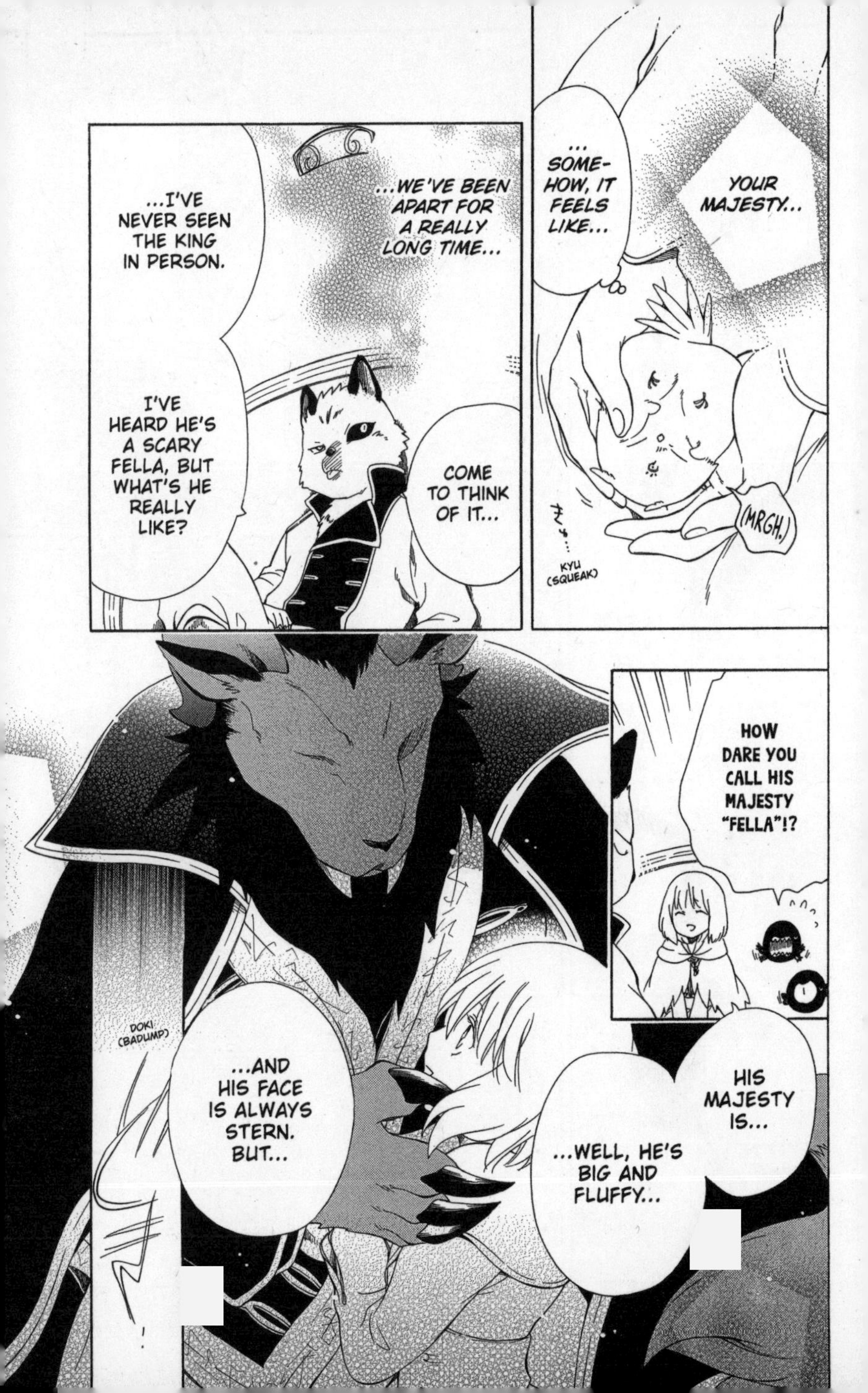
YOUR MAJESTY...
...SOME-HOW, IT FEELS LIKE...
(MRGH.)
KYU (SQUEAK)
...WE'VE BEEN APART FOR A REALLY LONG TIME...
COME TO THINK OF IT...
...I'VE NEVER SEEN THE KING IN PERSON.
I'VE HEARD HE'S A SCARY FELLA, BUT WHAT'S HE REALLY LIKE?
HOW DARE YOU CALL HIS MAJESTY "FELLA"!?
HIS MAJESTY IS...
...WELL, HE'S BIG AND FLUFFY...
...AND HIS FACE IS ALWAYS STERN. BUT...
DOKI (BADUMP)

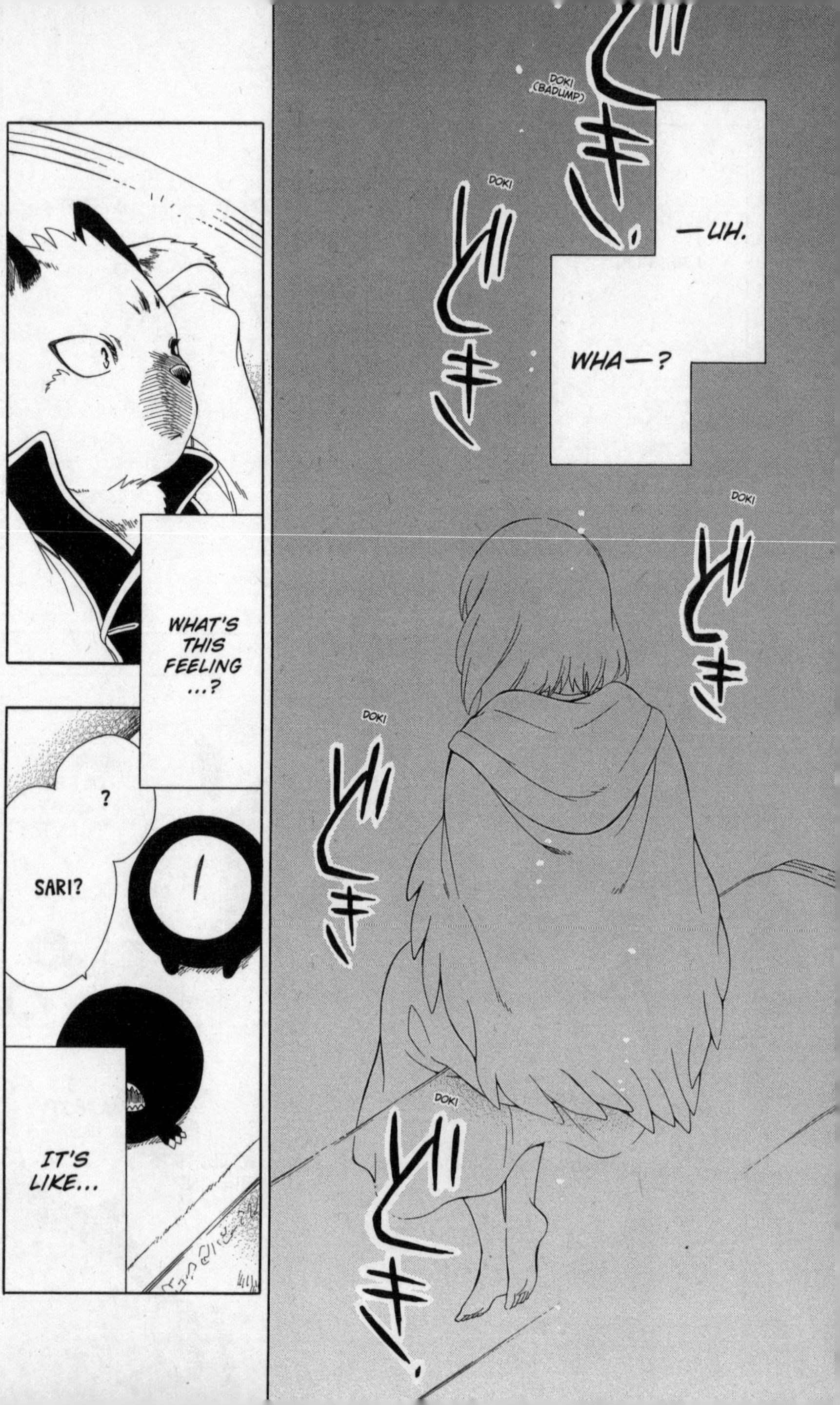

どきん
DOKI (BADUMP)
—UH.
WHA—?
DOKI
どき
DOKI
どき
DOKI
どき
DOKI
どき
WHAT'S THIS FEELING ...?
?
SARI?
IT'S LIKE...

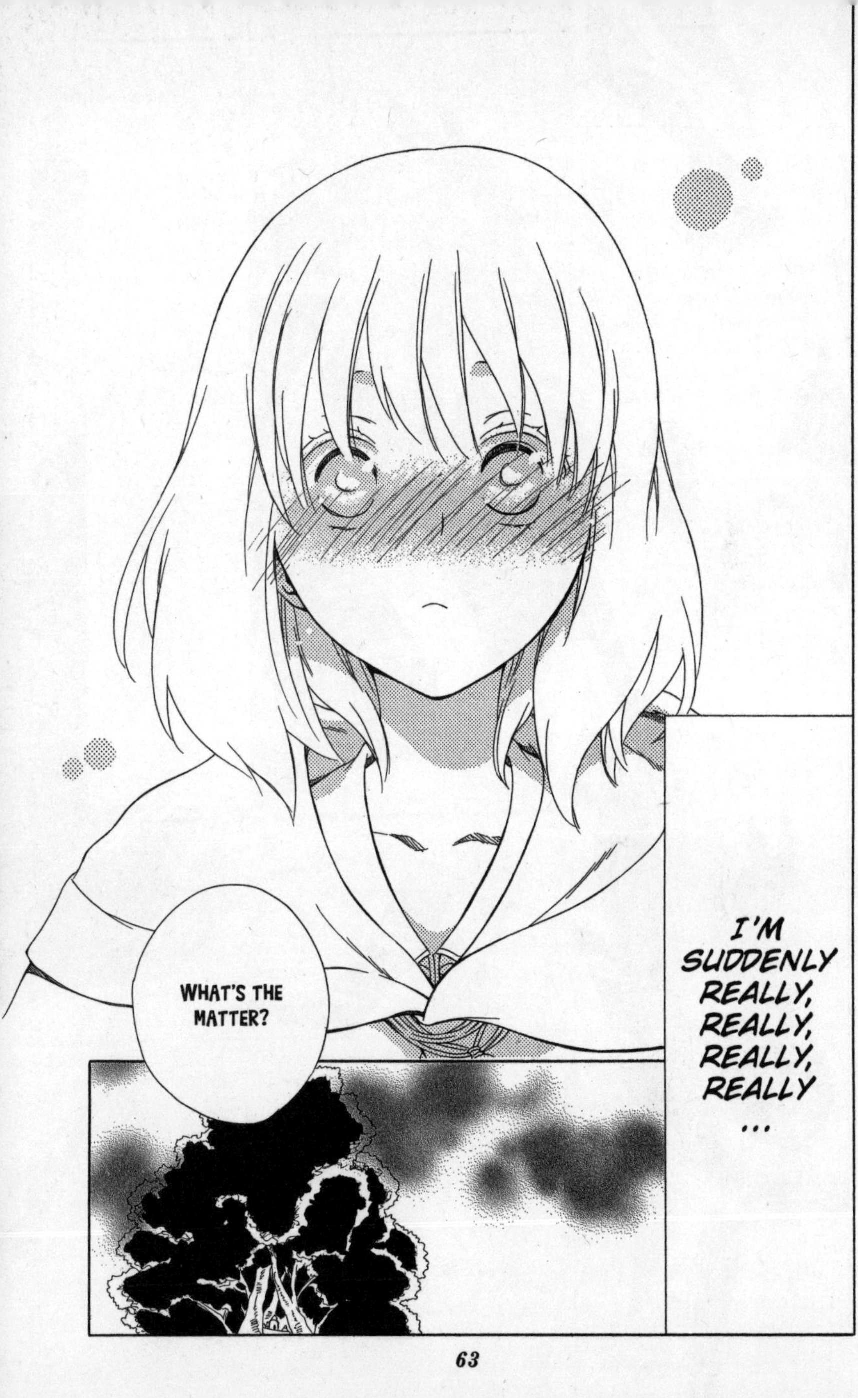
WHAT'S THE MATTER?
I'M SUDDENLY REALLY, REALLY, REALLY, REALLY ...

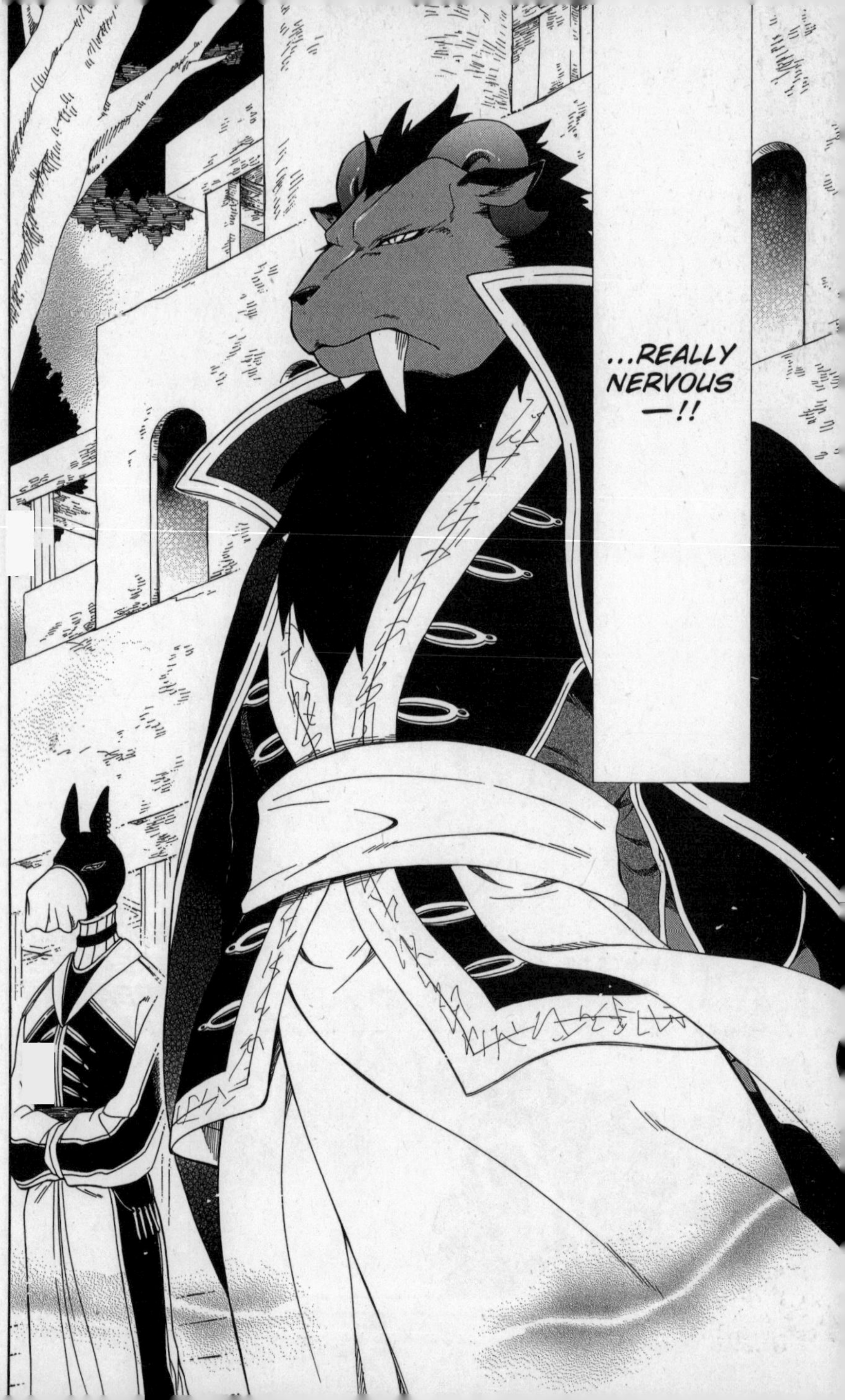
...REALLY NERVOUS—!!

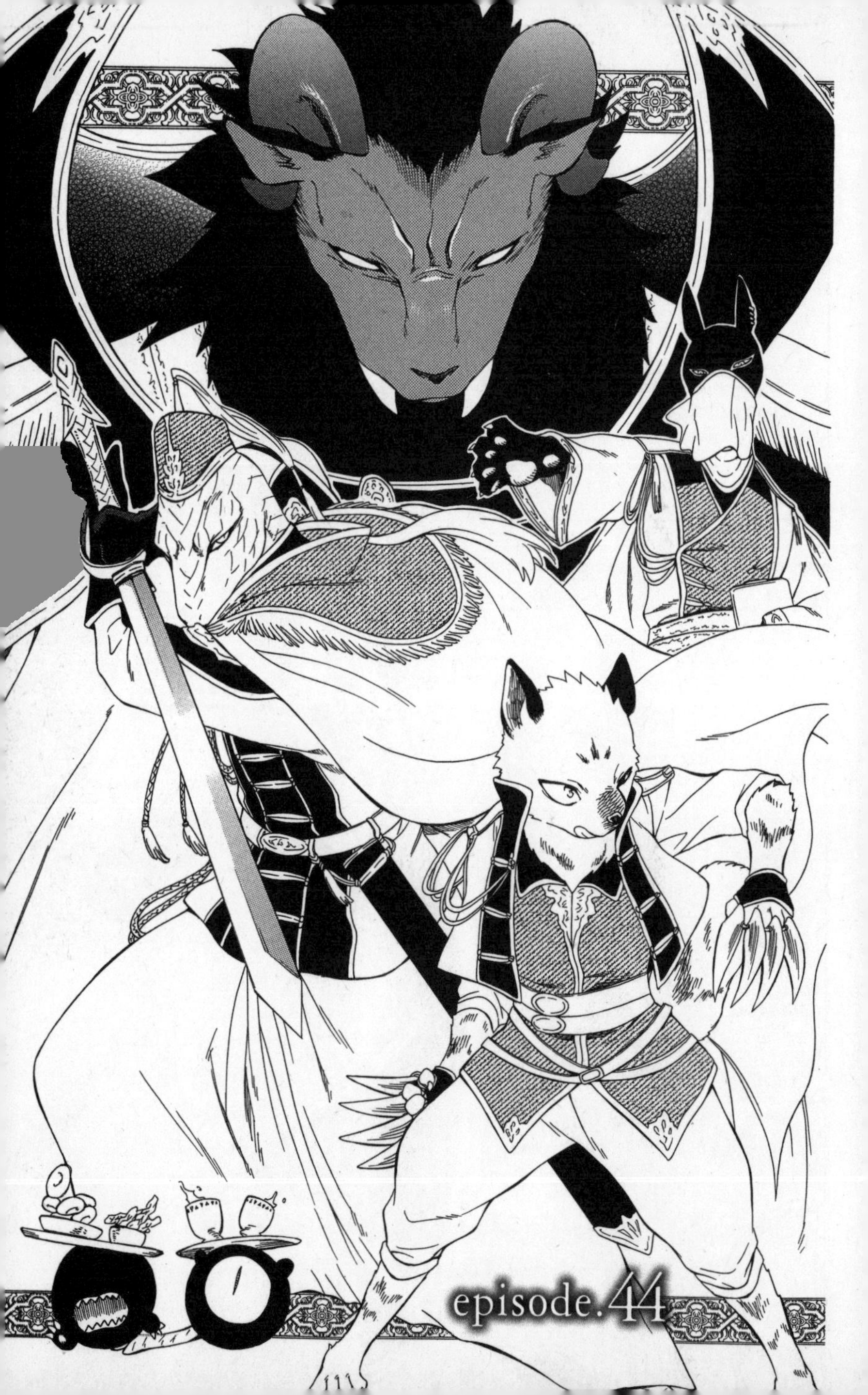
episode.44

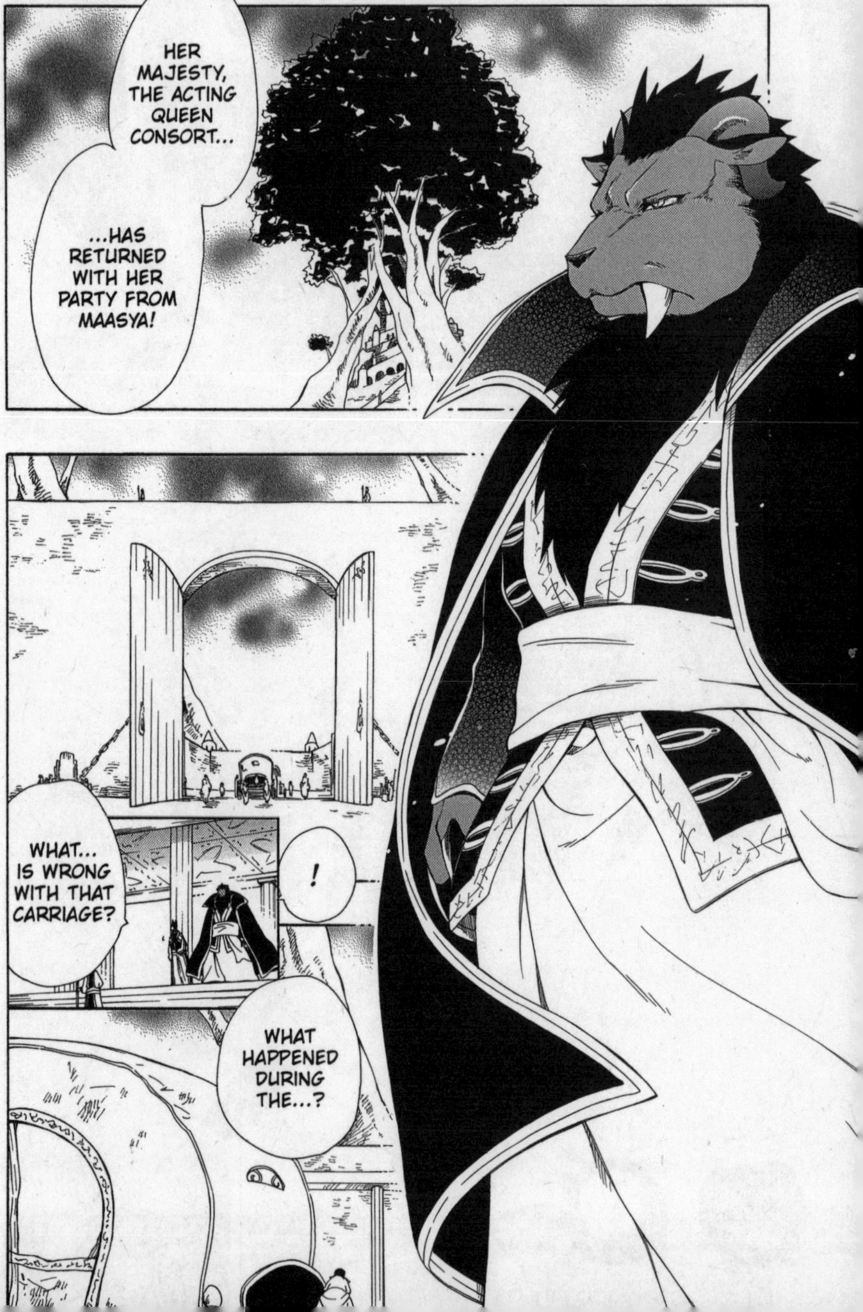
HER MAJESTY, THE ACTING QUEEN CONSORT...
...HAS RETURNED WITH HER PARTY FROM MAASYA!
!
WHAT... IS WRONG WITH THAT CARRIAGE?
WHAT HAPPENED DURING THE...?

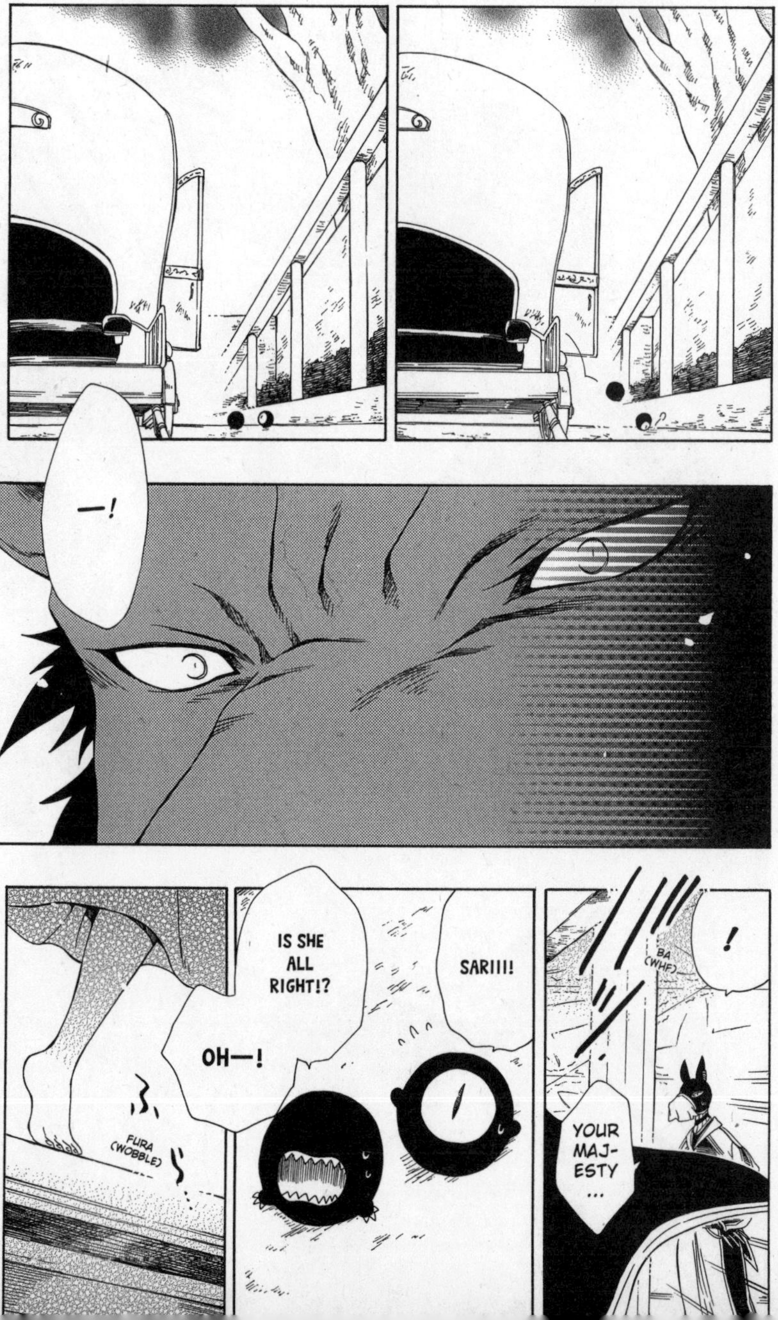
—!
BA (WHF)
!
YOUR MAJ-ESTY ...
SARIIII!
IS SHE ALL RIGHT!?
OH—!
FURA (WOBBLE)

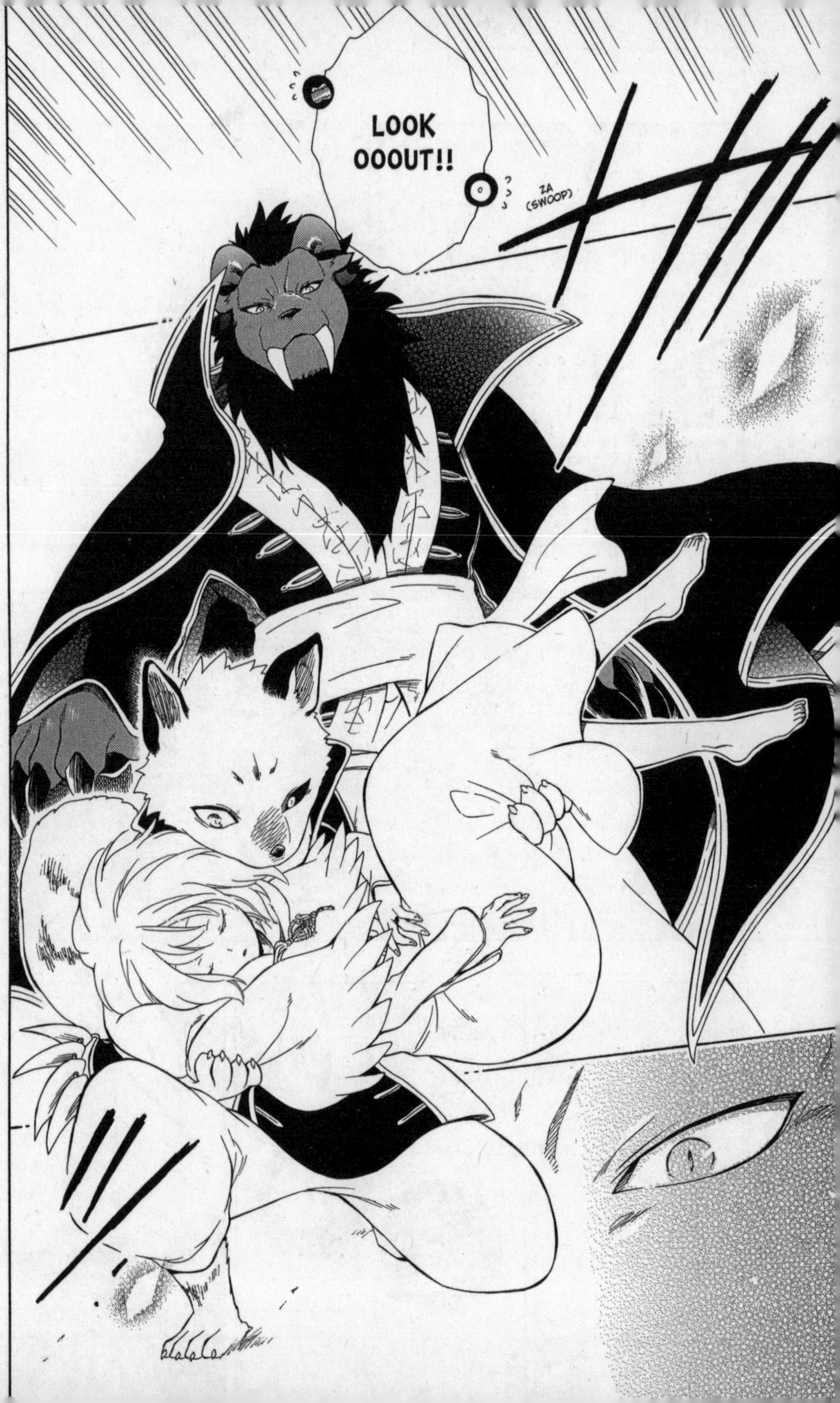
LOOK OOOUT!!
ZA (SWOOP)

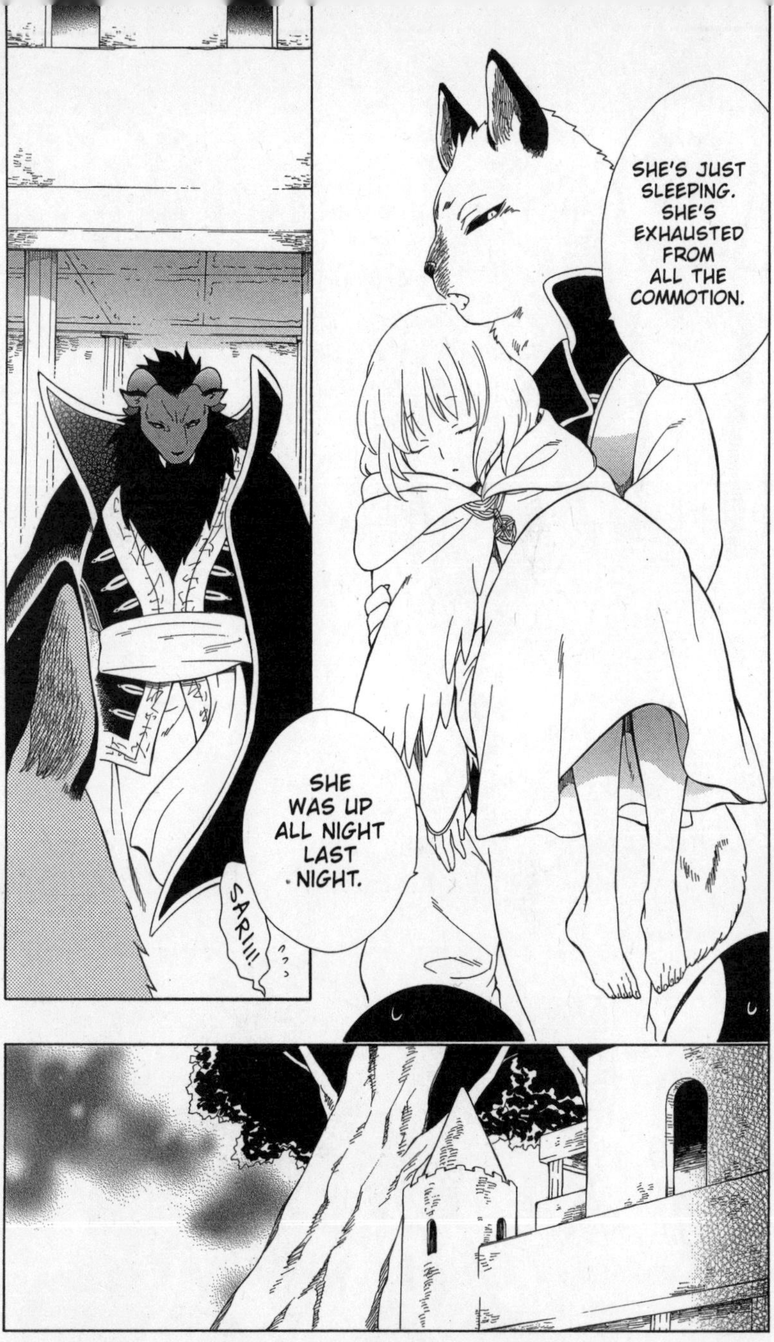
SHE'S JUST SLEEPING. SHE'S EXHAUSTED FROM ALL THE COMMOTION.
SARI!!!
SHE WAS UP ALL NIGHT LAST NIGHT.

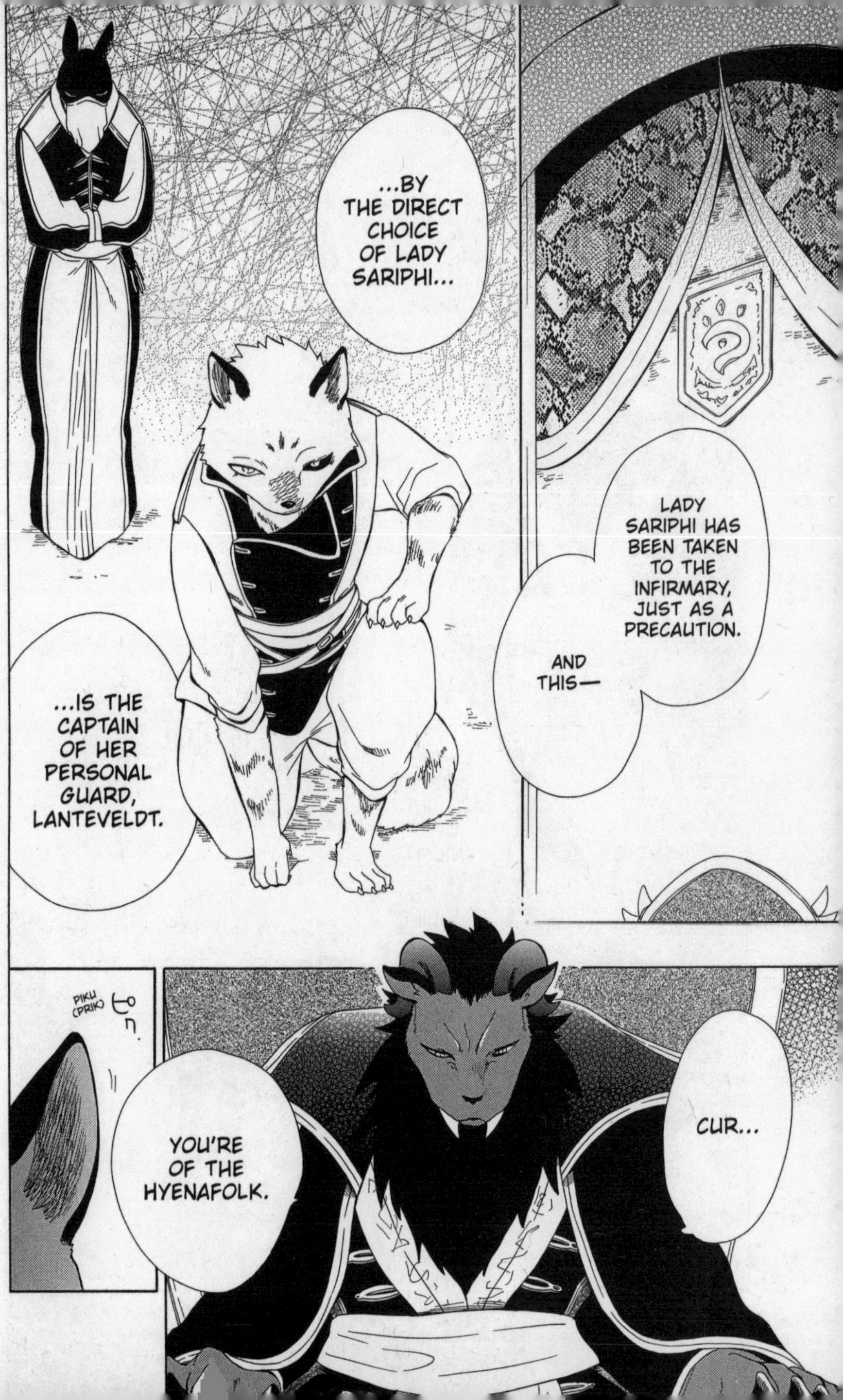
LADY SARIPHI HAS BEEN TAKEN TO THE INFIRMARY, JUST AS A PRECAUTION.
AND THIS—
...BY THE DIRECT CHOICE OF LADY SARIPHI...
...IS THE CAPTAIN OF HER PERSONAL GUARD, LANTEVELDT.
CUR...
YOU'RE OF THE HYENAFOLK.
PIKU (PRIK)

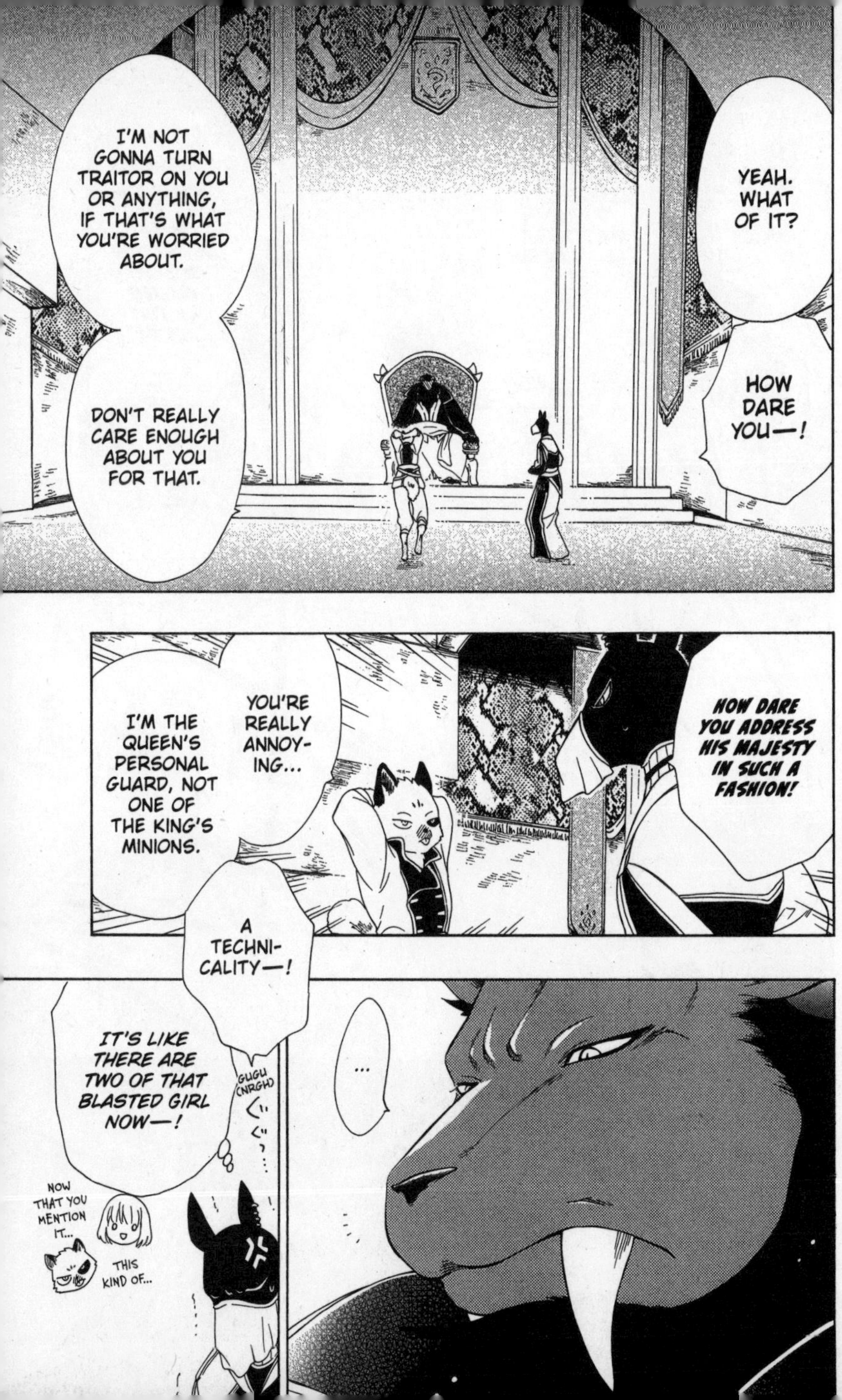
YEAH. WHAT OF IT?
HOW DARE YOU—!
I'M NOT GONNA TURN TRAITOR ON YOU OR ANYTHING, IF THAT'S WHAT YOU'RE WORRIED ABOUT.
DON'T REALLY CARE ENOUGH ABOUT YOU FOR THAT.
HOW DARE YOU ADDRESS HIS MAJESTY IN SUCH A FASHION!
YOU'RE REALLY ANNOY-ING...
I'M THE QUEEN'S PERSONAL GUARD, NOT ONE OF THE KING'S MINIONS.
A TECHNI-CALITY—!
...
GUGU (NRGH)
IT'S LIKE THERE ARE TWO OF THAT BLASTED GIRL NOW—!
NOW THAT YOU MENTION IT...
THIS KIND OF...

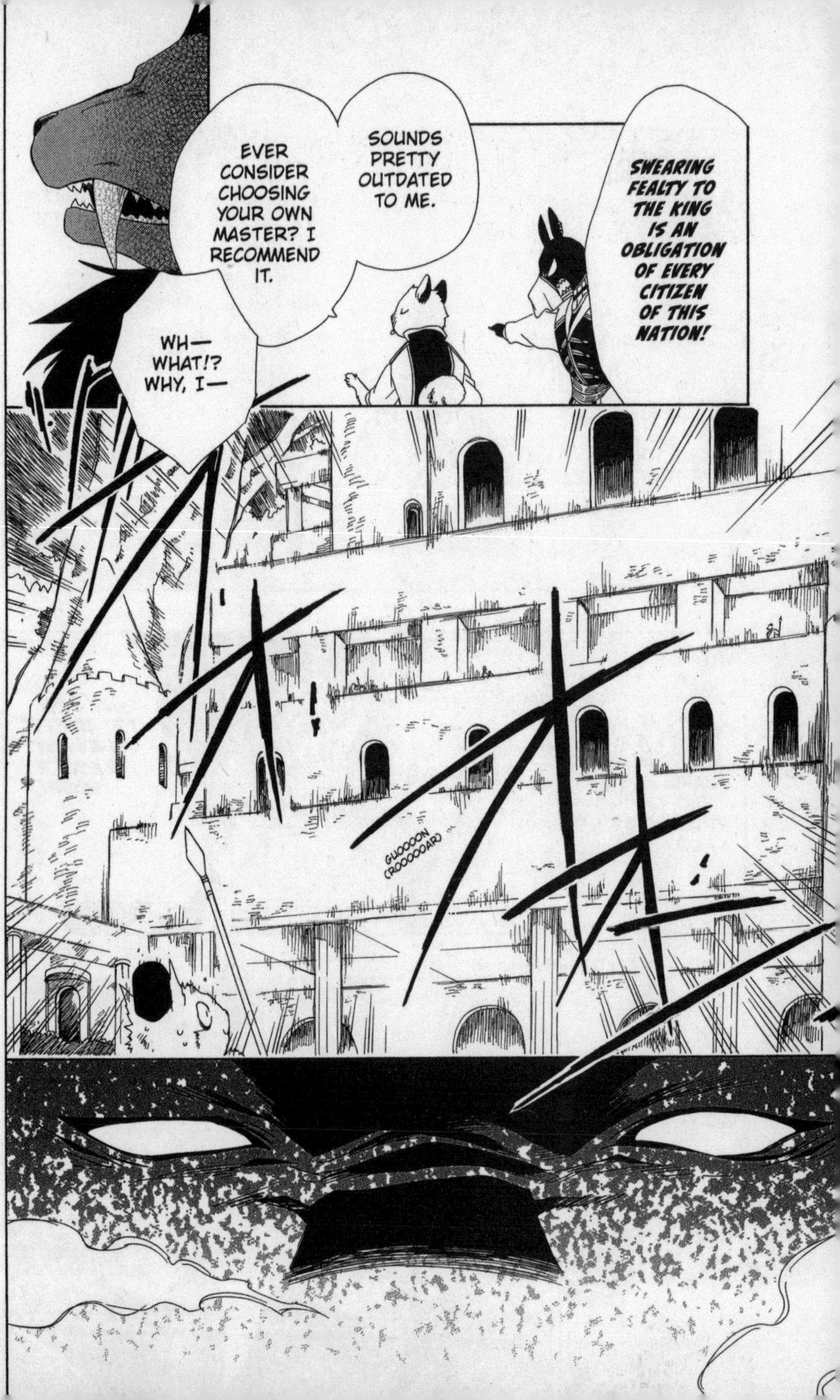
SWEARING FEALTY TO THE KING IS AN OBLIGATION OF EVERY CITIZEN OF THIS NATION!
SOUNDS PRETTY OUTDATED TO ME.
EVER CONSIDER CHOOSING YOUR OWN MASTER? I RECOMMEND IT.
WH— WHAT!? WHY, I—
GUOOOON (ROOOOOAR)

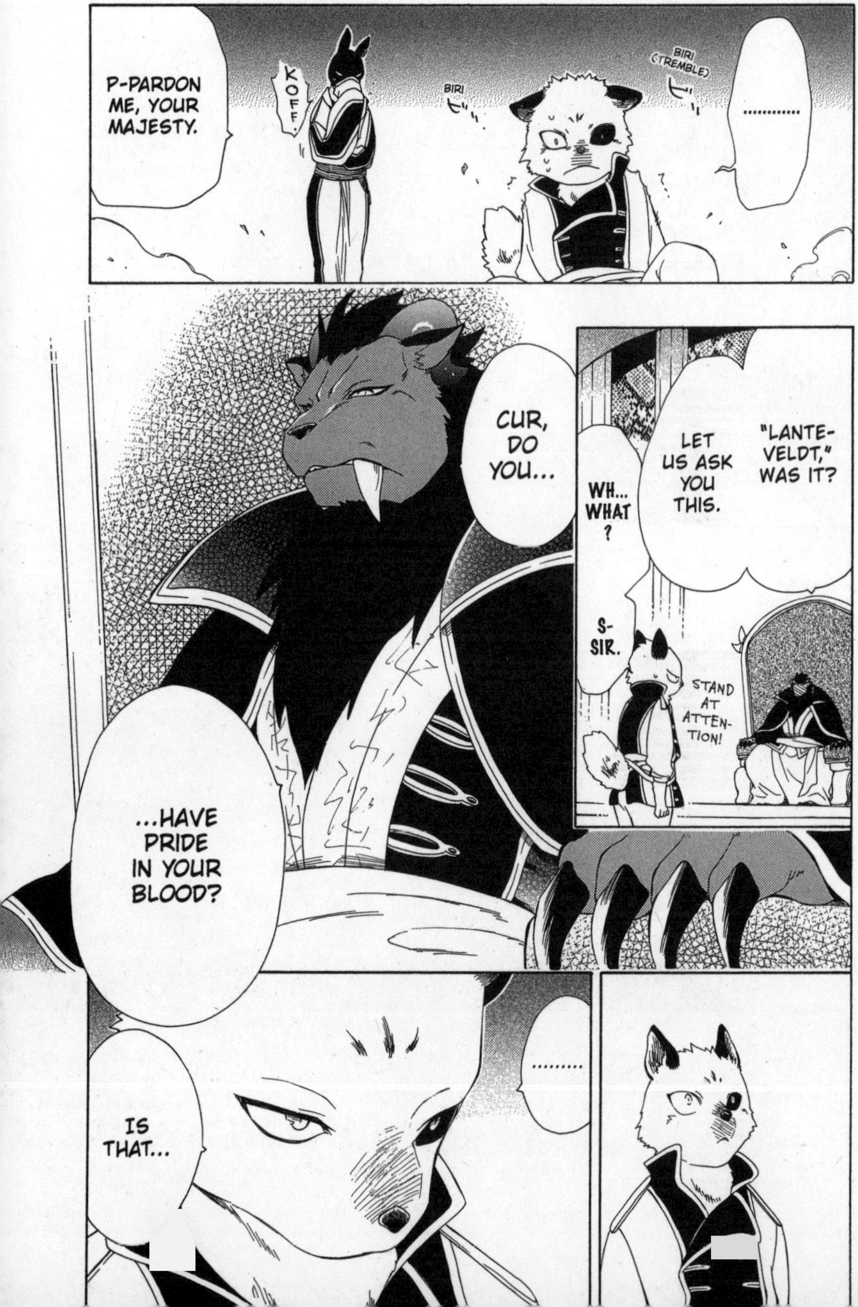
....
BIRI (TREMBLE)
BIRI
KOFF.
P-PARDON ME, YOUR MAJESTY.
"LANTE-VELDT," WAS IT?
LET US ASK YOU THIS.
WH... WHAT?
S-SIR.
STAND AT ATTEN-TION!
CUR, DO YOU...
...HAVE PRIDE IN YOUR BLOOD?
....
IS THAT...

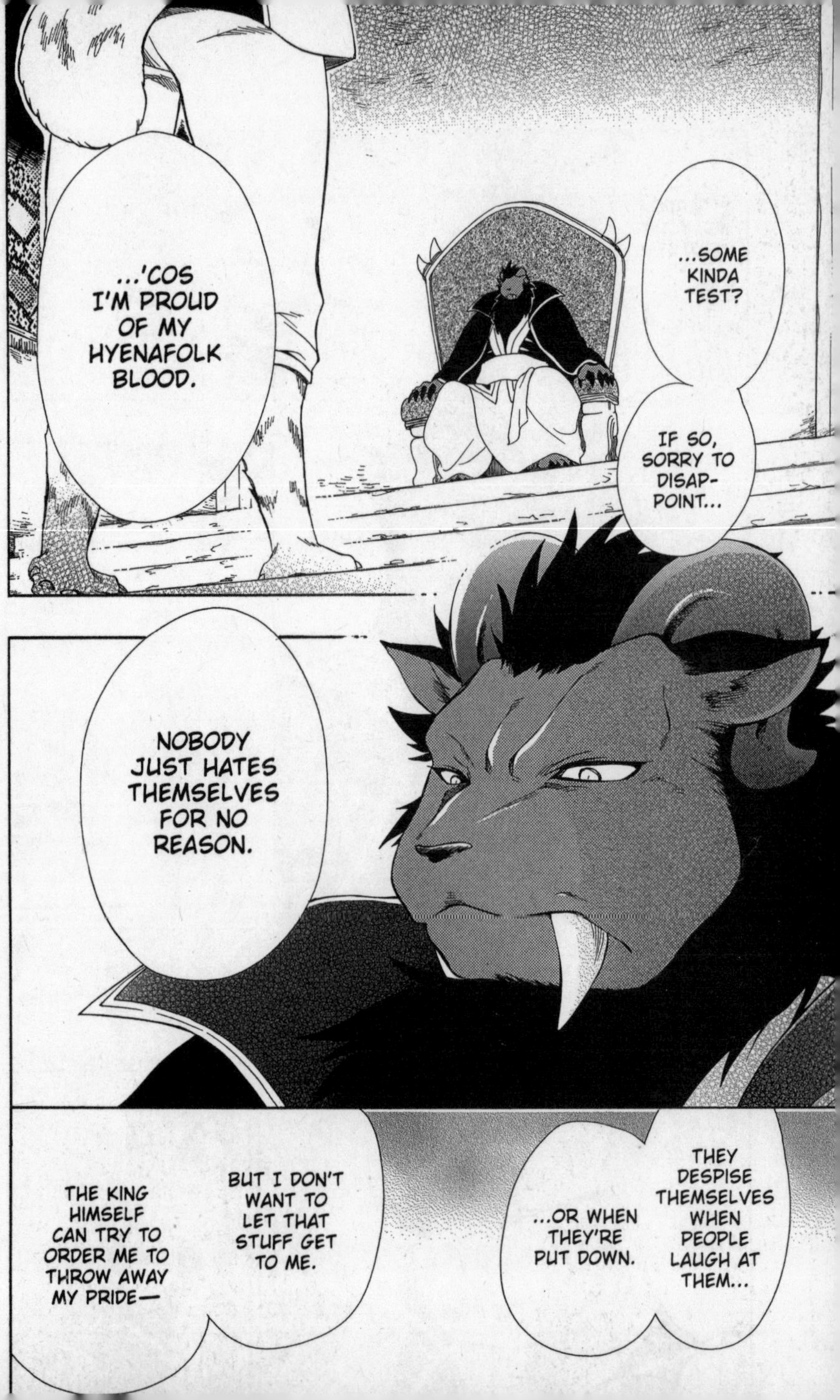
...SOME KINDA TEST?
IF SO, SORRY TO DISAP-POINT...
...'COS I'M PROUD OF MY HYENAFOLK BLOOD.
NOBODY JUST HATES THEMSELVES FOR NO REASON.
THEY DESPISE THEMSELVES WHEN PEOPLE LAUGH AT THEM...
...OR WHEN THEY'RE PUT DOWN.
BUT I DON'T WANT TO LET THAT STUFF GET TO ME.
THE KING HIMSELF CAN TRY TO ORDER ME TO THROW AWAY MY PRIDE—

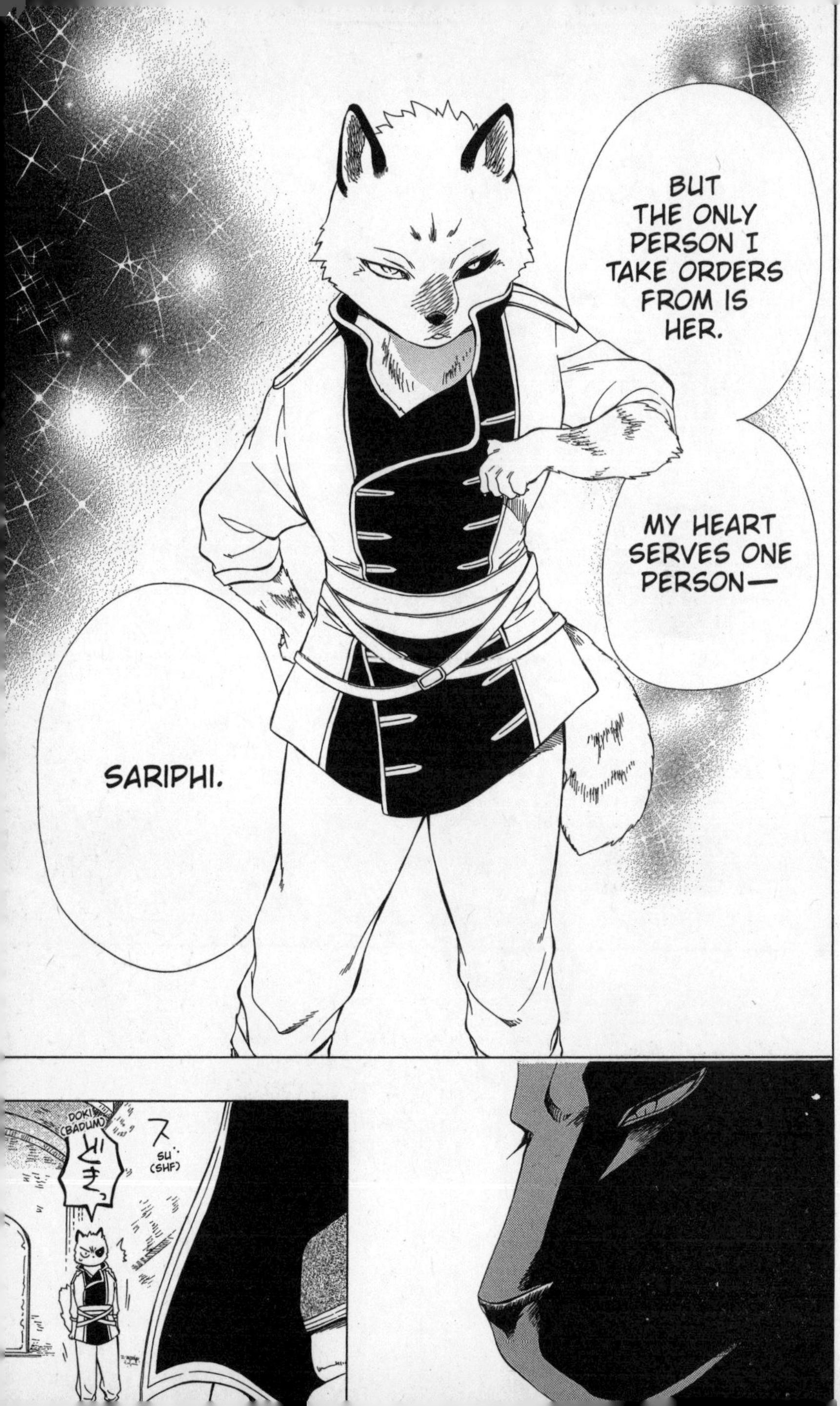
BUT THE ONLY PERSON I TAKE ORDERS FROM IS HER.
MY HEART SERVES ONE PERSON—
SARIPHI.
ス
SU (SHF)
どきっ
DOKI (BADUM)

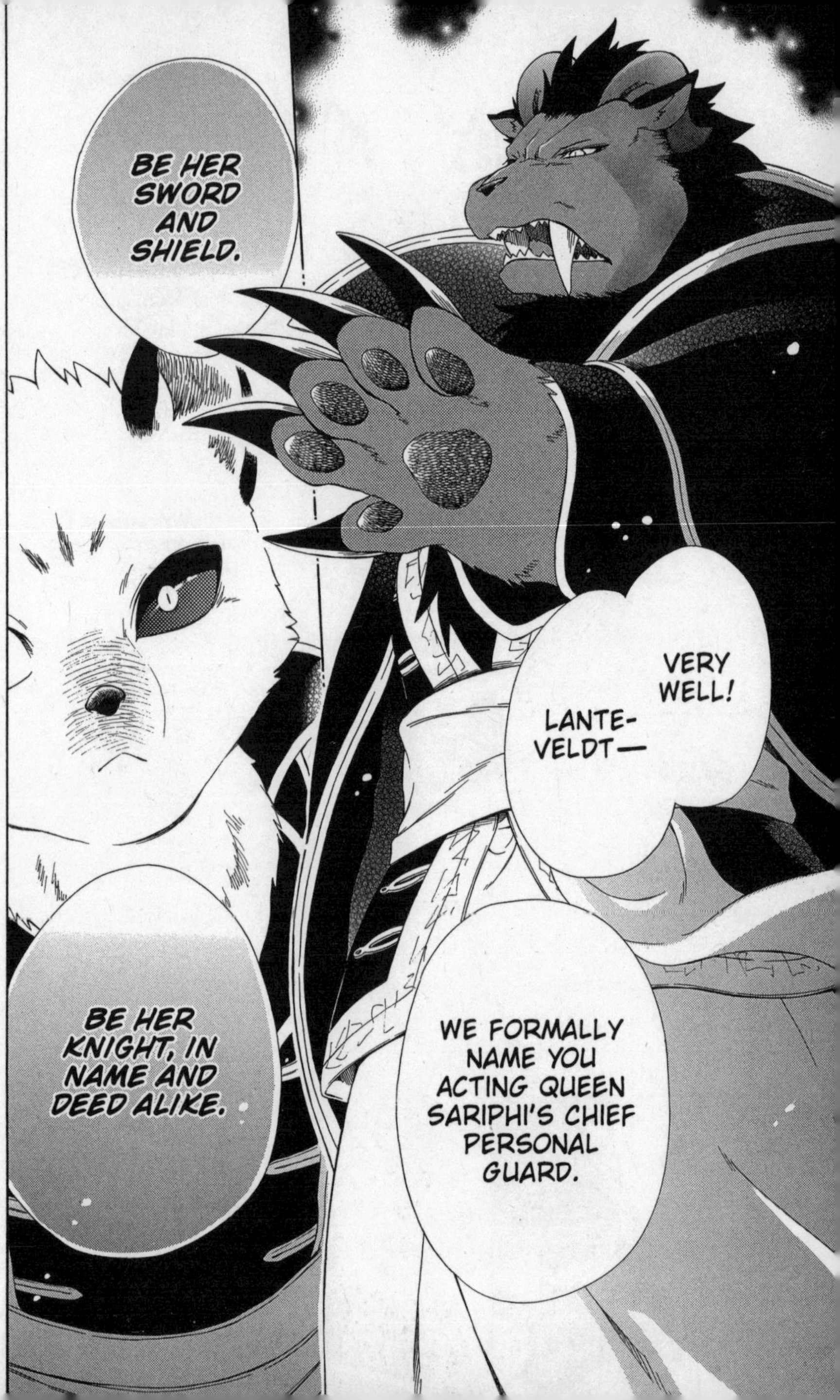
VERY WELL! LANTE-VELDT—
WE FORMALLY NAME YOU ACTING QUEEN SARIPHI'S CHIEF PERSONAL GUARD.
BE HER SWORD AND SHIELD.
BE HER KNIGHT, IN NAME AND DEED ALIKE.

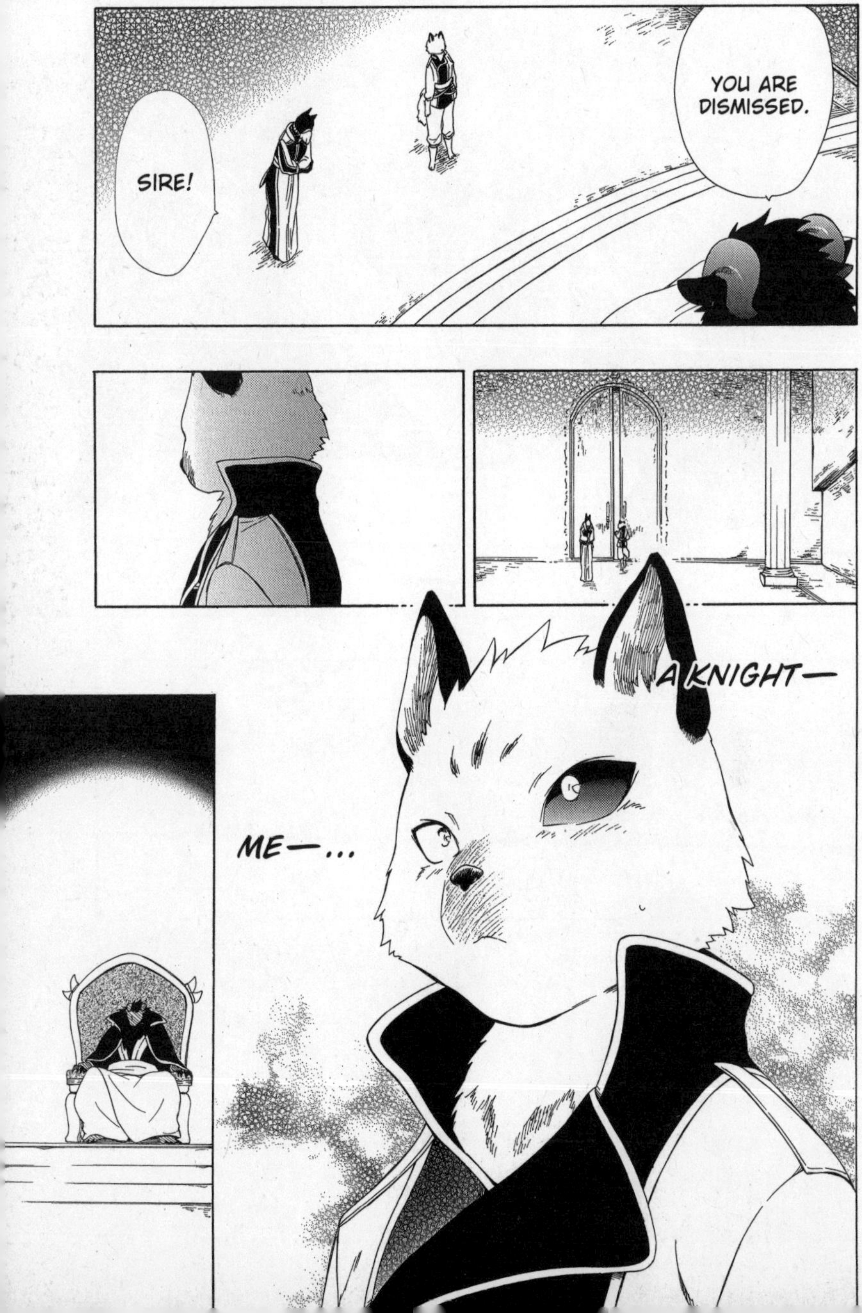
YOU ARE DISMISSED.
SIRE!
A KNIGHT—
ME—...

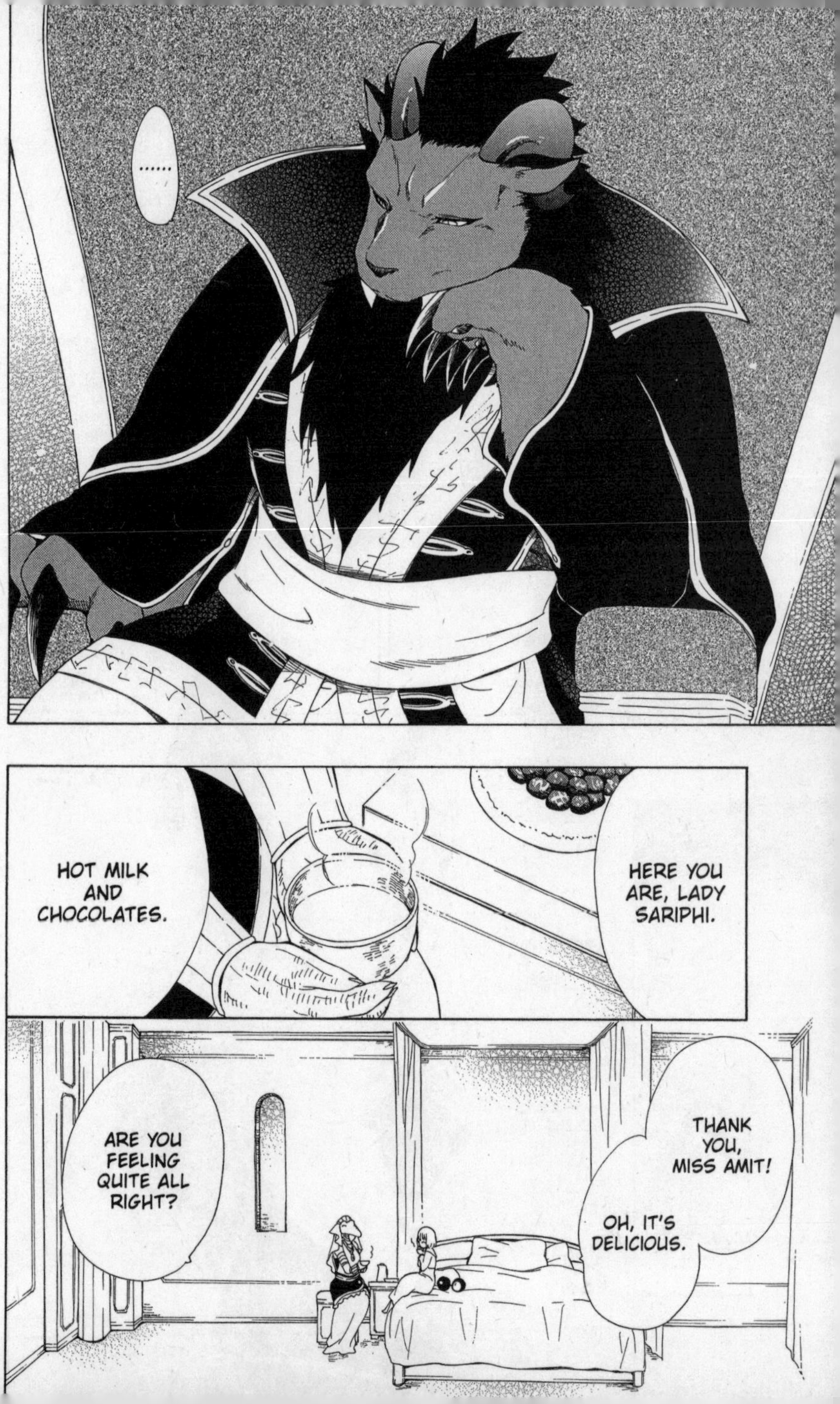
......
HERE YOU ARE, LADY SARIPHI.
HOT MILK AND CHOCOLATES.
THANK YOU, MISS AMIT!
OH, IT'S DELICIOUS.
ARE YOU FEELING QUITE ALL RIGHT?

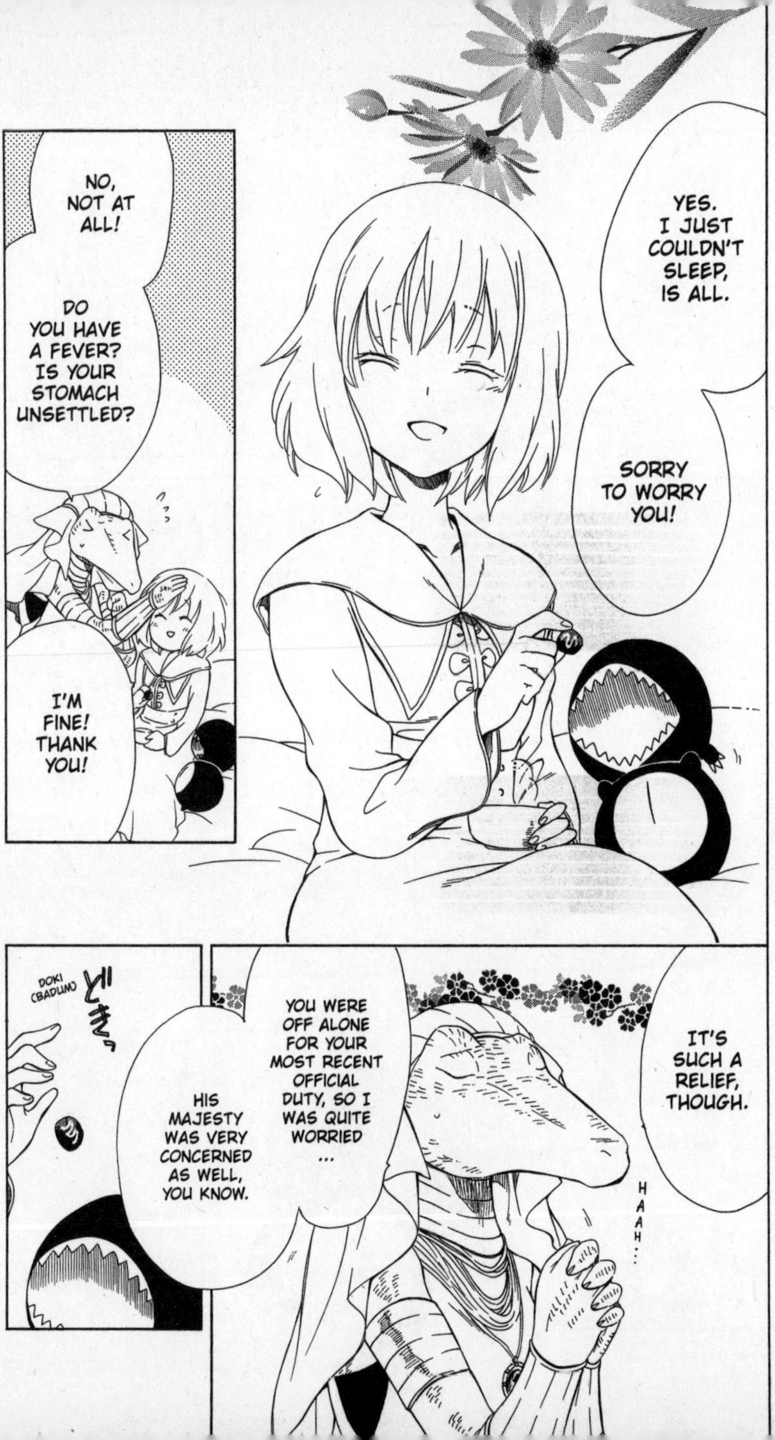
YES. I JUST COULDN'T SLEEP, IS ALL.
SORRY TO WORRY YOU!
NO, NOT AT ALL!
DO YOU HAVE A FEVER? IS YOUR STOMACH UNSETTLED?
I'M FINE! THANK YOU!
IT'S SUCH A RELIEF, THOUGH.
HAAAH...
YOU WERE OFF ALONE FOR YOUR MOST RECENT OFFICIAL DUTY, SO I WAS QUITE WORRIED ...
HIS MAJESTY WAS VERY CONCERNED AS WELL, YOU KNOW.
DOKI (BADUM)

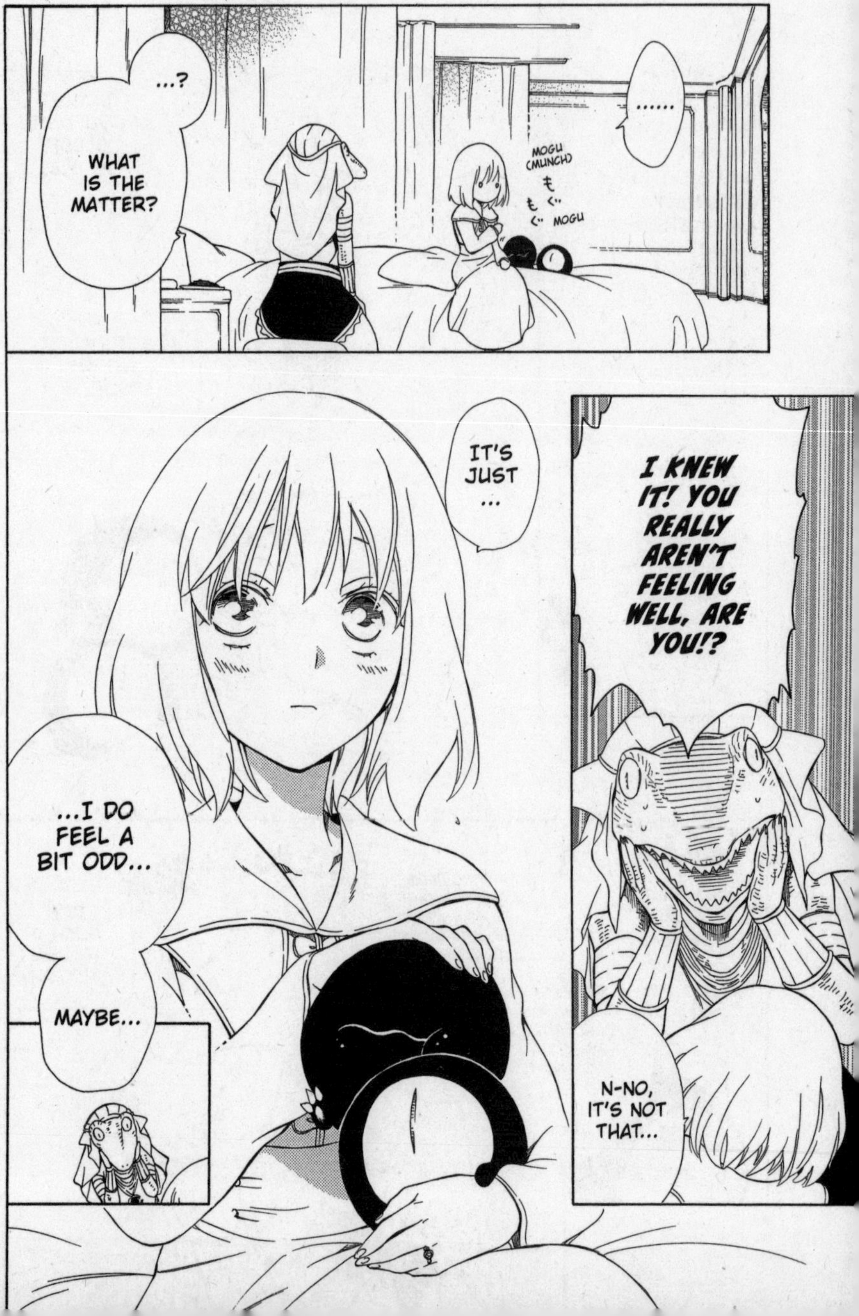
......
MOGU (MUNCH)
もぐもぐ
MOGU
...? WHAT IS THE MATTER?
IT'S JUST...
...I DO FEEL A BIT ODD...
MAYBE...
I KNEW IT! YOU REALLY AREN'T FEELING WELL, ARE YOU!?
N-NO, IT'S NOT THAT...

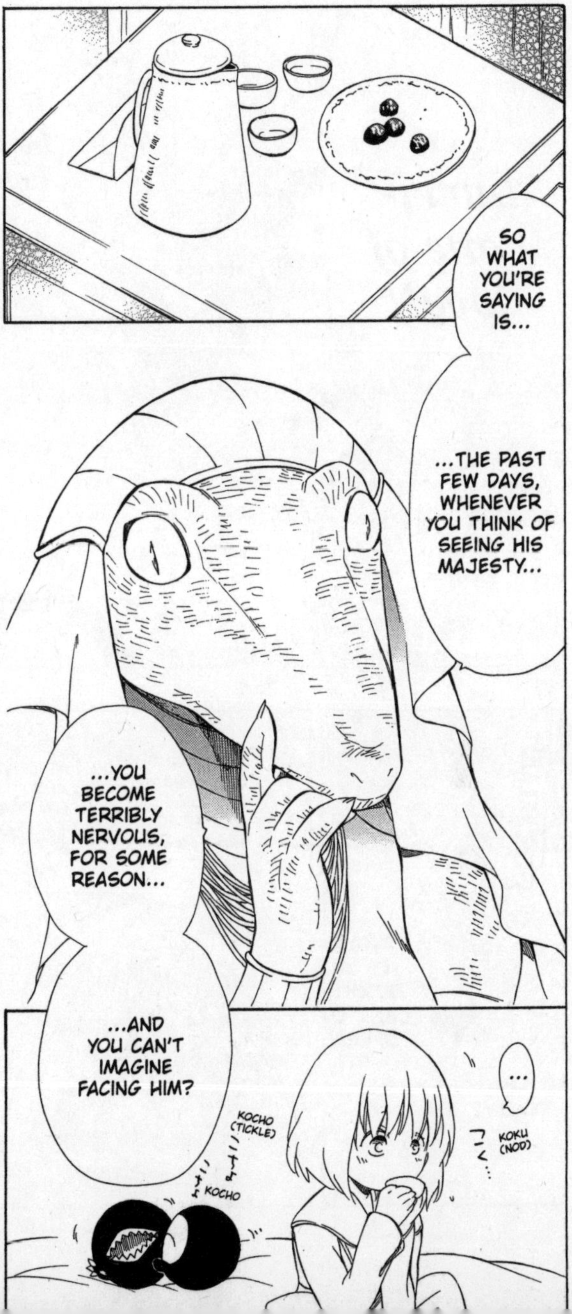
SO WHAT YOU'RE SAYING IS...
...THE PAST FEW DAYS, WHENEVER YOU THINK OF SEEING HIS MAJESTY...
...YOU BECOME TERRIBLY NERVOUS, FOR SOME REASON...
...AND YOU CAN'T IMAGINE FACING HIM?
...
KOKU (NOD)
KOCHO (TICKLE)
KOCHO

LANTEVELDT

I'D BEEN PLANNING THE APPEARANCE OF SARIPHI'S BODYGUARD FOR QUITE A WHILE, AND ALTHOUGH I'D KNOWN FOR A LONG TIME HE WOULD BE HYENAFOLK, THE CHARACTER HIMSELF WASN'T COMING TOGETHER. HIS BIRTH WAS VERY DIFFICULT. I WENT THROUGH CONCEPTS LIKE "CRUSTY OLD MAN" AND "FOPPISH OLD MAN" BEFORE LANDING ON THE SASSY YOUNG GUY HE IS.

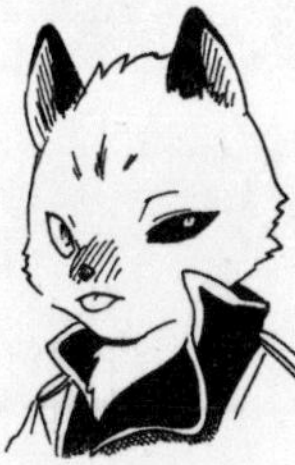

HE'S ABOUT 5'7" AND ROUGHLY SIXTEEN YEARS OLD—A YEAR OLDER THAN SARIPHI AND FULL OF MISCHIEF.

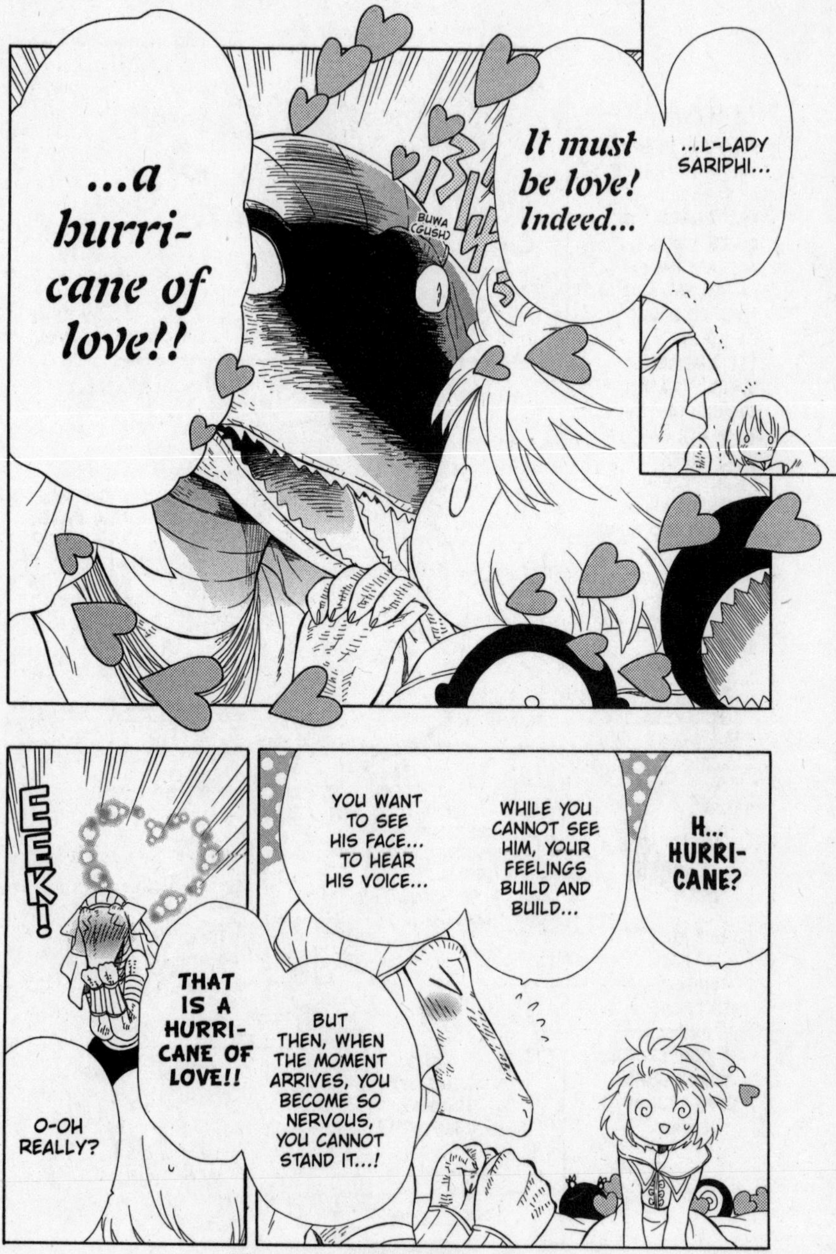
...L-LADY SARIPHI...
It must be love! Indeed...
BUWA (GUSH)
...a hurri-cane of love!!
H... HURRI-CANE?
WHILE YOU CANNOT SEE HIM, YOUR FEELINGS BUILD AND BUILD...
YOU WANT TO SEE HIS FACE... TO HEAR HIS VOICE...
BUT THEN, WHEN THE MOMENT ARRIVES, YOU BECOME SO NERVOUS, YOU CANNOT STAND IT...!
THAT IS A HURRI-CANE OF LOVE!!
EEK!
O-OH REALLY?

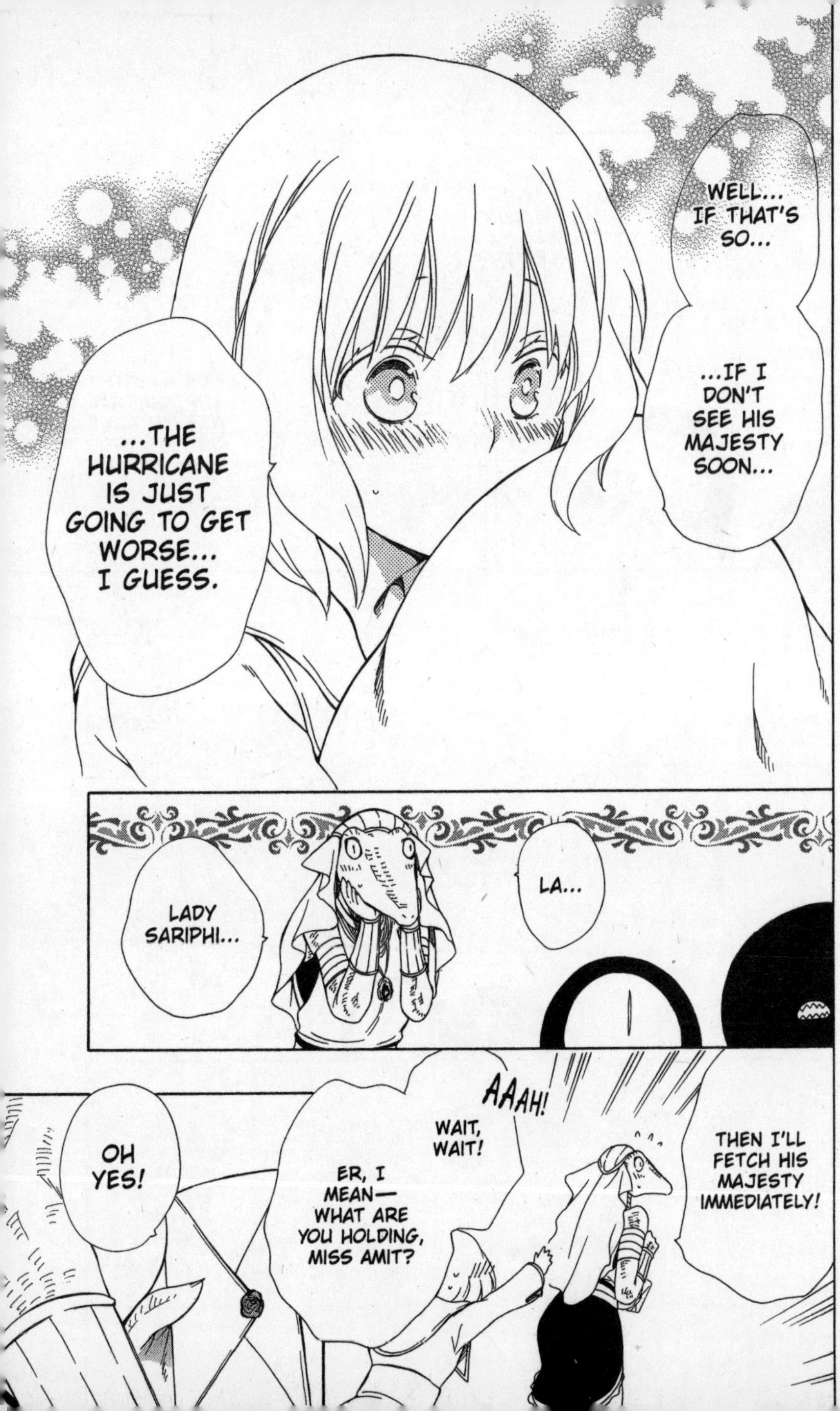
WELL... IF THAT'S SO...
...IF I DON'T SEE HIS MAJESTY SOON...
...THE HURRICANE IS JUST GOING TO GET WORSE... I GUESS.
LA...
LADY SARIPHI...
THEN I'LL FETCH HIS MAJESTY IMMEDIATELY!
AAAH!
WAIT, WAIT!
ER, I MEAN— WHAT ARE YOU HOLDING, MISS AMIT?
OH YES!

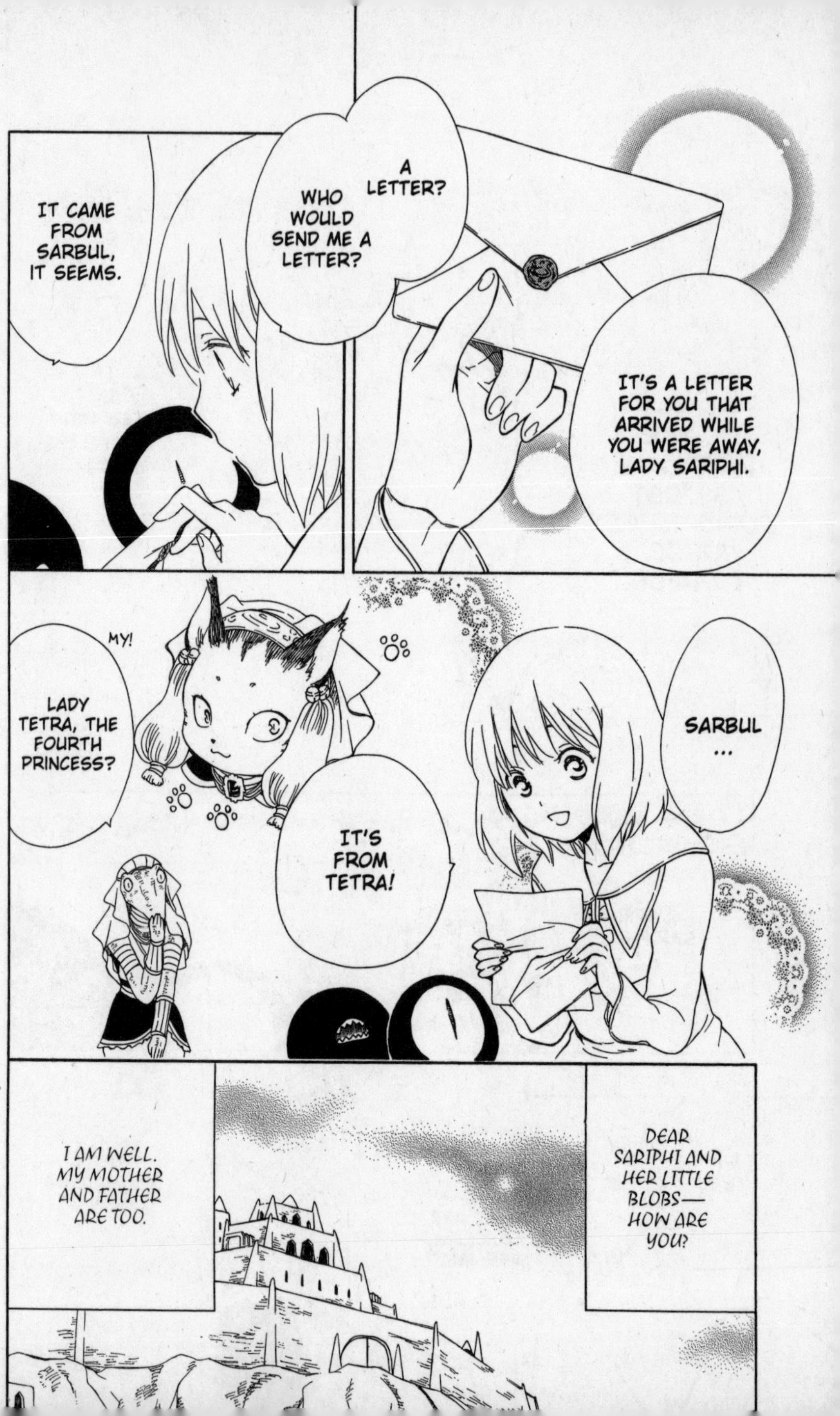
IT'S A LETTER FOR YOU THAT ARRIVED WHILE YOU WERE AWAY, LADY SARIPHI.
A LETTER? WHO WOULD SEND ME A LETTER?
IT CAME FROM SARBUL, IT SEEMS.
SARBUL ...
IT'S FROM TETRA!
MY! LADY TETRA, THE FOURTH PRINCESS?
DEAR SARIPHI AND HER LITTLE BLOBS—HOW ARE YOU?
I AM WELL. MY MOTHER AND FATHER ARE TOO.

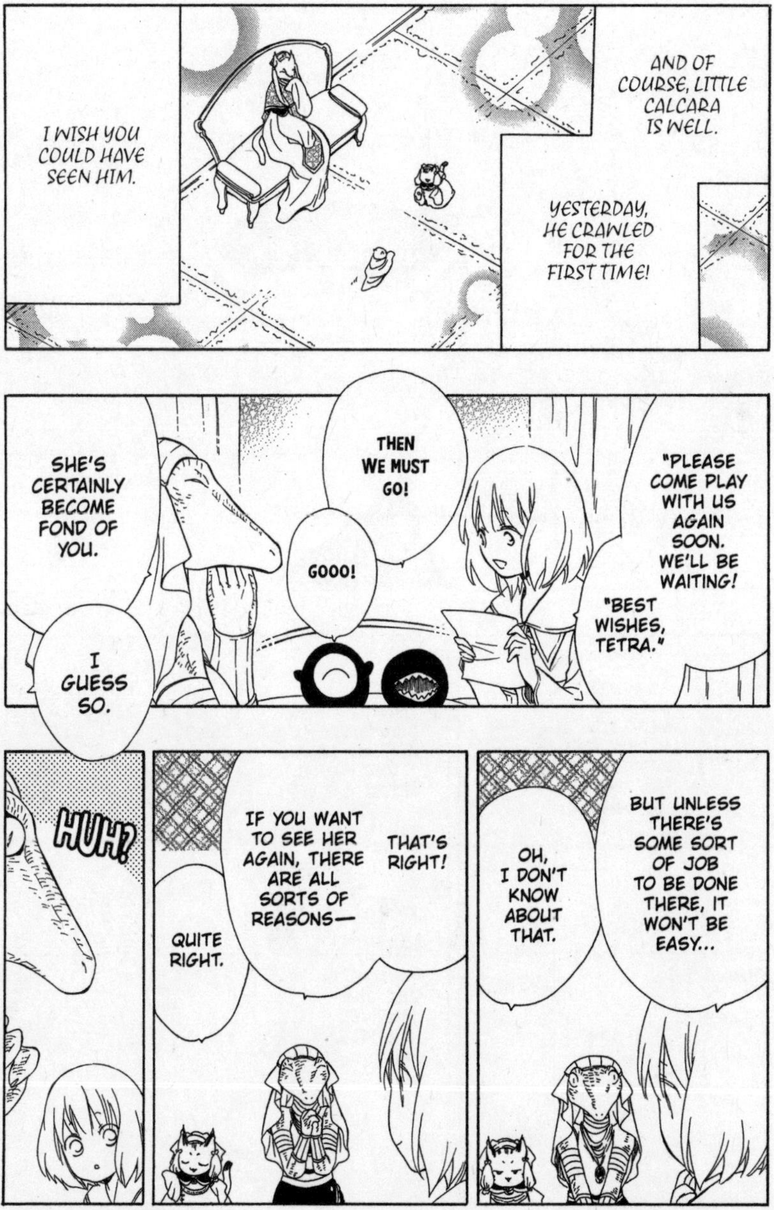
AND OF COURSE, LITTLE CALCARA IS WELL.
YESTERDAY, HE CRAWLED FOR THE FIRST TIME!
I WISH YOU COULD HAVE SEEN HIM.
"PLEASE COME PLAY WITH US AGAIN SOON. WE'LL BE WAITING!
"BEST WISHES, TETRA."
THEN WE MUST GO!
GOOO!
SHE'S CERTAINLY BECOME FOND OF YOU.
I GUESS SO.
BUT UNLESS THERE'S SOME SORT OF JOB TO BE DONE THERE, IT WON'T BE EASY...
OH, I DON'T KNOW ABOUT THAT.
THAT'S RIGHT!
IF YOU WANT TO SEE HER AGAIN, THERE ARE ALL SORTS OF REASONS—
QUITE RIGHT.
HUH?

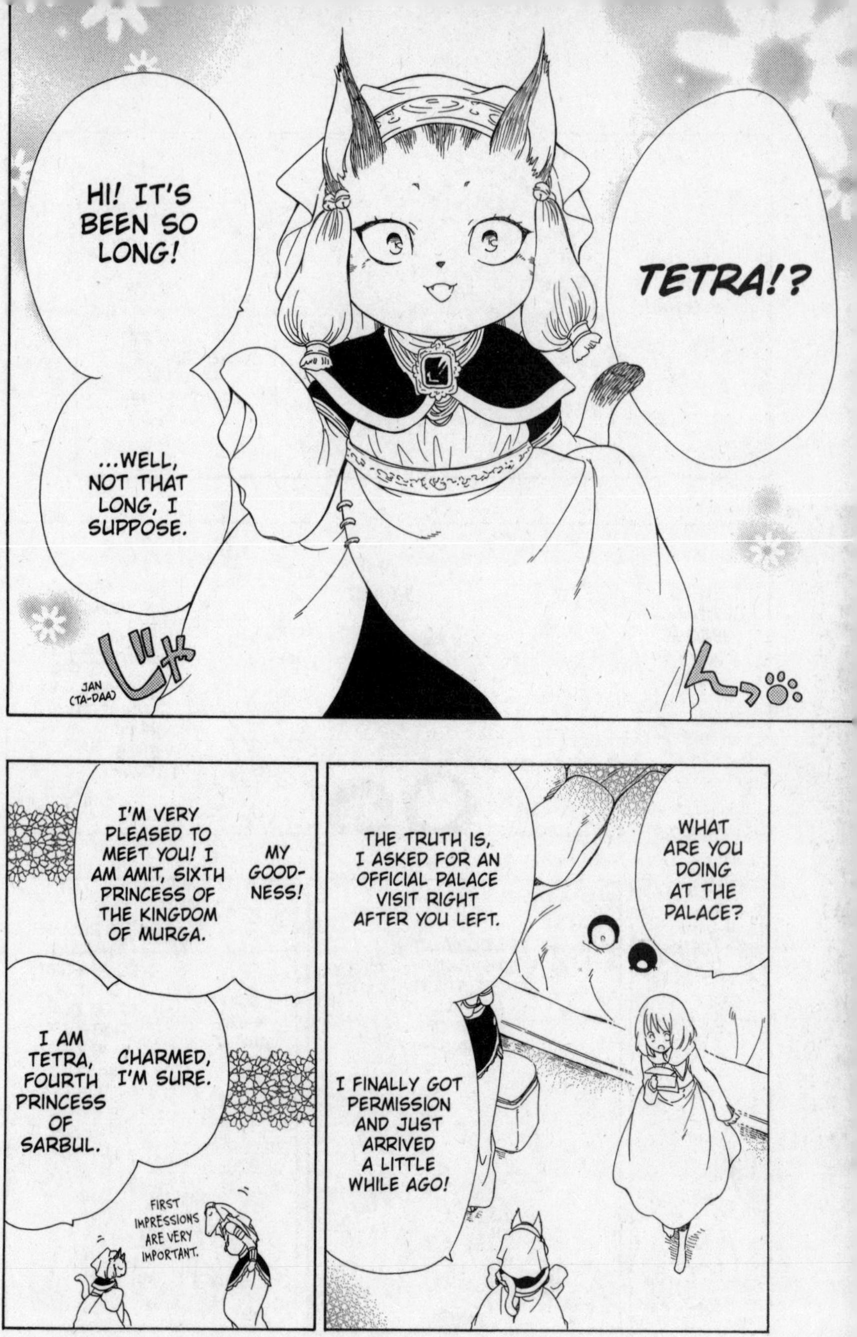
TETRA!?
HI! IT'S BEEN SO LONG!
...WELL, NOT THAT LONG, I SUPPOSE.
JAN (TA-DAA)
WHAT ARE YOU DOING AT THE PALACE?
THE TRUTH IS, I ASKED FOR AN OFFICIAL PALACE VISIT RIGHT AFTER YOU LEFT.
I FINALLY GOT PERMISSION AND JUST ARRIVED A LITTLE WHILE AGO!
MY GOODNESS!
I'M VERY PLEASED TO MEET YOU! I AM AMIT, SIXTH PRINCESS OF THE KINGDOM OF MURGA.
CHARMED, I'M SURE.
I AM TETRA, FOURTH PRINCESS OF SARBUL.
FIRST IMPRESSIONS ARE VERY IMPORTANT.

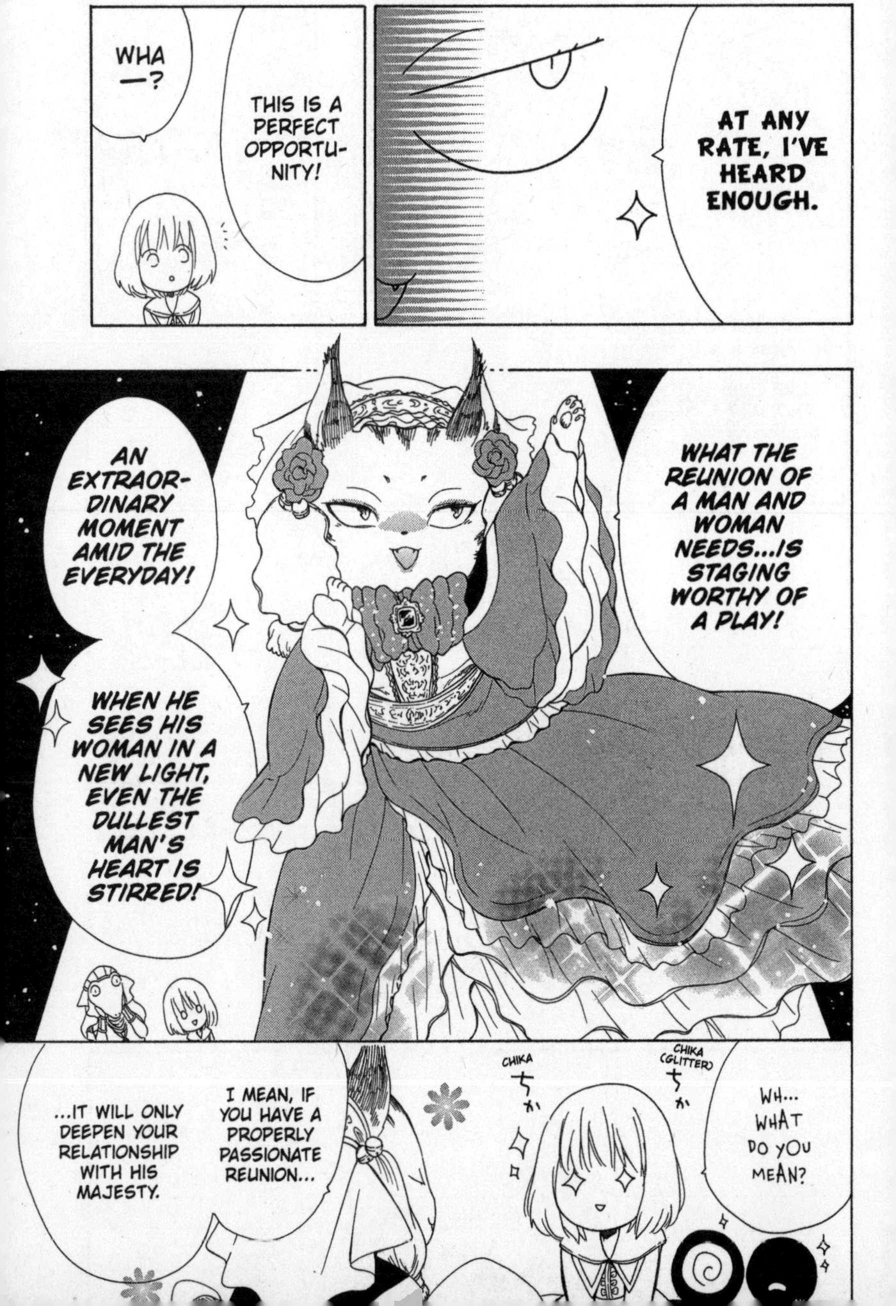
AT ANY RATE, I'VE HEARD ENOUGH.
THIS IS A PERFECT OPPORTU-NITY!
WHA—?
WHAT THE REUNION OF A MAN AND WOMAN NEEDS...IS STAGING WORTHY OF A PLAY!
AN EXTRAOR-DINARY MOMENT AMID THE EVERYDAY!
WHEN HE SEES HIS WOMAN IN A NEW LIGHT, EVEN THE DULLEST MAN'S HEART IS STIRRED!
WH... WHAT DO YOU MEAN?
ちか CHIKA (GLITTER)
ちか CHIKA
I MEAN, IF YOU HAVE A PROPERLY PASSIONATE REUNION...
...IT WILL ONLY DEEPEN YOUR RELATIONSHIP WITH HIS MAJESTY.

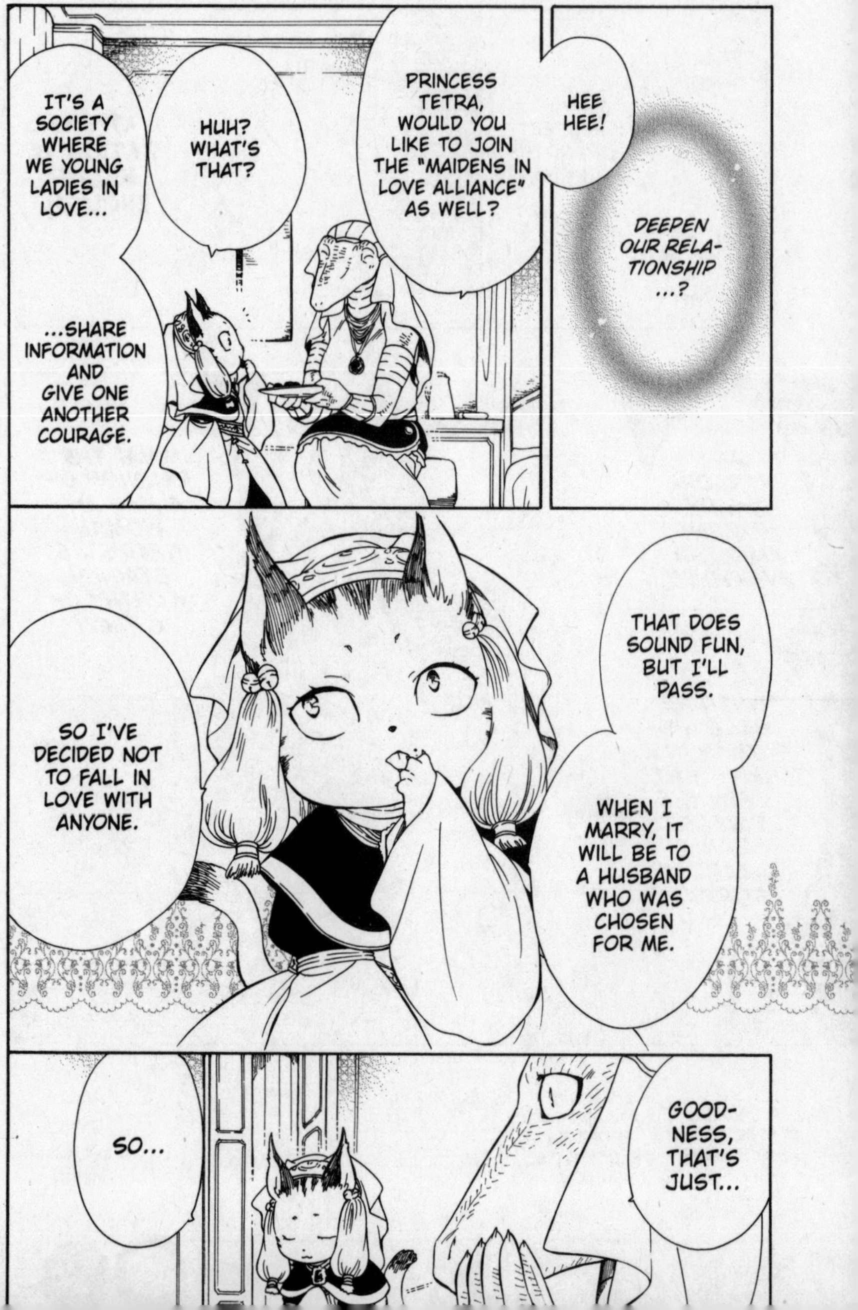
HEE HEE!
DEEPEN OUR RELATIONSHIP...?
PRINCESS TETRA, WOULD YOU LIKE TO JOIN THE "MAIDENS IN LOVE ALLIANCE" AS WELL?
HUH? WHAT'S THAT?
IT'S A SOCIETY WHERE WE YOUNG LADIES IN LOVE...
...SHARE INFORMATION AND GIVE ONE ANOTHER COURAGE.
THAT DOES SOUND FUN, BUT I'LL PASS.
WHEN I MARRY, IT WILL BE TO A HUSBAND WHO WAS CHOSEN FOR ME.
SO I'VE DECIDED NOT TO FALL IN LOVE WITH ANYONE.
GOODNESS, THAT'S JUST...
SO...

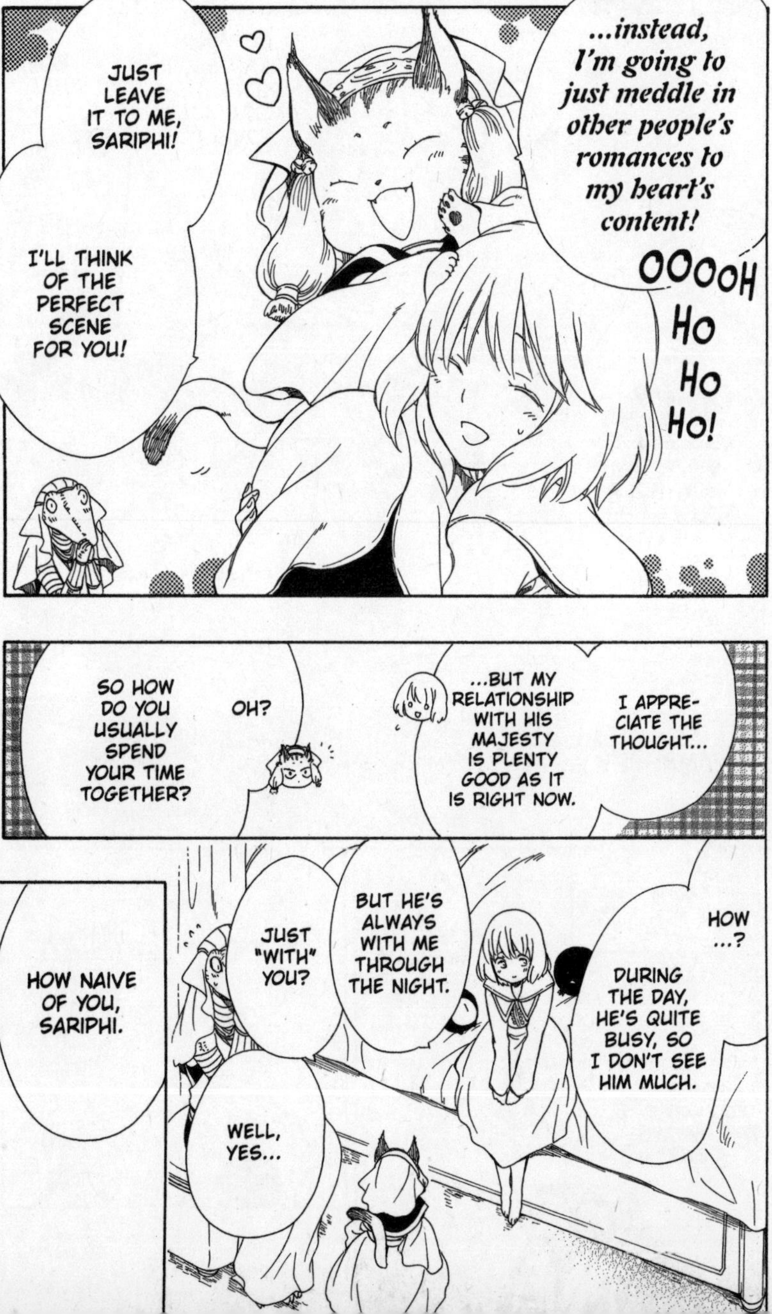
...instead, I'm going to just meddle in other people's romances to my heart's content!
OOOOH HO HO HO!
JUST LEAVE IT TO ME, SARIPHI!
I'LL THINK OF THE PERFECT SCENE FOR YOU!
I APPRE-CIATE THE THOUGHT...
...BUT MY RELATIONSHIP WITH HIS MAJESTY IS PLENTY GOOD AS IT IS RIGHT NOW.
OH?
SO HOW DO YOU USUALLY SPEND YOUR TIME TOGETHER?
HOW ...?
DURING THE DAY, HE'S QUITE BUSY, SO I DON'T SEE HIM MUCH.
BUT HE'S ALWAYS WITH ME THROUGH THE NIGHT.
JUST "WITH" YOU?
WELL, YES...
HOW NAIVE OF YOU, SARIPHI.

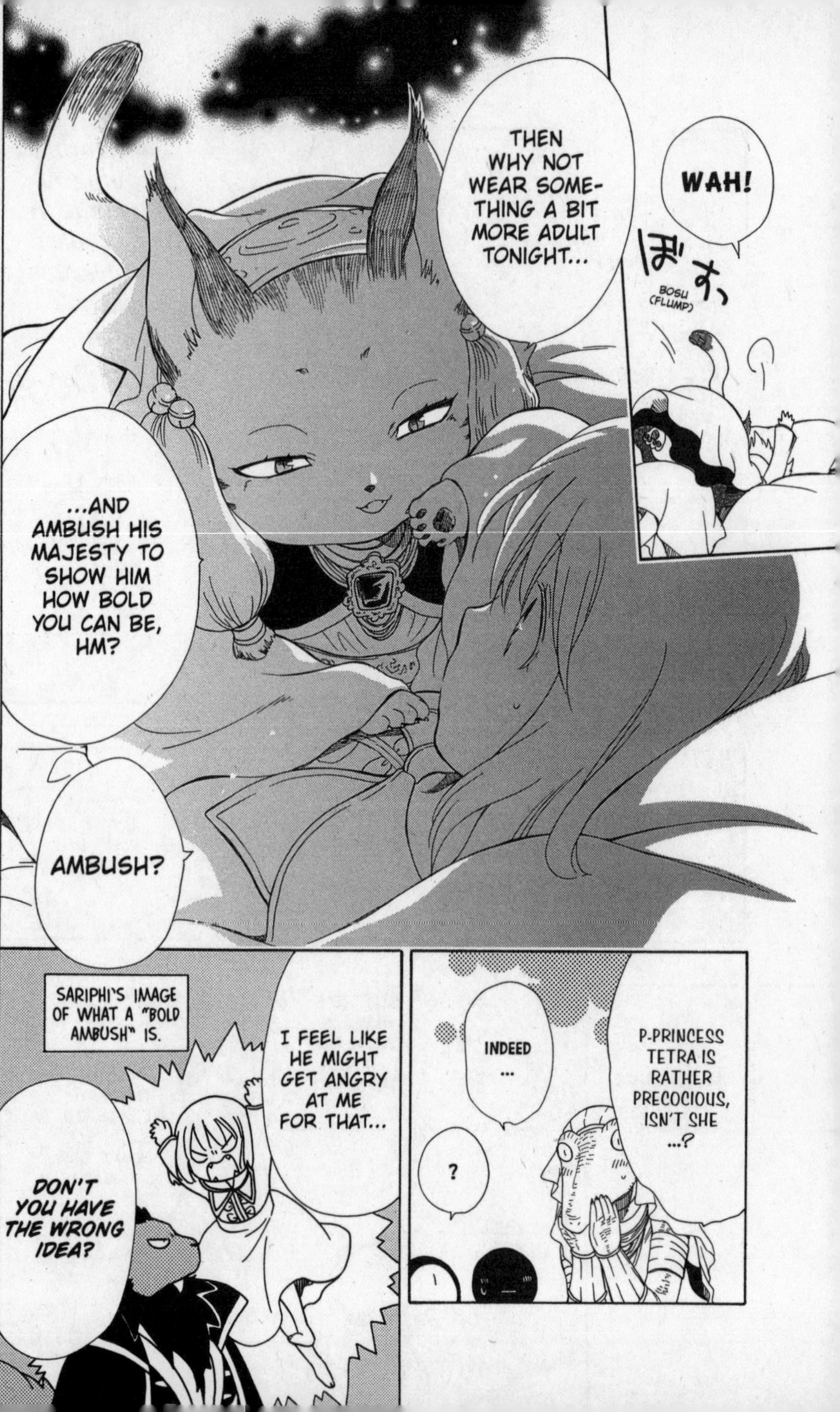
WAH!
ぼすっ
BOSU (FLUMP)
THEN WHY NOT WEAR SOME-THING A BIT MORE ADULT TONIGHT...
...AND AMBUSH HIS MAJESTY TO SHOW HIM HOW BOLD YOU CAN BE, HM?
AMBUSH?
P-PRINCESS TETRA IS RATHER PRECOCIOUS, ISN'T SHE ...?
INDEED ...
?
SARIPHI'S IMAGE OF WHAT A "BOLD AMBUSH" IS.
I FEEL LIKE HE MIGHT GET ANGRY AT ME FOR THAT...
DON'T YOU HAVE THE WRONG IDEA?

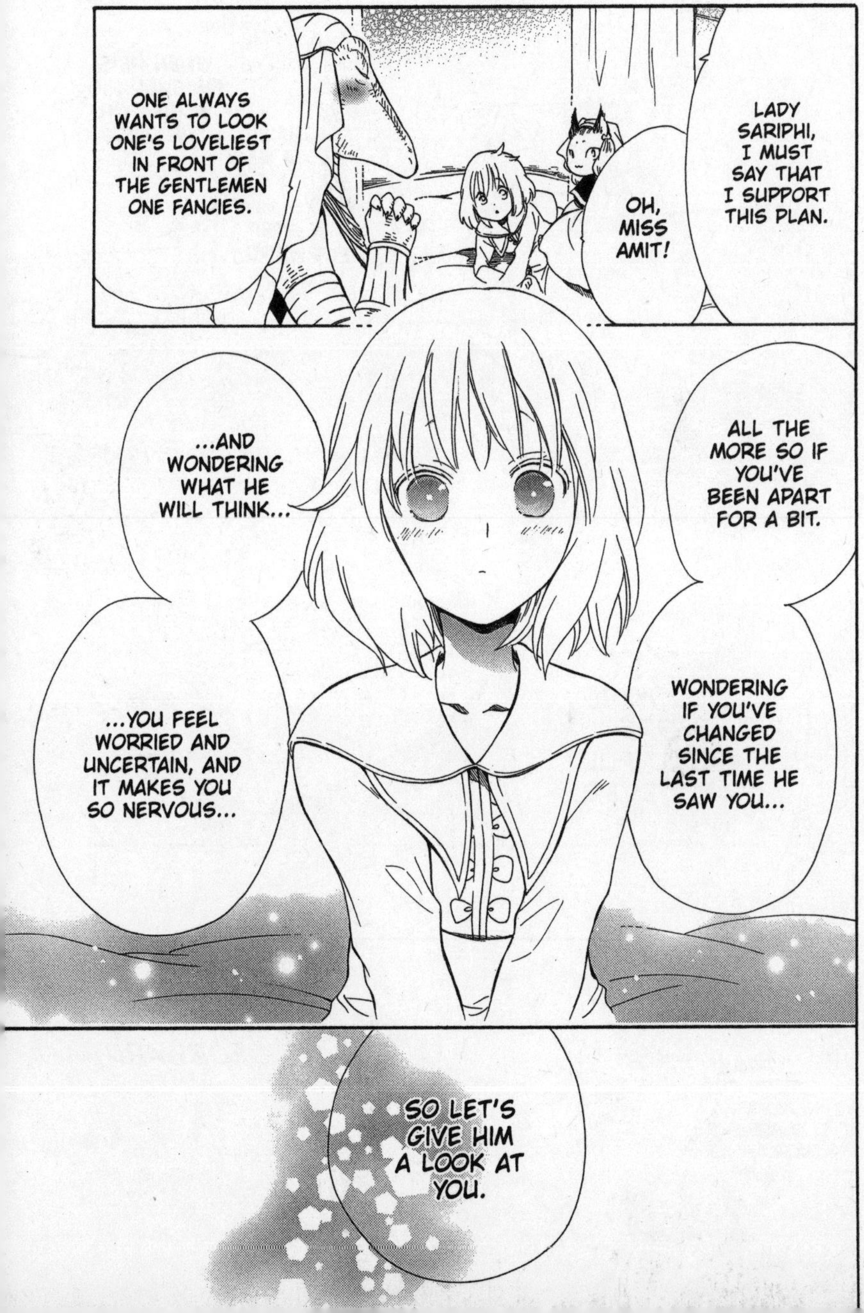
LADY SARIPHI, I MUST SAY THAT I SUPPORT THIS PLAN.
OH, MISS AMIT!
ONE ALWAYS WANTS TO LOOK ONE'S LOVELIEST IN FRONT OF THE GENTLEMEN ONE FANCIES.
ALL THE MORE SO IF YOU'VE BEEN APART FOR A BIT.
WONDERING IF YOU'VE CHANGED SINCE THE LAST TIME HE SAW YOU...
...AND WONDERING WHAT HE WILL THINK...
...YOU FEEL WORRIED AND UNCERTAIN, AND IT MAKES YOU SO NERVOUS...
SO LET'S GIVE HIM A LOOK AT YOU.

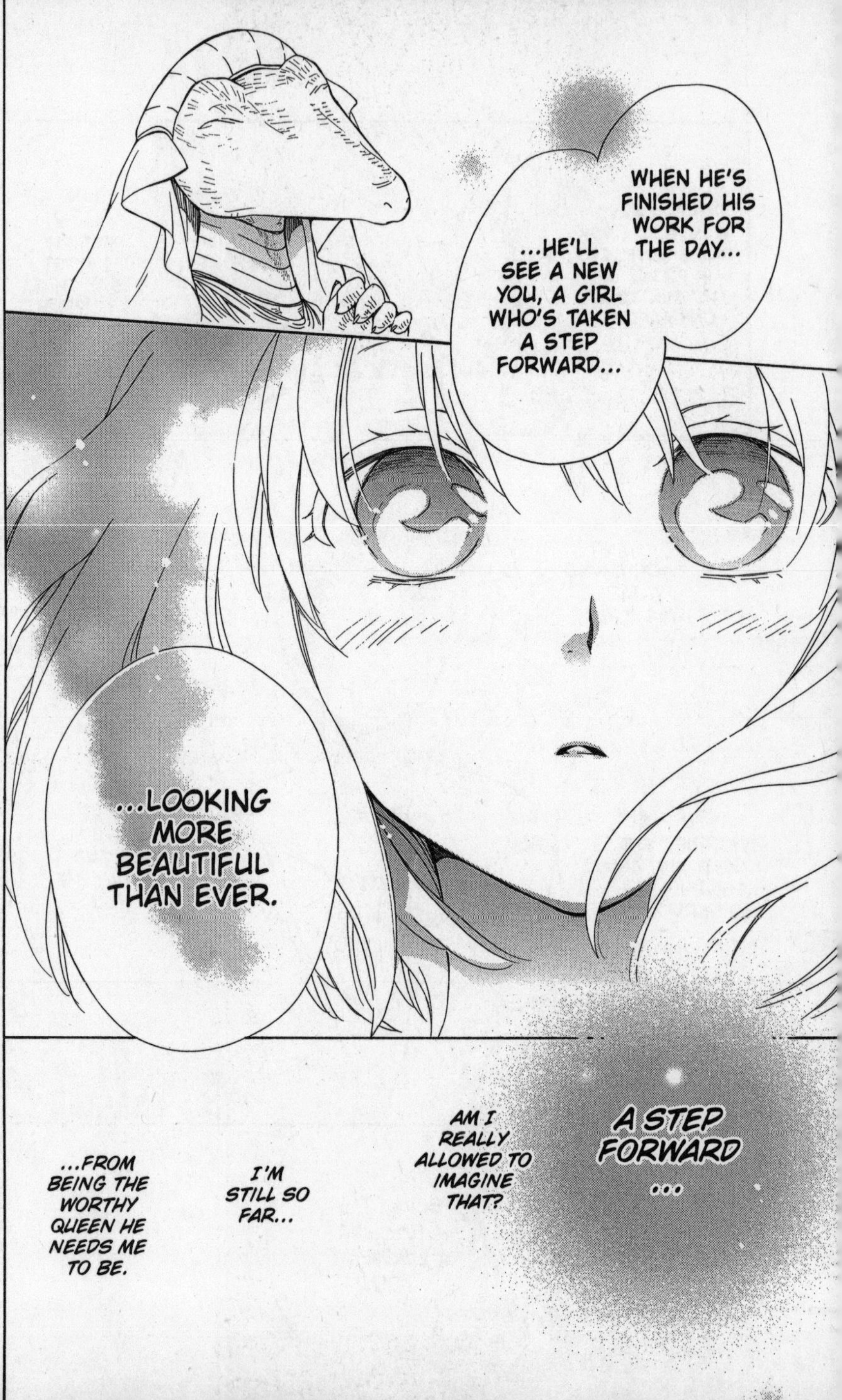
WHEN HE'S FINISHED HIS WORK FOR THE DAY...
...HE'LL SEE A NEW YOU, A GIRL WHO'S TAKEN A STEP FORWARD...
...LOOKING MORE BEAUTIFUL THAN EVER.
A STEP FORWARD...
AM I REALLY ALLOWED TO IMAGINE THAT?
I'M STILL SO FAR...
...FROM BEING THE WORTHY QUEEN HE NEEDS ME TO BE.

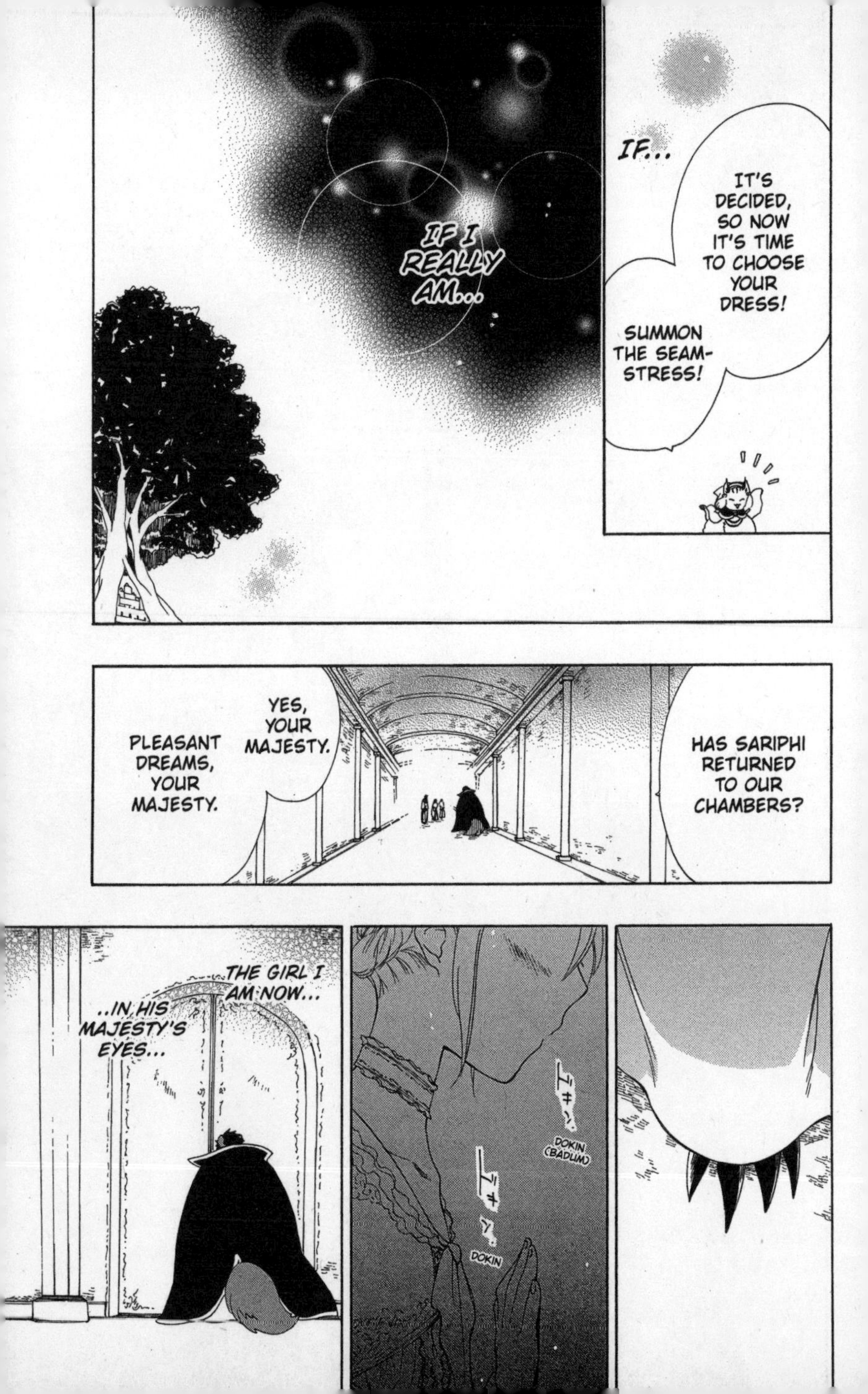
IF...
IT'S DECIDED, SO NOW IT'S TIME TO CHOOSE YOUR DRESS!
SUMMON THE SEAM-STRESS!
IF I REALLY AM...
HAS SARIPHI RETURNED TO OUR CHAMBERS?
YES, YOUR MAJESTY.
PLEASANT DREAMS, YOUR MAJESTY.
DOKIN (BADUM)
DOKIN
THE GIRL I AM NOW...
..IN HIS MAJESTY'S EYES...

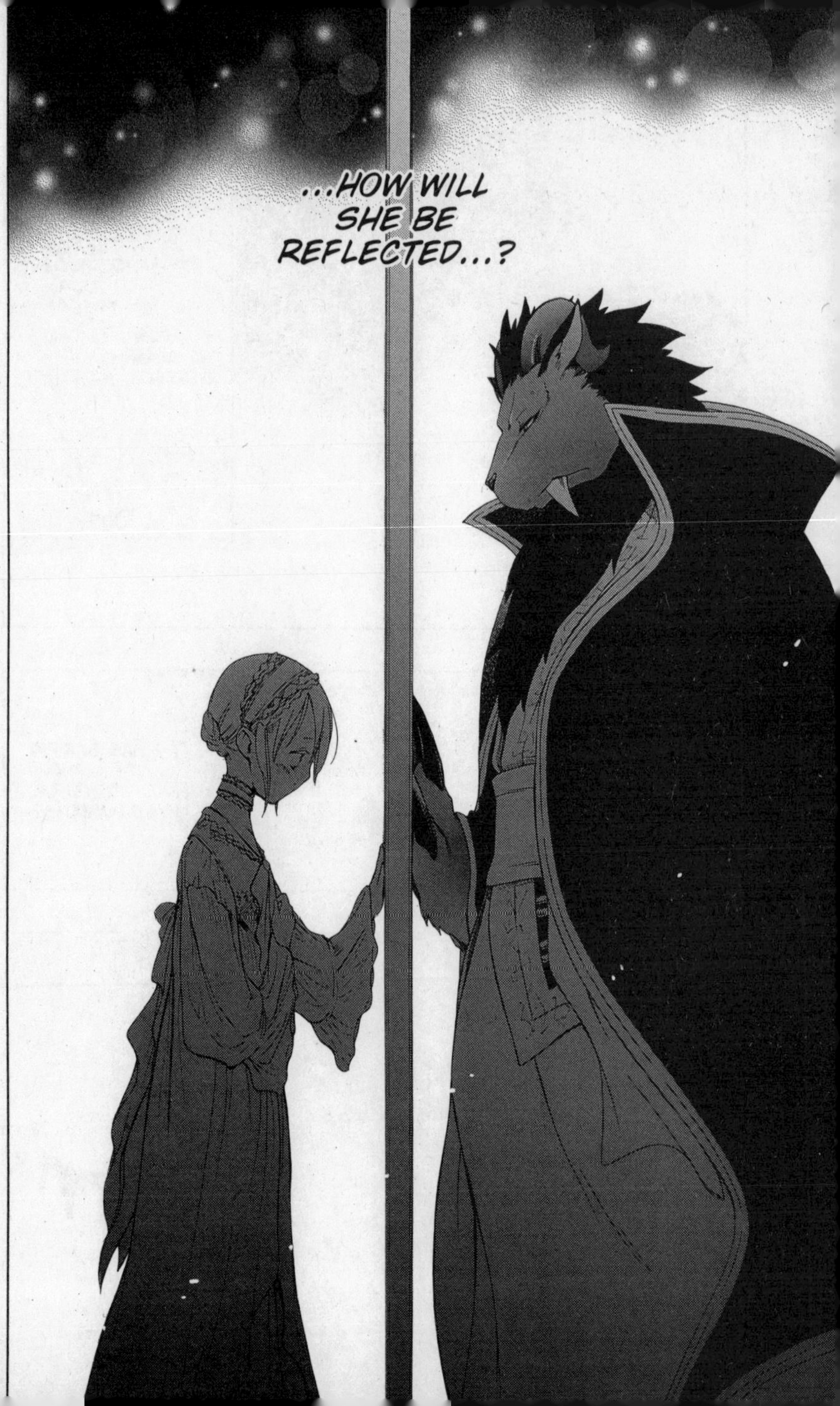
...HOW WILL SHE BE REFLECTED...?

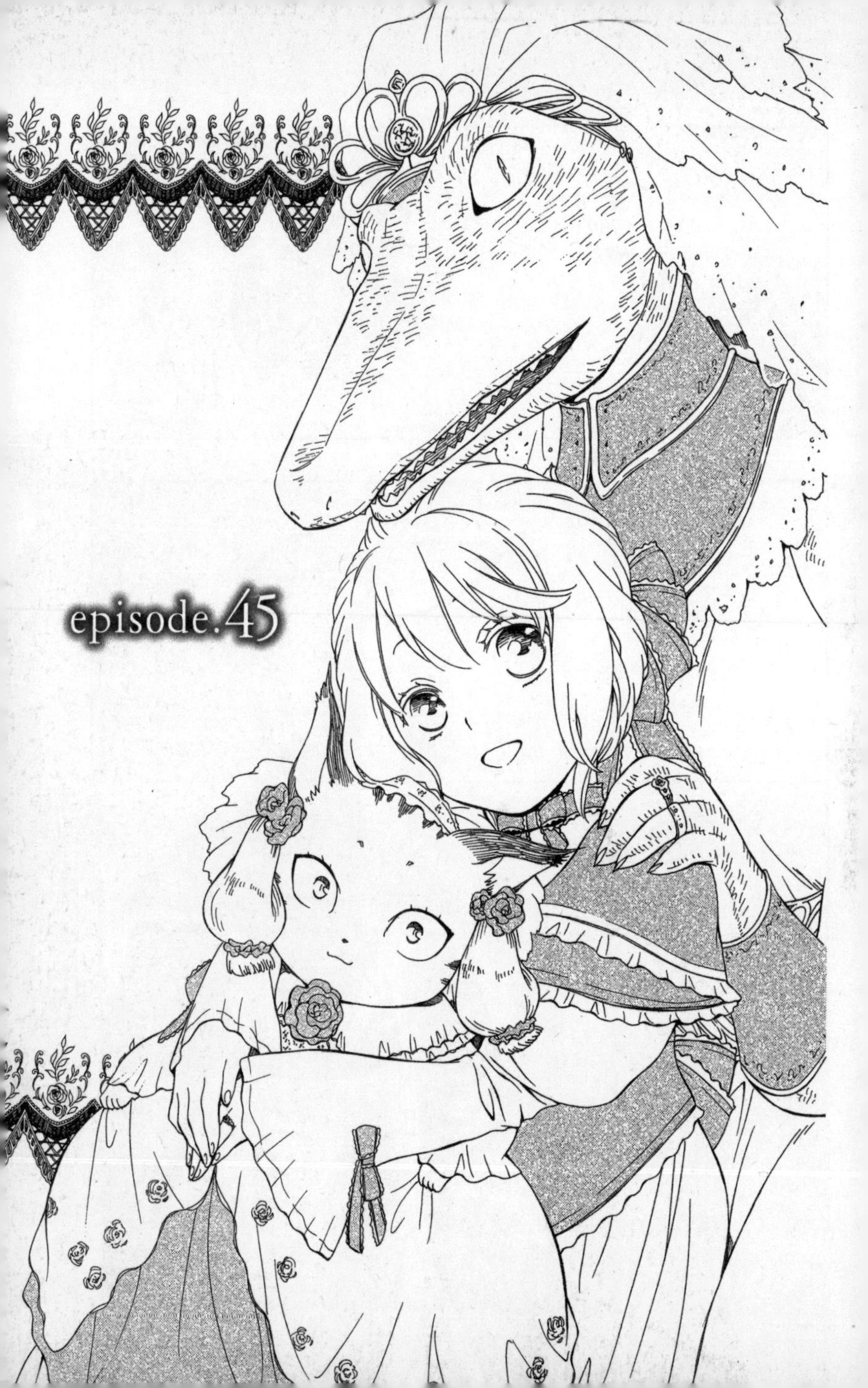
episode.45

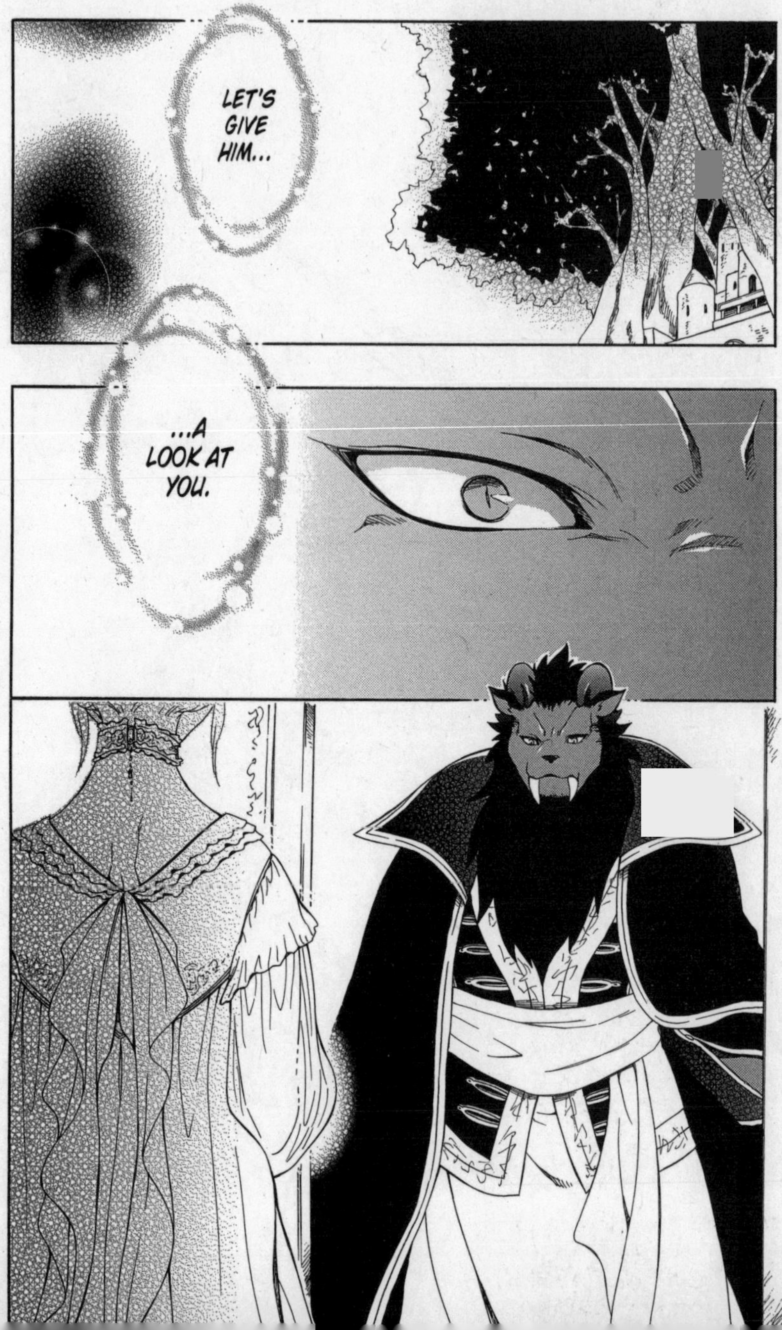
LET'S GIVE HIM...
...A LOOK AT YOU.

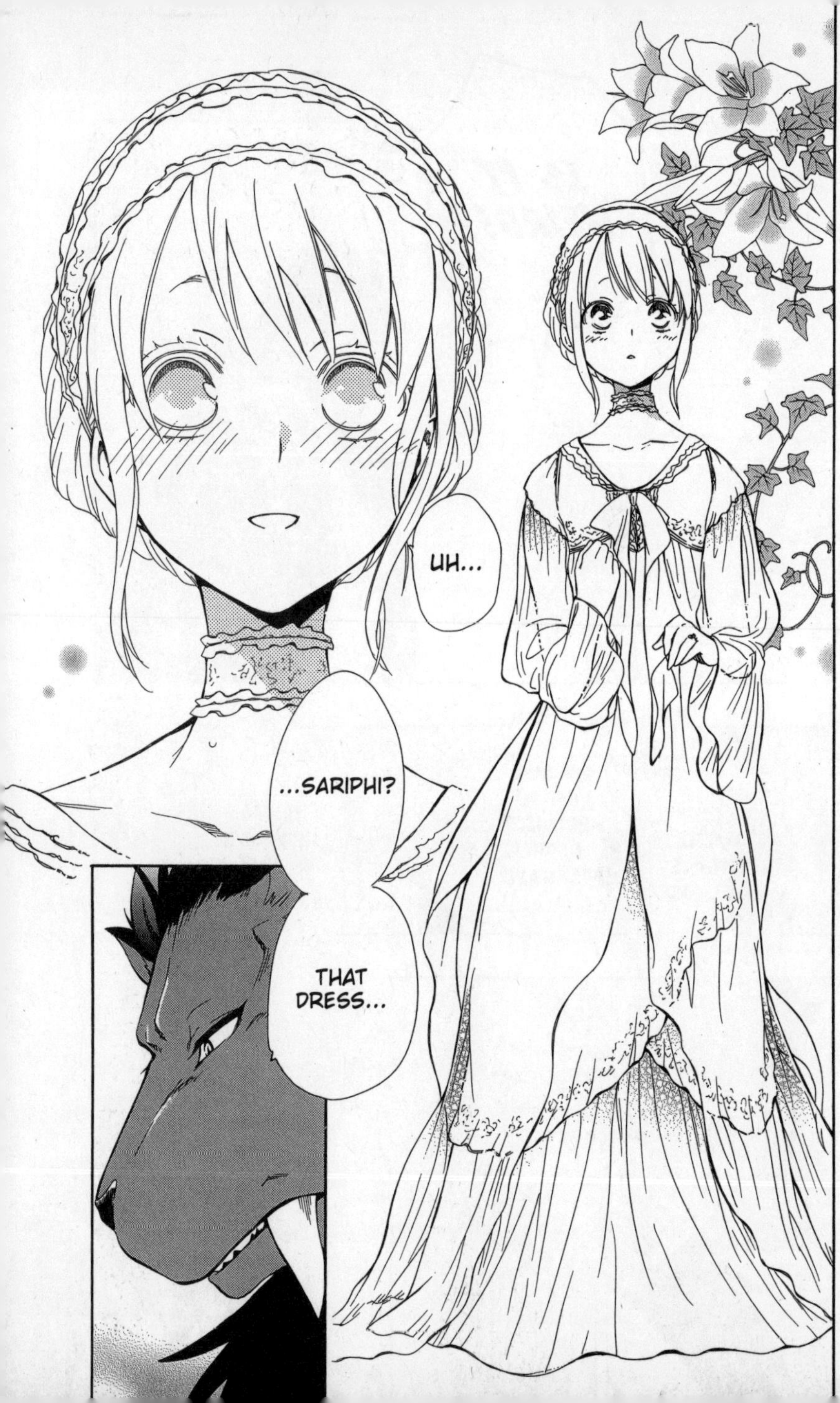
UH...
...SARIPHI?
THAT DRESS...

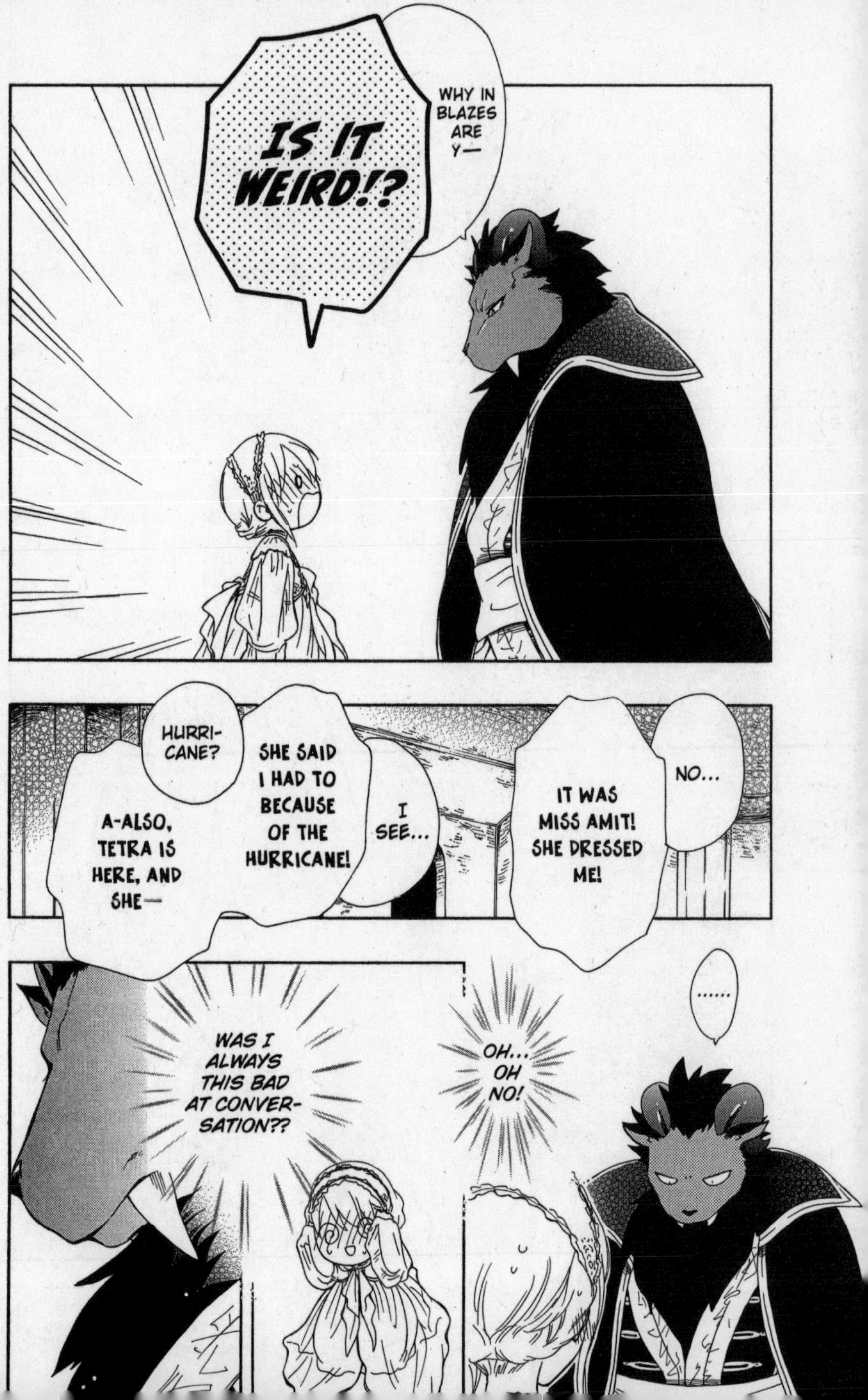
WHY IN BLAZES ARE Y—
IS IT WEIRD!?
NO...
IT WAS MISS AMIT! SHE DRESSED ME!
I SEE...
SHE SAID I HAD TO BECAUSE OF THE HURRICANE!
HURRI-CANE?
A-ALSO, TETRA IS HERE, AND SHE—
......
OH... OH NO!
WAS I ALWAYS THIS BAD AT CONVER-SATION??

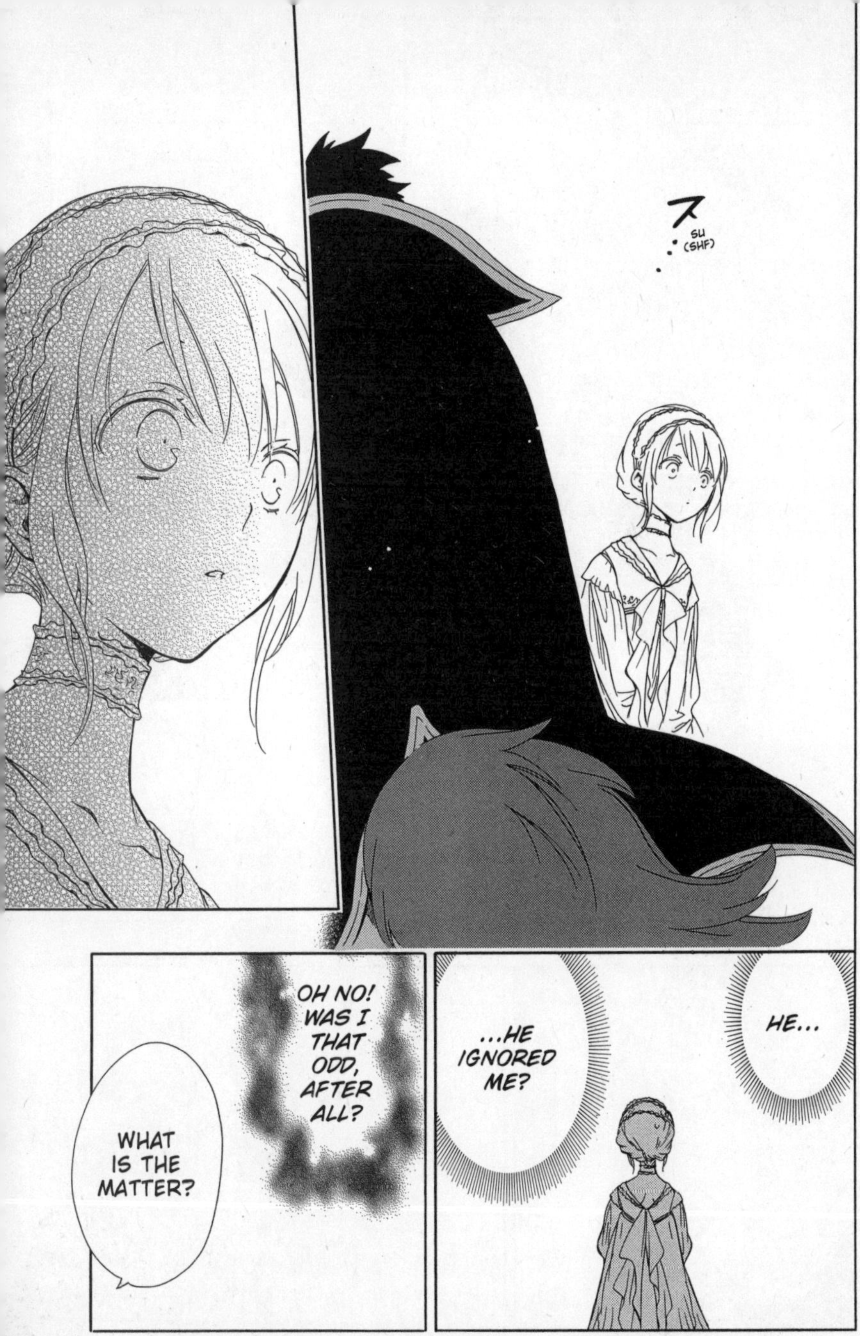
ス
SU (SHF)
HE...
...HE IGNORED ME?
OH NO! WAS I THAT ODD, AFTER ALL?
WHAT IS THE MATTER?

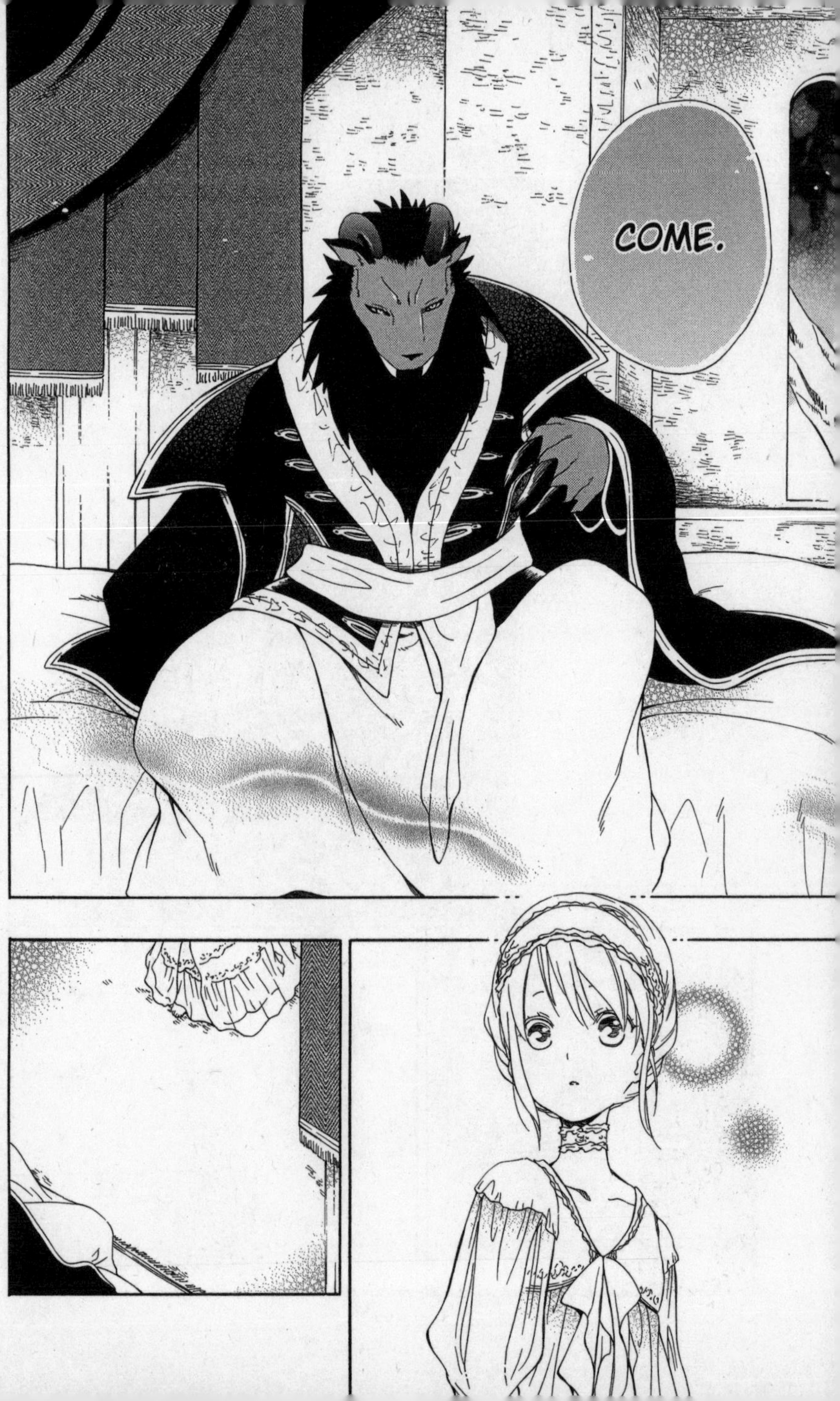
COME.

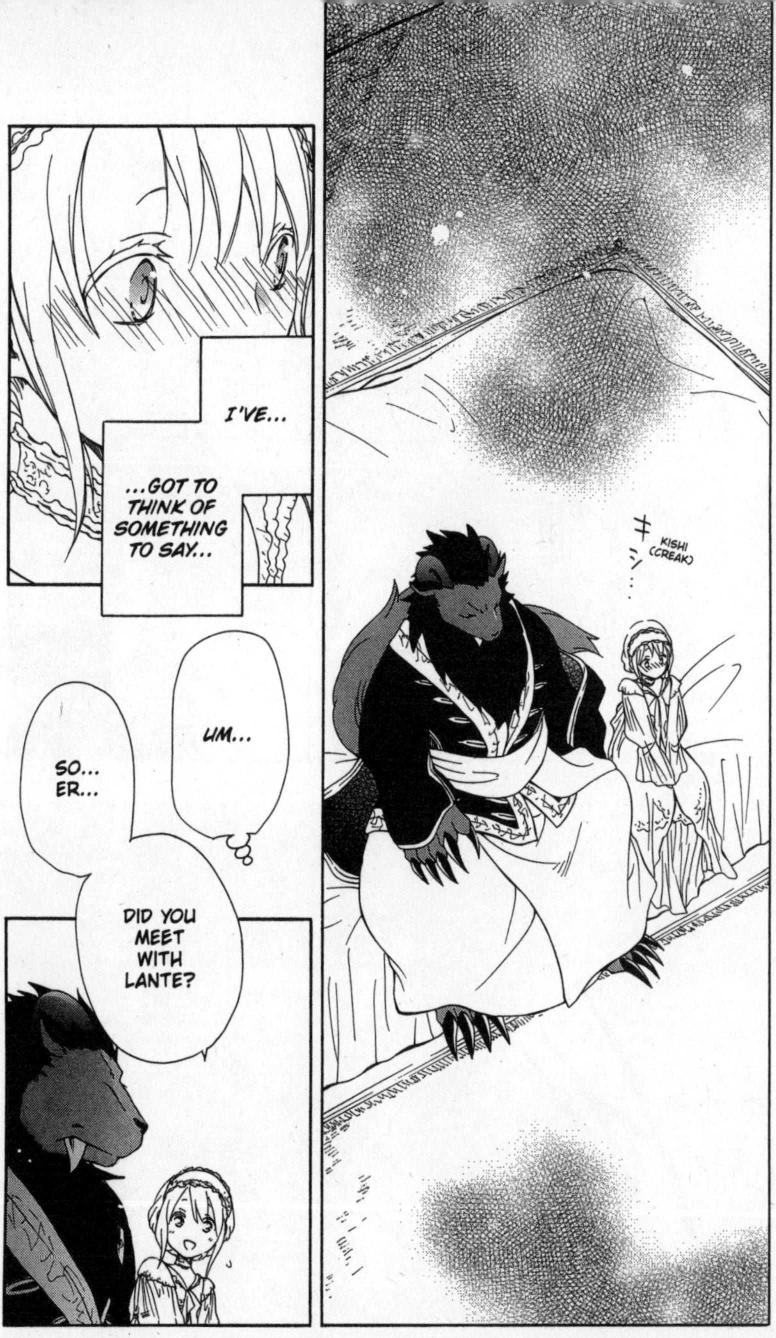
キシ…
KISHI (CREAK)
I'VE...
...GOT TO THINK OF SOMETHING TO SAY...
UM...
SO... ER...
DID YOU MEET WITH LANTE?

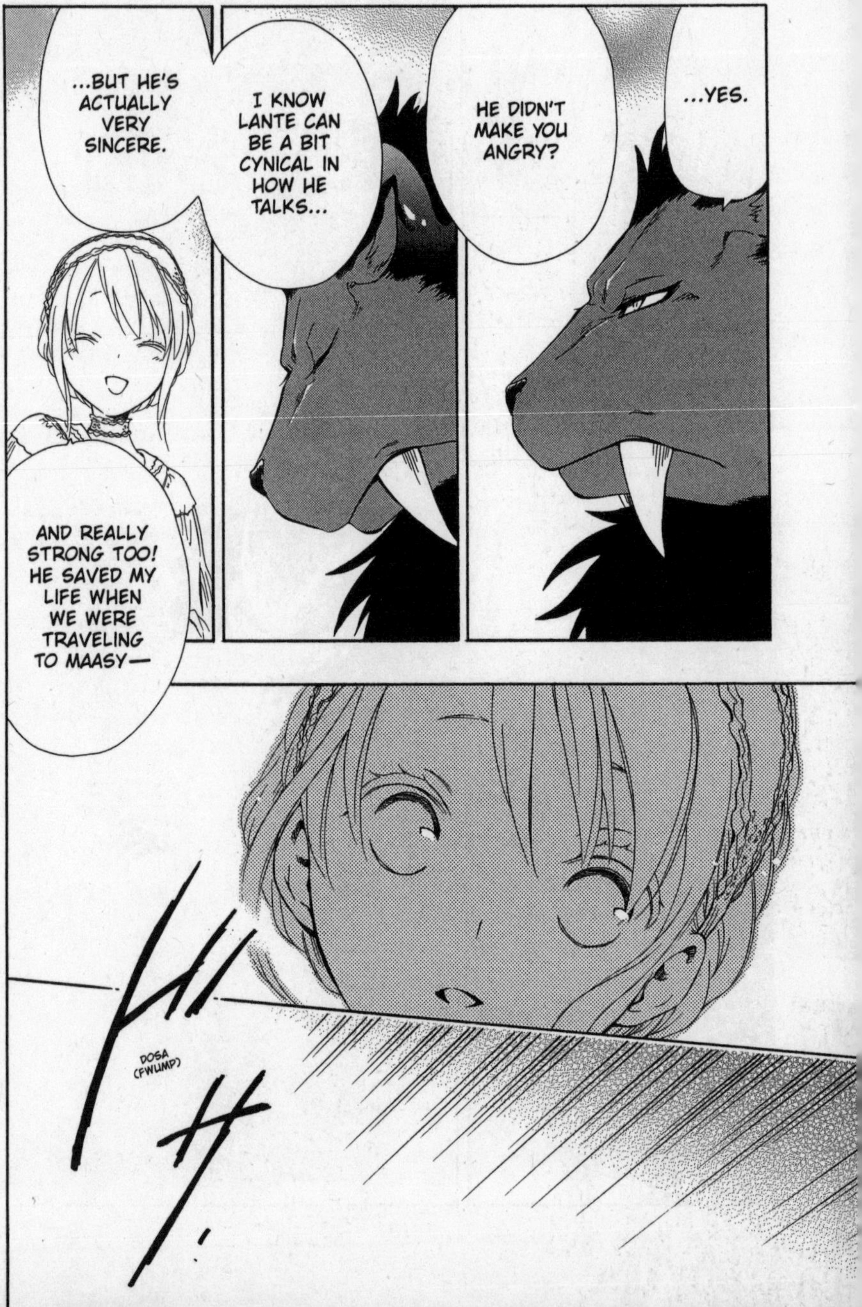
...YES.
HE DIDN'T MAKE YOU ANGRY?
I KNOW LANTE CAN BE A BIT CYNICAL IN HOW HE TALKS...
...BUT HE'S ACTUALLY VERY SINCERE.
AND REALLY STRONG TOO! HE SAVED MY LIFE WHEN WE WERE TRAVELING TO MAASY—
DOSA (FWUMP)

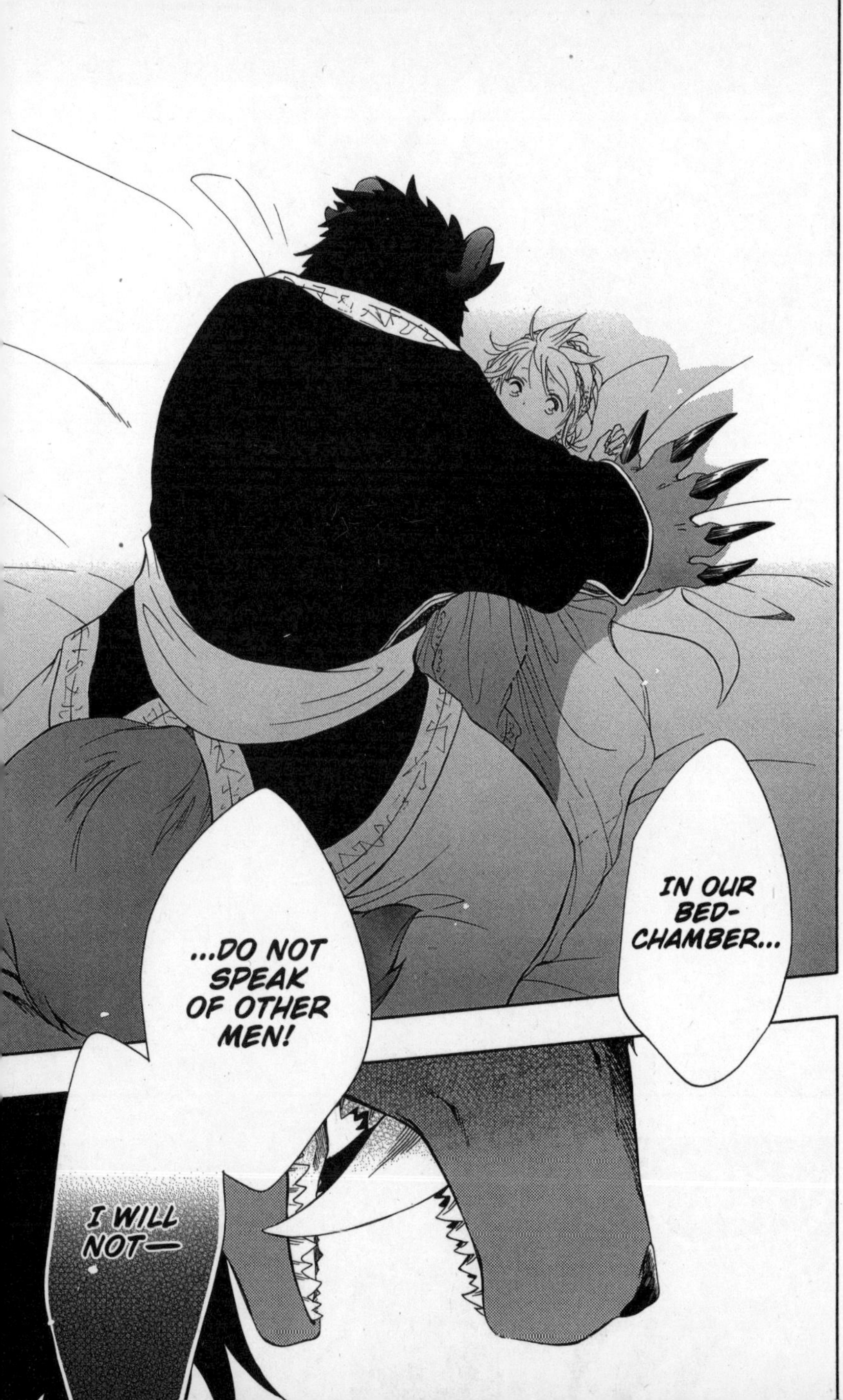
IN OUR BED-CHAMBER...
...DO NOT SPEAK OF OTHER MEN!
I WILL NOT—

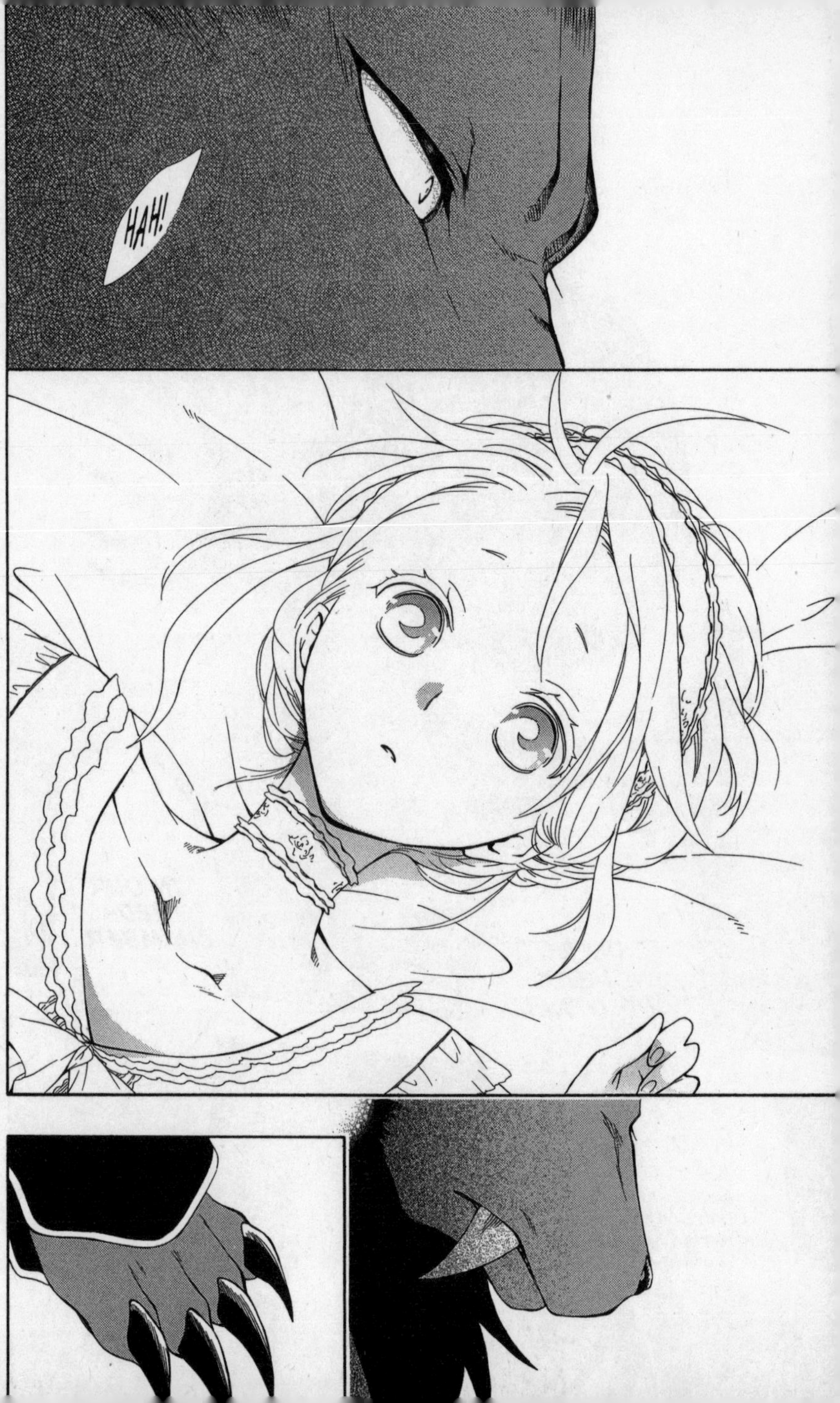
HAH!

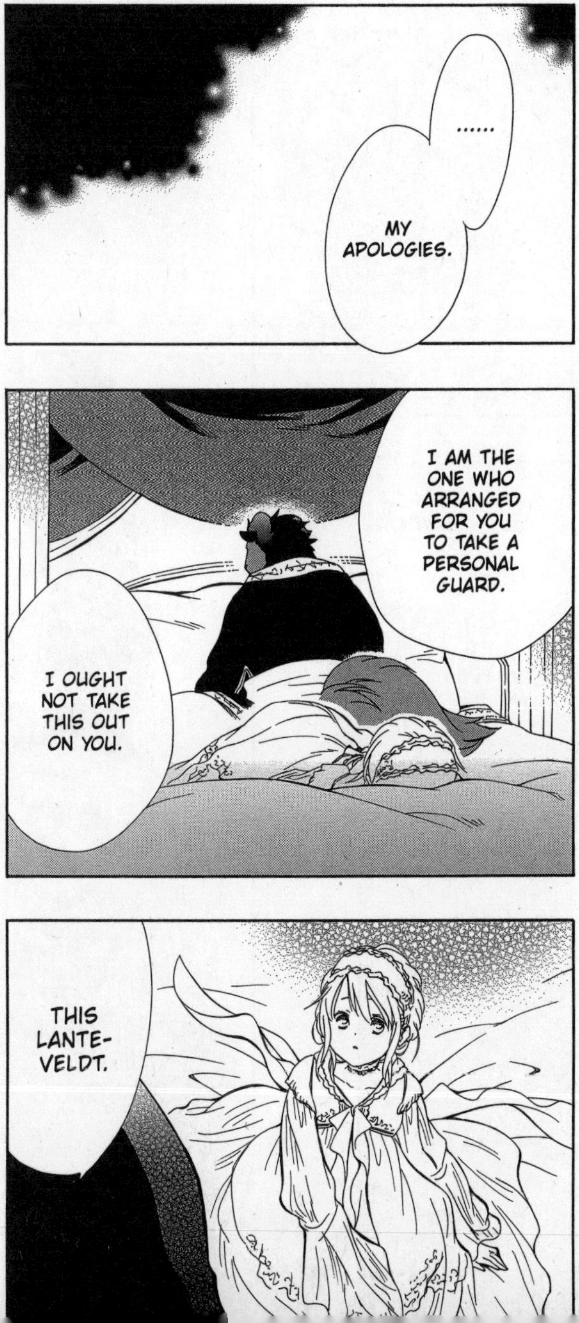
......
MY APOLOGIES.
I AM THE ONE WHO ARRANGED FOR YOU TO TAKE A PERSONAL GUARD.
I OUGHT NOT TAKE THIS OUT ON YOU.
THIS LANTE-VELDT.

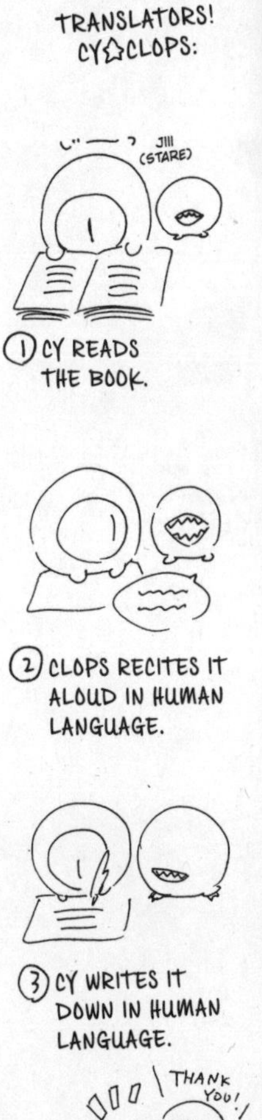
TRANSLATORS! CY☆CLOPS:
JIII (STARE)
① CY READS THE BOOK.
② CLOPS RECITES IT ALOUD IN HUMAN LANGUAGE.
③ CY WRITES IT DOWN IN HUMAN LANGUAGE.
THANK YOU!
④ THEN TO SARIPHI!
ALSO, FOR SIMPLE WRITING, SARI'S GOTTEN BETTER, SO SHE CAN READ IT BY HERSELF.

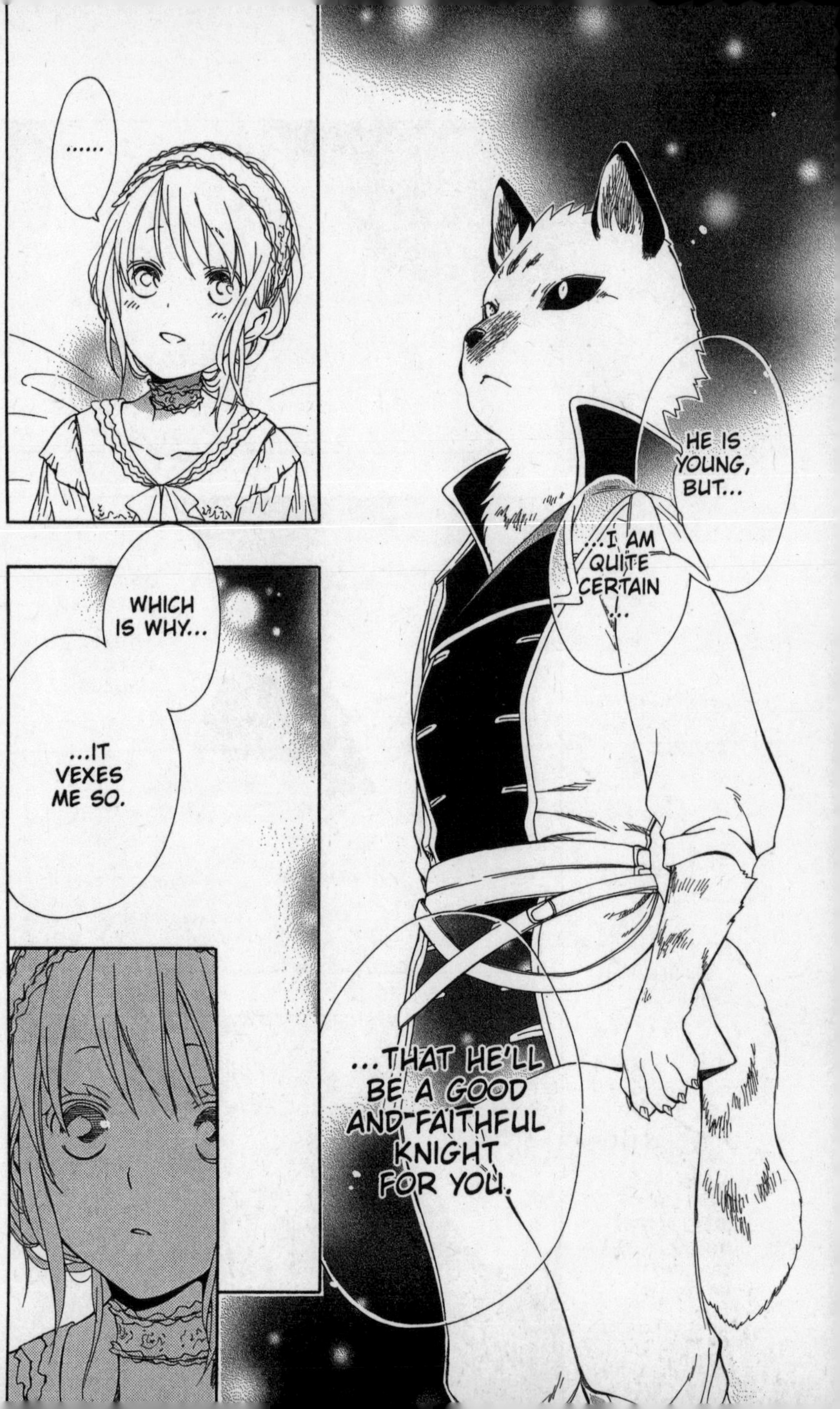
HE IS YOUNG, BUT...
...I AM QUITE CERTAIN...
...THAT HE'LL BE A GOOD AND FAITHFUL KNIGHT FOR YOU.
......
WHICH IS WHY...
...IT VEXES ME SO.

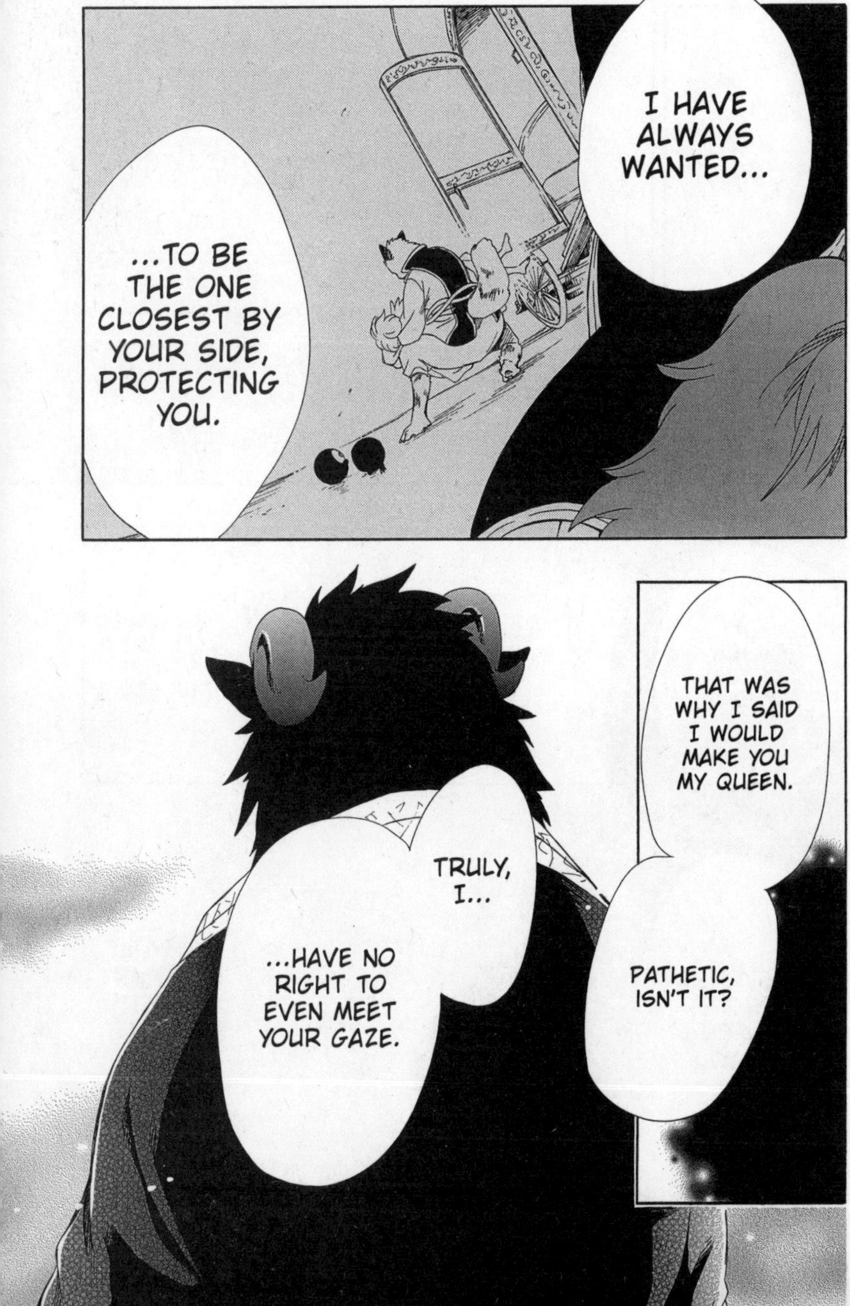
I HAVE ALWAYS WANTED...
...TO BE THE ONE CLOSEST BY YOUR SIDE, PROTECTING YOU.
THAT WAS WHY I SAID I WOULD MAKE YOU MY QUEEN.
PATHETIC, ISN'T IT?
TRULY, I...
...HAVE NO RIGHT TO EVEN MEET YOUR GAZE.

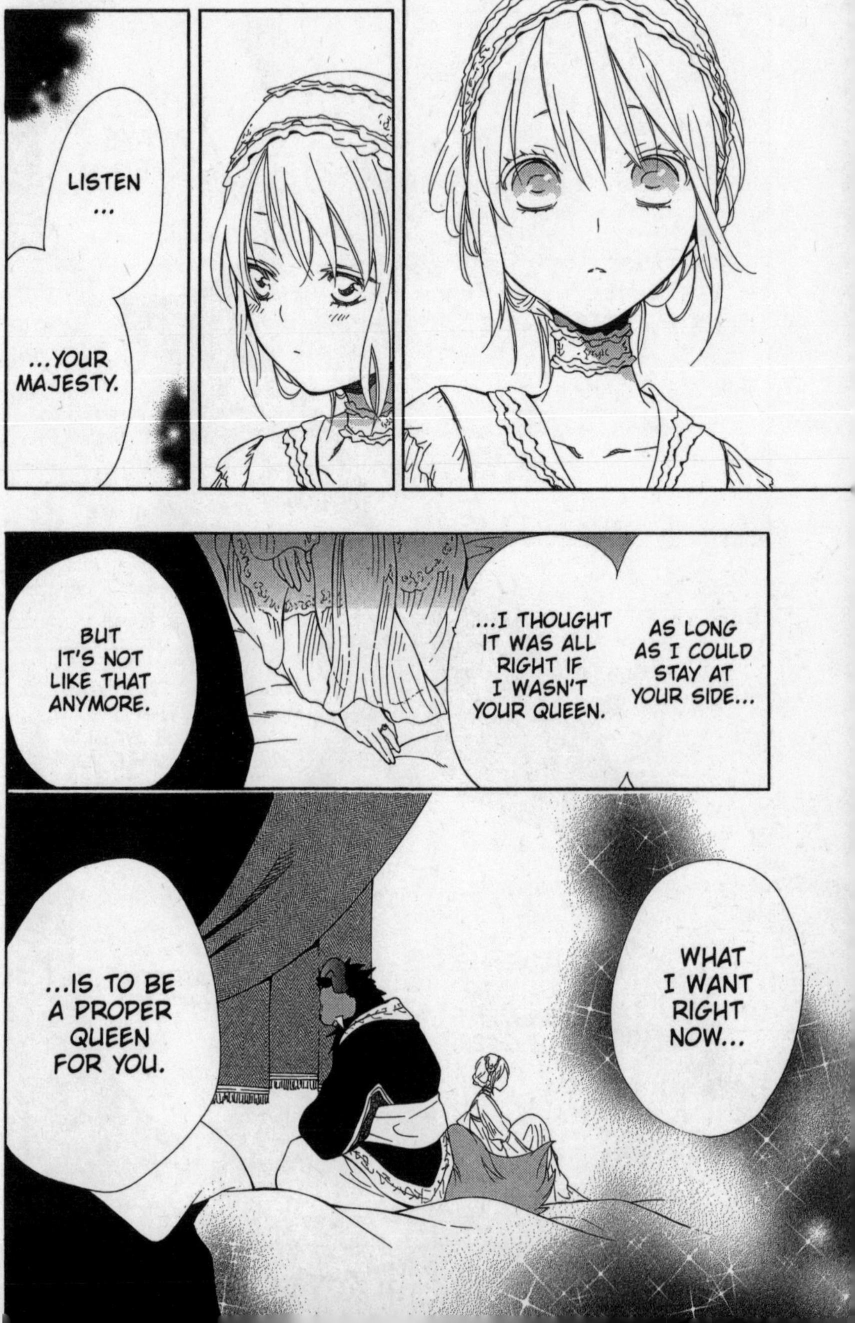
LISTEN...
...YOUR MAJESTY.
AS LONG AS I COULD STAY AT YOUR SIDE...
...I THOUGHT IT WAS ALL RIGHT IF I WASN'T YOUR QUEEN.
BUT IT'S NOT LIKE THAT ANYMORE.
WHAT I WANT RIGHT NOW...
...IS TO BE A PROPER QUEEN FOR YOU.

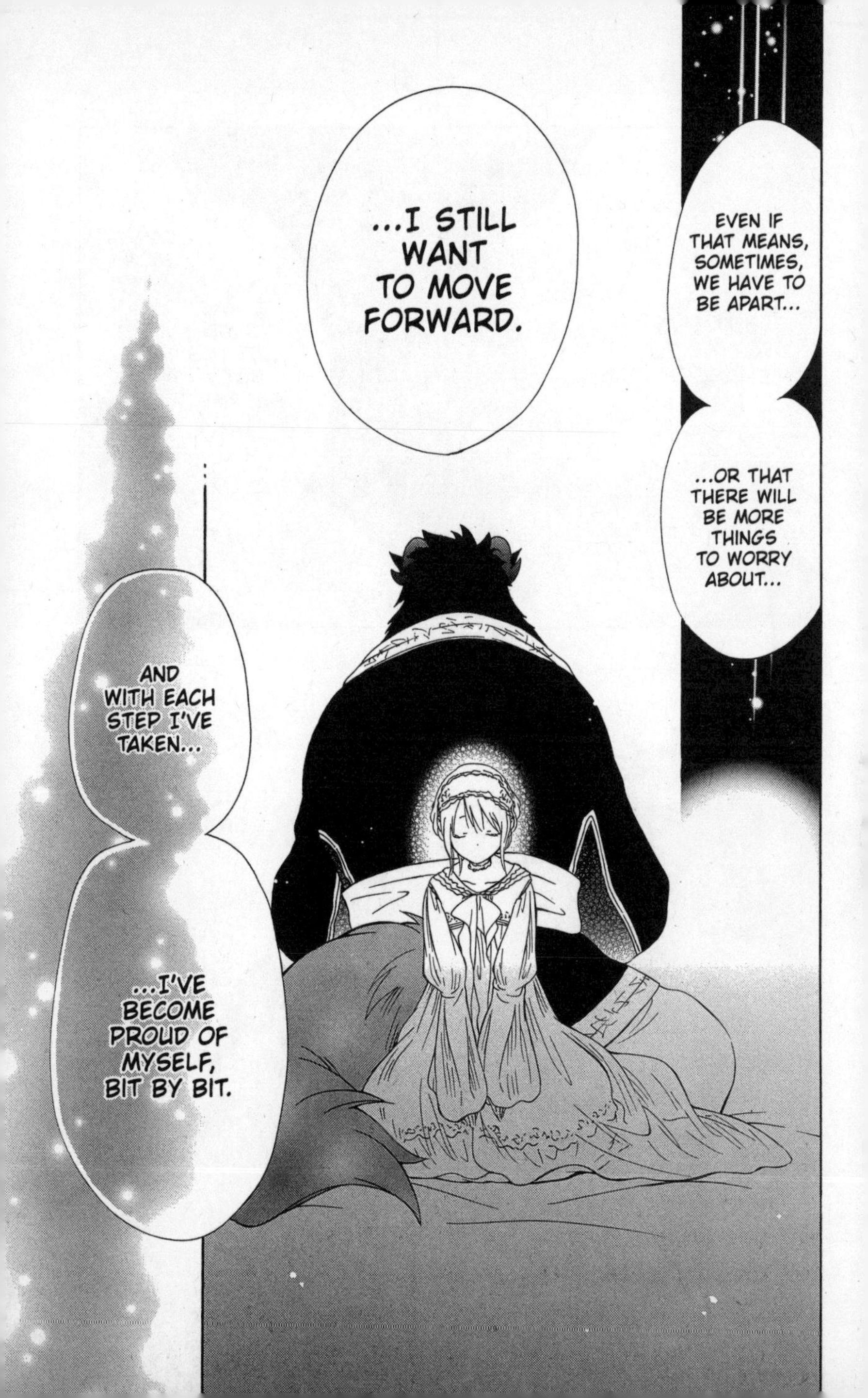
EVEN IF THAT MEANS, SOMETIMES, WE HAVE TO BE APART...
...OR THAT THERE WILL BE MORE THINGS TO WORRY ABOUT...
...I STILL WANT TO MOVE FORWARD.
AND WITH EACH STEP I'VE TAKEN...
...I'VE BECOME PROUD OF MYSELF, BIT BY BIT.

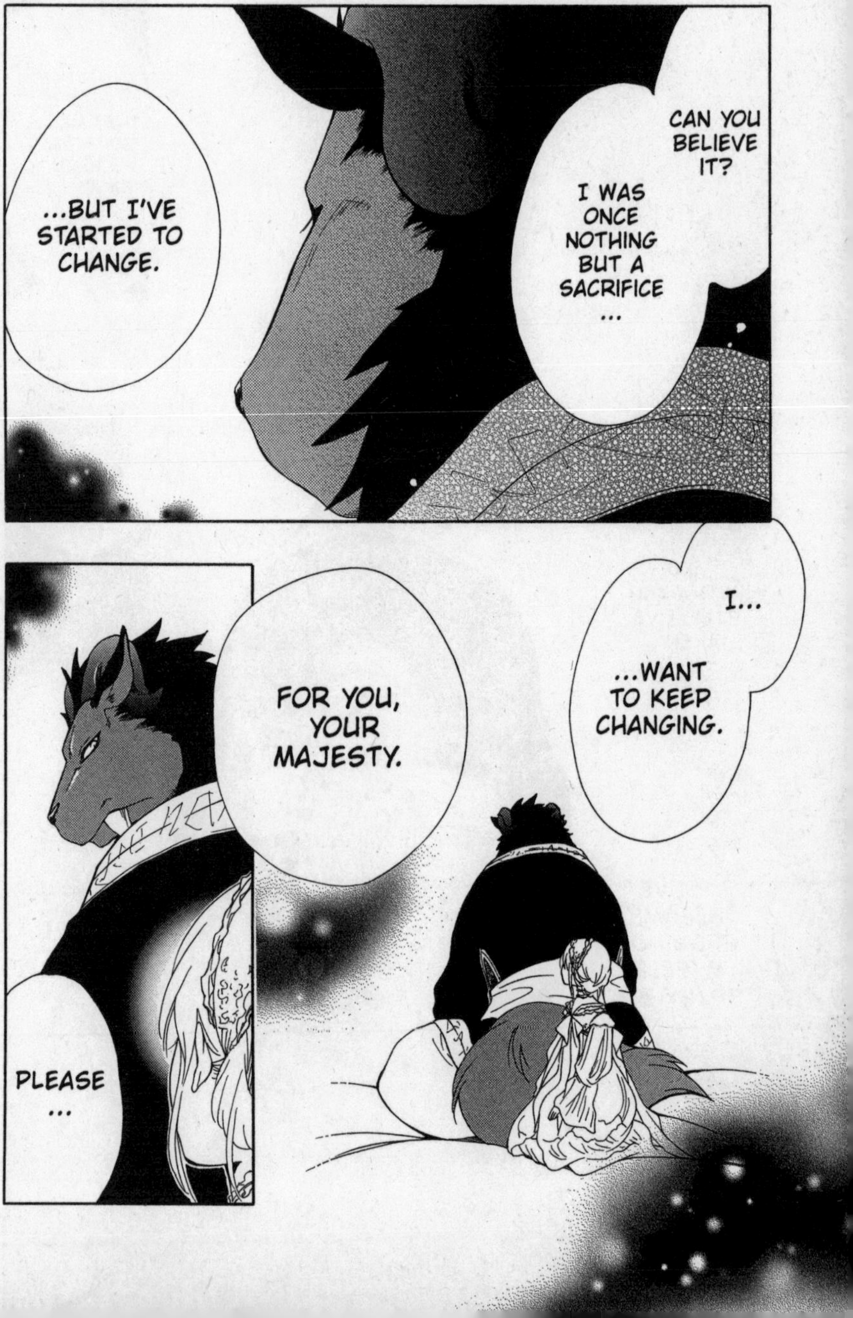
CAN YOU BELIEVE IT?
I WAS ONCE NOTHING BUT A SACRIFICE...
...BUT I'VE STARTED TO CHANGE.
I...
...WANT TO KEEP CHANGING.
FOR YOU, YOUR MAJESTY.
PLEASE...

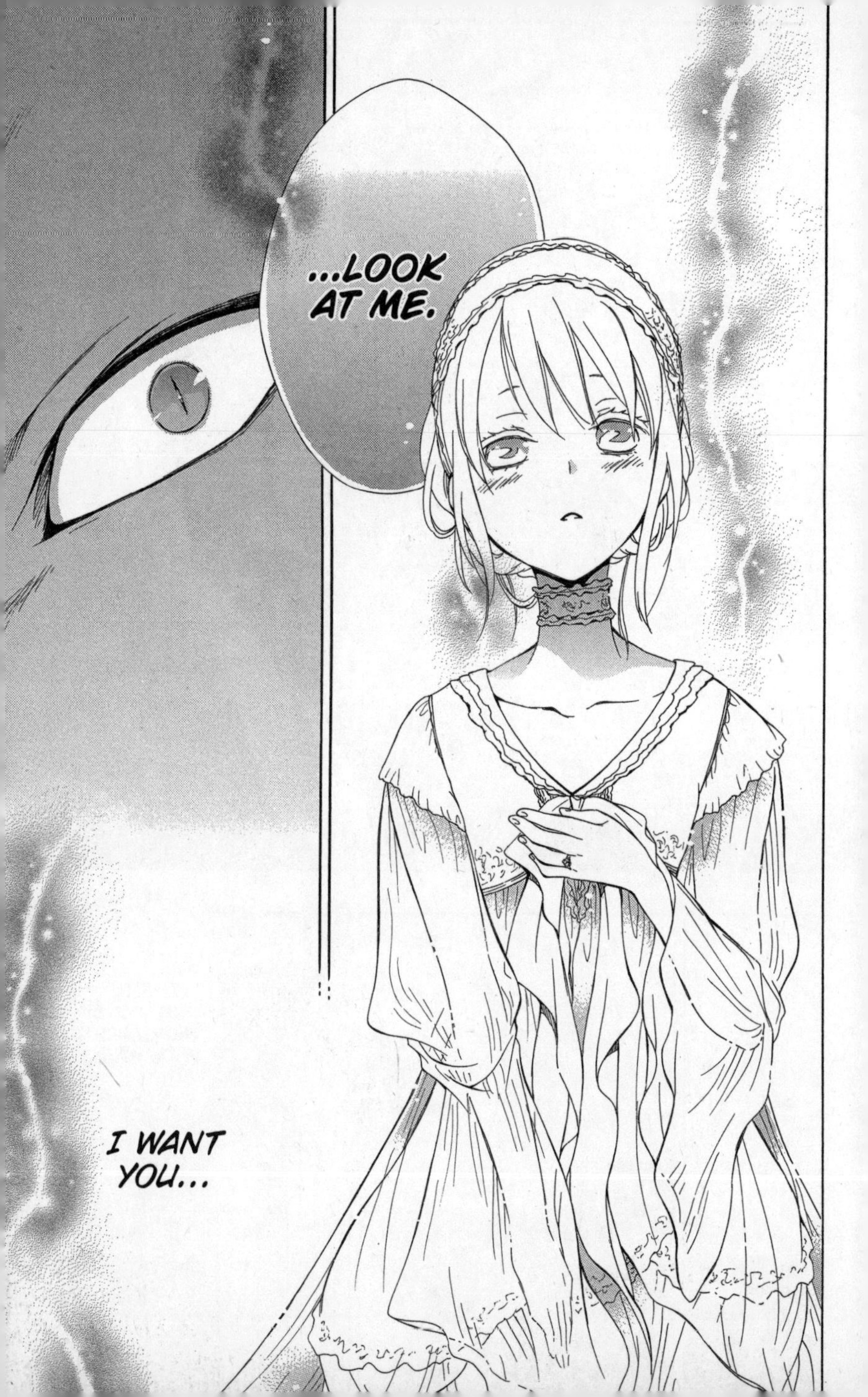
...LOOK AT ME.
I WANT YOU...

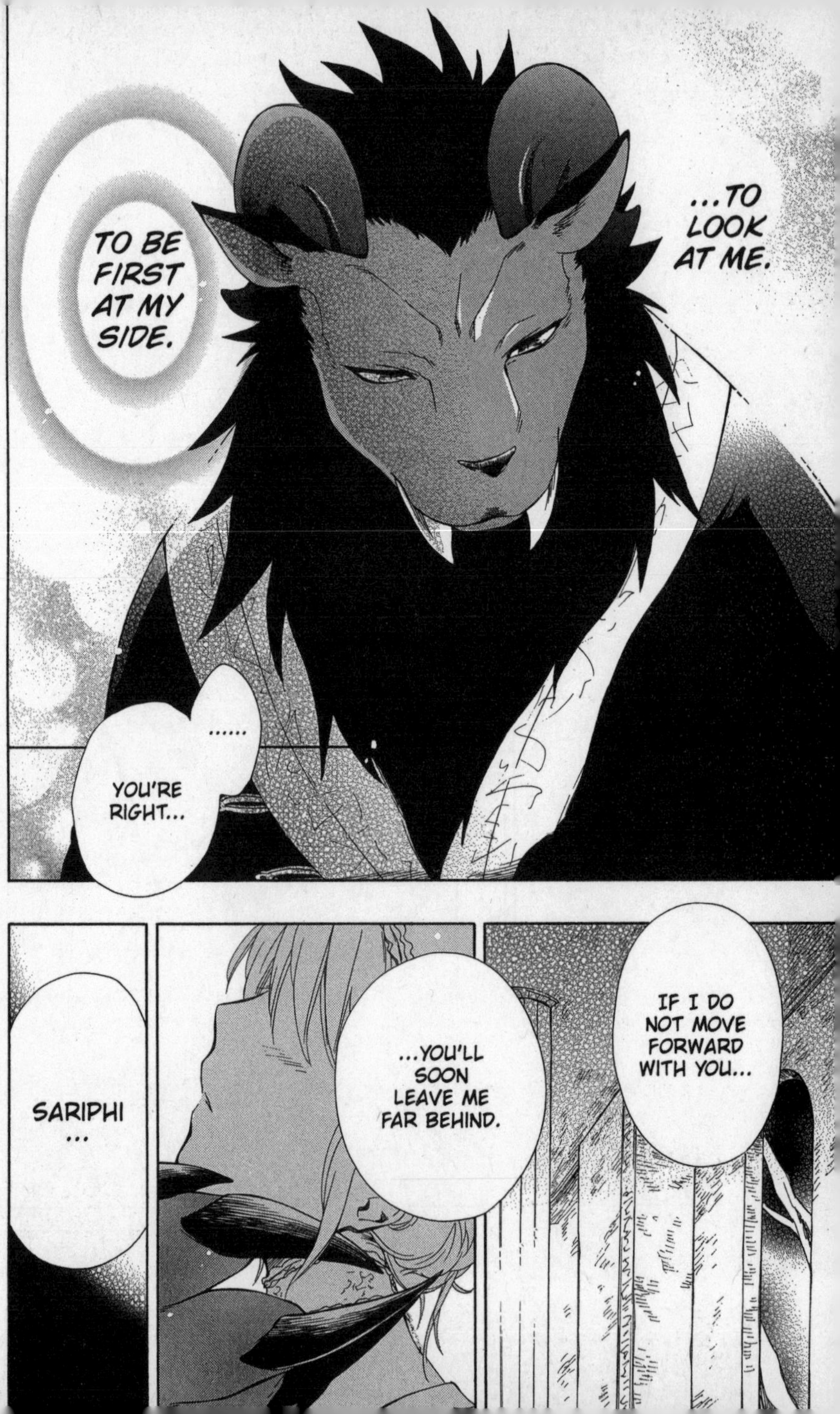
...TO LOOK AT ME.
TO BE FIRST AT MY SIDE.
......
YOU'RE RIGHT...
IF I DO NOT MOVE FORWARD WITH YOU...
...YOU'LL SOON LEAVE ME FAR BEHIND.
SARIPHI ...

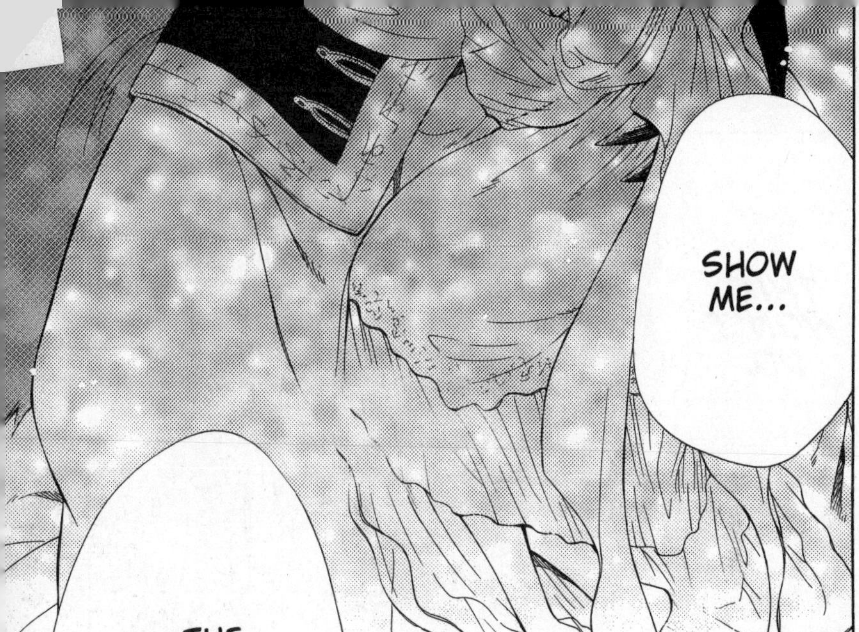
SHOW ME...
...THE PROUD FORM OF MY QUEEN.

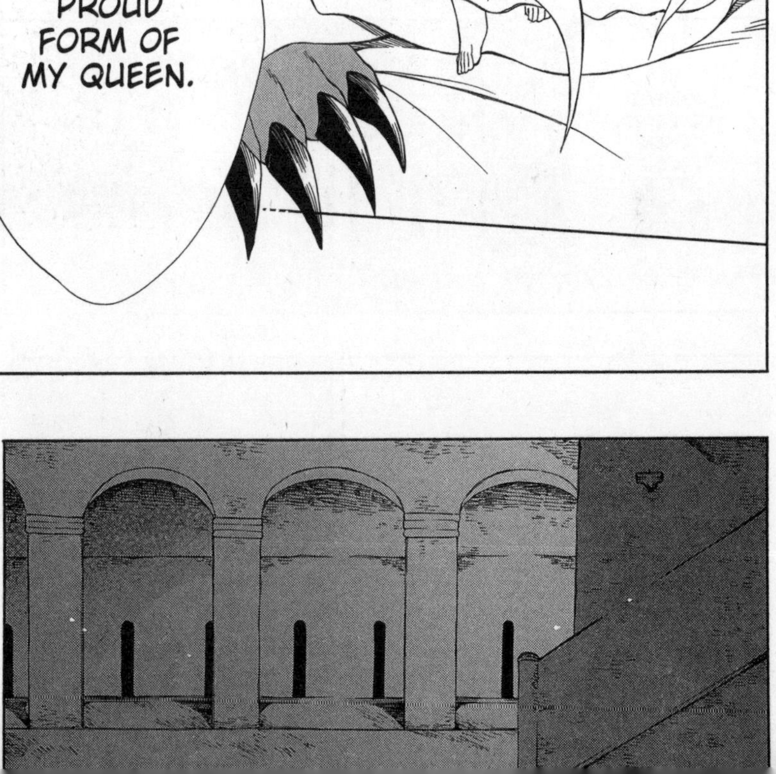

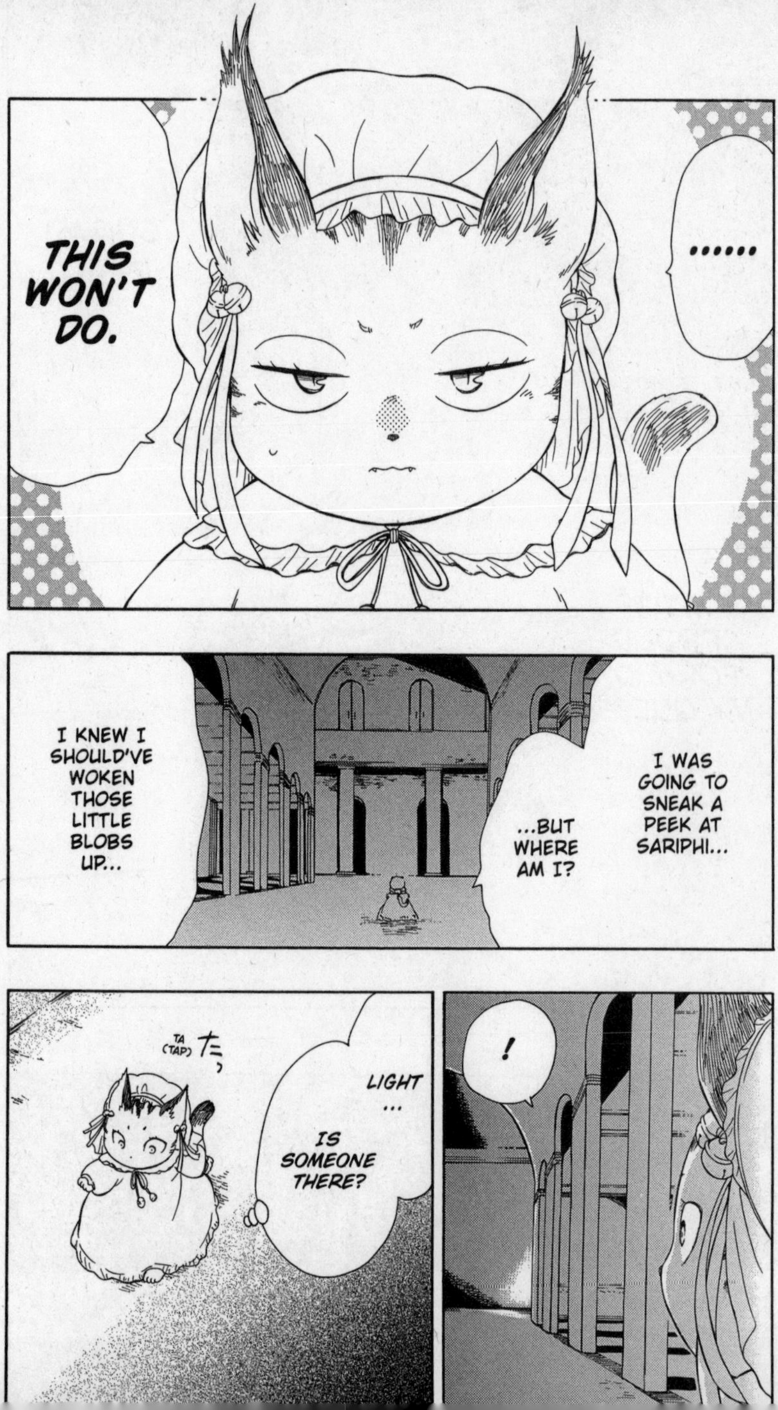
......
THIS WON'T DO.
I WAS GOING TO SNEAK A PEEK AT SARIPHI...
...BUT WHERE AM I?
I KNEW I SHOULD'VE WOKEN THOSE LITTLE BLOBS UP...
!
LIGHT ...
IS SOMEONE THERE?
TA (TAP)

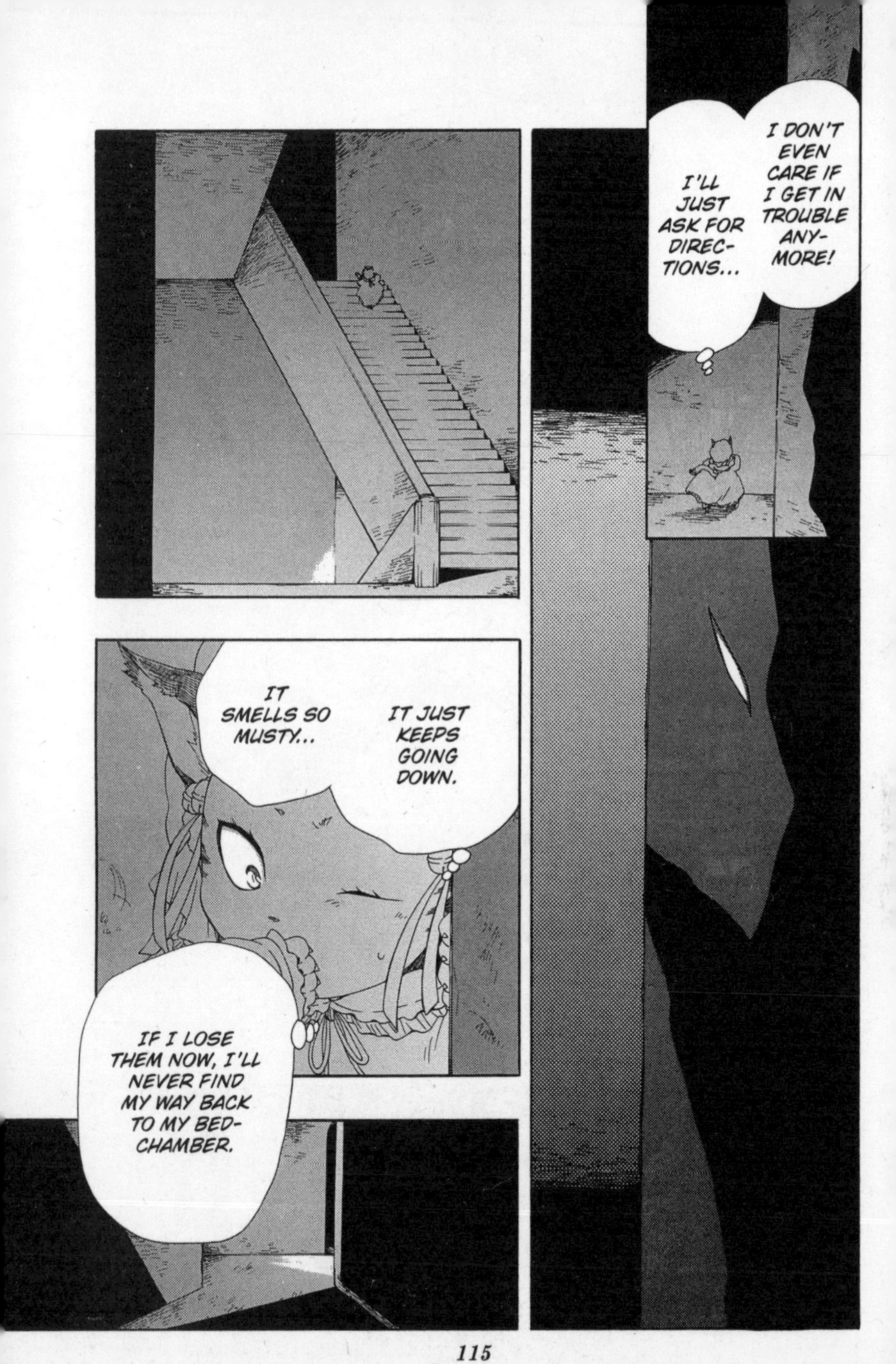
I DON'T EVEN CARE IF I GET IN TROUBLE ANYMORE!
I'LL JUST ASK FOR DIRECTIONS...
IT SMELLS SO MUSTY...
IT JUST KEEPS GOING DOWN.
IF I LOSE THEM NOW, I'LL NEVER FIND MY WAY BACK TO MY BEDCHAMBER.

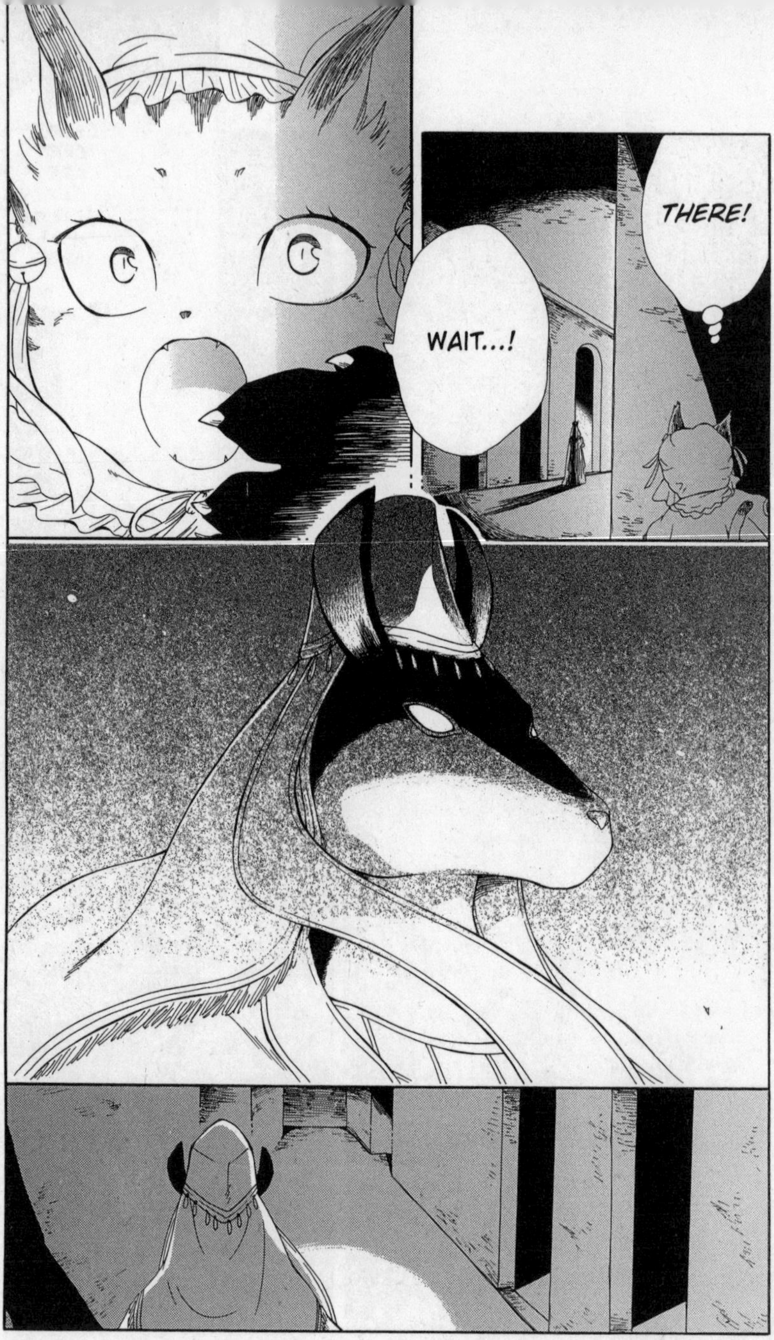
THERE!
WAIT...!

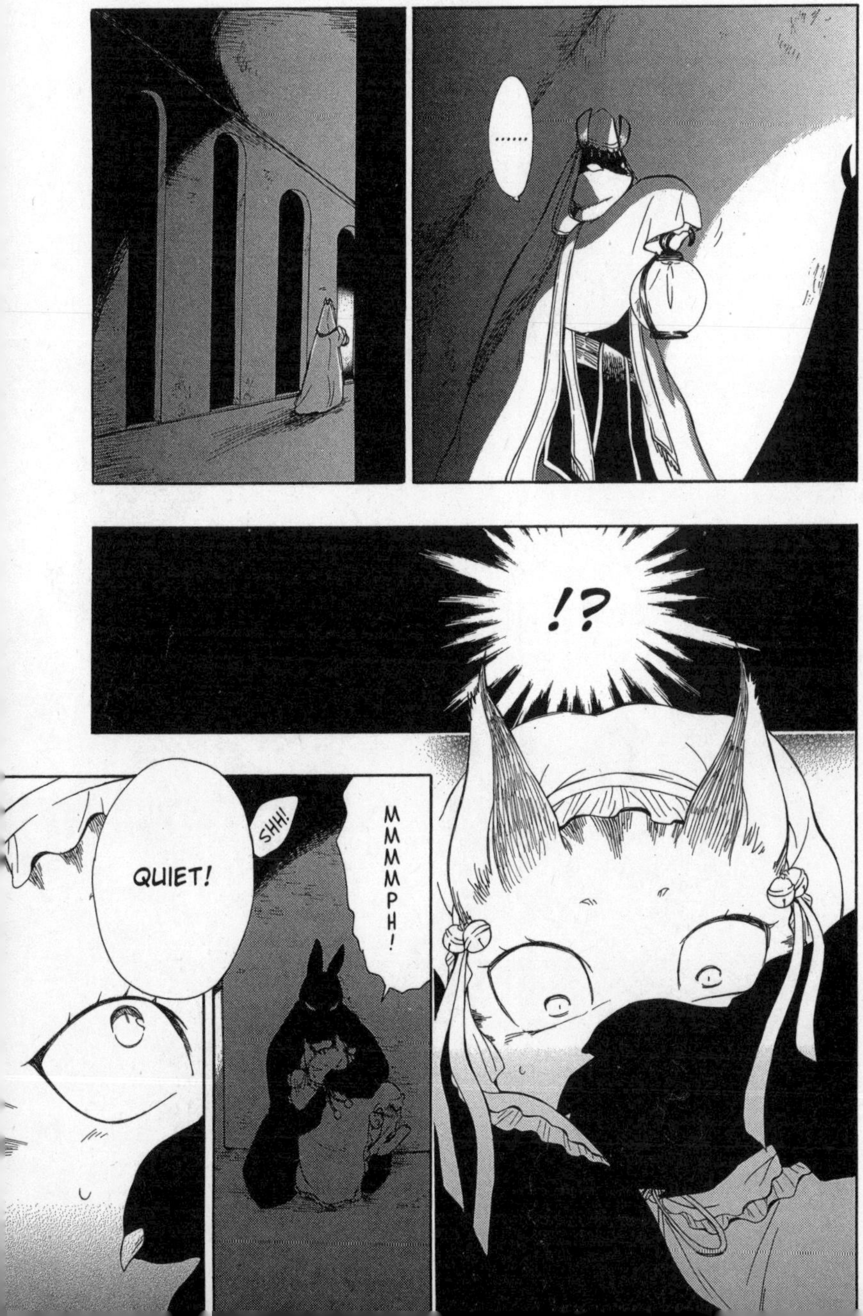
......
!?
MMMMPH!
SHH!
QUIET!

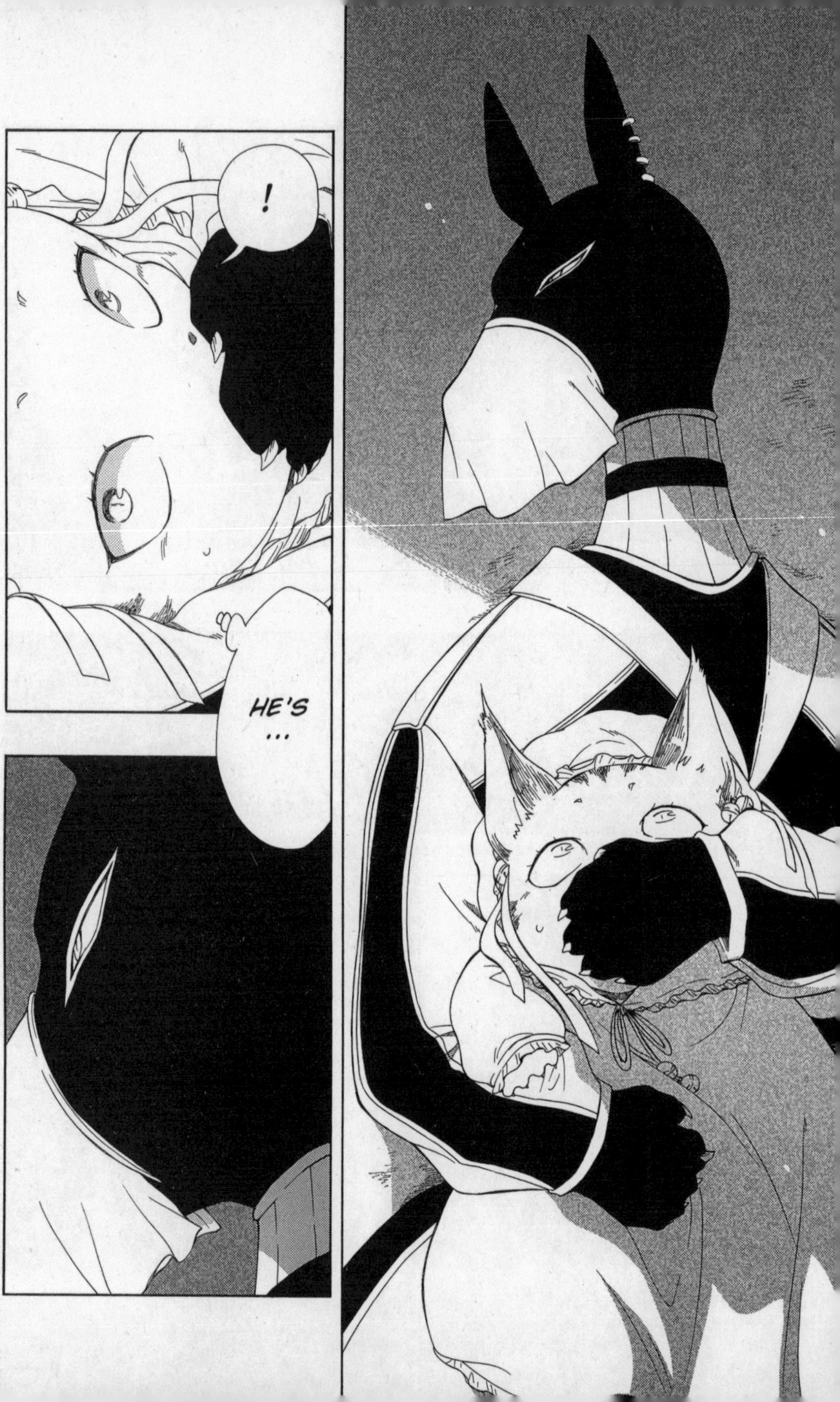
!
HE'S ...

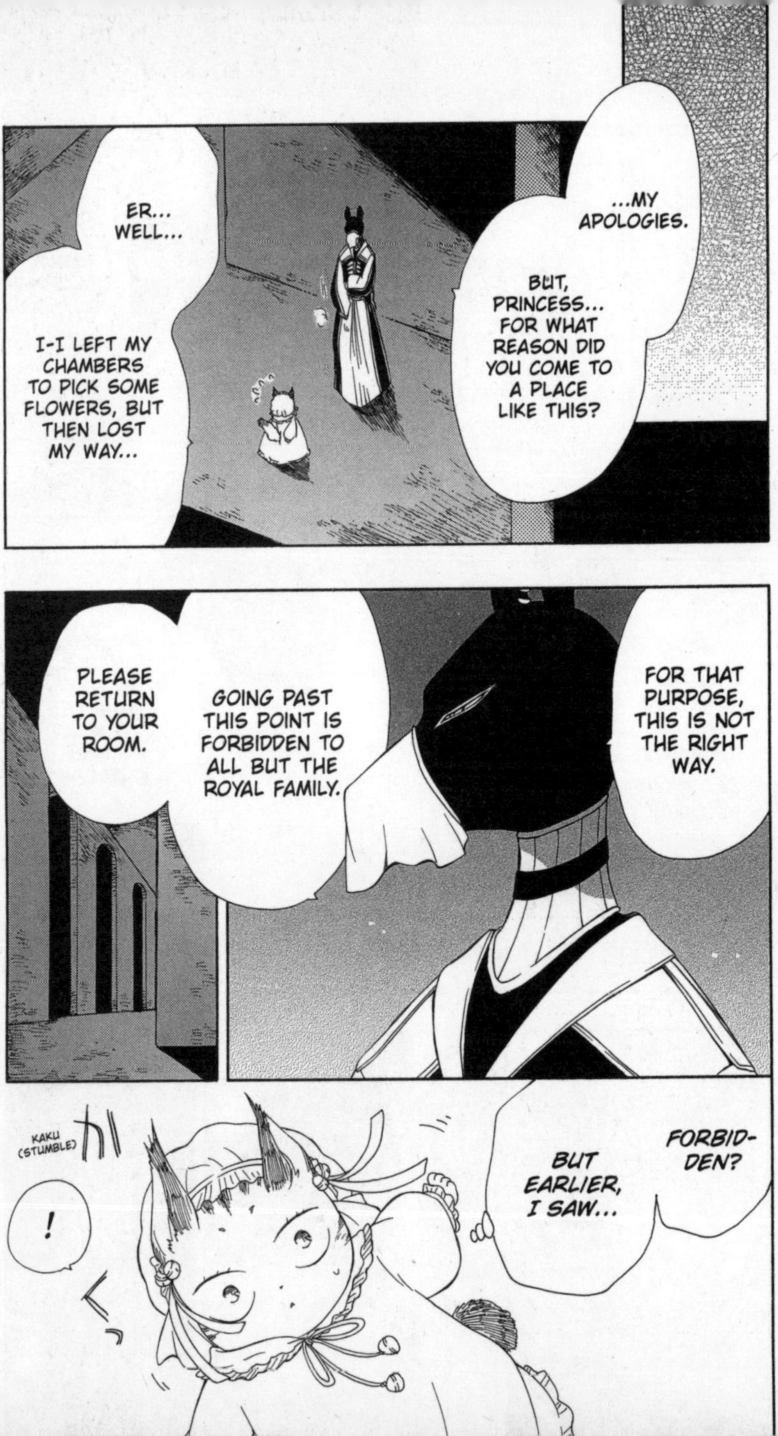
...MY APOLOGIES.
BUT, PRINCESS... FOR WHAT REASON DID YOU COME TO A PLACE LIKE THIS?
ER... WELL...
I-I LEFT MY CHAMBERS TO PICK SOME FLOWERS, BUT THEN LOST MY WAY...
FOR THAT PURPOSE, THIS IS NOT THE RIGHT WAY.
GOING PAST THIS POINT IS FORBIDDEN TO ALL BUT THE ROYAL FAMILY.
PLEASE RETURN TO YOUR ROOM.
FORBID-DEN?
BUT EARLIER, I SAW...
KAKU (STUMBLE)
!

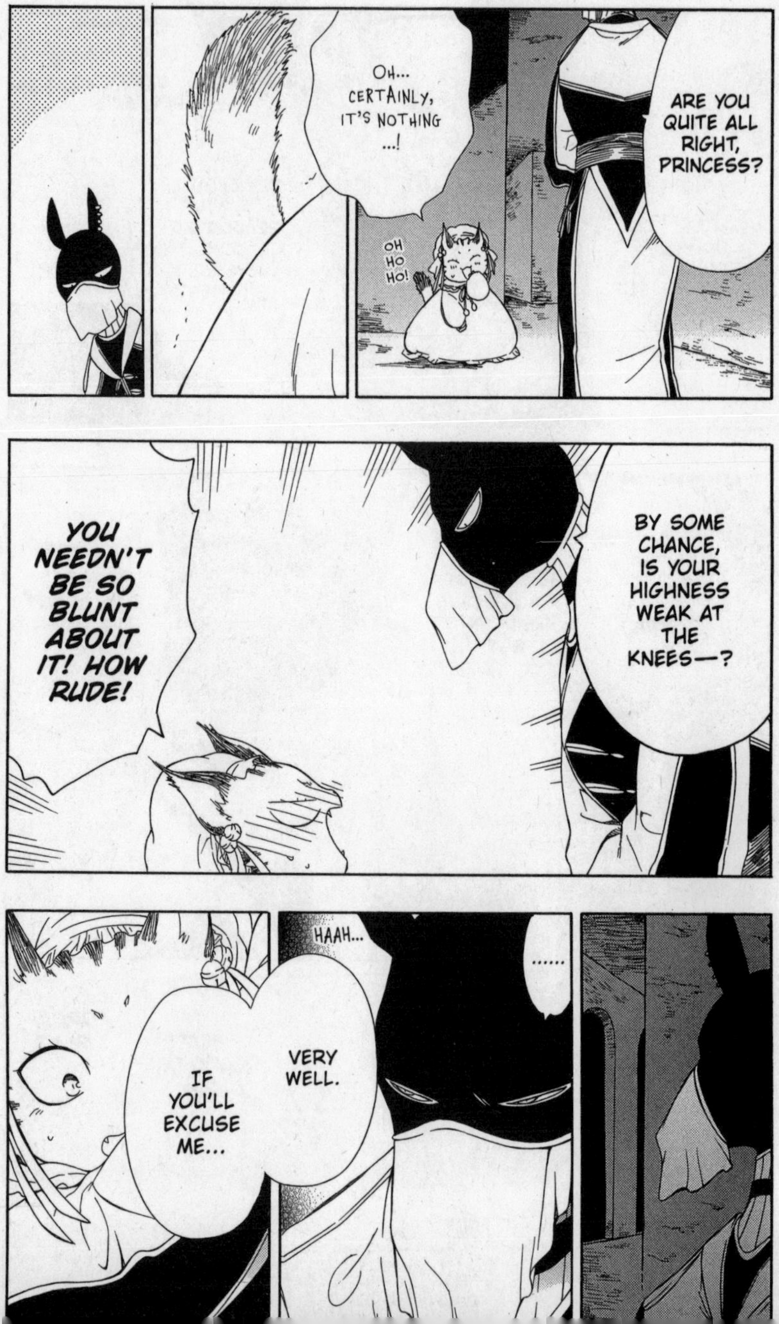
ARE YOU QUITE ALL RIGHT, PRINCESS?
OH... CERTAINLY, IT'S NOTHING ...!
OH HO HO!
BY SOME CHANCE, IS YOUR HIGHNESS WEAK AT THE KNEES—?
YOU NEEDN'T BE SO BLUNT ABOUT IT! HOW RUDE!
......
HAAH...
VERY WELL.
IF YOU'LL EXCUSE ME...

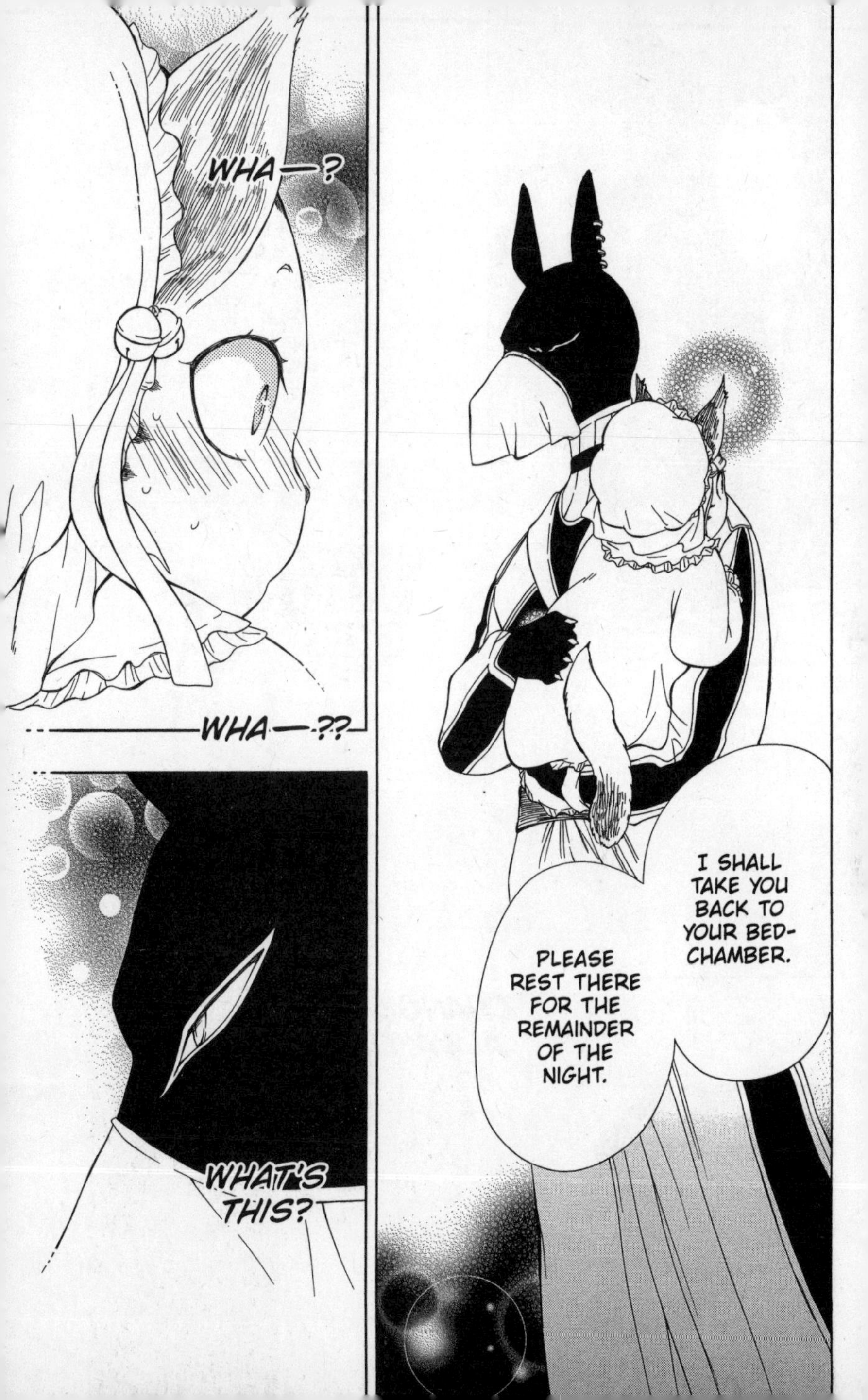
I SHALL TAKE YOU BACK TO YOUR BED-CHAMBER.
PLEASE REST THERE FOR THE REMAINDER OF THE NIGHT.
WHA—?
WHA—??
WHAT'S THIS?

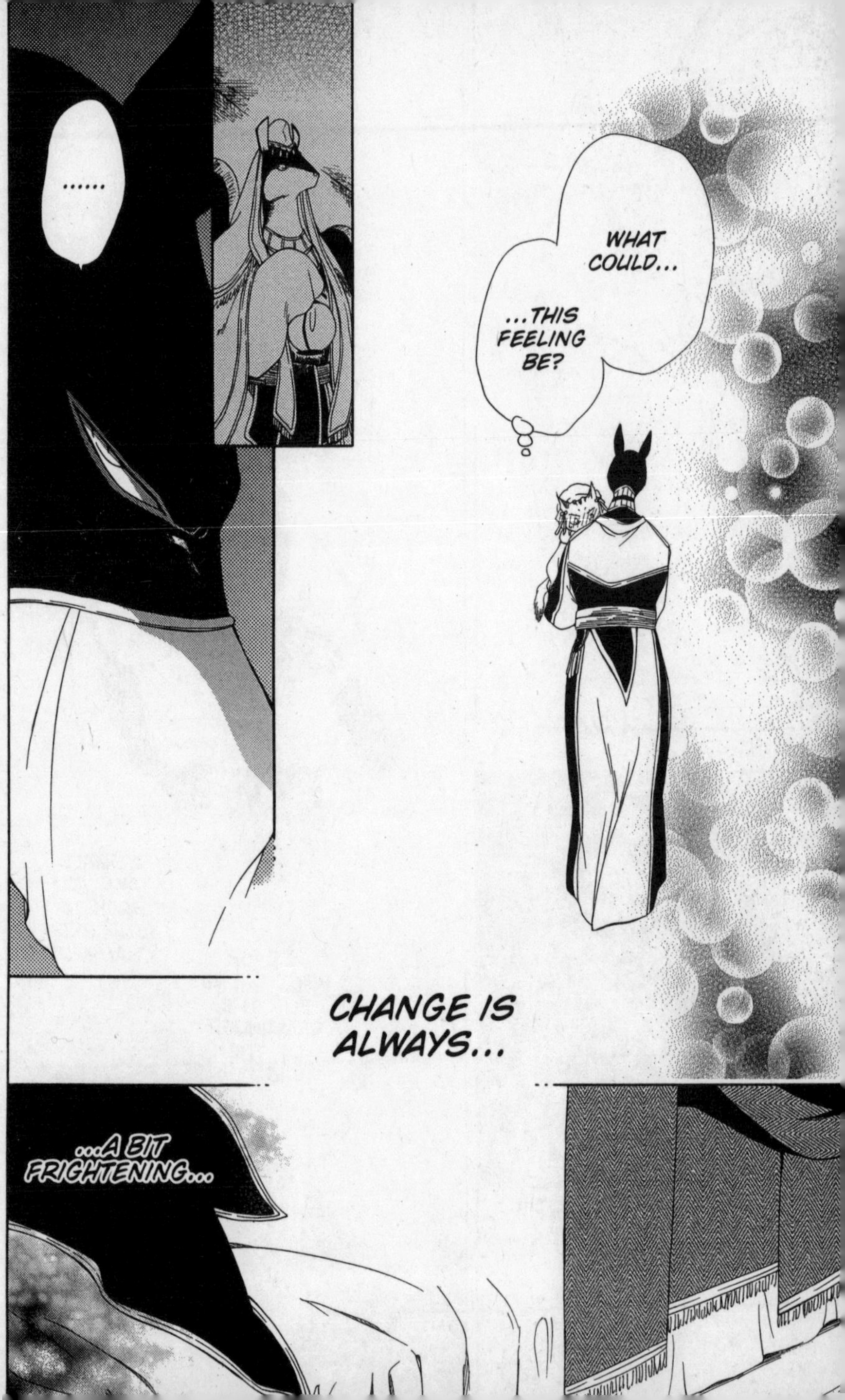
WHAT COULD...
...THIS FEELING BE?
......
CHANGE IS ALWAYS...
...A BIT FRIGHTENING...

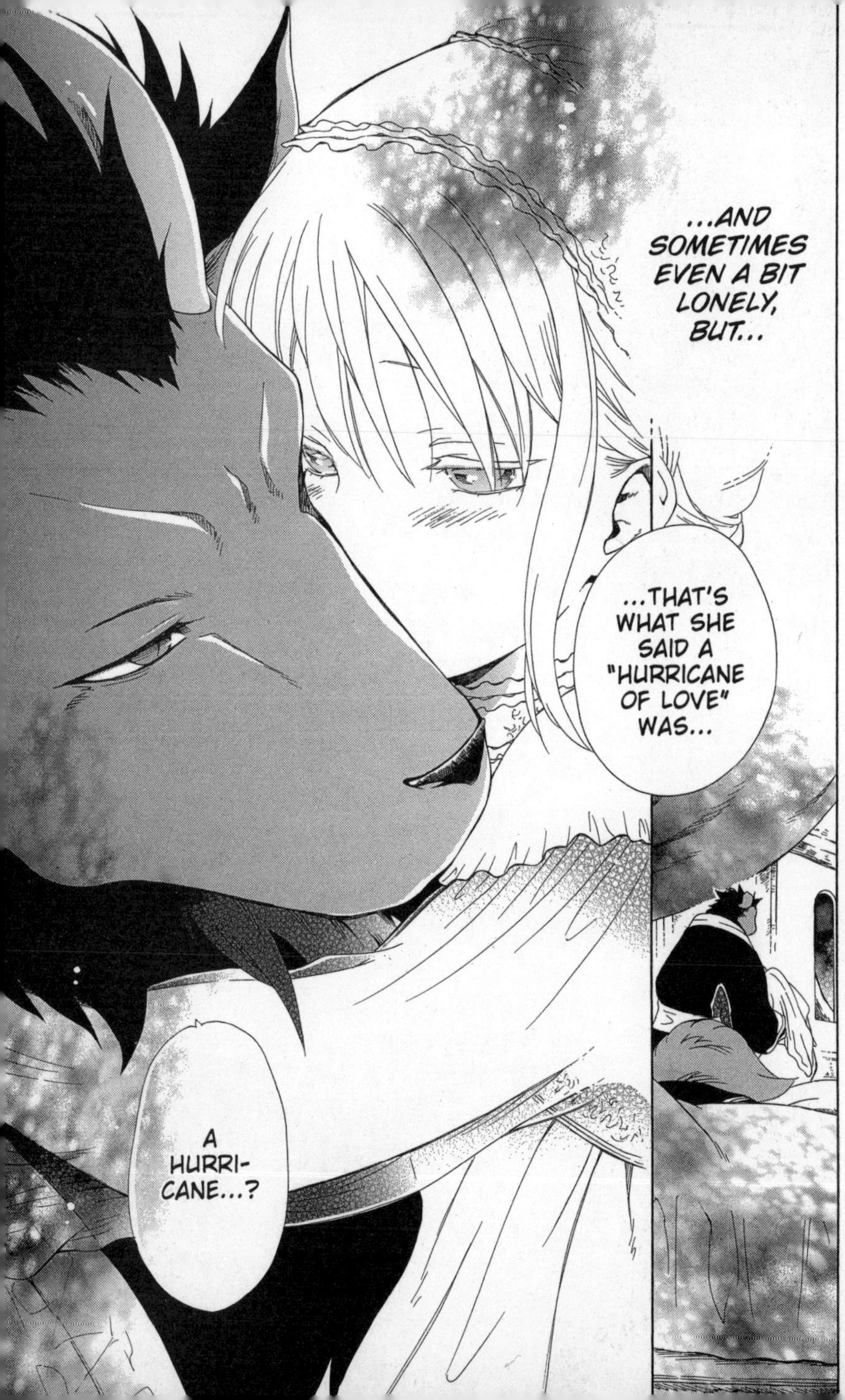
...AND SOMETIMES EVEN A BIT LONELY, BUT...
...THAT'S WHAT SHE SAID A "HURRICANE OF LOVE" WAS...
A HURRI-CANE...?

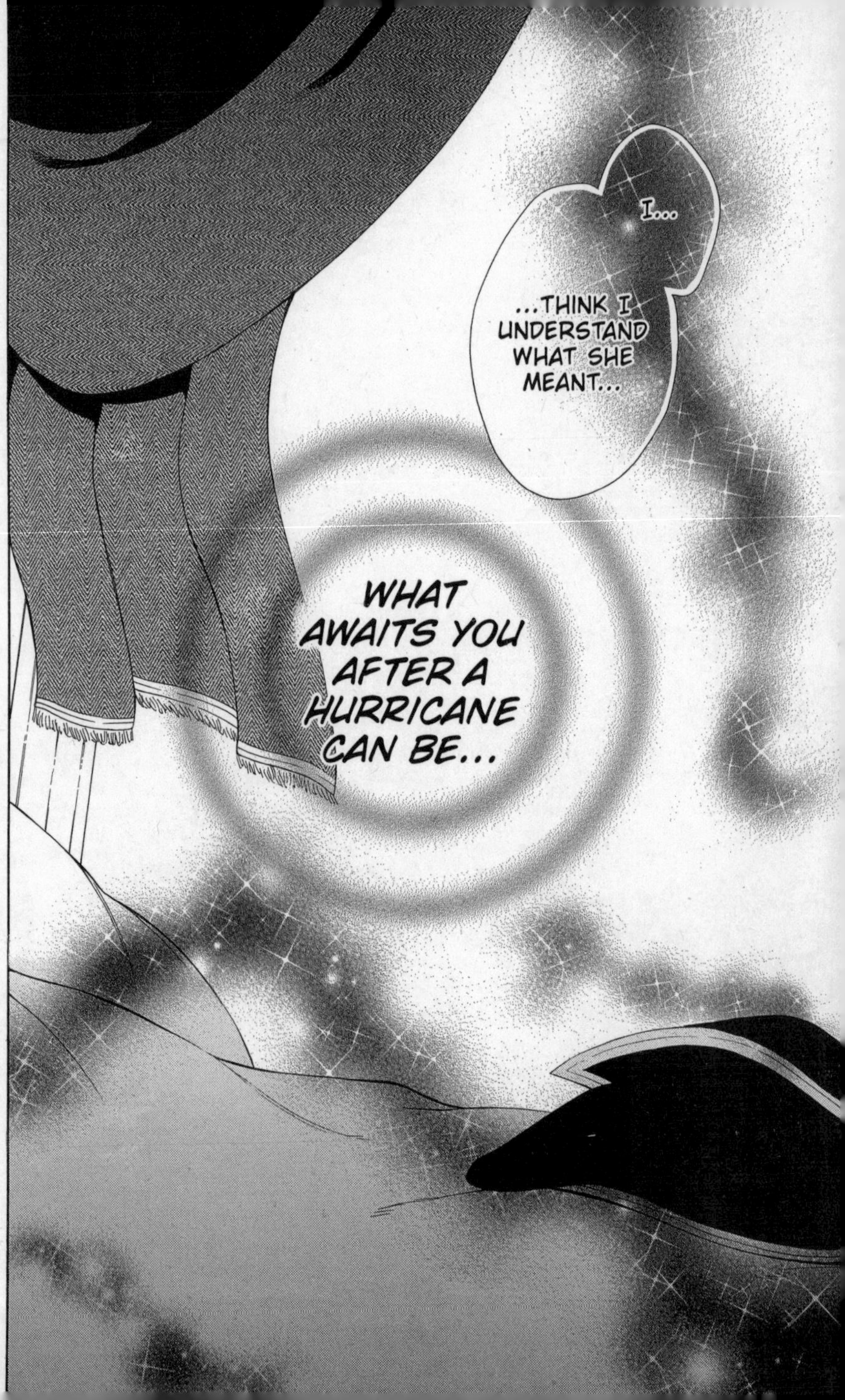
I...
...THINK I UNDERSTAND WHAT SHE MEANT...
WHAT AWAITS YOU AFTER A HURRICANE CAN BE...

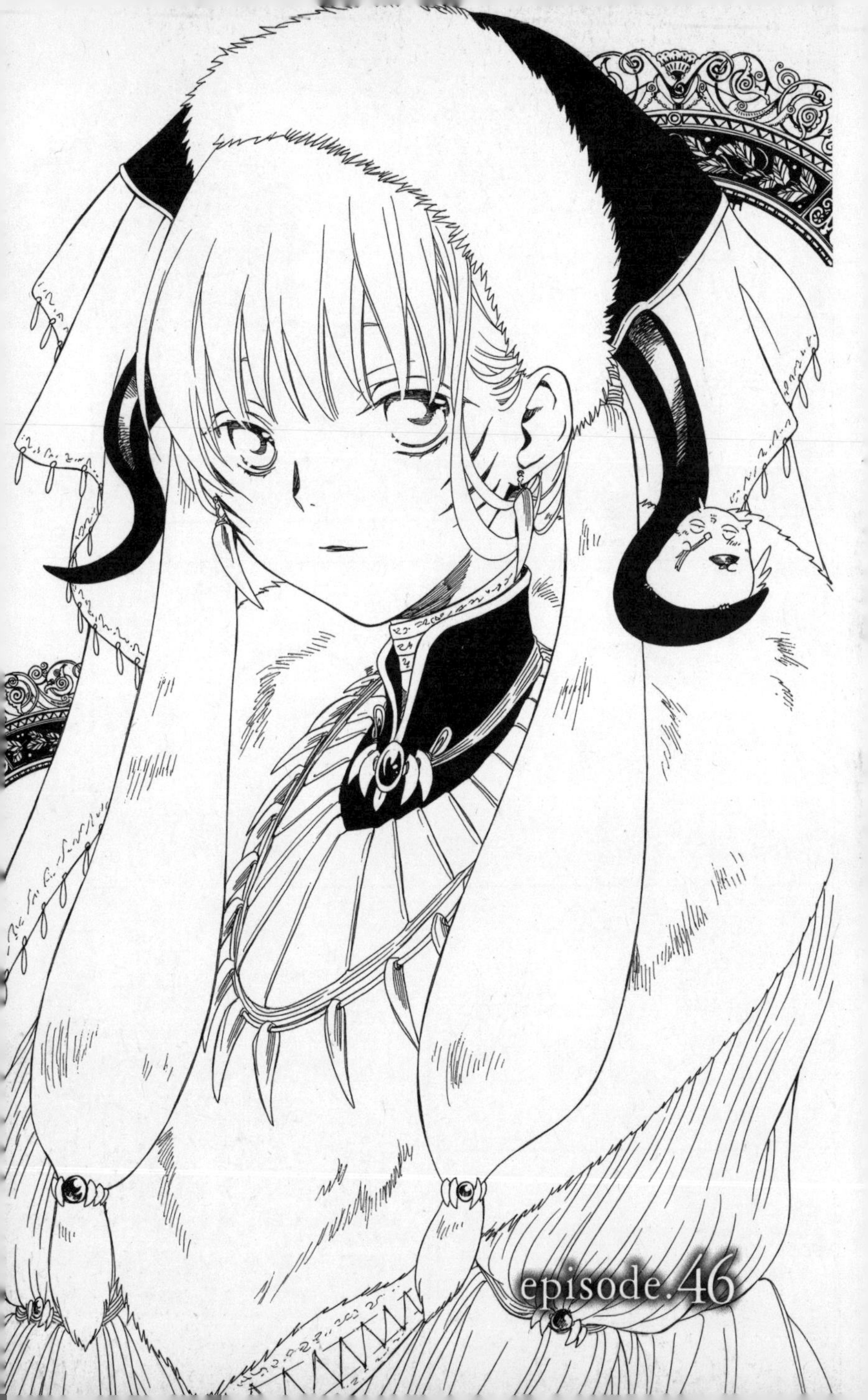
episode.46

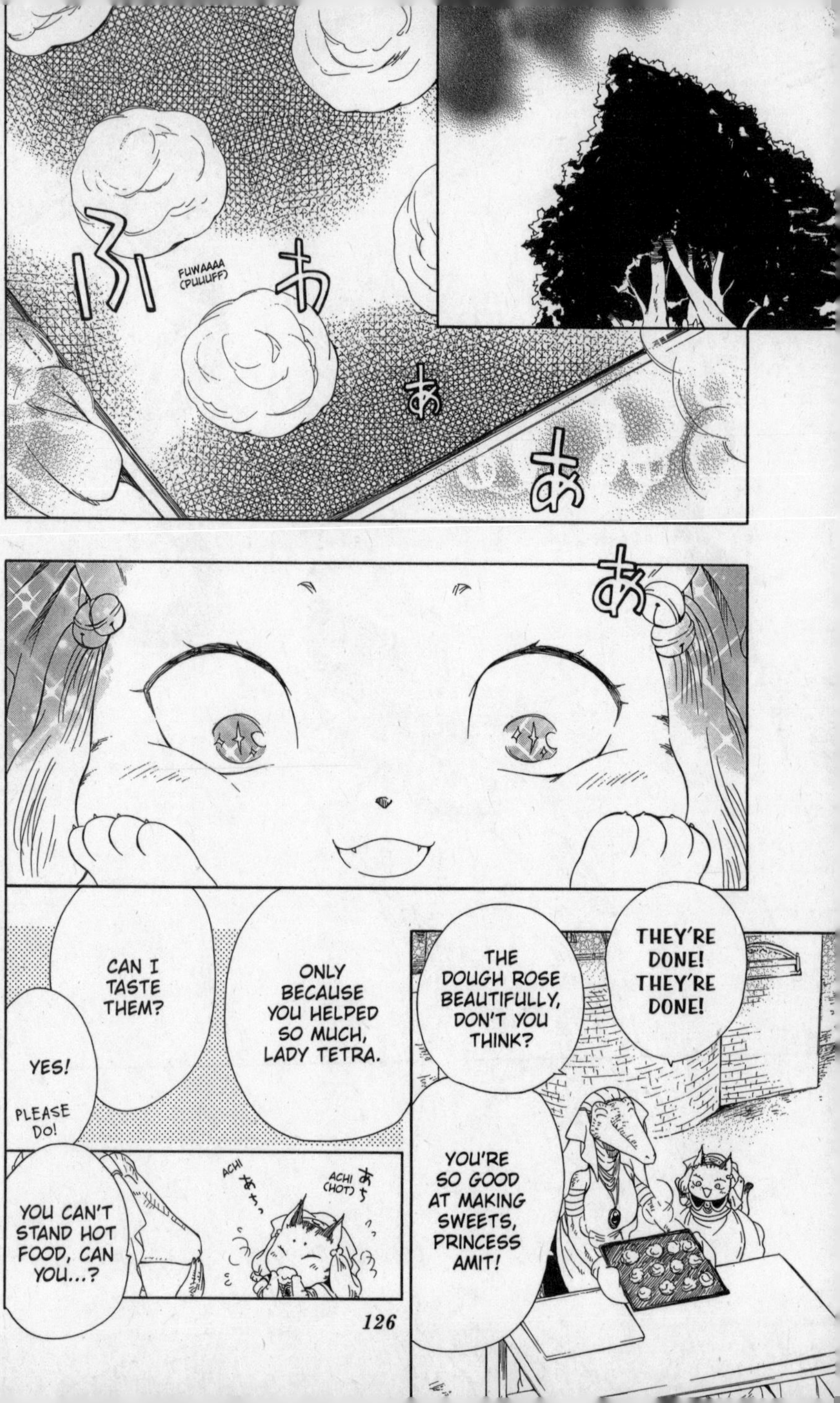
ふぁぁぁ
FUWAAAA (PUUUFF)
あ
THEY'RE DONE! THEY'RE DONE!
THE DOUGH ROSE BEAUTIFULLY, DON'T YOU THINK?
YOU'RE SO GOOD AT MAKING SWEETS, PRINCESS AMIT!
ONLY BECAUSE YOU HELPED SO MUCH, LADY TETRA.
CAN I TASTE THEM?
YES!
PLEASE DO!
あち
ACHI (HOT)
あちっ
ACHI
YOU CAN'T STAND HOT FOOD, CAN YOU...?

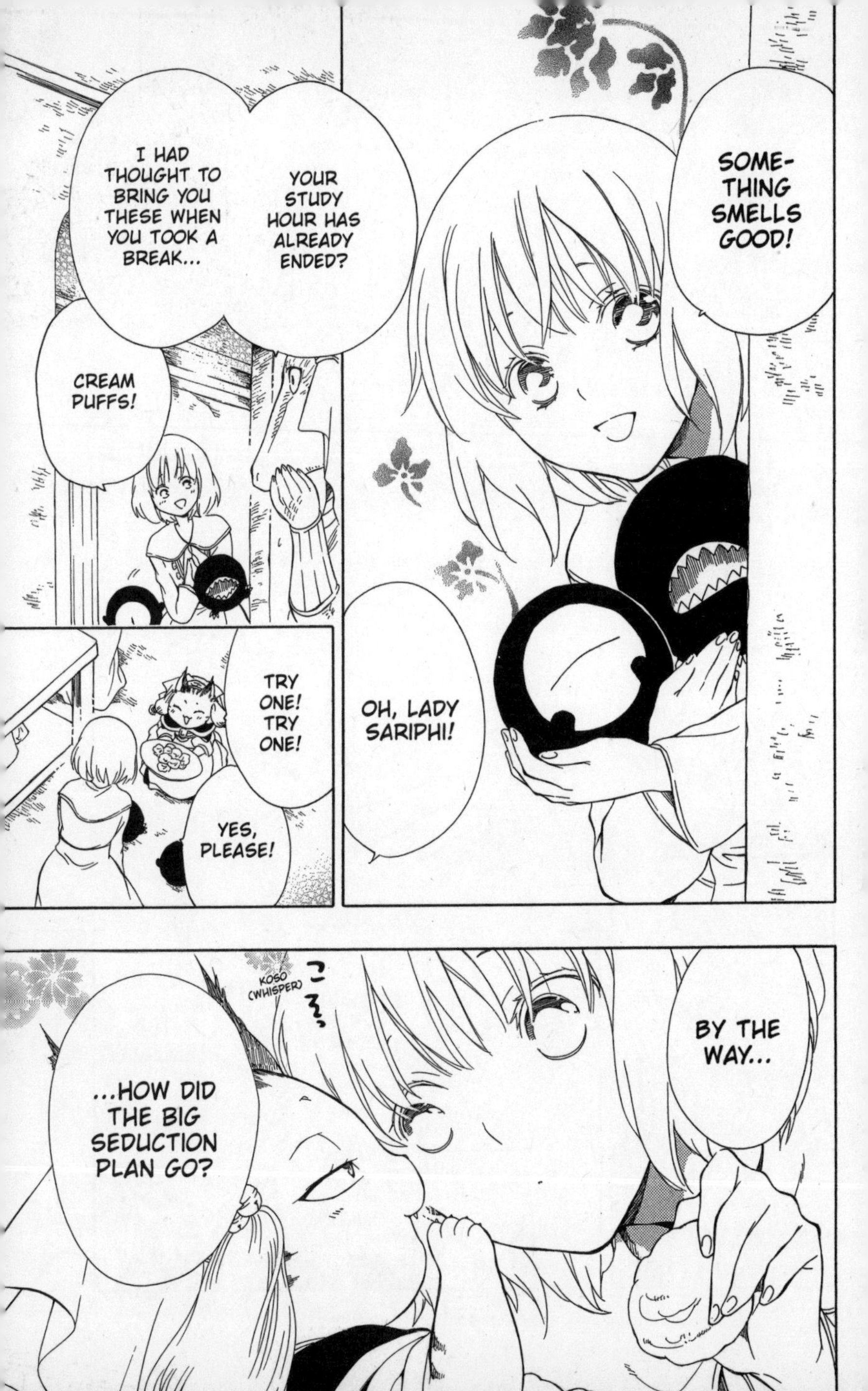
SOME-THING SMELLS GOOD!
OH, LADY SARIPHI!
YOUR STUDY HOUR HAS ALREADY ENDED?
I HAD THOUGHT TO BRING YOU THESE WHEN YOU TOOK A BREAK...
CREAM PUFFS!
TRY ONE! TRY ONE!
YES, PLEASE!
BY THE WAY...
こそ
KOSO (WHISPER)
...HOW DID THE BIG SEDUCTION PLAN GO?

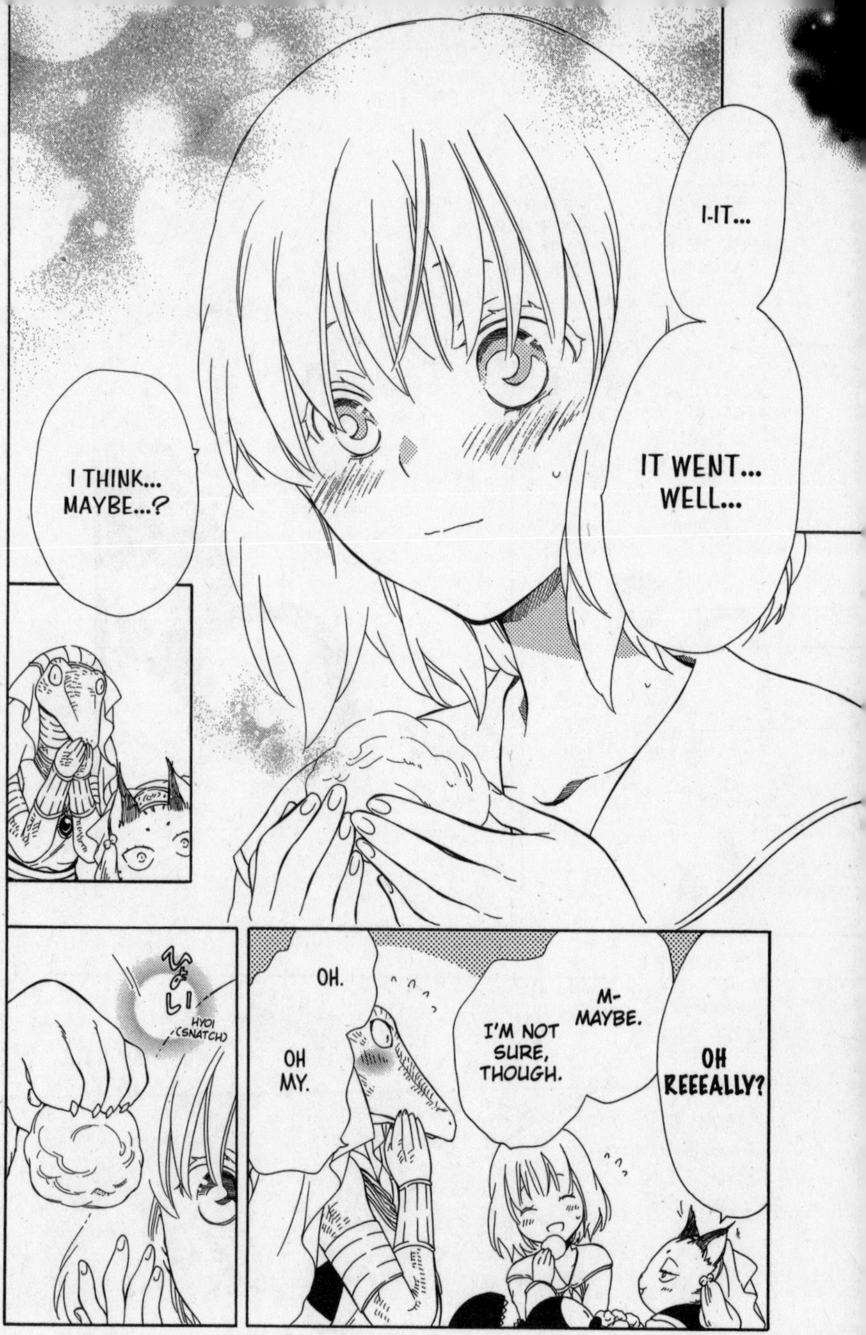
I-IT...
IT WENT... WELL...
I THINK... MAYBE...?
OH REEEALLY?
M- MAYBE.
I'M NOT SURE, THOUGH.
OH.
OH MY.
ひょい
HYOI (SNATCH)

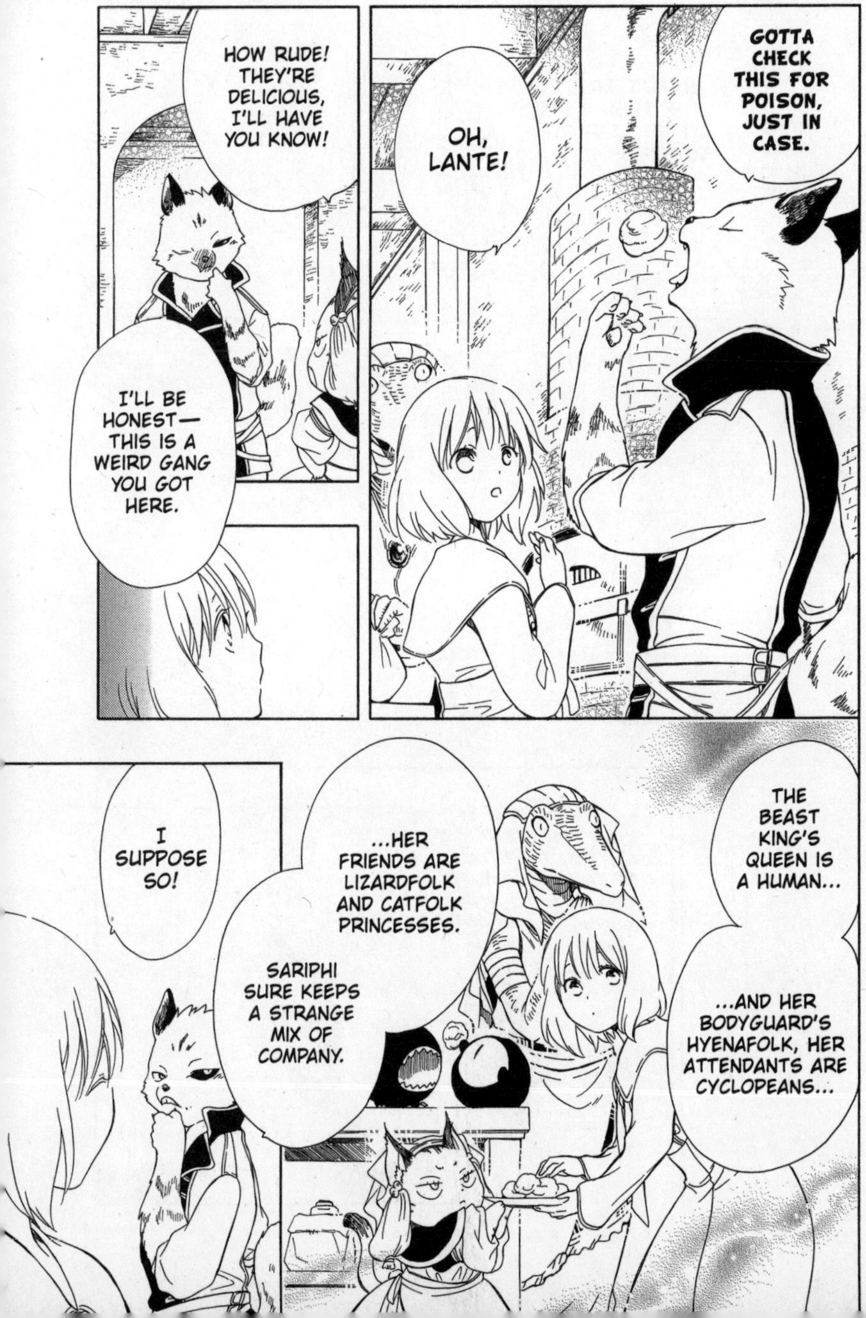
GOTTA CHECK THIS FOR POISON, JUST IN CASE.
OH, LANTE!
HOW RUDE! THEY'RE DELICIOUS, I'LL HAVE YOU KNOW!
I'LL BE HONEST—THIS IS A WEIRD GANG YOU GOT HERE.
THE BEAST KING'S QUEEN IS A HUMAN...
...AND HER BODYGUARD'S HYENAFOLK, HER ATTENDANTS ARE CYCLOPEANS...
...HER FRIENDS ARE LIZARDFOLK AND CATFOLK PRINCESSES.
SARIPHI SURE KEEPS A STRANGE MIX OF COMPANY.
I SUPPOSE SO!

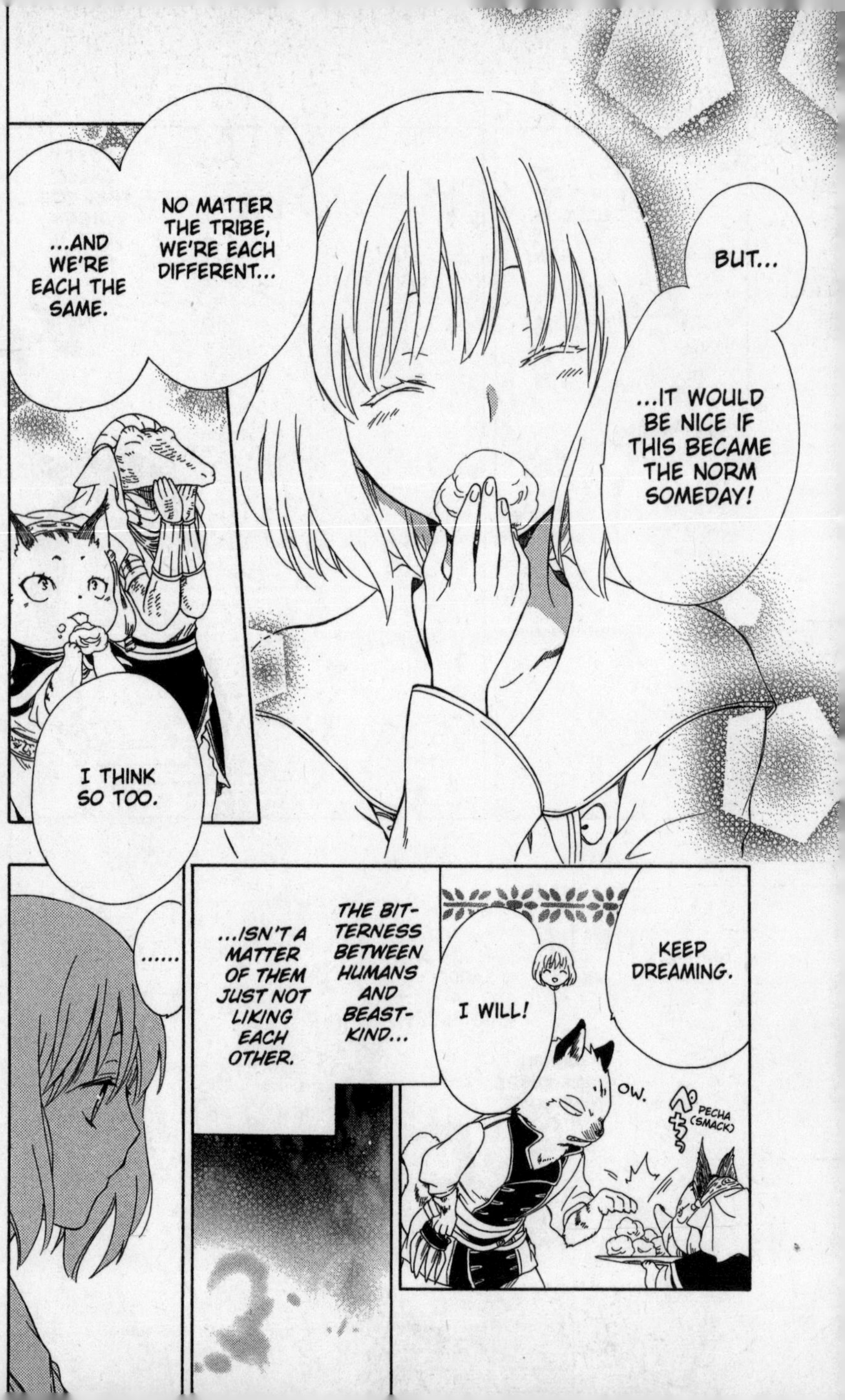
NO MATTER THE TRIBE, WE'RE EACH DIFFERENT...
...AND WE'RE EACH THE SAME.
BUT...
...IT WOULD BE NICE IF THIS BECAME THE NORM SOMEDAY!
I THINK SO TOO.
KEEP DREAMING.
I WILL!
OW.
PECHA (SMACK)
THE BIT-TERNESS BETWEEN HUMANS AND BEAST-KIND...
...ISN'T A MATTER OF THEM JUST NOT LIKING EACH OTHER.
......

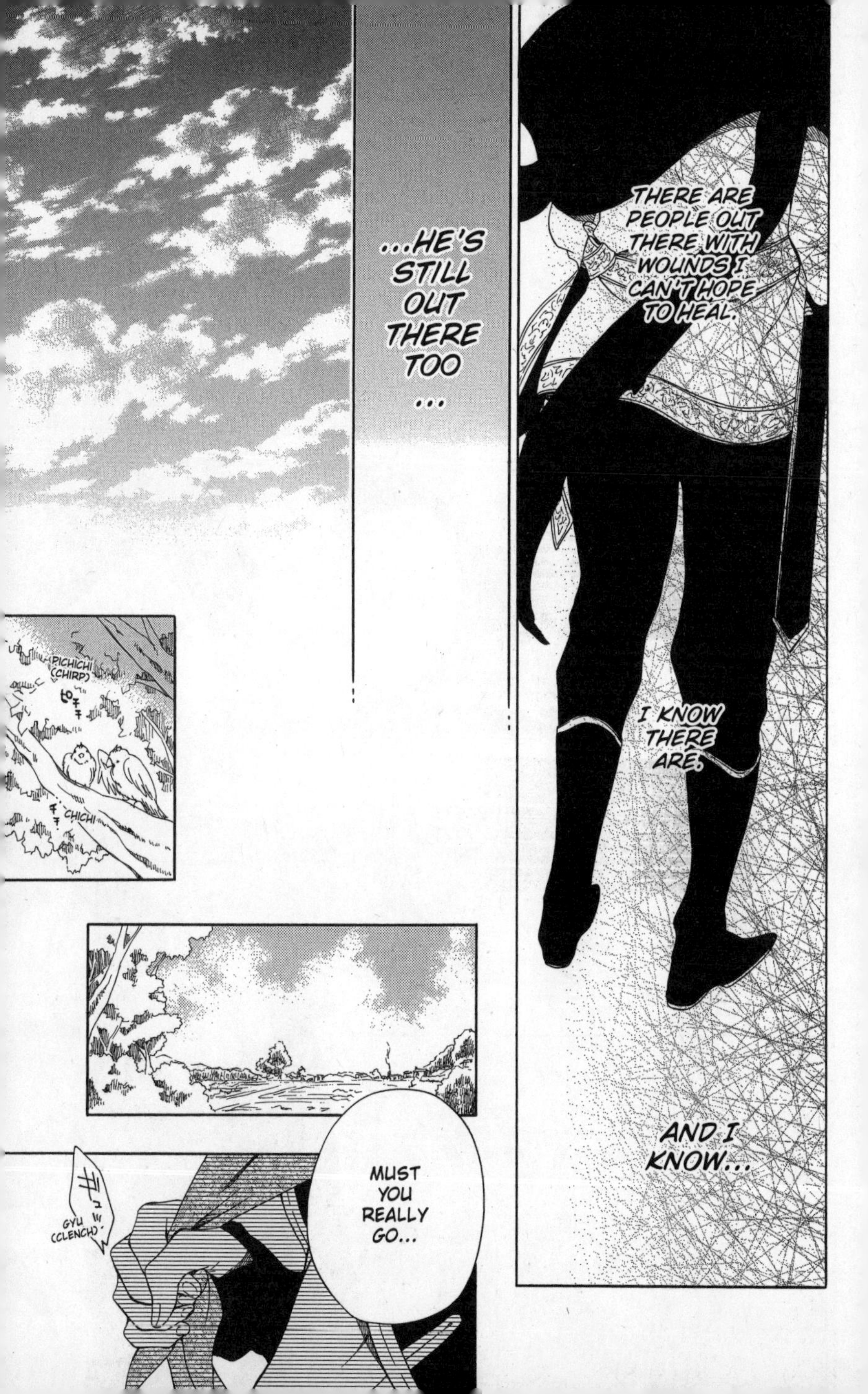
THERE ARE PEOPLE OUT THERE WITH WOUNDS I CAN'T HOPE TO HEAL.
I KNOW THERE ARE.
AND I KNOW...
...HE'S STILL OUT THERE TOO...
PICHICHI (CHIRP)
CHICHI
MUST YOU REALLY GO...
GYU (CLENCH)

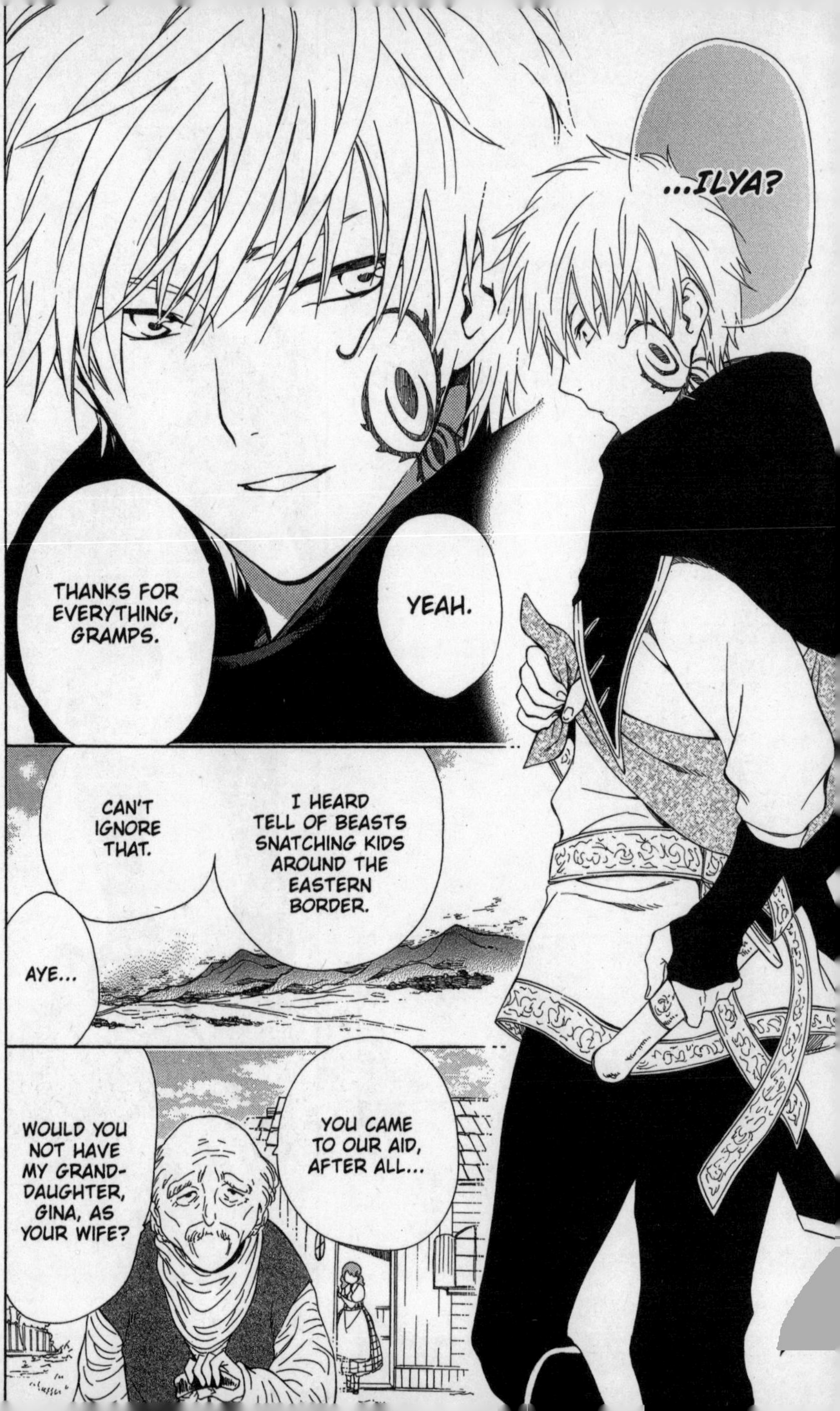
...ILYA?
YEAH.
THANKS FOR EVERYTHING, GRAMPS.
I HEARD TELL OF BEASTS SNATCHING KIDS AROUND THE EASTERN BORDER.
CAN'T IGNORE THAT.
AYE...
YOU CAME TO OUR AID, AFTER ALL...
WOULD YOU NOT HAVE MY GRAND-DAUGHTER, GINA, AS YOUR WIFE?

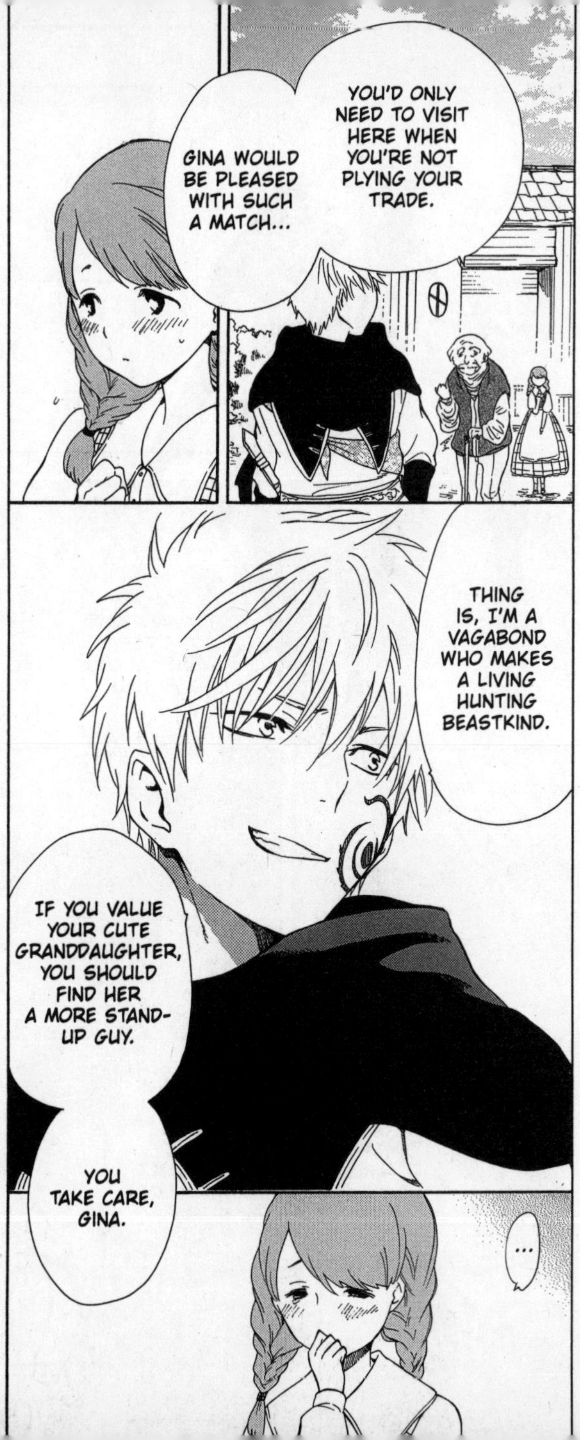
YOU'D ONLY NEED TO VISIT HERE WHEN YOU'RE NOT PLYING YOUR TRADE.
GINA WOULD BE PLEASED WITH SUCH A MATCH...
THING IS, I'M A VAGABOND WHO MAKES A LIVING HUNTING BEASTKIND.
IF YOU VALUE YOUR CUTE GRANDDAUGHTER, YOU SHOULD FIND HER A MORE STAND-UP GUY.
YOU TAKE CARE, GINA.
...

THIS VOLUME SEES THE APPEARANCE OF THIS GUY, WHO HASN'T SHOWN UP SINCE VOLUME 3. I'D ALWAYS HOPED TO SEE HIM AGAIN, BUT WHEN ILYA FIRST APPEARED, I HAD NO IDEA I'D BE ABLE TO KEEP GOING FOR EIGHT VOLUMES. THE FACT HE'S IN VOLUME 8 MAKES ME AWFULLY HAPPY. HOPEFULLY, THE NEXT TIME HE APPEARS, HE'LL GET TO SEE SARIPHI AGAIN.

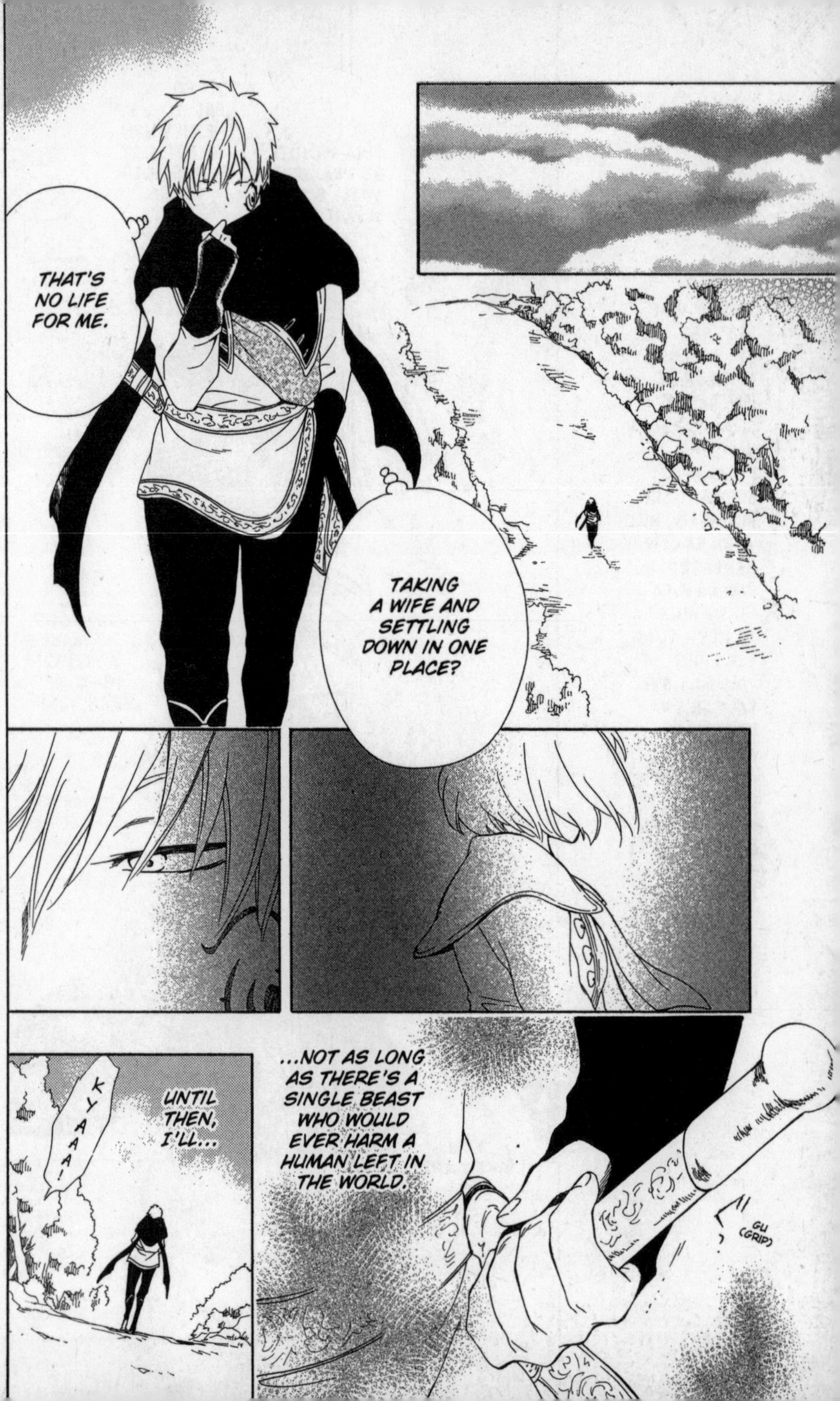
TAKING A WIFE AND SETTLING DOWN IN ONE PLACE?
THAT'S NO LIFE FOR ME.
...NOT AS LONG AS THERE'S A SINGLE BEAST WHO WOULD EVER HARM A HUMAN LEFT IN THE WORLD.
GU (GRIP)
UNTIL THEN, I'LL...
KYAAAA!

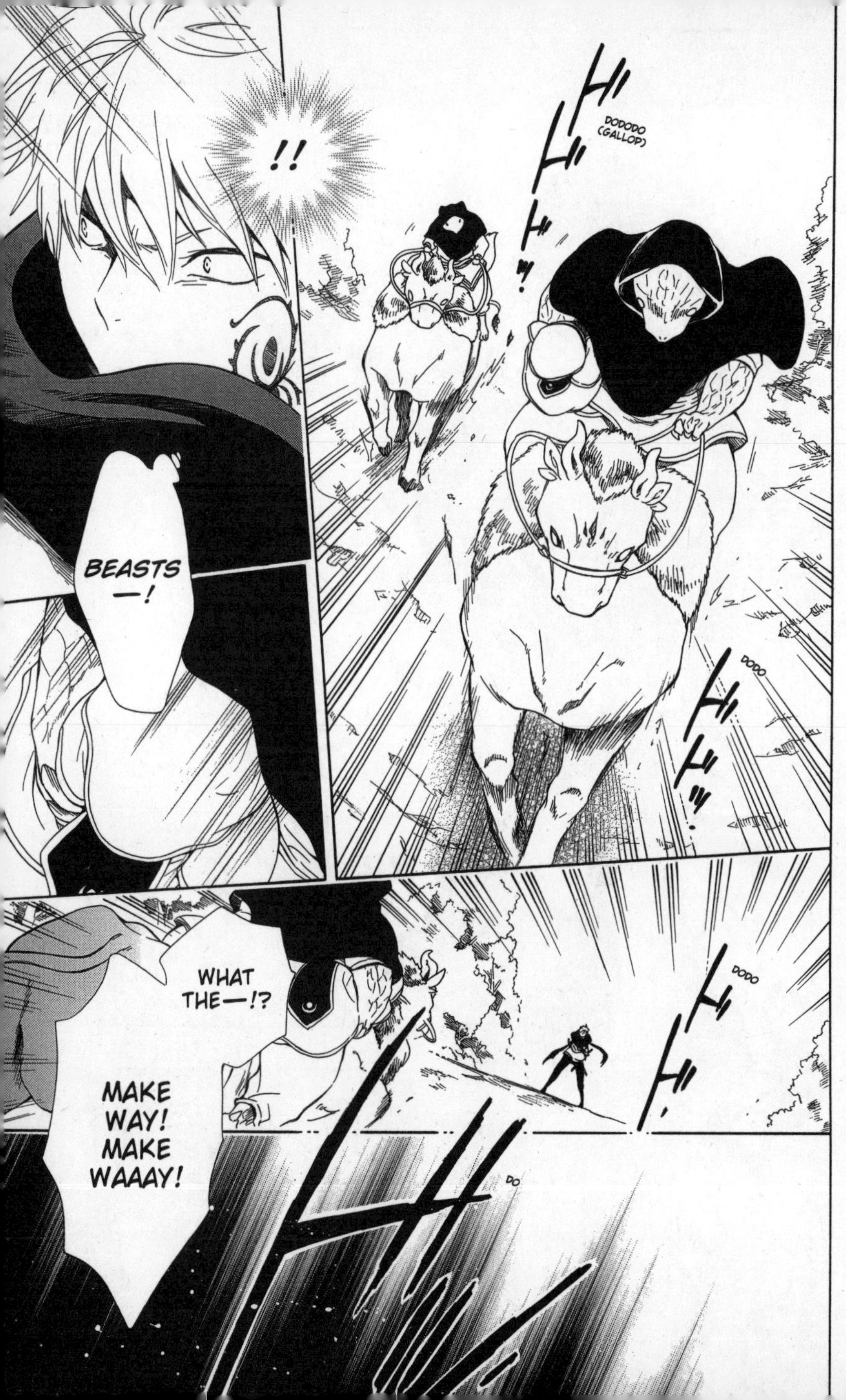
DODODO (GALLOP)
DODO
!!
BEASTS—!
DODO
WHAT THE—!?
DO
MAKE WAY! MAKE WAAAY!

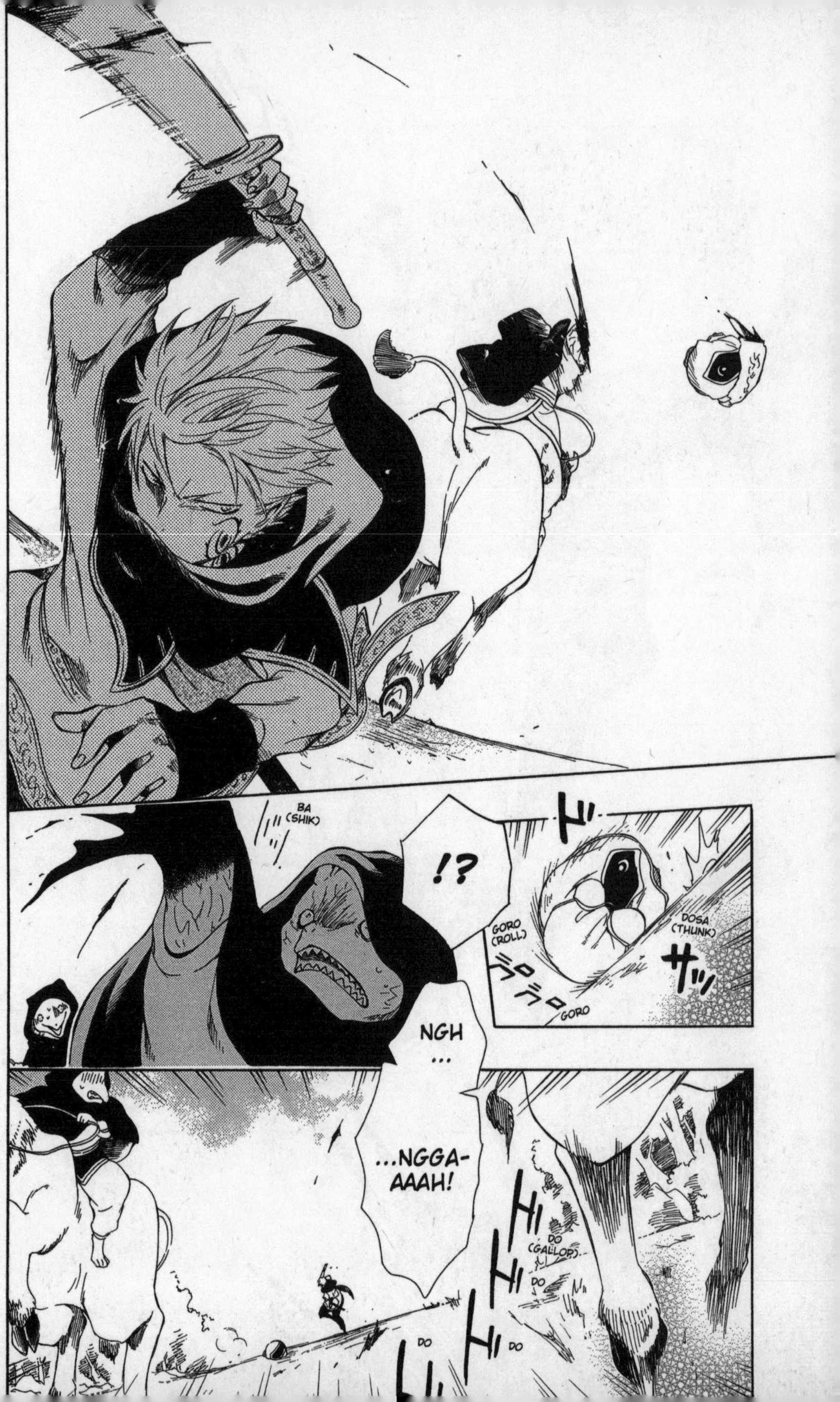
DOSA (THUNK)
GORO (ROLL)
GORO
BA (SHIK)
!?
NGH ...
...NGGA-AAAH!
DO (GALLOP)
DO
DO
DO

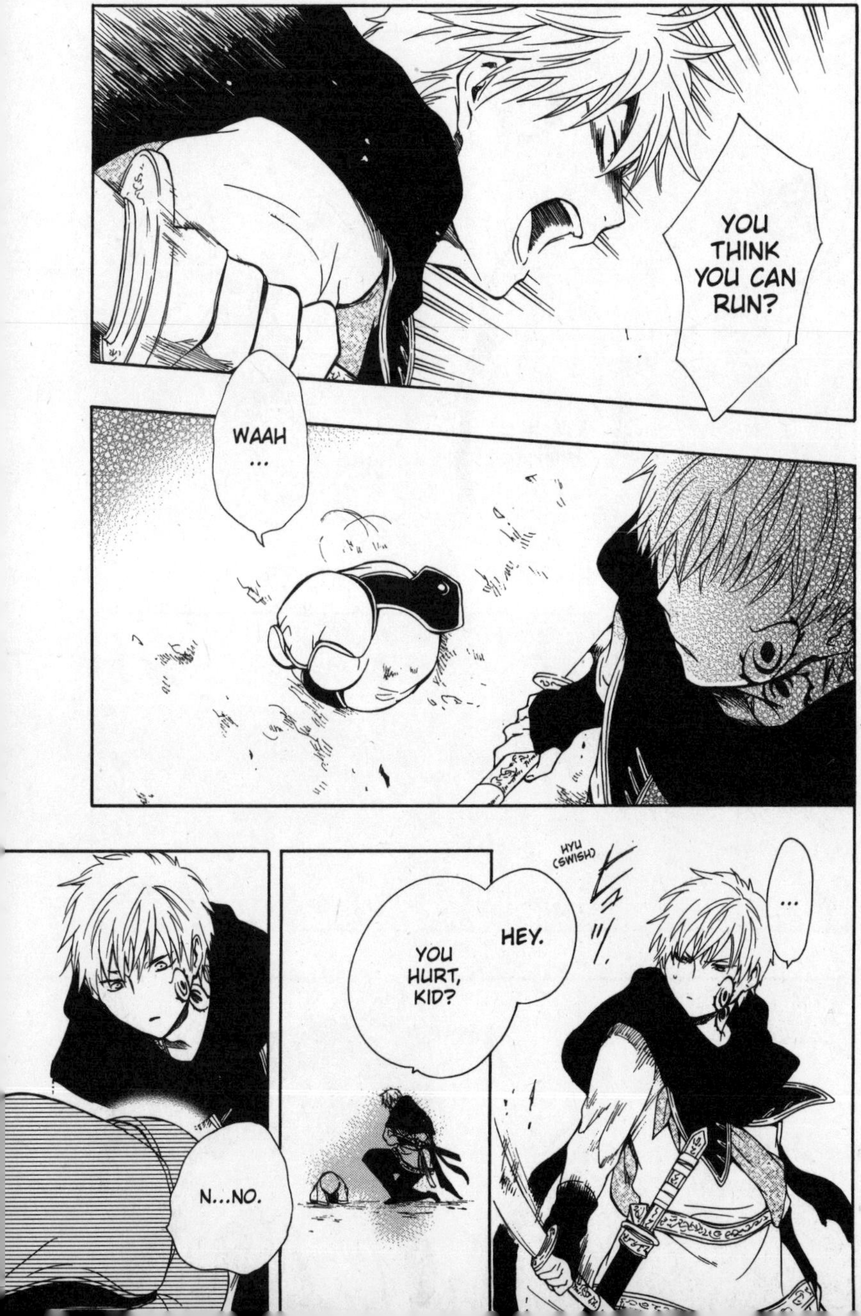
YOU THINK YOU CAN RUN?
WAAH ...
...
HYU (SWISH)
HEY.
YOU HURT, KID?
N...NO.

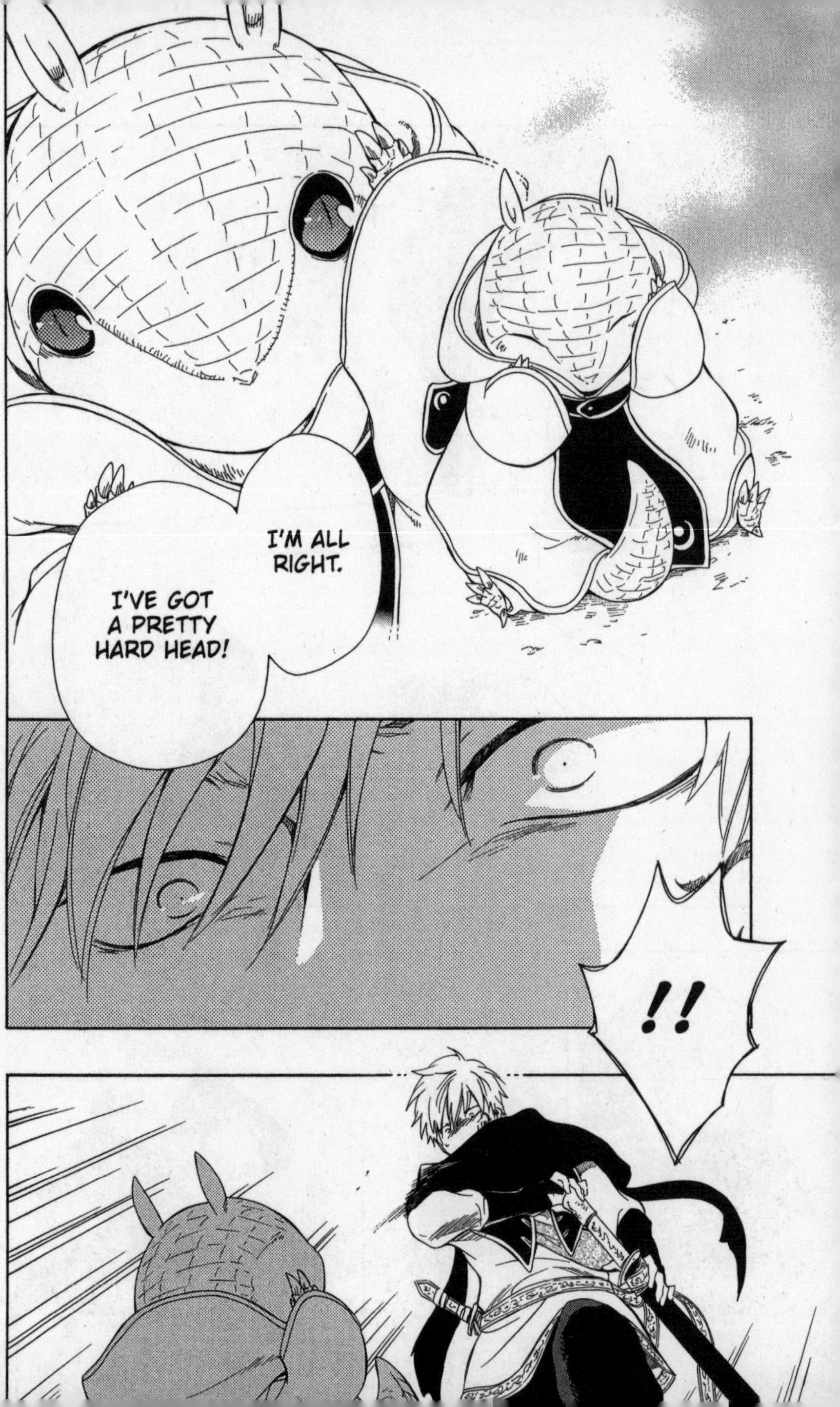
I'M ALL RIGHT.
I'VE GOT A PRETTY HARD HEAD!
!!

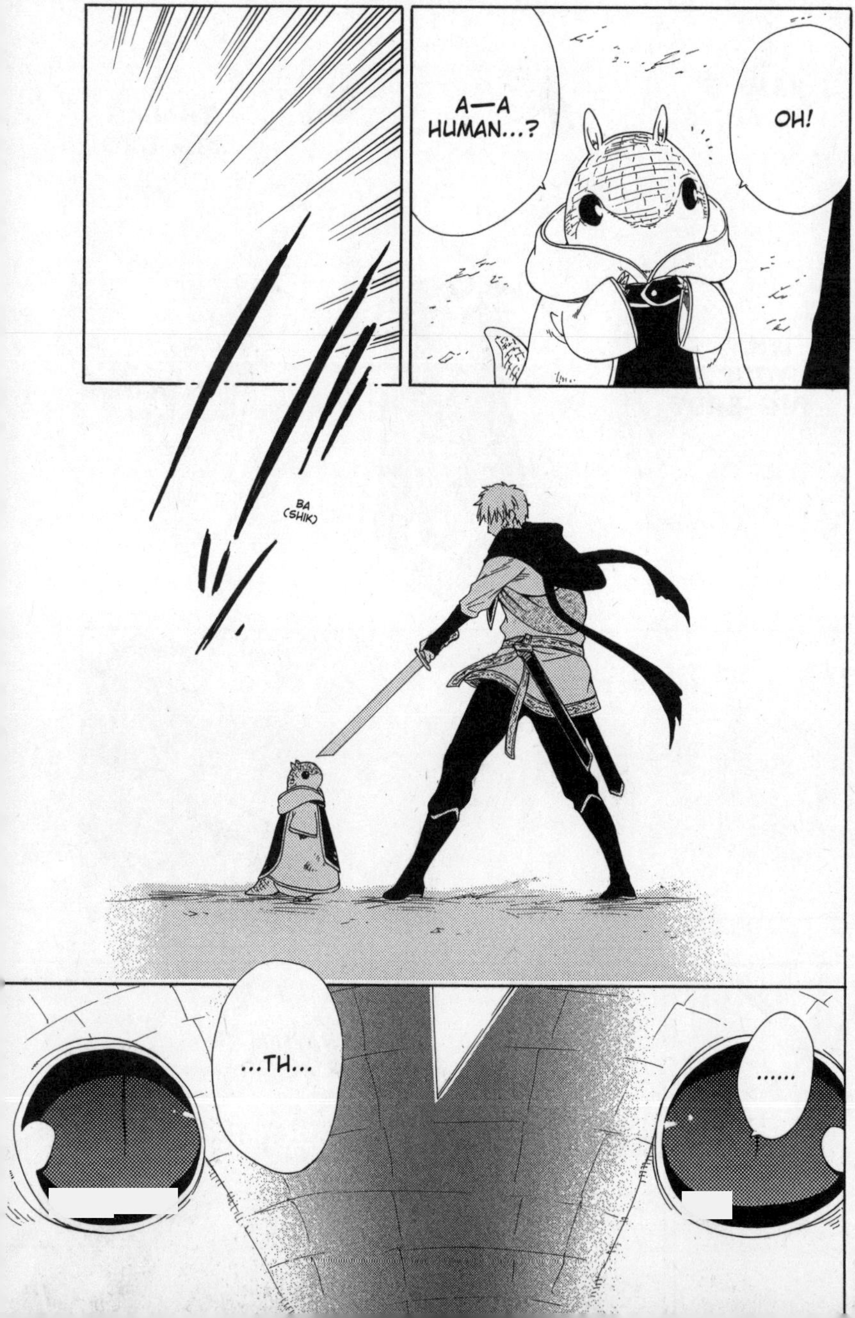
OH!
A—A HUMAN...?
BA (SHIK)
......
...TH...

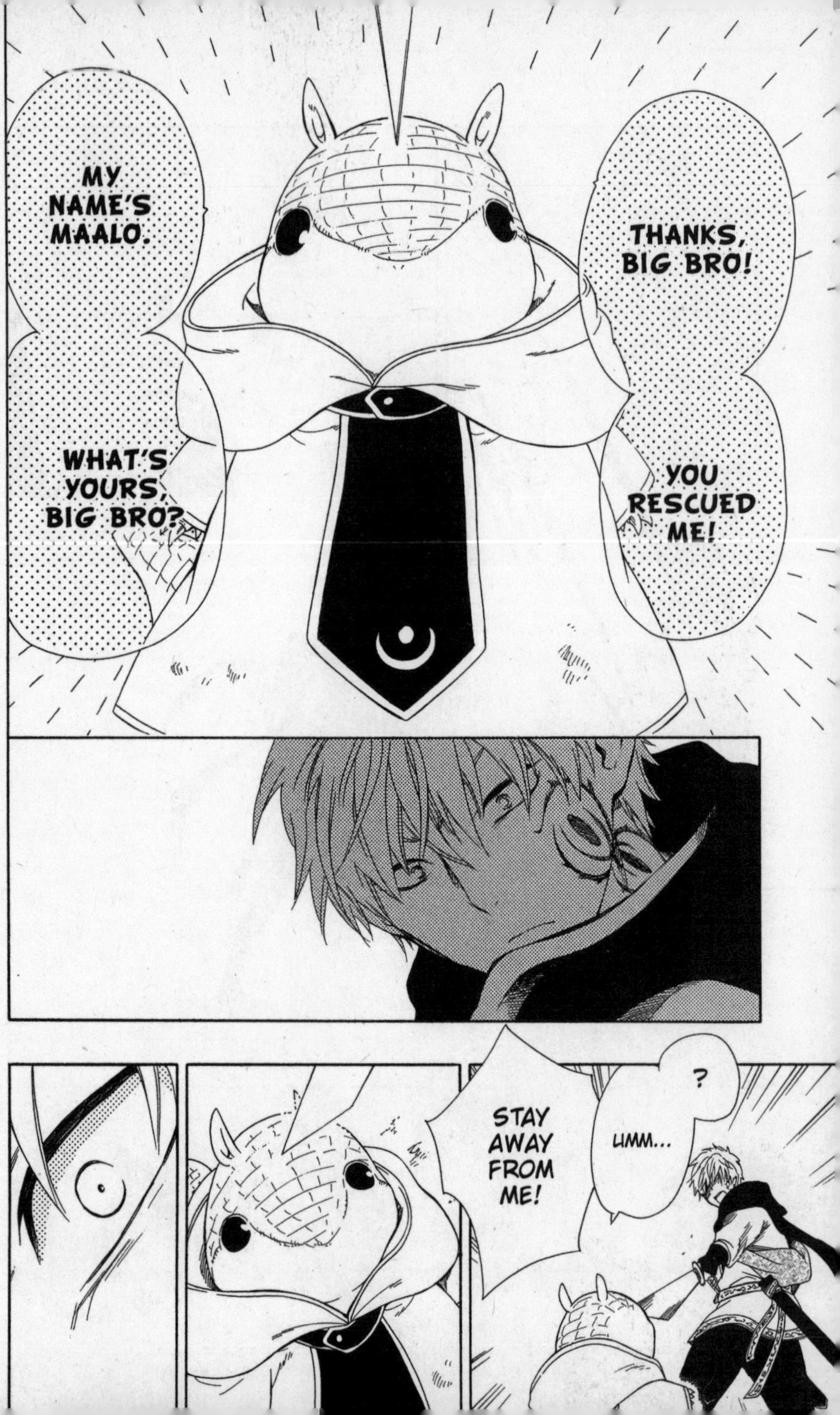
THANKS, BIG BRO!
YOU RESCUED ME!
MY NAME'S MAALO.
WHAT'S YOURS, BIG BRO?
?
UMM...
STAY AWAY FROM ME!

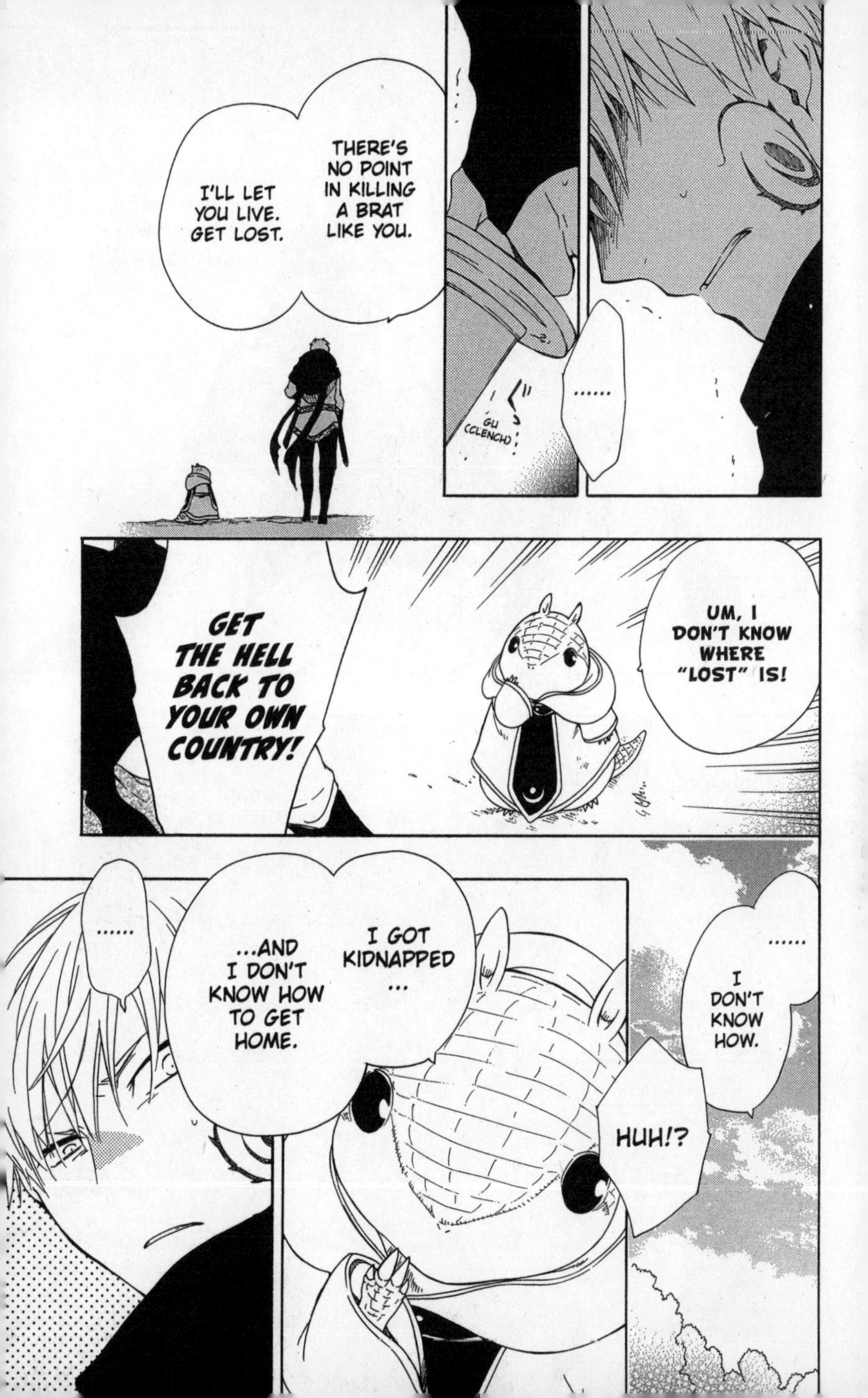
......
GU (CLENCH)
THERE'S NO POINT IN KILLING A BRAT LIKE YOU.
I'LL LET YOU LIVE. GET LOST.
UM, I DON'T KNOW WHERE "LOST" IS!
GET THE HELL BACK TO YOUR OWN COUNTRY!
...... I DON'T KNOW HOW.
HUH!?
I GOT KIDNAPPED...
...AND I DON'T KNOW HOW TO GET HOME.
......

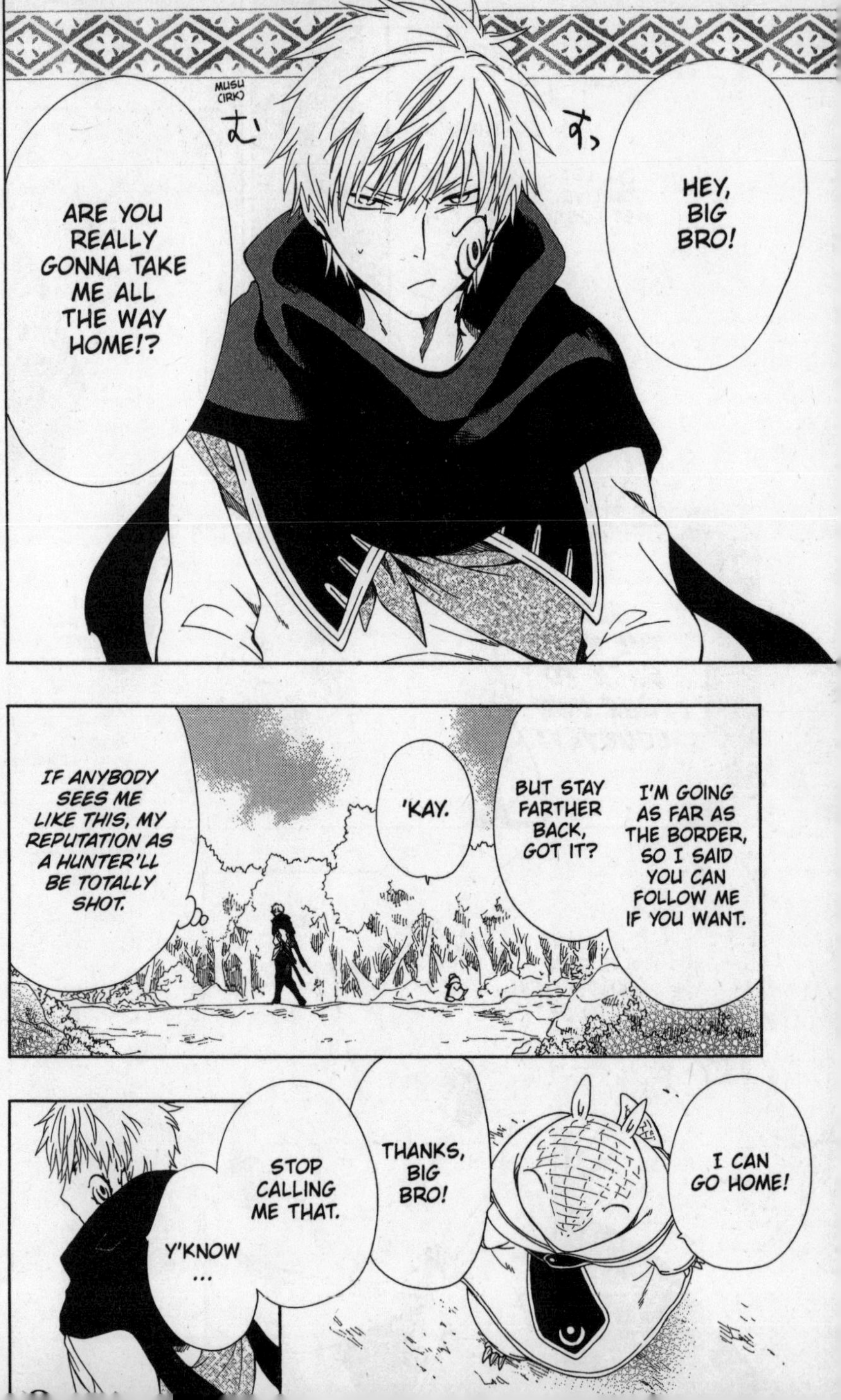

HEY, BIG BRO!
むすっ
MUSU (IRK)
ARE YOU REALLY GONNA TAKE ME ALL THE WAY HOME!?
I'M GOING AS FAR AS THE BORDER, SO I SAID YOU CAN FOLLOW ME IF YOU WANT.
BUT STAY FARTHER BACK, GOT IT?
'KAY.
IF ANYBODY SEES ME LIKE THIS, MY REPUTATION AS A HUNTER'LL BE TOTALLY SHOT.
I CAN GO HOME!
THANKS, BIG BRO!
STOP CALLING ME THAT.
Y'KNOW ...

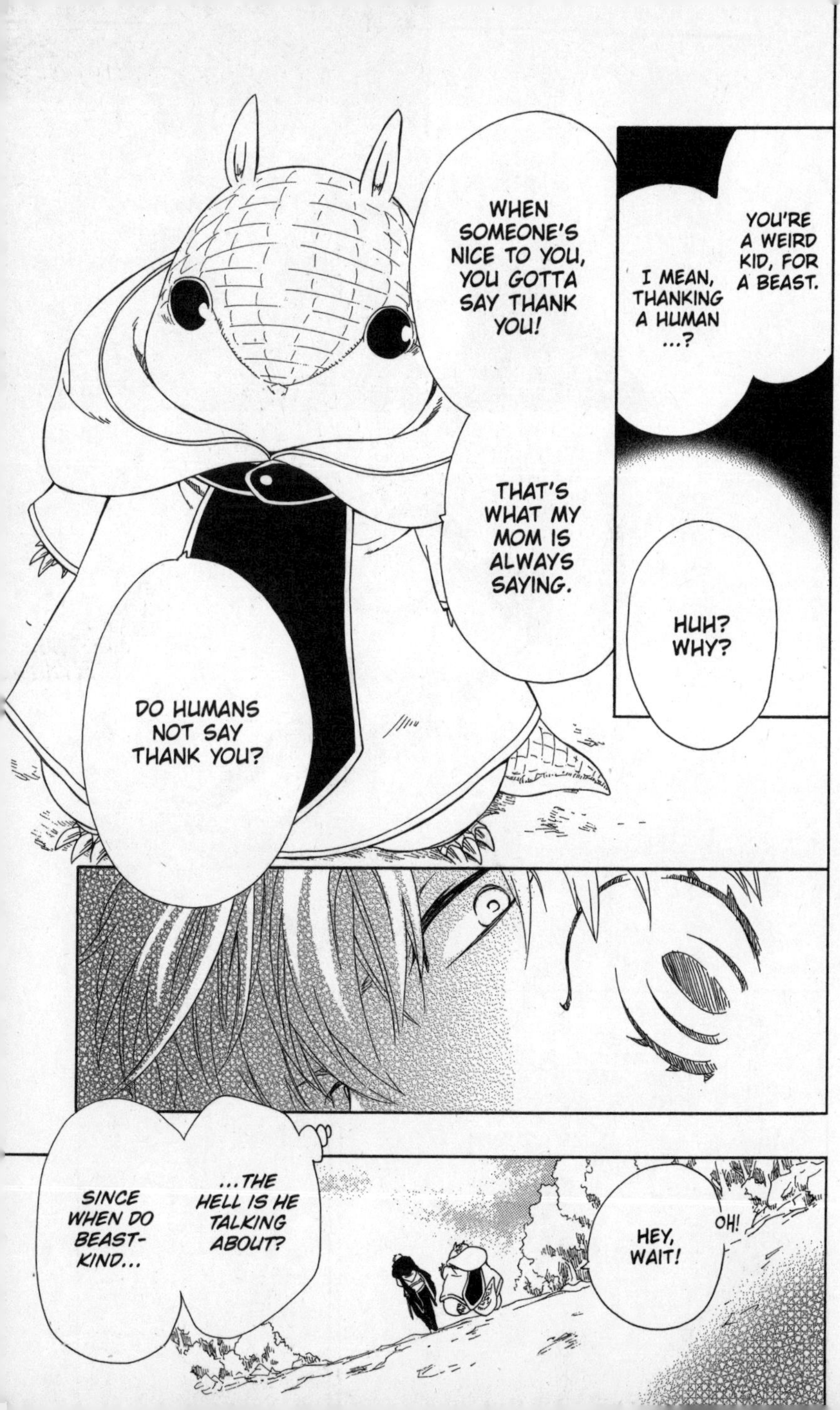
YOU'RE A WEIRD KID, FOR A BEAST.
I MEAN, THANKING A HUMAN ...?
HUH? WHY?
WHEN SOMEONE'S NICE TO YOU, YOU GOTTA SAY THANK YOU!
THAT'S WHAT MY MOM IS ALWAYS SAYING.
DO HUMANS NOT SAY THANK YOU?
OH!
HEY, WAIT!
...THE HELL IS HE TALKING ABOUT?
SINCE WHEN DO BEAST-KIND...

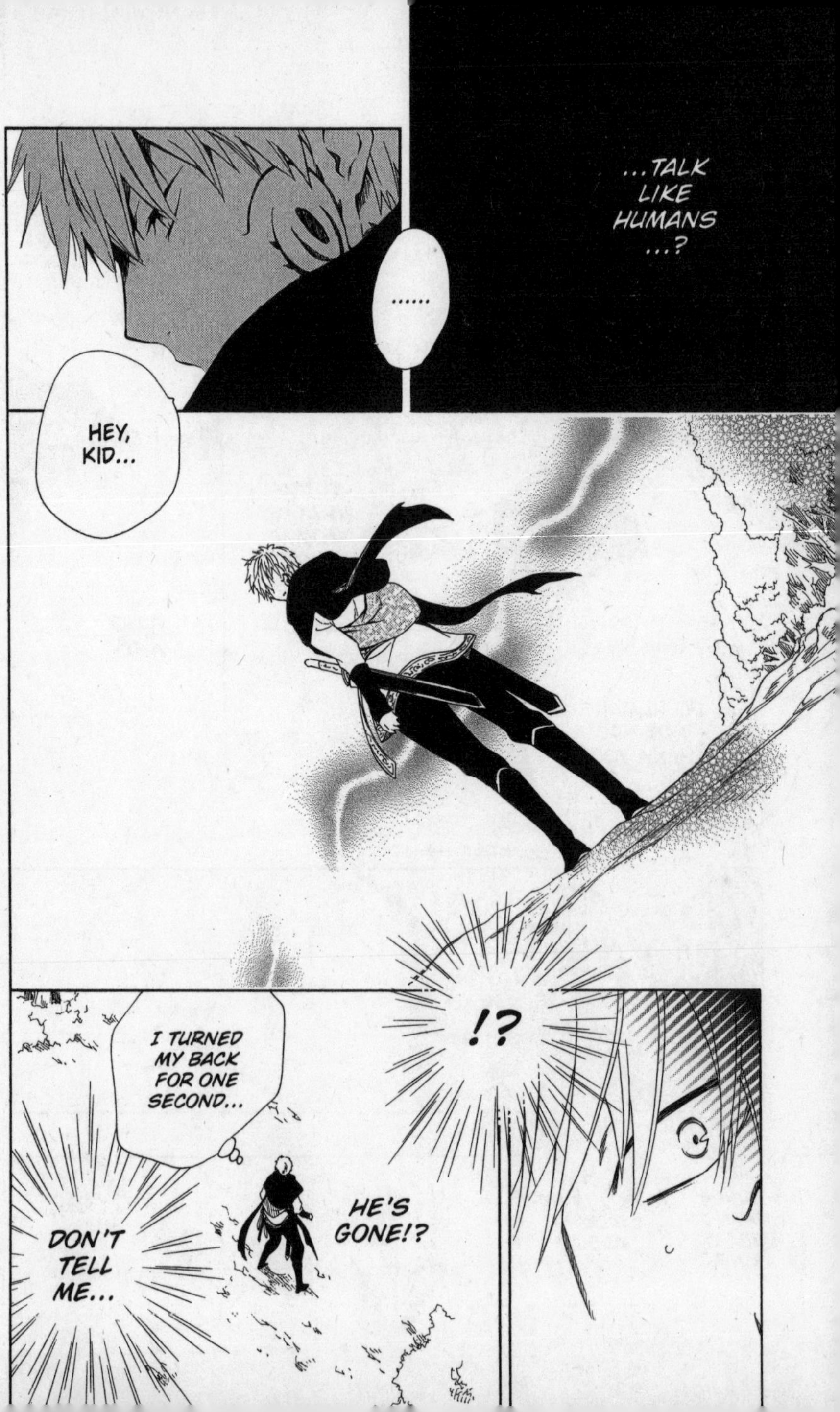
...TALK LIKE HUMANS ...?
......
HEY, KID...
!?
I TURNED MY BACK FOR ONE SECOND...
HE'S GONE!?
DON'T TELL ME...

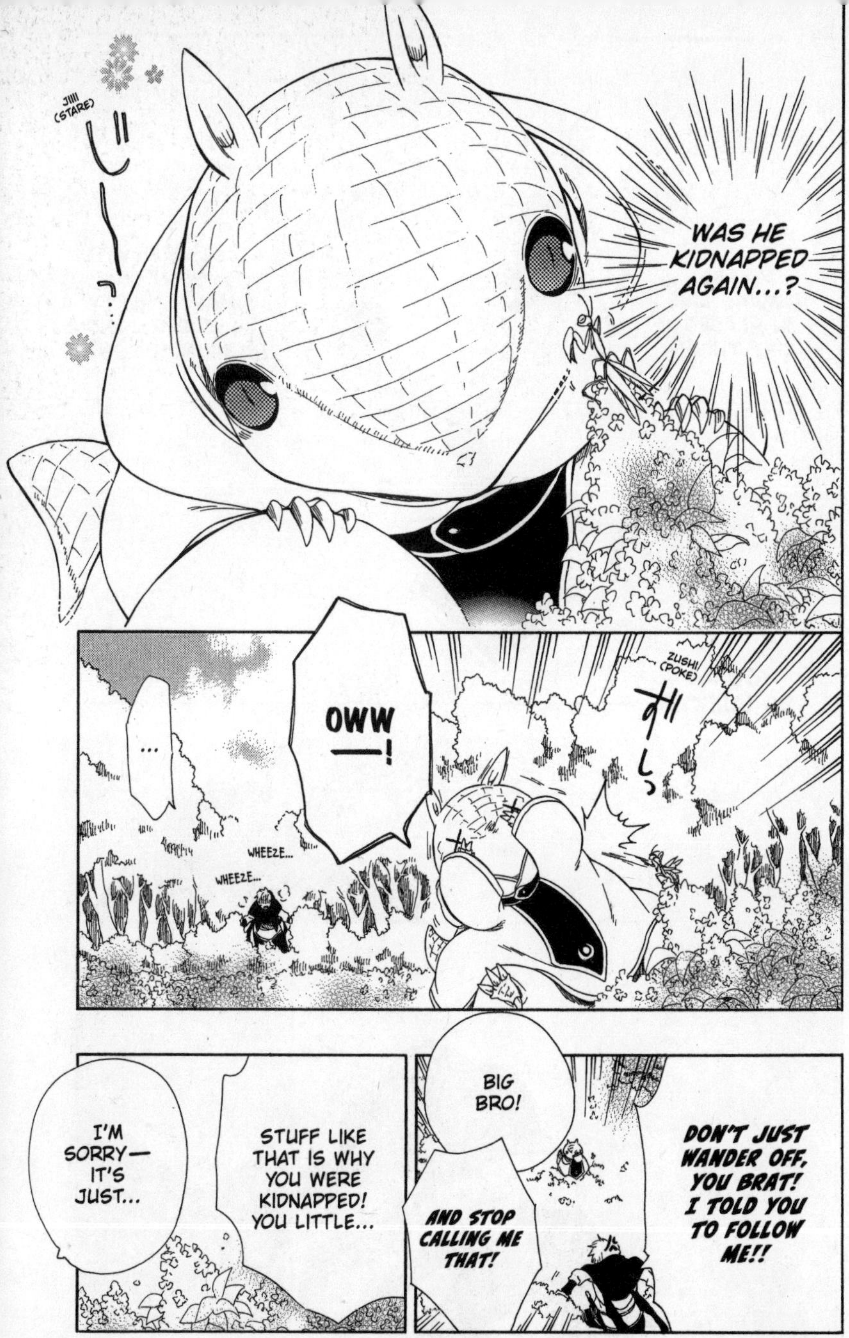
WAS HE KIDNAPPED AGAIN...?
JIIII (STARE)
ZUSHI (POKE)
OWW—!
...
WHEEZE...
WHEEZE...
DON'T JUST WANDER OFF, YOU BRAT! I TOLD YOU TO FOLLOW ME!!
BIG BRO!
AND STOP CALLING ME THAT!
STUFF LIKE THAT IS WHY YOU WERE KIDNAPPED! YOU LITTLE...
I'M SORRY— IT'S JUST...

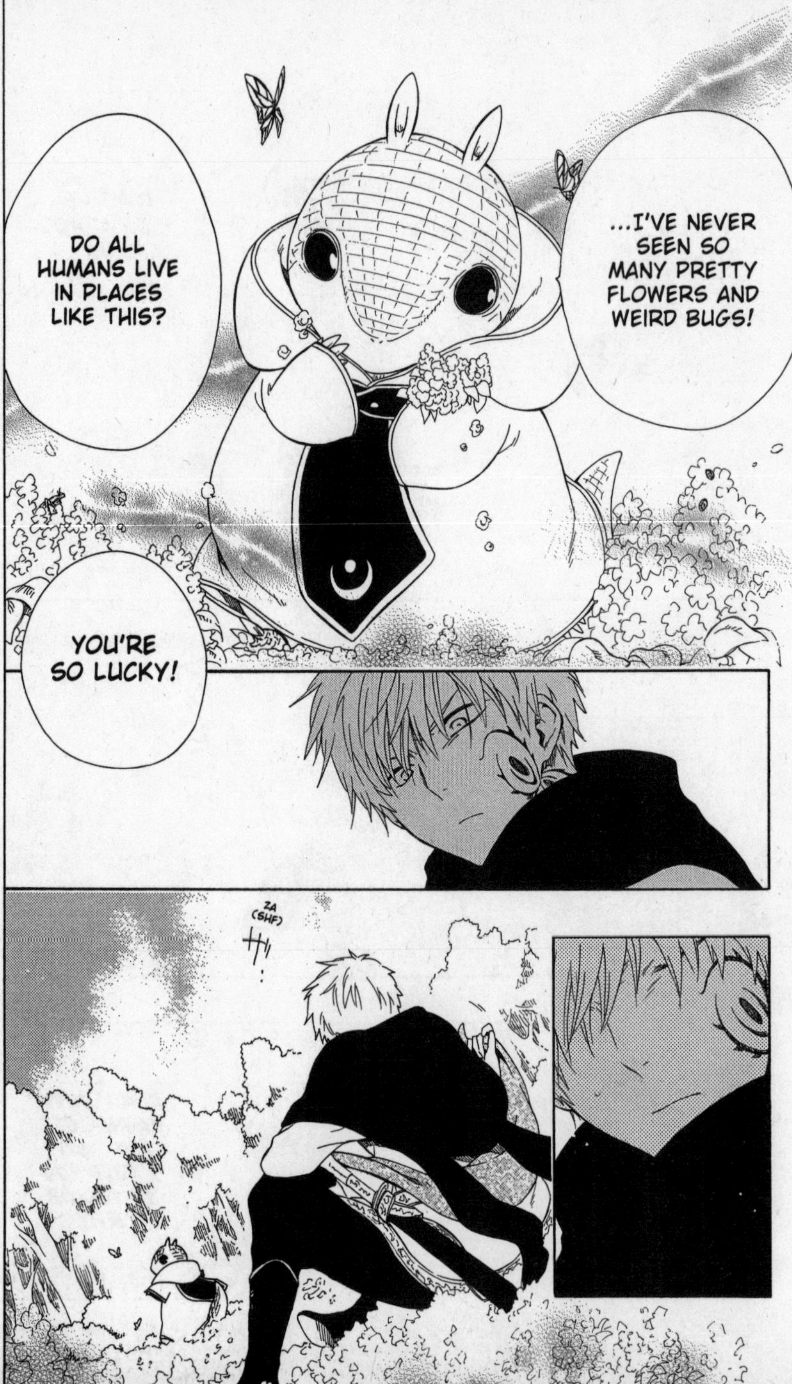
...I'VE NEVER SEEN SO MANY PRETTY FLOWERS AND WEIRD BUGS!
DO ALL HUMANS LIVE IN PLACES LIKE THIS?
YOU'RE SO LUCKY!
ZA (SHF)

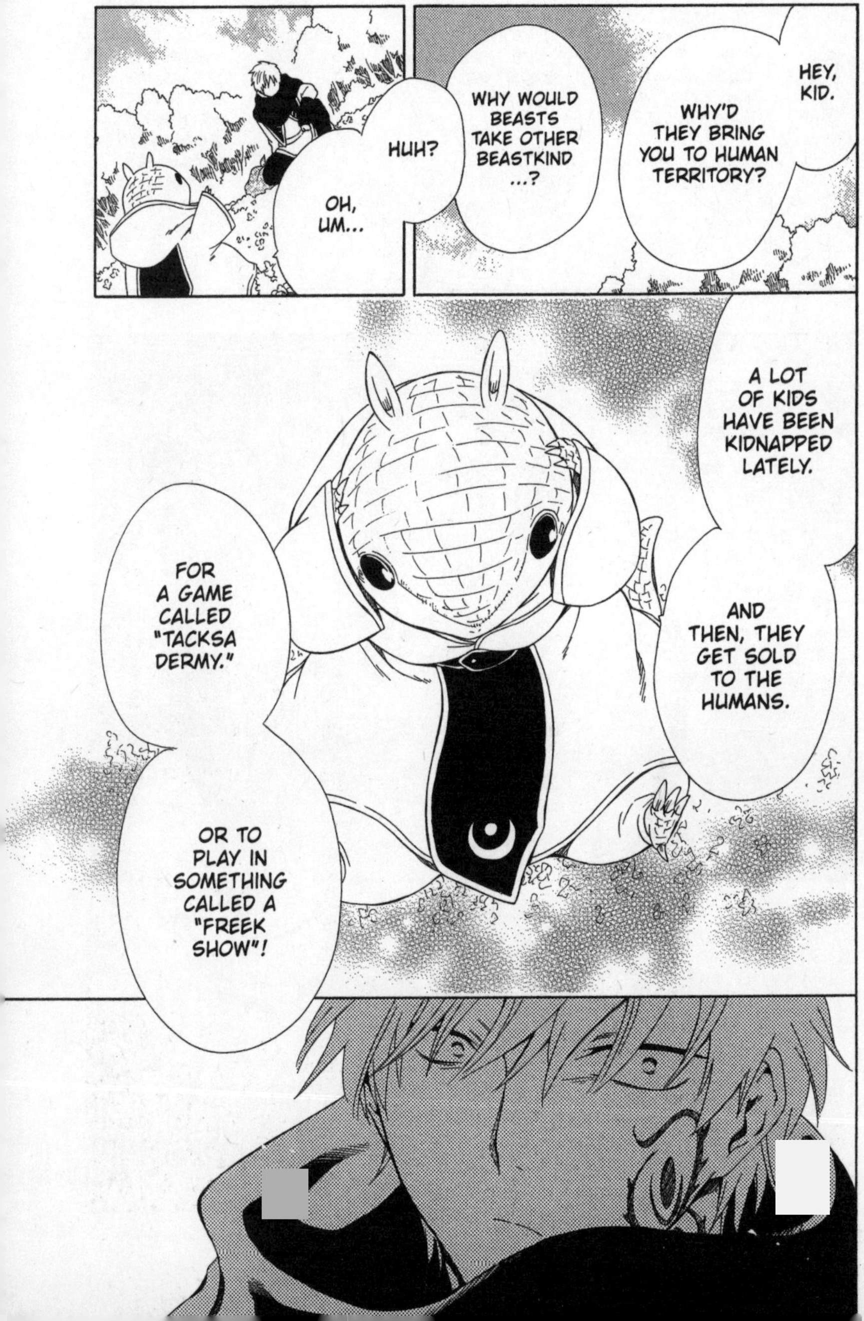
HEY, KID.
WHY'D THEY BRING YOU TO HUMAN TERRITORY?
WHY WOULD BEASTS TAKE OTHER BEASTKIND ...?
HUH?
OH, UM...
A LOT OF KIDS HAVE BEEN KIDNAPPED LATELY.
AND THEN, THEY GET SOLD TO THE HUMANS.
FOR A GAME CALLED "TACKSA DERMY."
OR TO PLAY IN SOMETHING CALLED A "FREEK SHOW"!

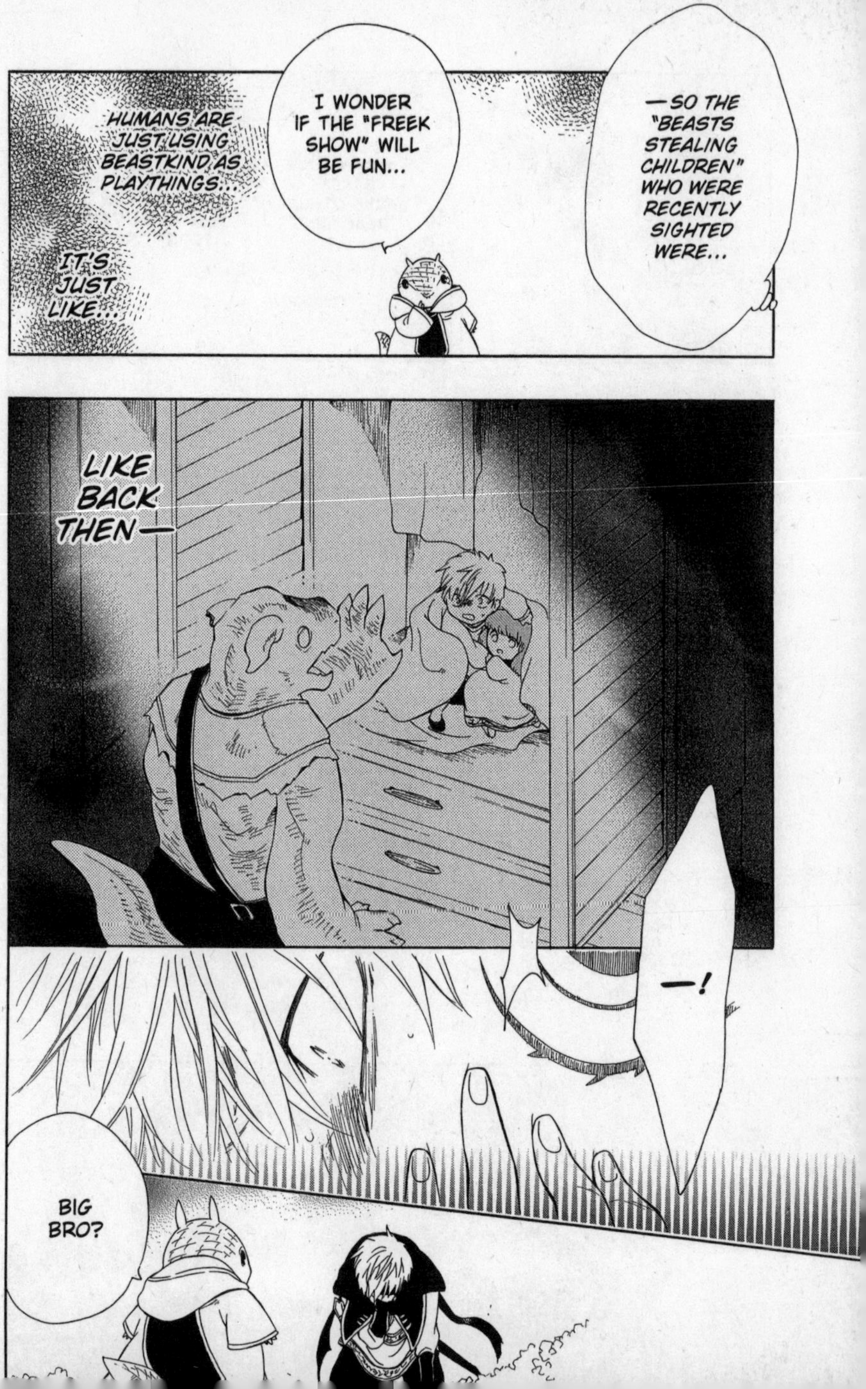
—SO THE "BEASTS STEALING CHILDREN" WHO WERE RECENTLY SIGHTED WERE...
I WONDER IF THE "FREEK SHOW" WILL BE FUN...
HUMANS ARE JUST USING BEASTKIND AS PLAYTHINGS...
IT'S JUST LIKE...
LIKE BACK THEN—
—!
BIG BRO?

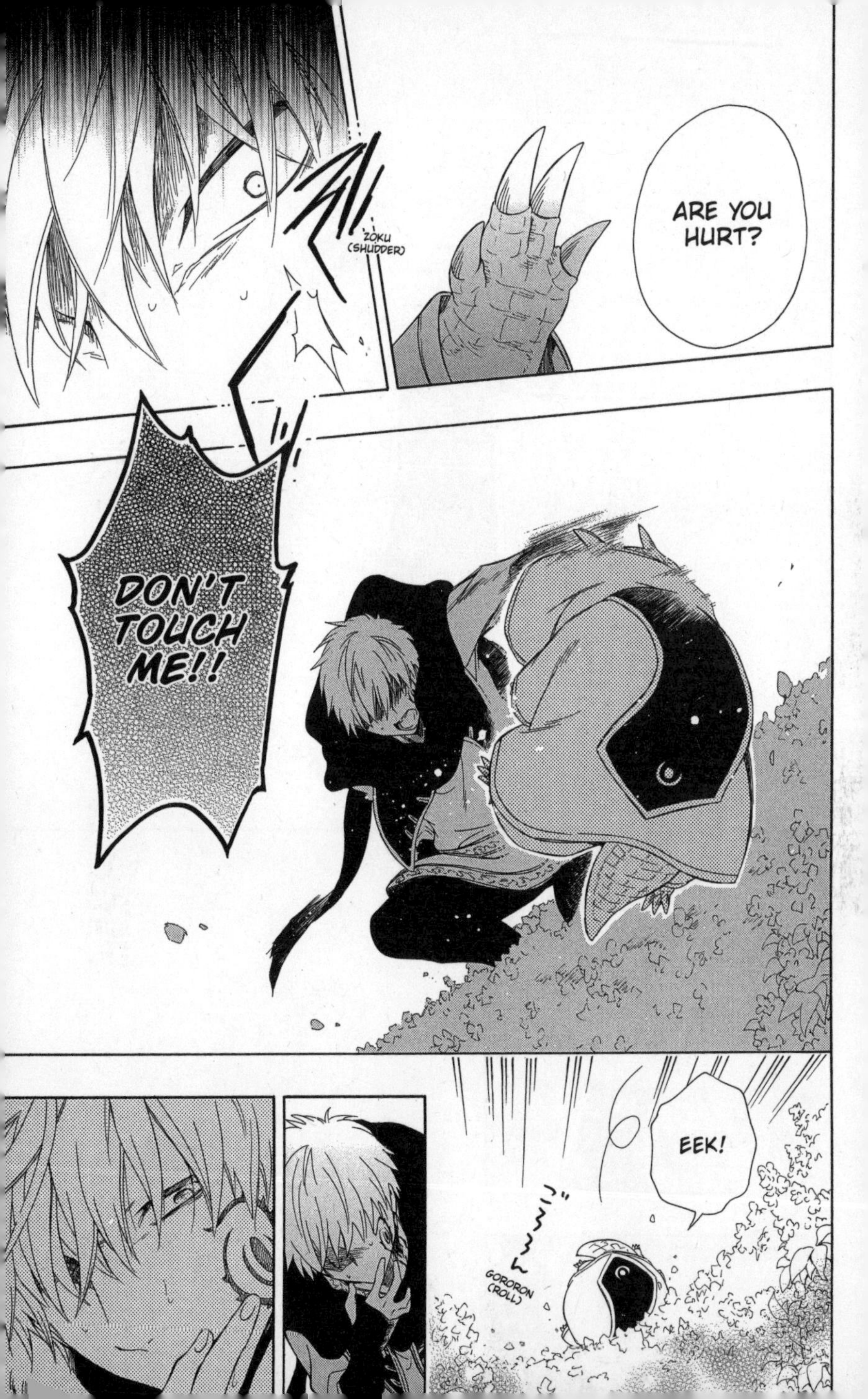
ARE YOU HURT?
ZOKU (SHUDDER)
DON'T TOUCH ME!!
EEK!
GORORON (ROLL)

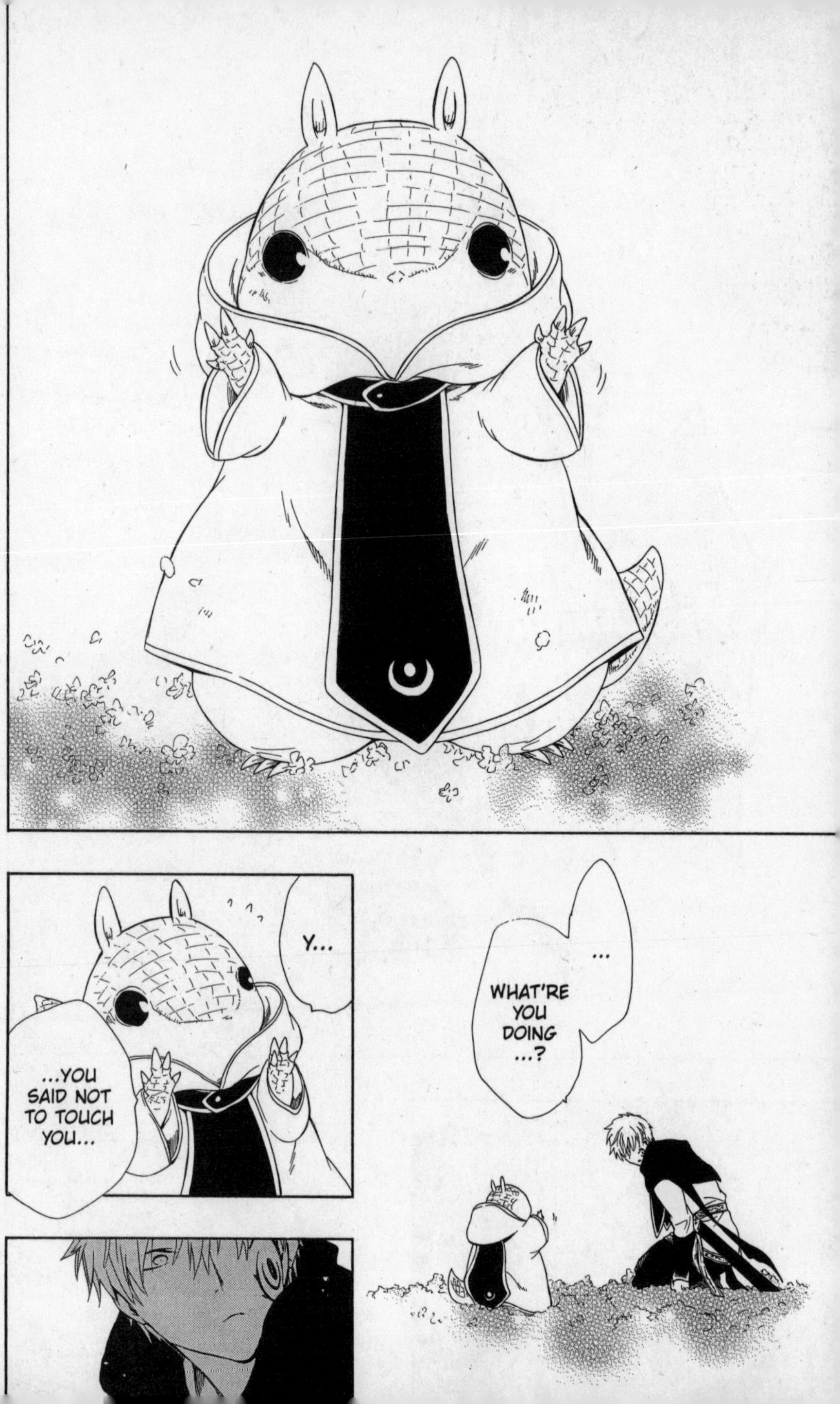
...
WHAT'RE YOU DOING ...?
Y...
...YOU SAID NOT TO TOUCH YOU...

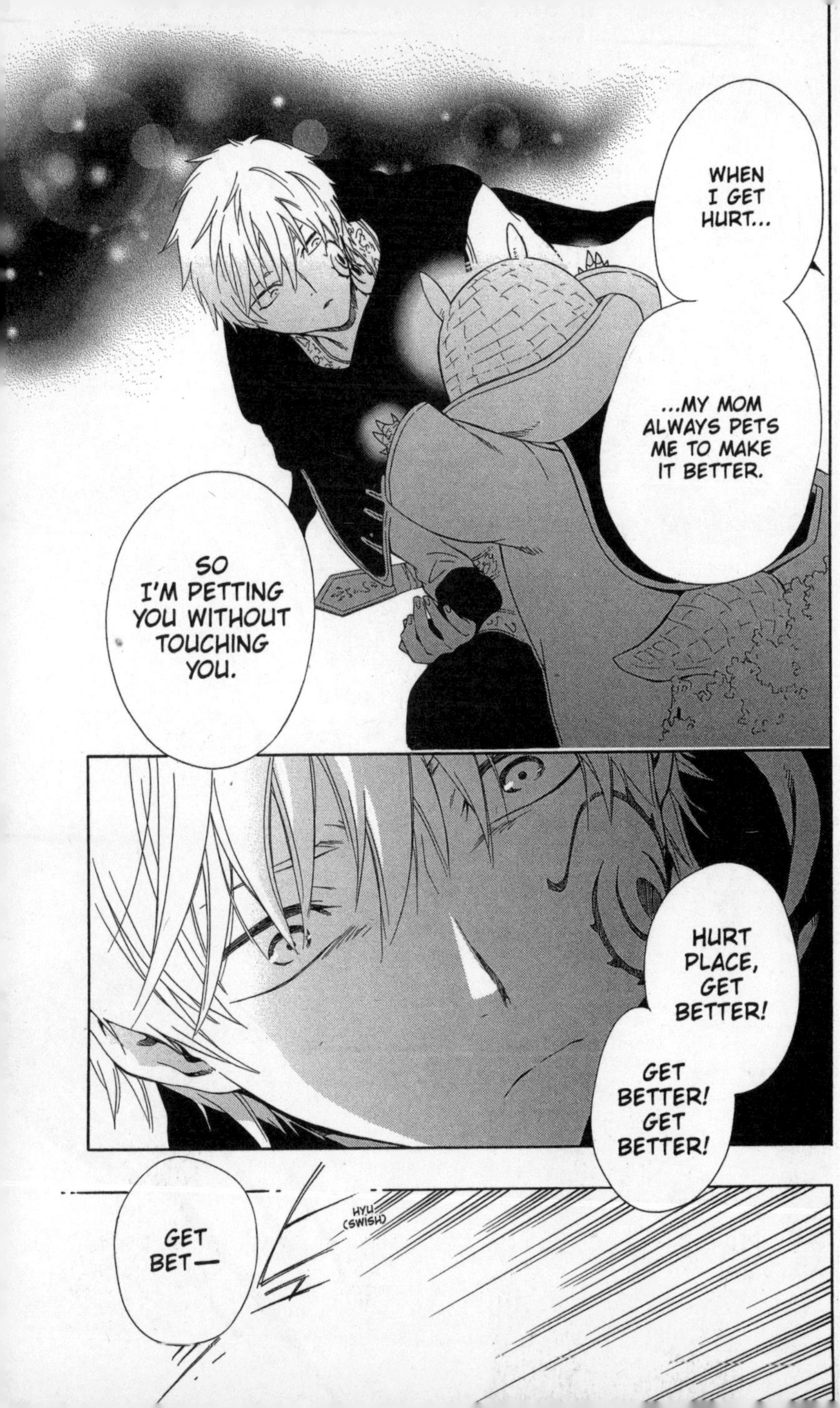
WHEN I GET HURT...
...MY MOM ALWAYS PETS ME TO MAKE IT BETTER.
SO I'M PETTING YOU WITHOUT TOUCHING YOU.
HURT PLACE, GET BETTER!
GET BETTER! GET BETTER!
HYU (SWISH)
GET BET—

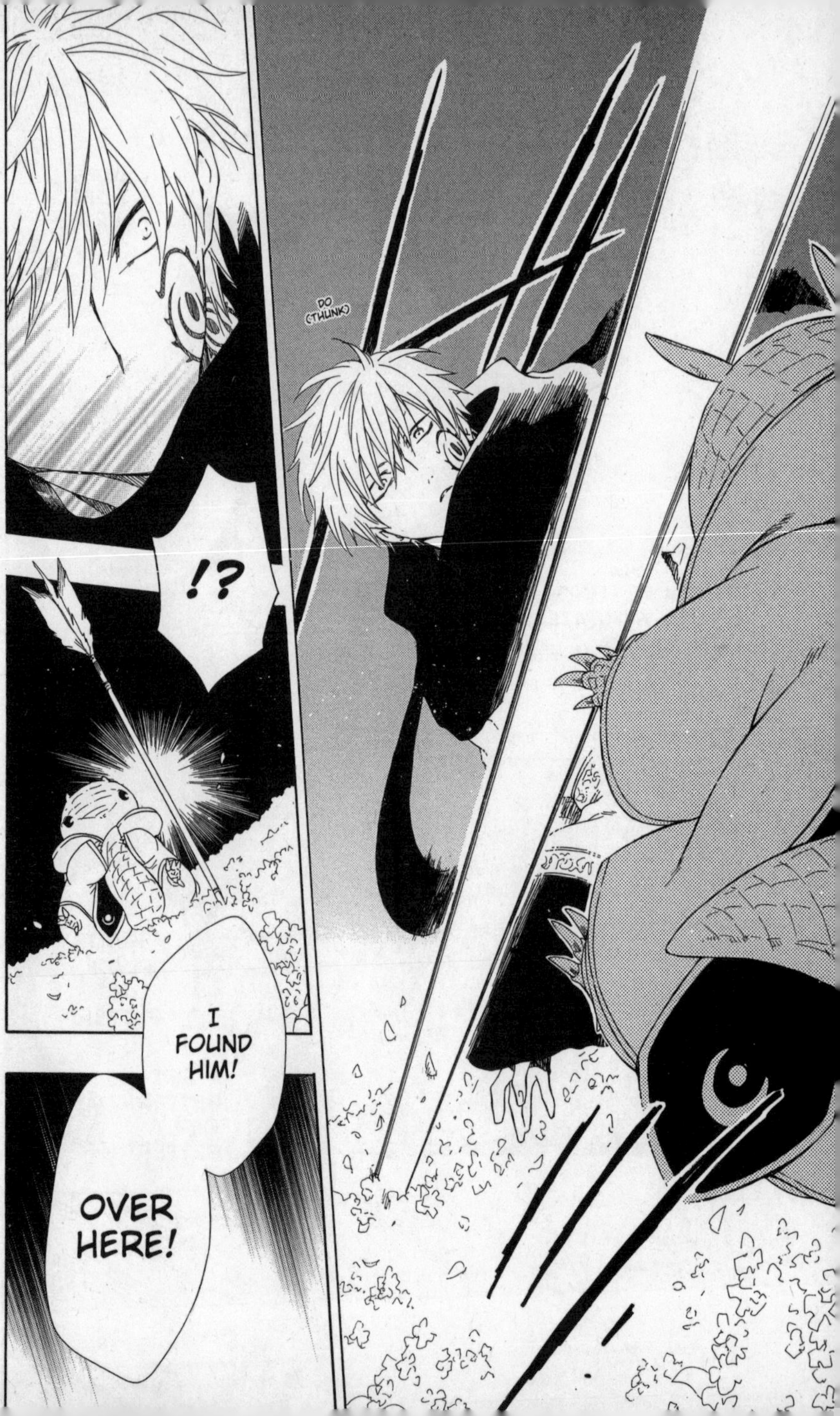
DO (THUNK)
!?
I FOUND HIM!
OVER HERE!

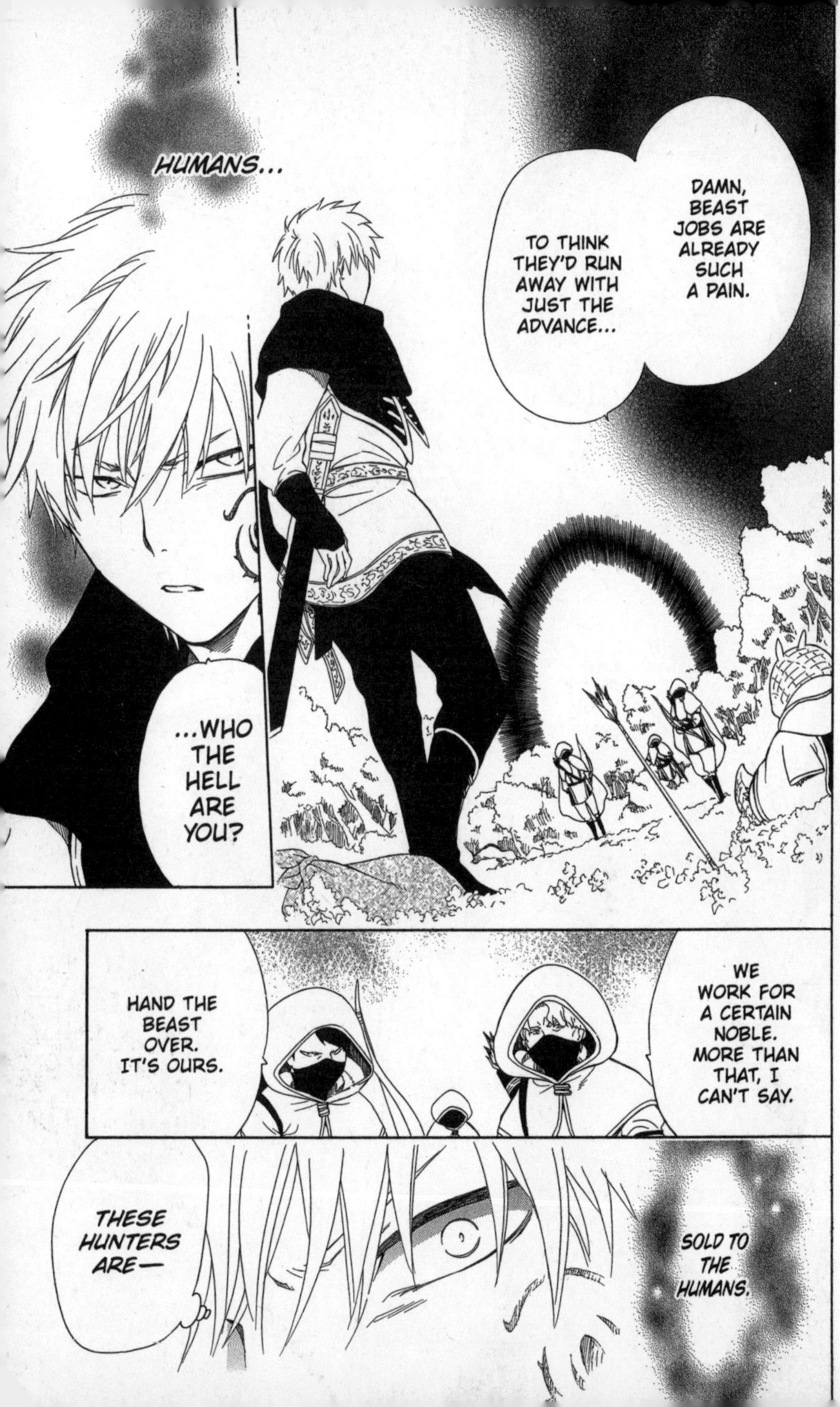
DAMN, BEAST JOBS ARE ALREADY SUCH A PAIN.
TO THINK THEY'D RUN AWAY WITH JUST THE ADVANCE...
HUMANS...
...WHO THE HELL ARE YOU?
WE WORK FOR A CERTAIN NOBLE. MORE THAN THAT, I CAN'T SAY.
HAND THE BEAST OVER. IT'S OURS.
THESE HUNTERS ARE—
SOLD TO THE HUMANS.

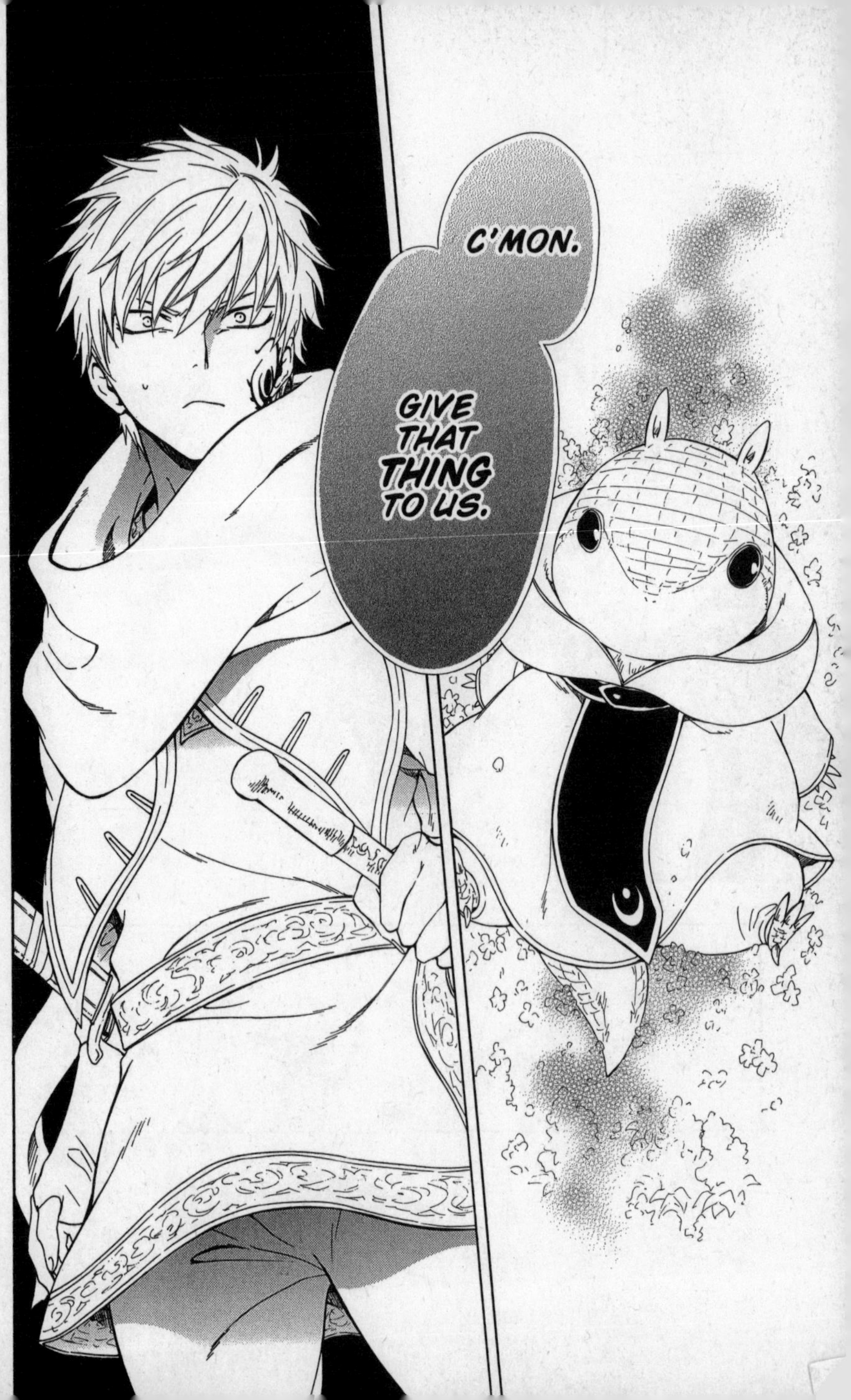
C'MON.
GIVE THAT THING TO US.

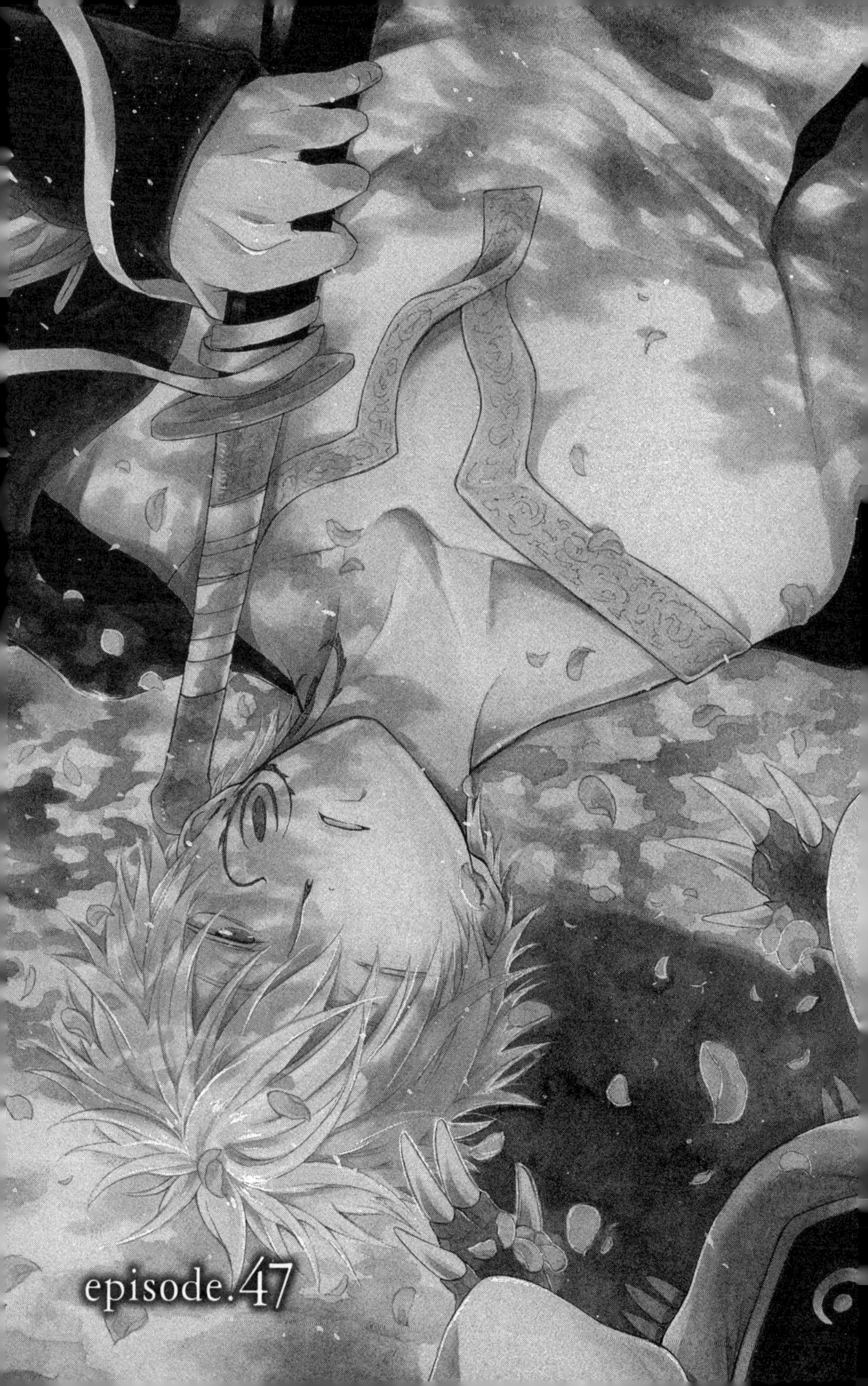
episode.47

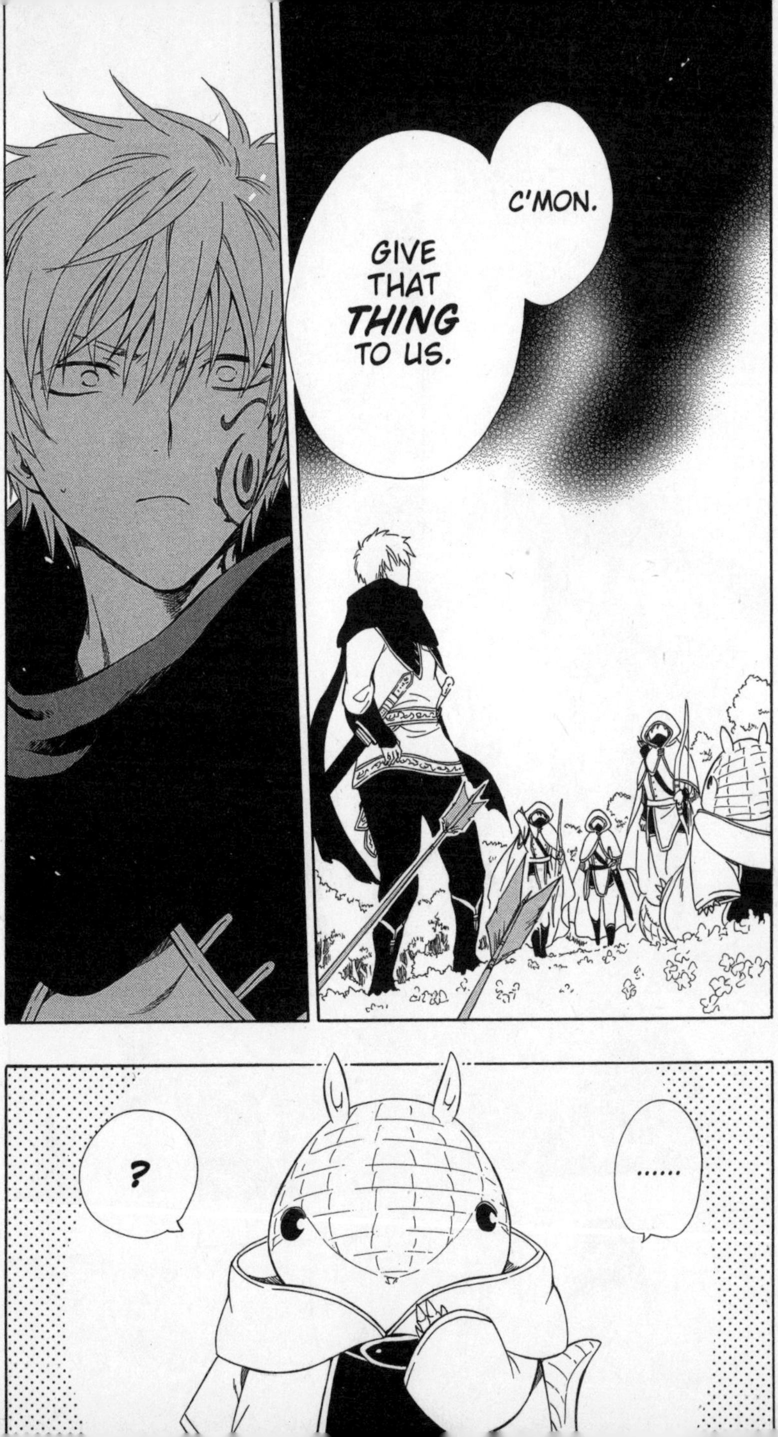
C'MON.
GIVE THAT THING TO US.
......
?

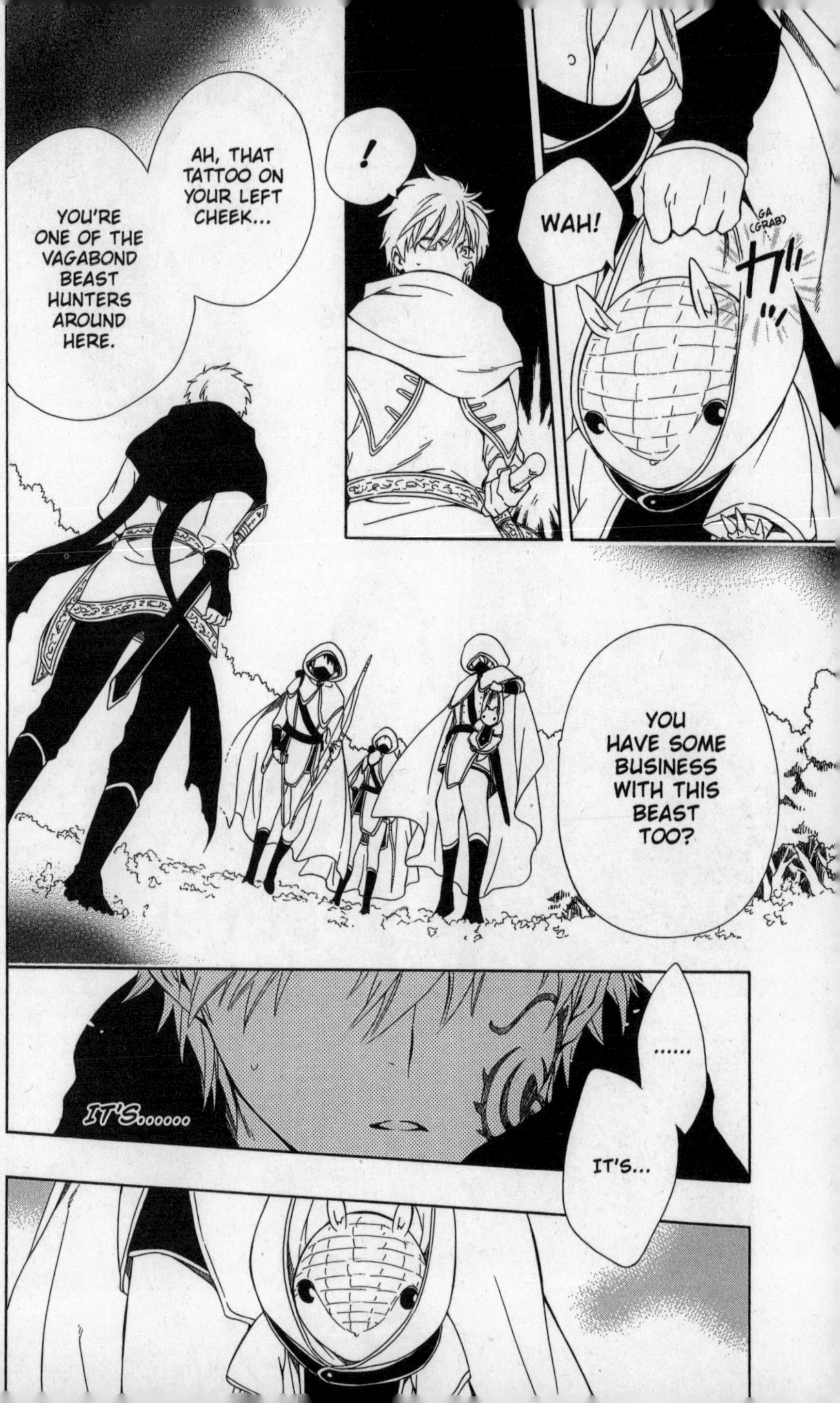
WAH!
GA (GRAB)
!
AH, THAT TATTOO ON YOUR LEFT CHEEK...
YOU'RE ONE OF THE VAGABOND BEAST HUNTERS AROUND HERE.
YOU HAVE SOME BUSINESS WITH THIS BEAST TOO?
......
IT'S...
IT'S......

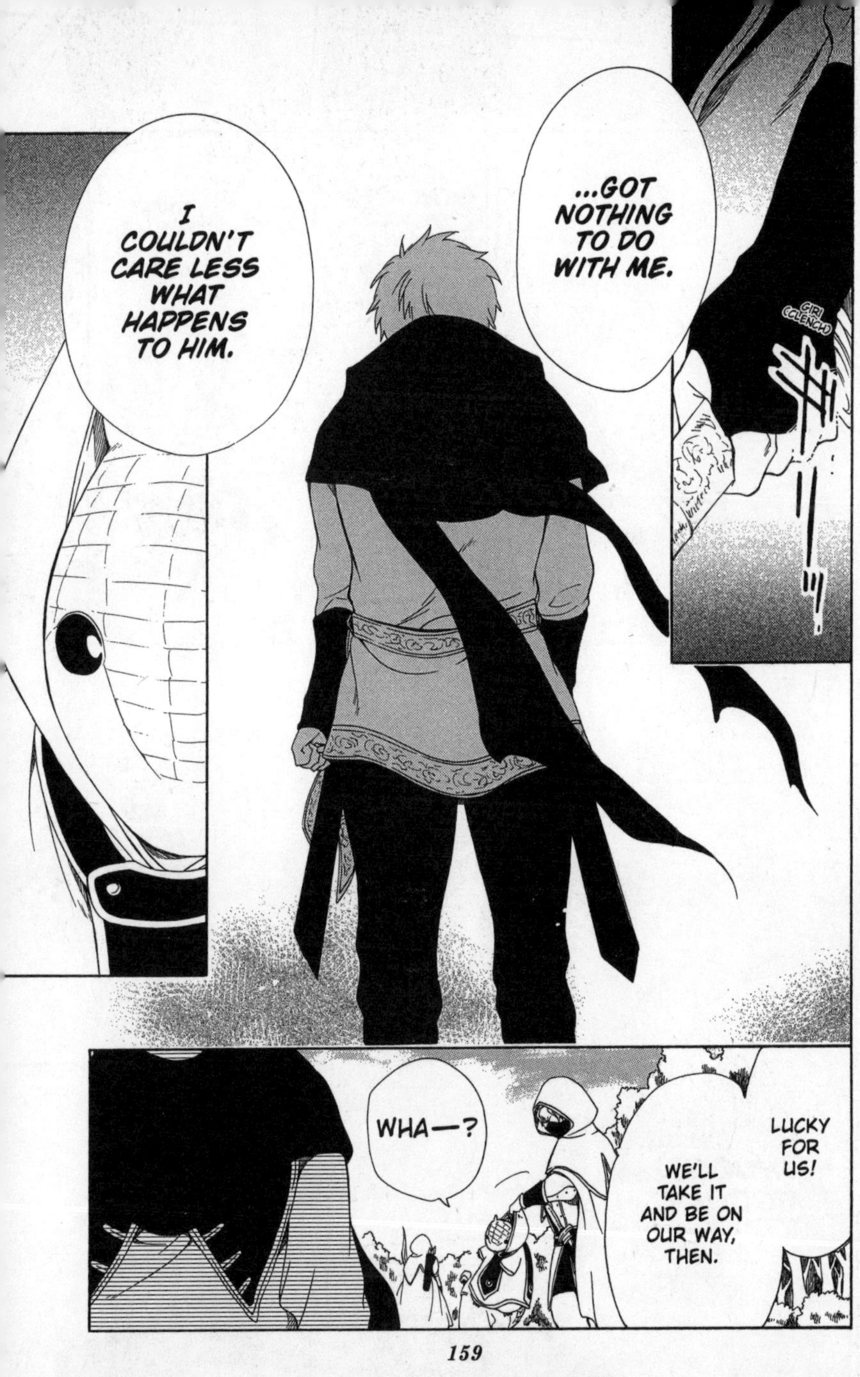
...GOT NOTHING TO DO WITH ME.
GIRI (CLENCH)
I COULDN'T CARE LESS WHAT HAPPENS TO HIM.
LUCKY FOR US!
WE'LL TAKE IT AND BE ON OUR WAY, THEN.
WHA—?

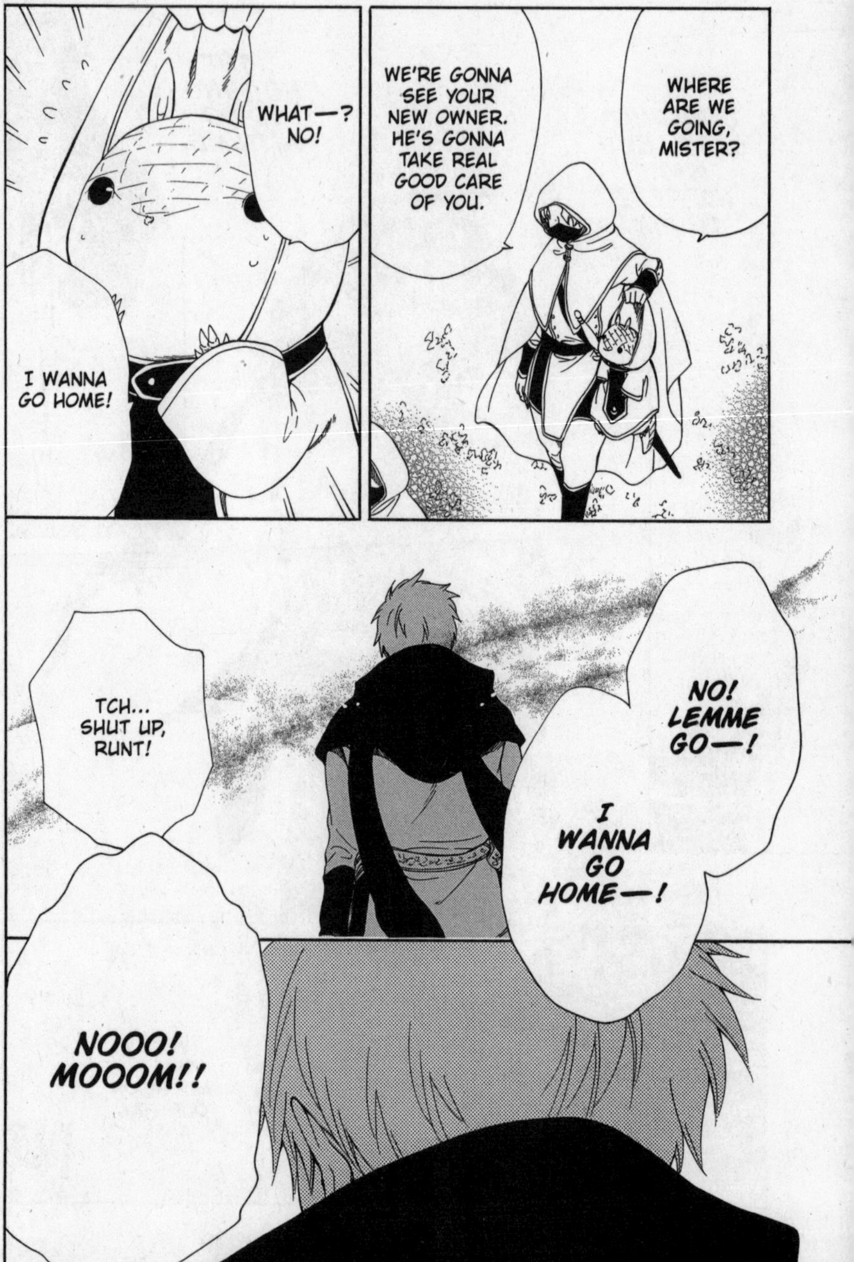
WHERE ARE WE GOING, MISTER?
WE'RE GONNA SEE YOUR NEW OWNER. HE'S GONNA TAKE REAL GOOD CARE OF YOU.
WHAT—? NO!
I WANNA GO HOME!
NO! LEMME GO—!
I WANNA GO HOME—!
TCH... SHUT UP, RUNT!
NOOO! MOOOM!!

THUS DOES VOLUME 8 COME TO AN END. GOSH, VOLUME 8 ALREADY? THAT MUST MEAN NEXT IS VOLUME 9! I WILL NEVER TAKE BEING ABLE TO CREATE COMICS FOR GRANTED, AND EVEN AS I'LL CONTINUE TO DO MY BEST AT IT, I'M ALREADY DEEPLY GRATEFUL FOR SO MUCH. I HOPE WE'LL MEET AGAIN IN THE NEXT VOLUME. FAREWELL! YIKES, THIS PEN IS REALLY STARTING TO GIVE OUT...!

TOMOFUJI

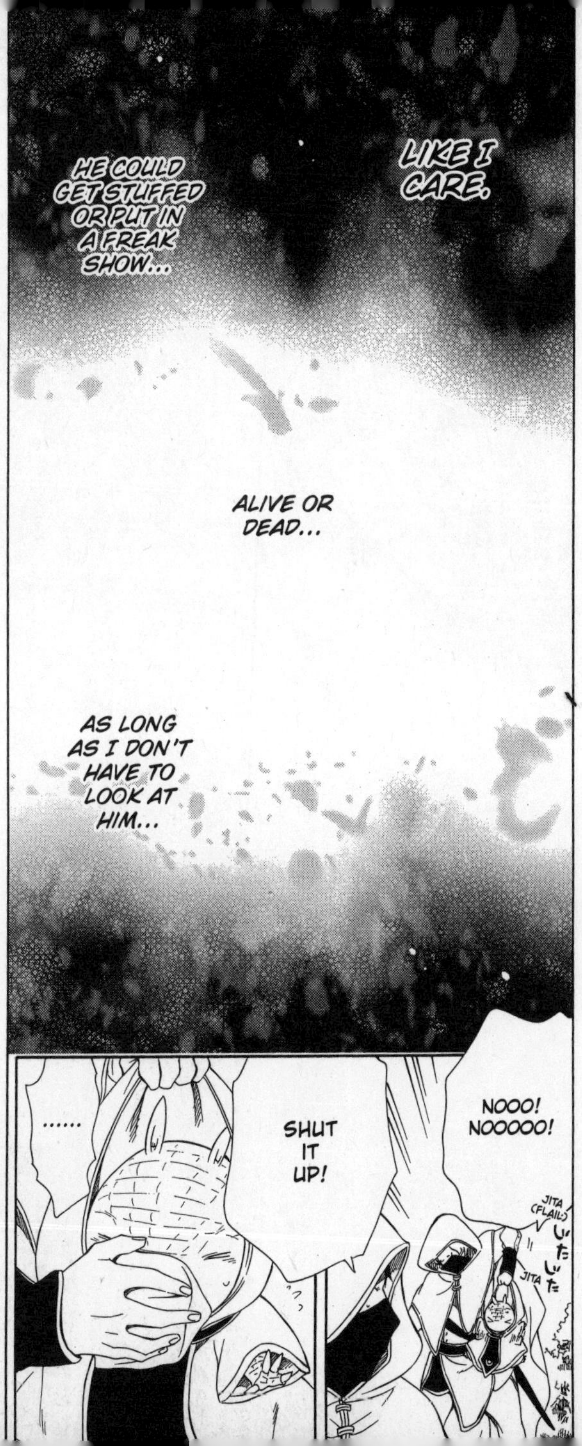
LIKE I CARE.
HE COULD GET STUFFED OR PUT IN A FREAK SHOW...
ALIVE OR DEAD...
AS LONG AS I DON'T HAVE TO LOOK AT HIM...
NOOO! NOOOOO!
JITA (FLAIL:)
JITA
SHUT IT UP!
......

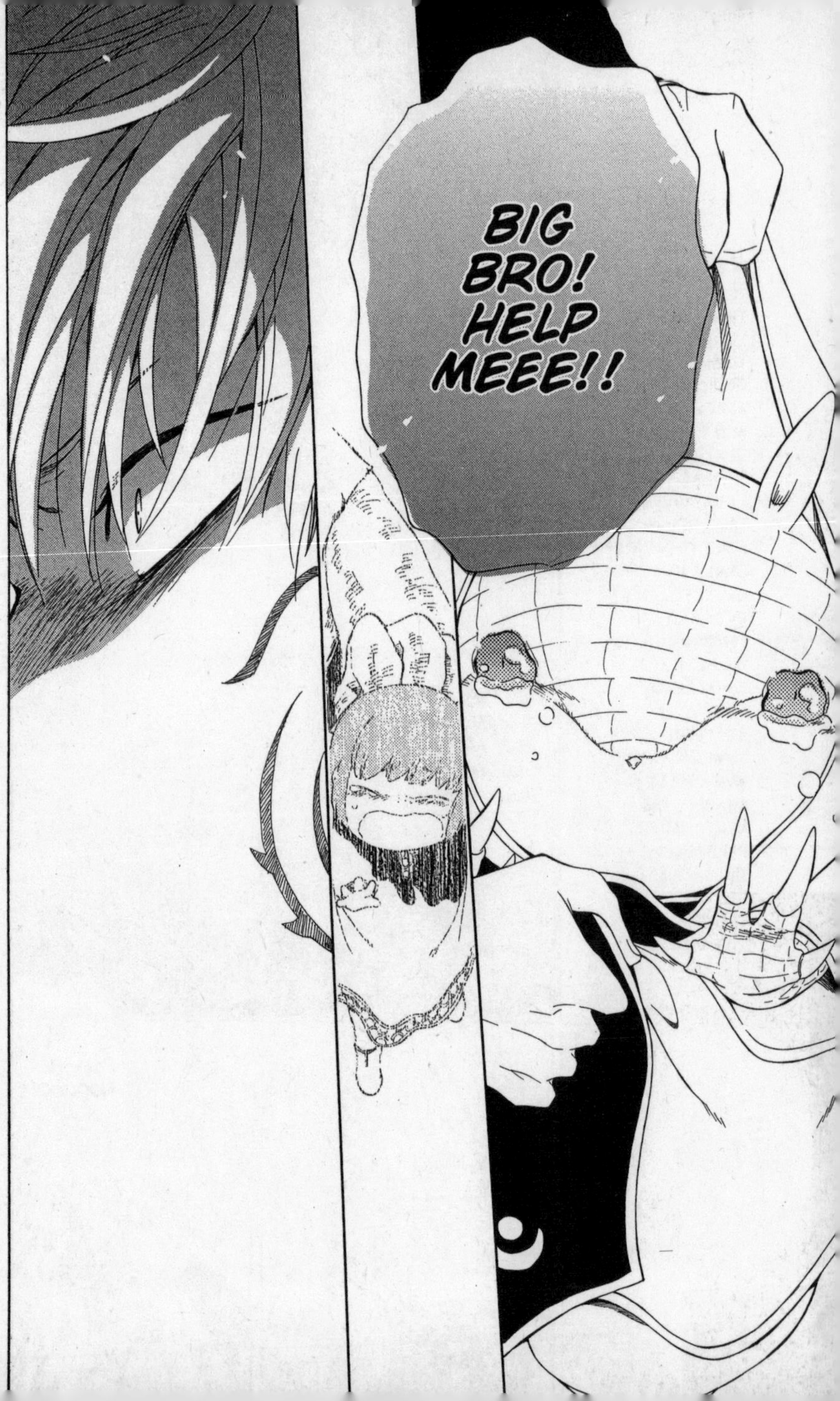
BIG BRO! HELP MEEE!!

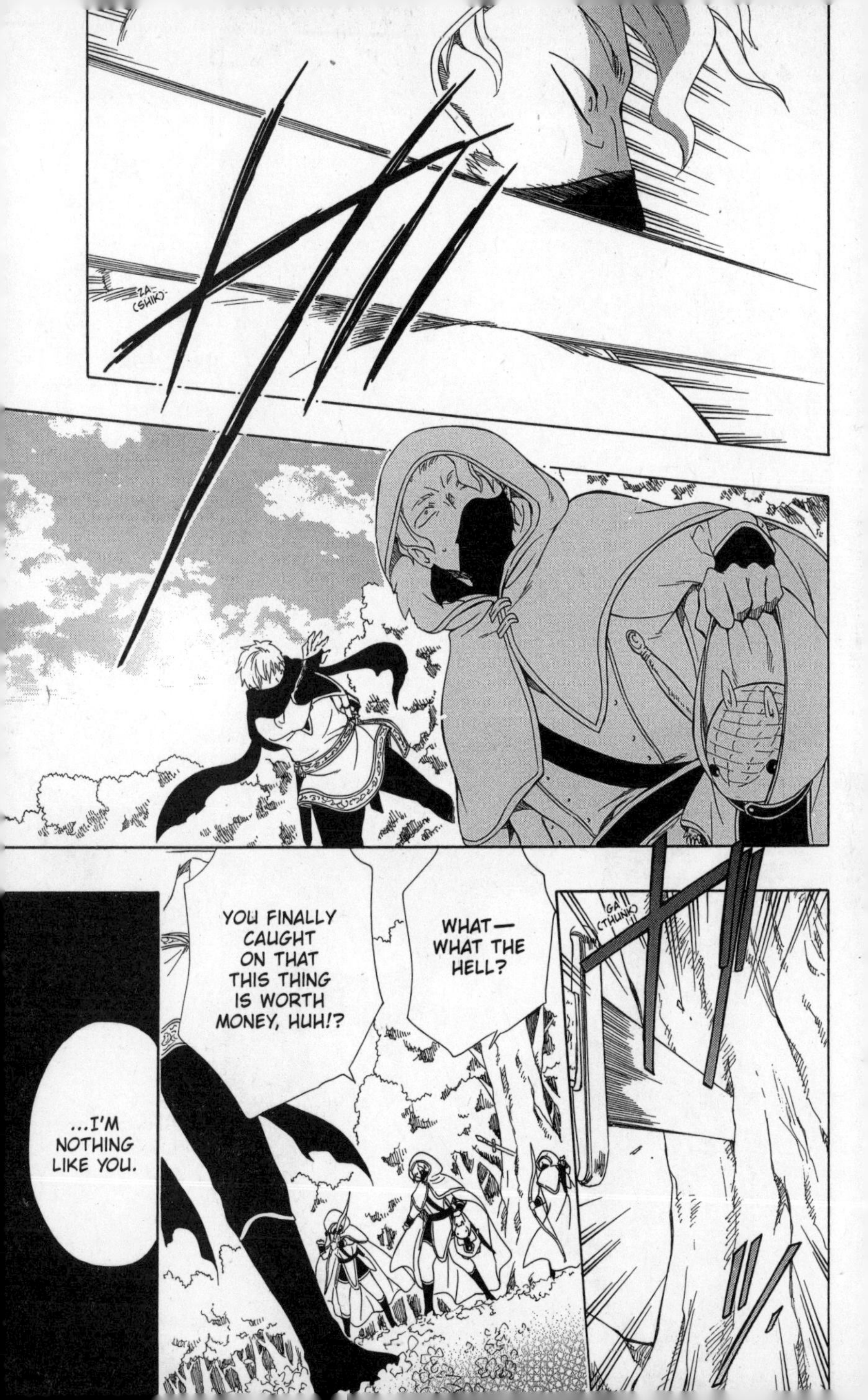
ZA- (SHIK)
GA (THUNK)
WHAT— WHAT THE HELL?
YOU FINALLY CAUGHT ON THAT THIS THING IS WORTH MONEY, HUH!?
...I'M NOTHING LIKE YOU.

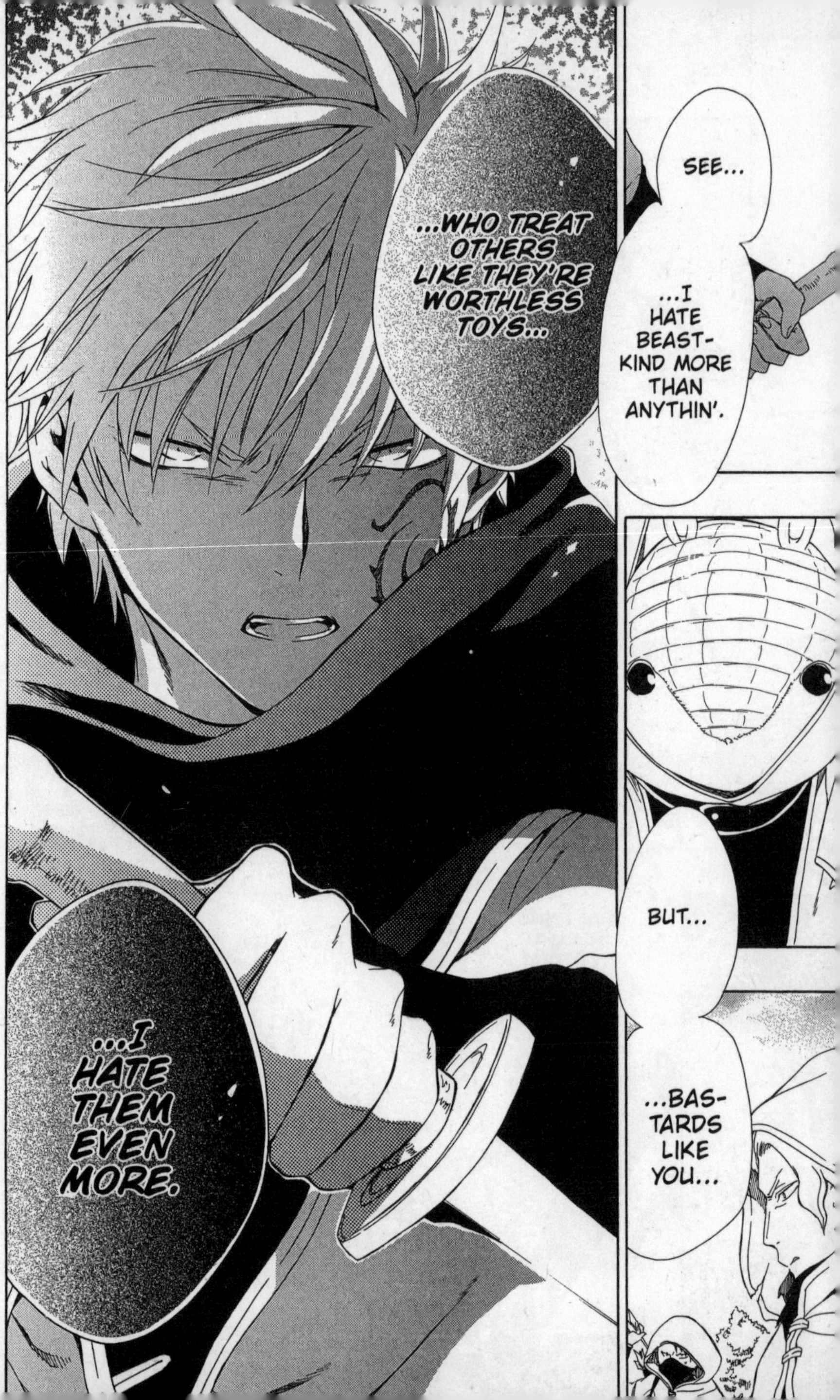
SEE...
...I HATE BEAST-KIND MORE THAN ANYTHIN'.
BUT...
...BAS-TARDS LIKE YOU...
...WHO TREAT OTHERS LIKE THEY'RE WORTHLESS TOYS...
...I HATE THEM EVEN MORE.

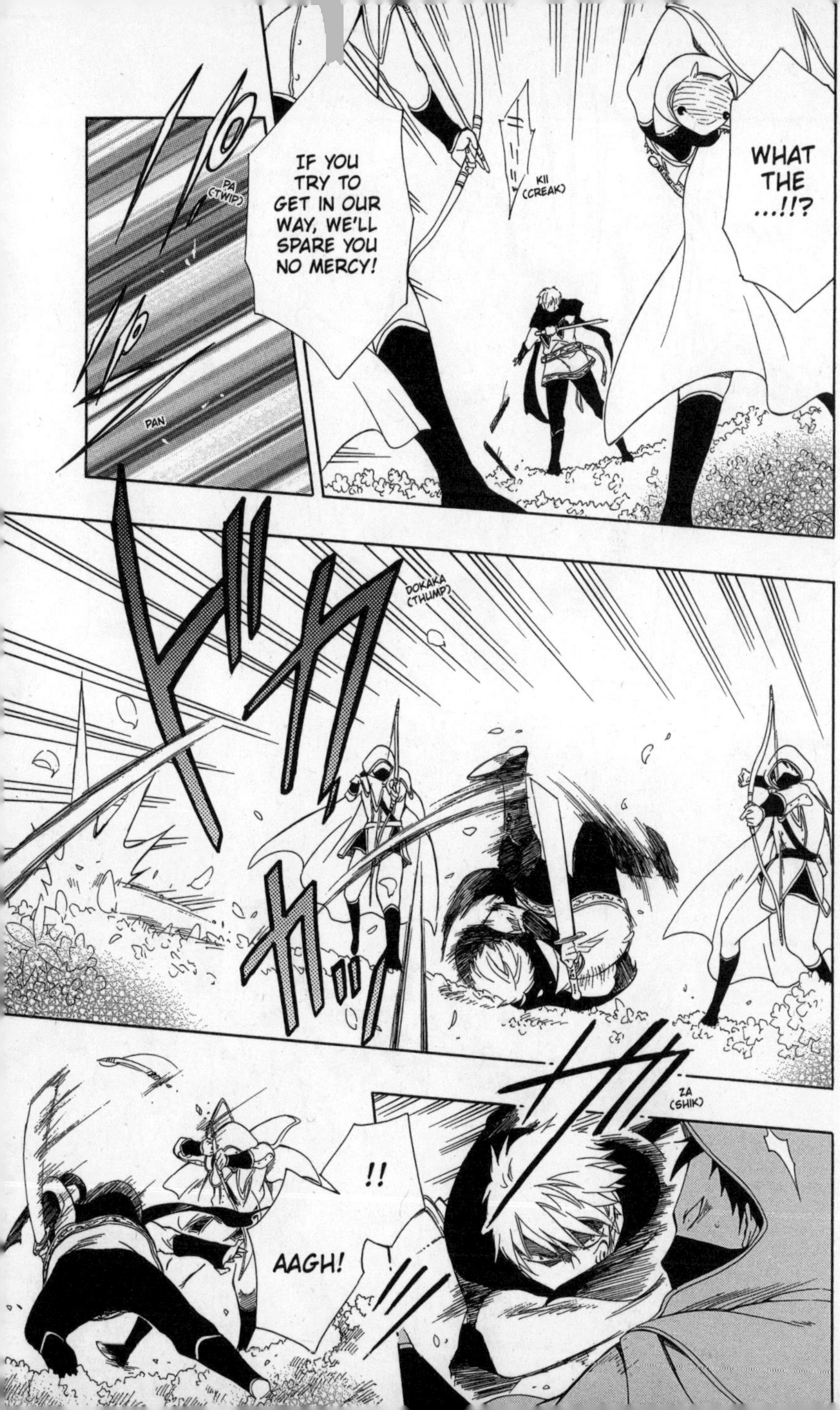
WHAT THE ...!!?
IF YOU TRY TO GET IN OUR WAY, WE'LL SPARE YOU NO MERCY!
KII (CREAK)
PA (TWIP)
PAN
DOKAKA (THUMP)
ZA (SHIK)
!!
AAGH!

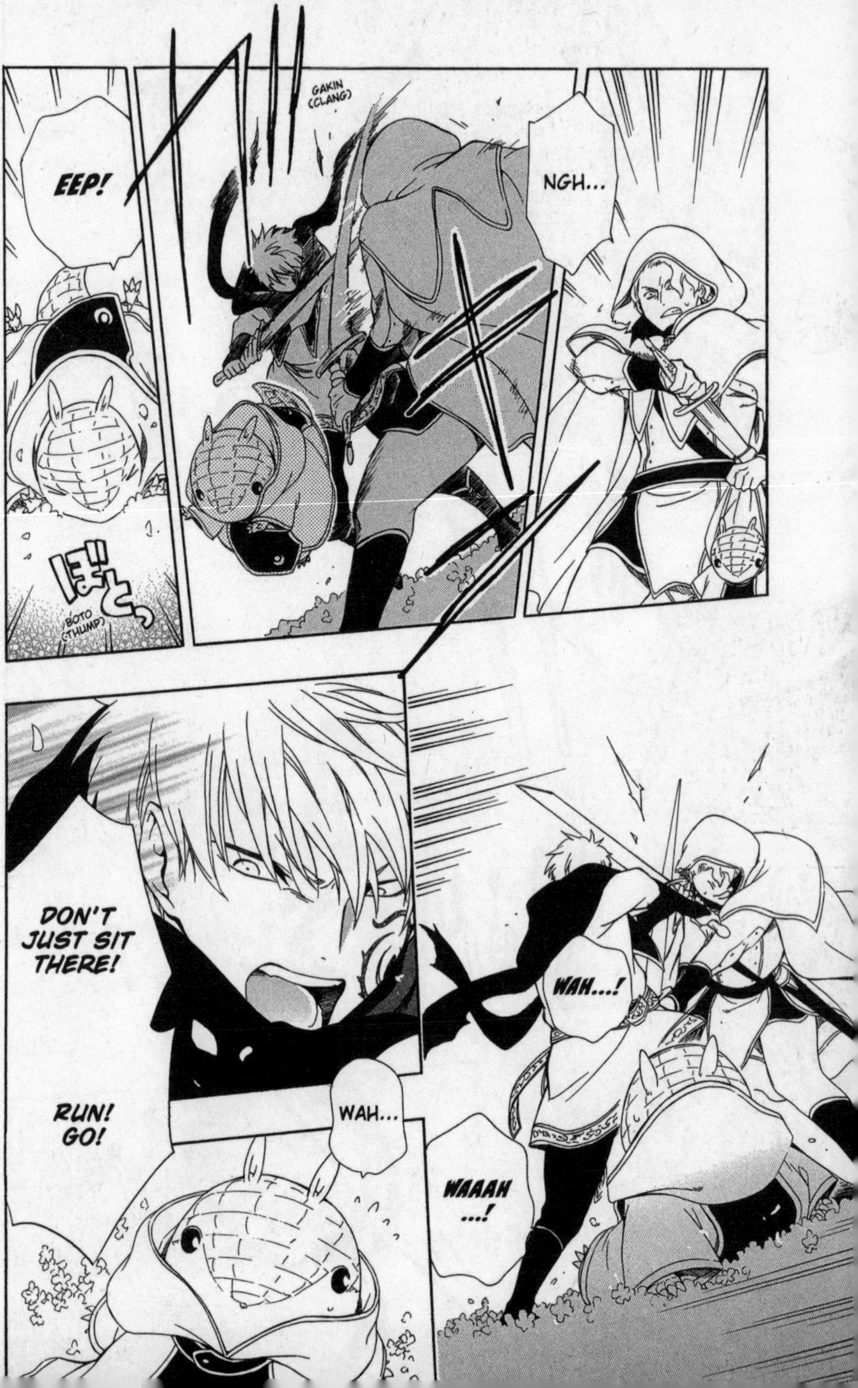
NGH...
GAKIN (CLANG)
EEP!
ぼとっ
BOTO (THUMP)
WAH...!
WAAAH ...!
DON'T JUST SIT THERE!
RUN! GO!
WAH...

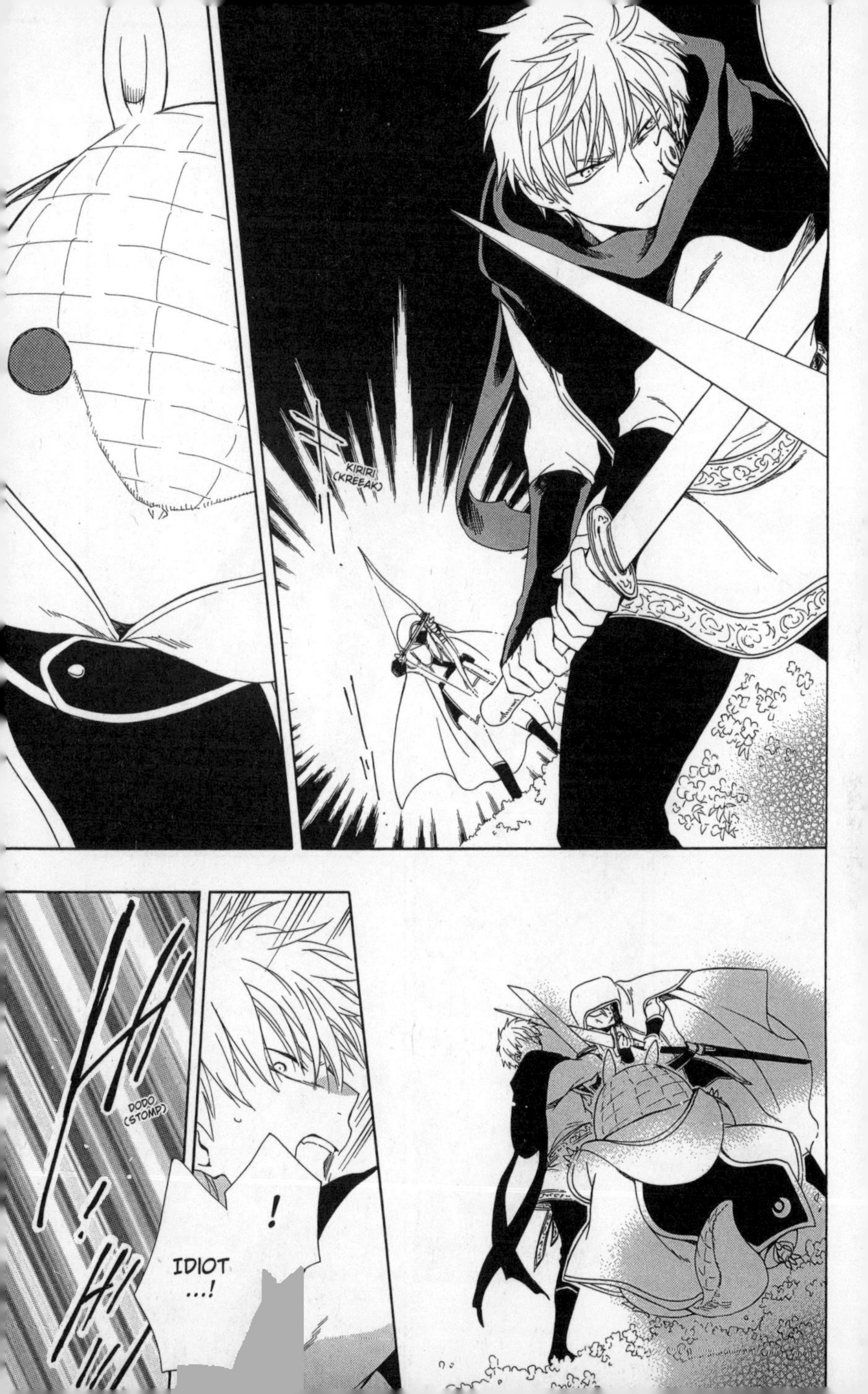
KIRIRI (KREEAK)
DODO (STOMP)
!
IDIOT ...!

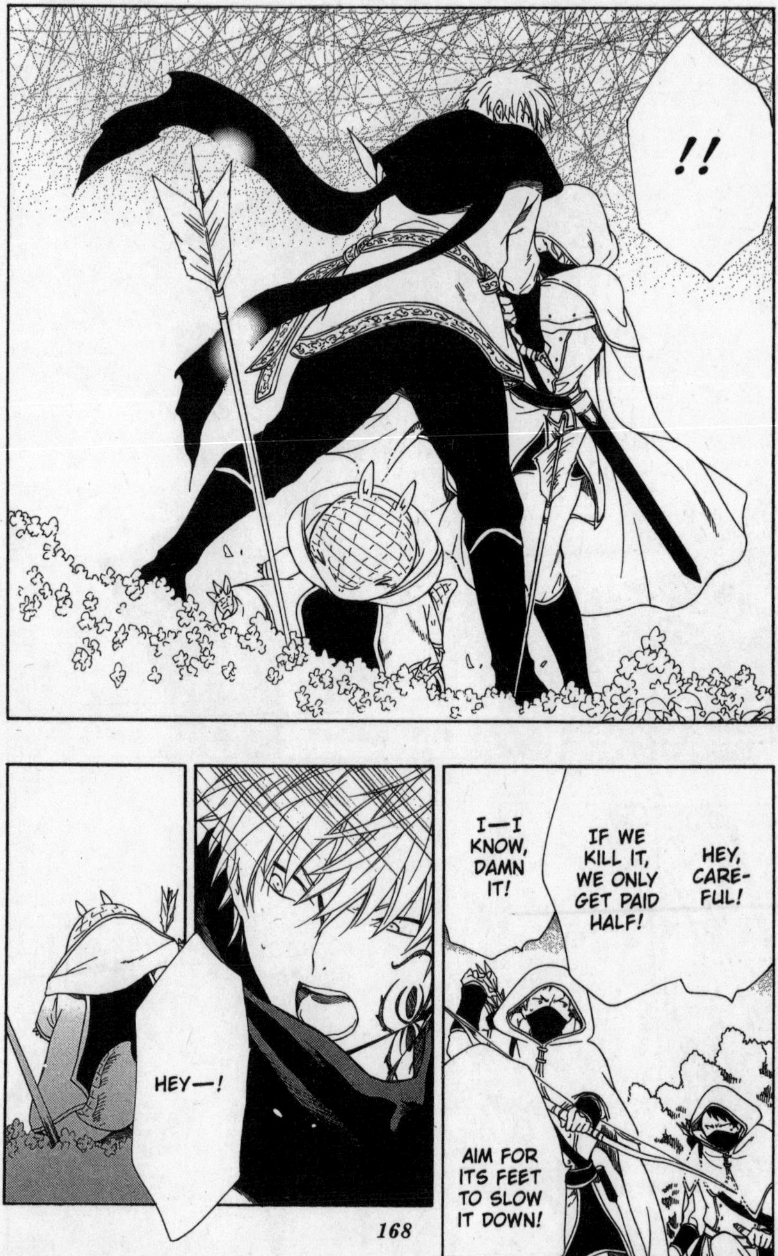
!!
HEY, CARE-FUL!
IF WE KILL IT, WE ONLY GET PAID HALF!
I—I KNOW, DAMN IT!
AIM FOR ITS FEET TO SLOW IT DOWN!
HEY—!

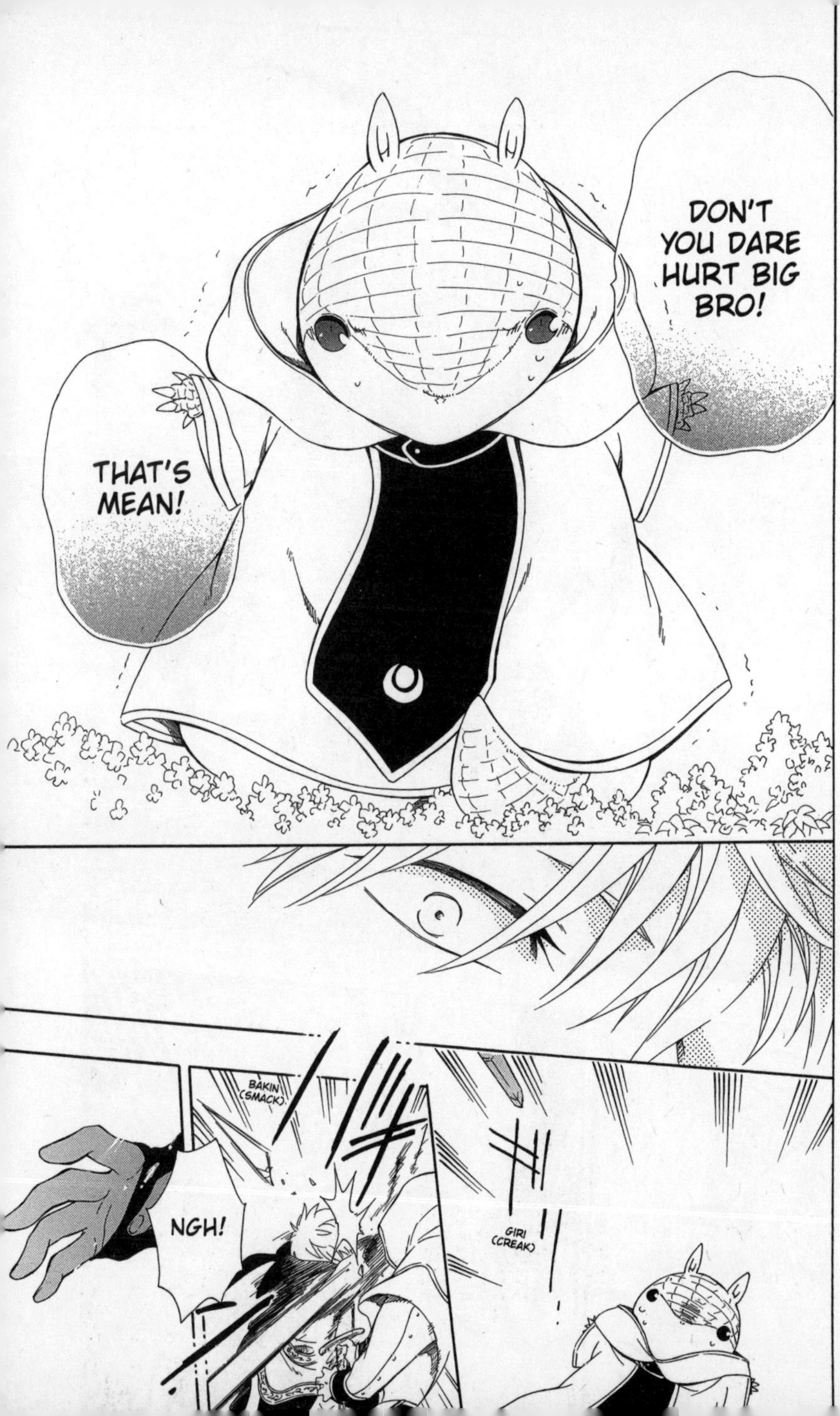
DON'T YOU DARE HURT BIG BRO!
THAT'S MEAN!
BAKIN (SMACK)
GIRI (CREAK)
NGH!

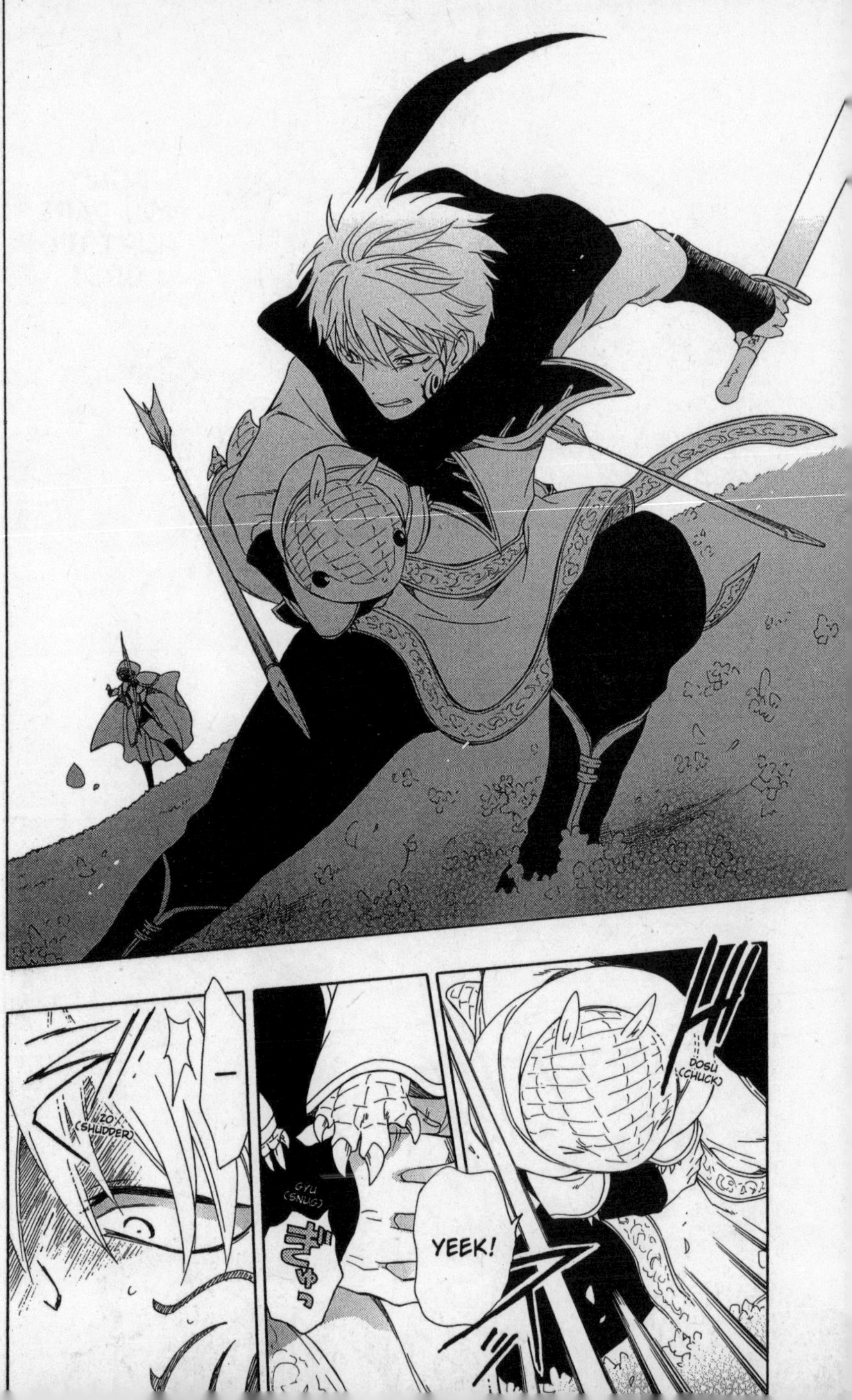
DOSU
(CHUCK)
GYU
(SNUG)
YEEK!
ZO
(SHUDDER)

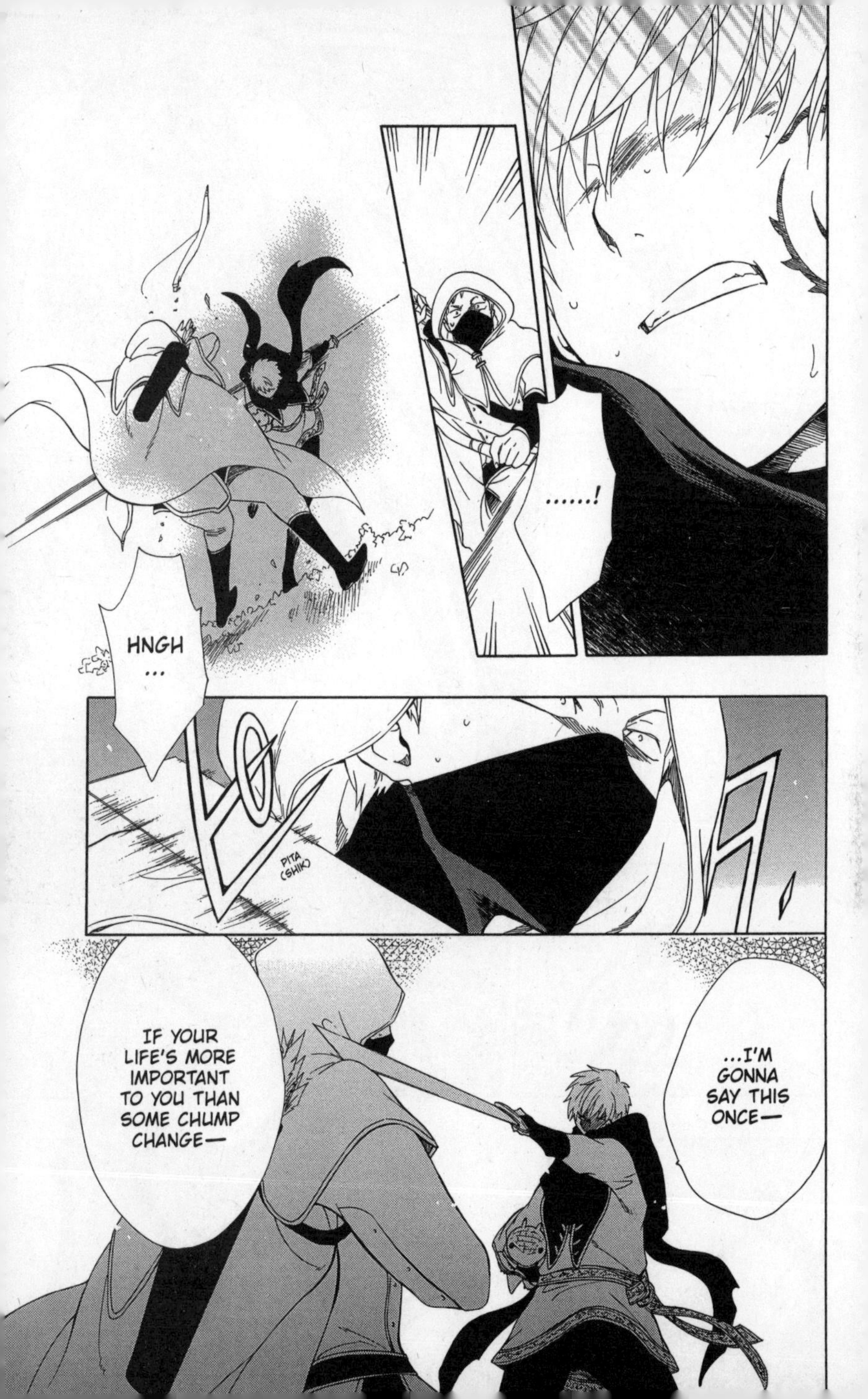
......!
HNGH ...
PITA (SHIK)
...I'M GONNA SAY THIS ONCE—
IF YOUR LIFE'S MORE IMPORTANT TO YOU THAN SOME CHUMP CHANGE—

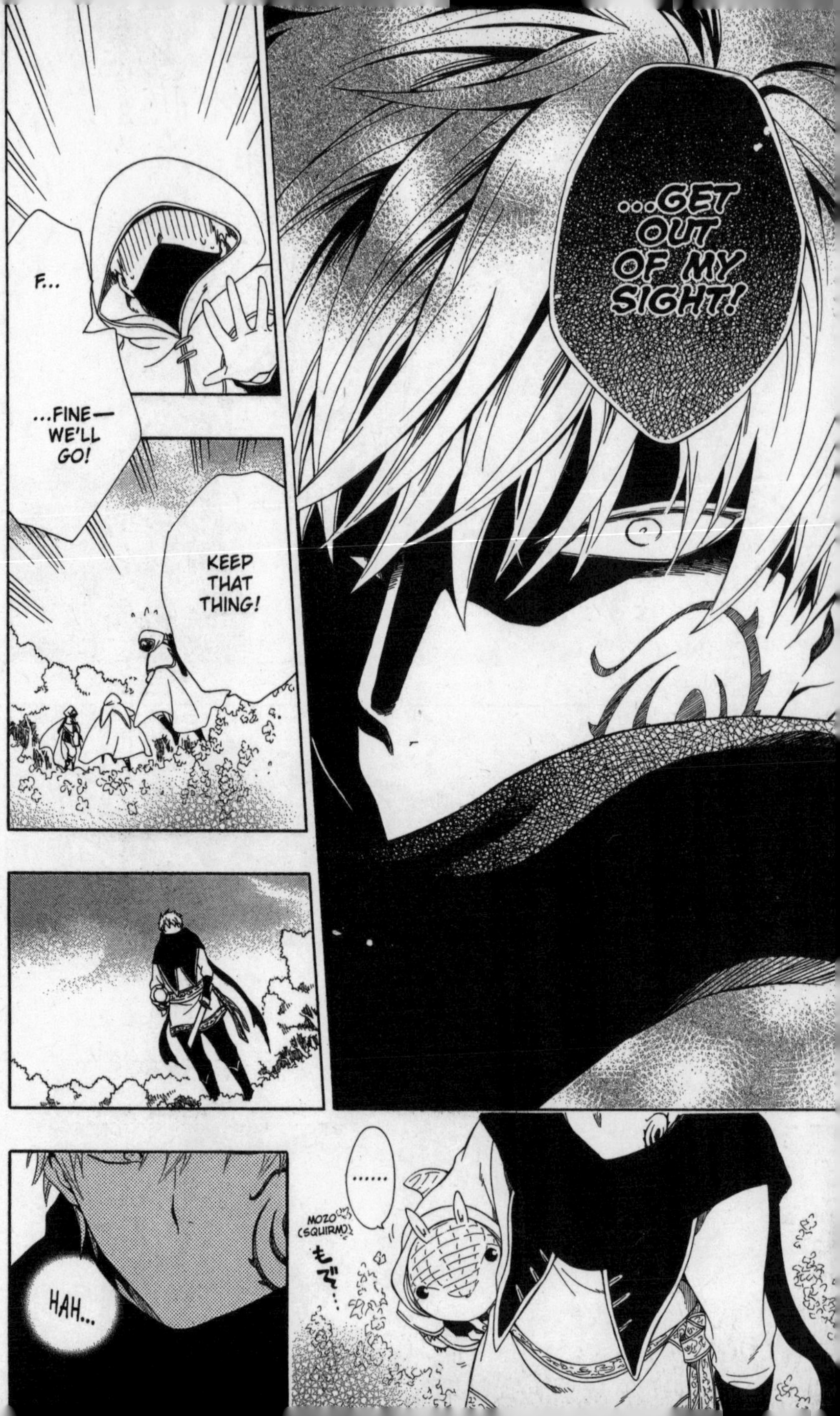
...GET OUT OF MY SIGHT!
F...
...FINE— WE'LL GO!
KEEP THAT THING!
......
MOZO (SQUIRM)
もぞ...
HAH...

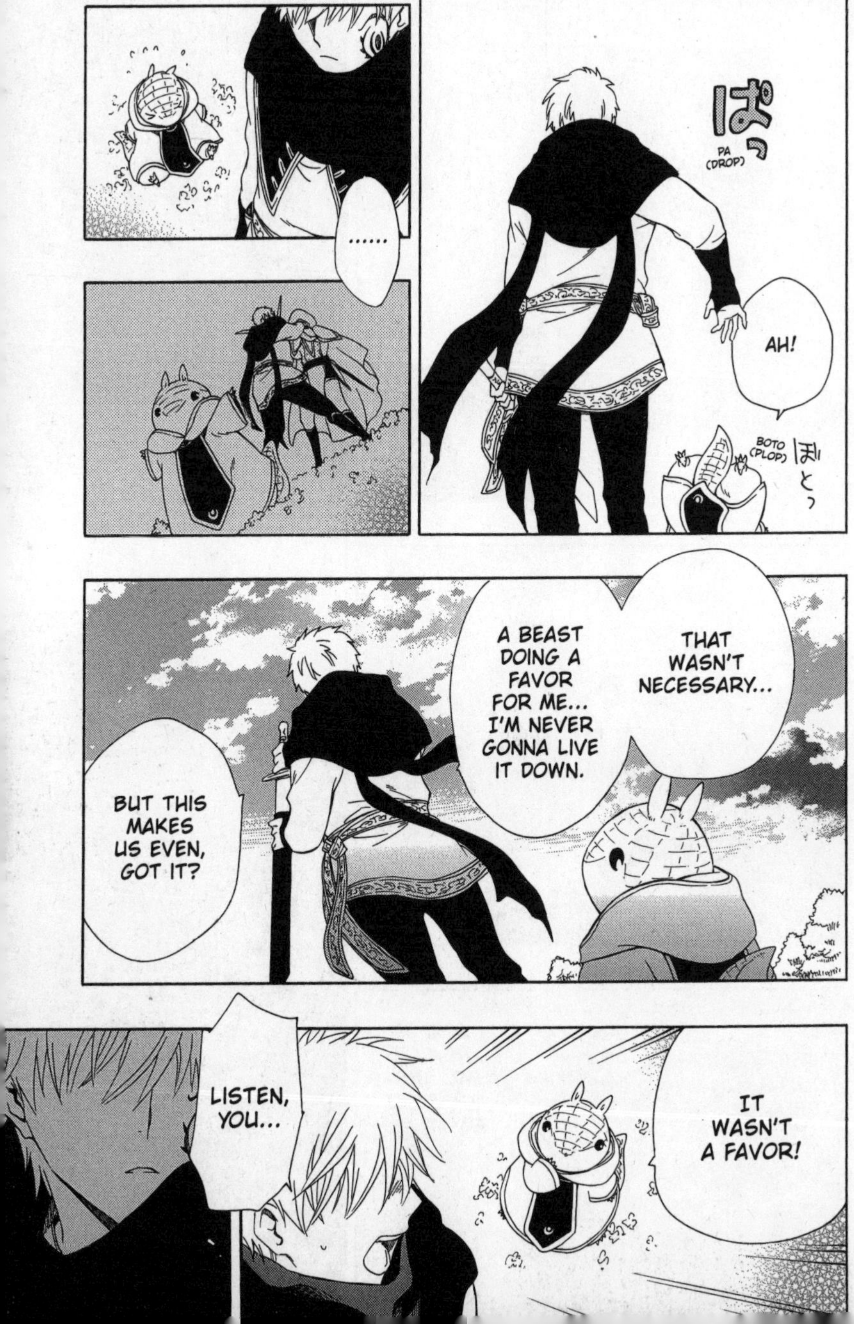
ぱっ
PA (DROP)
AH!
BOTO (PLOP)
ぼとっ
......
THAT WASN'T NECESSARY...
A BEAST DOING A FAVOR FOR ME... I'M NEVER GONNA LIVE IT DOWN.
BUT THIS MAKES US EVEN, GOT IT?
IT WASN'T A FAVOR!
LISTEN, YOU...

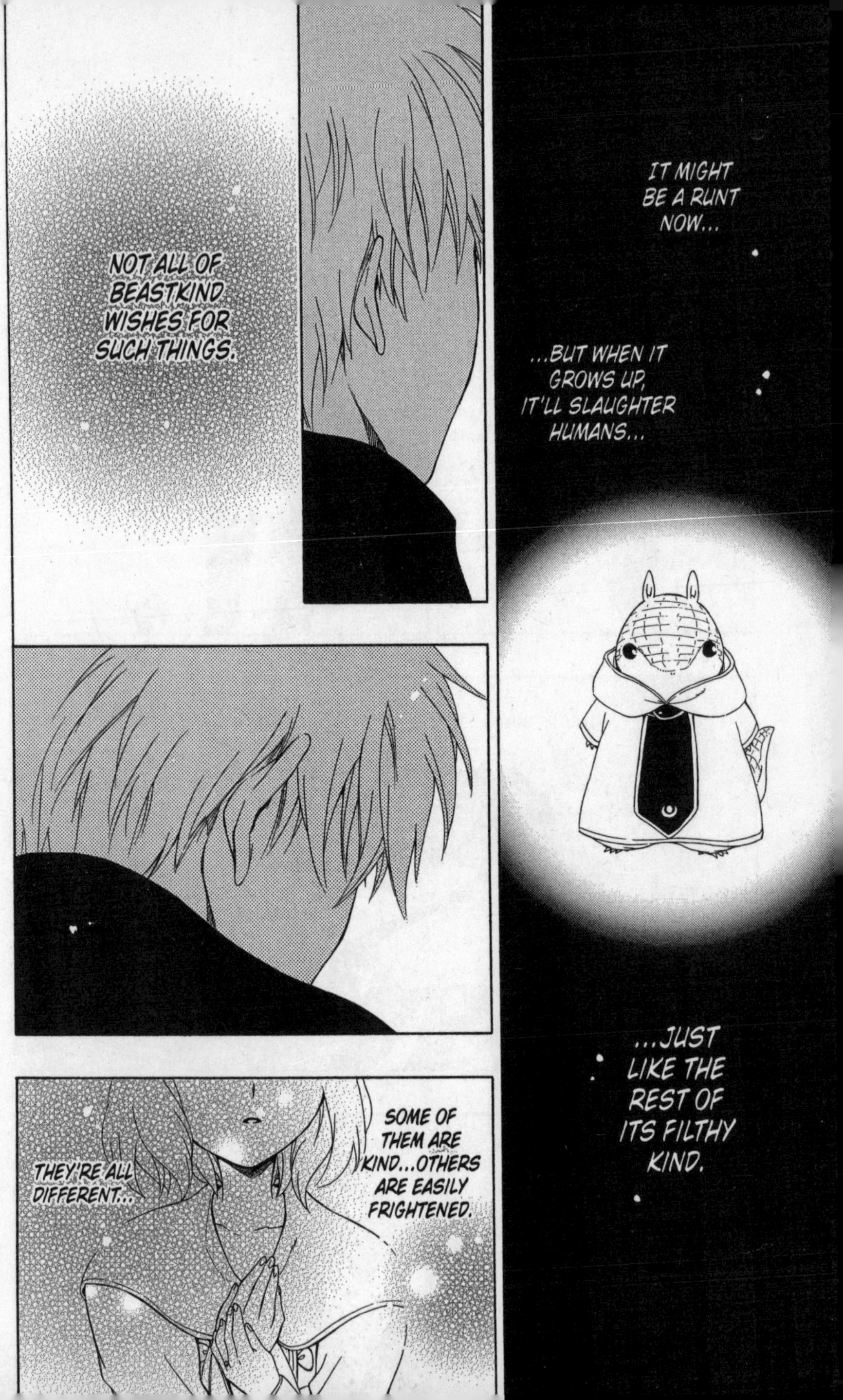
IT MIGHT BE A RUNT NOW...
...BUT WHEN IT GROWS UP, IT'LL SLAUGHTER HUMANS...
...JUST LIKE THE REST OF ITS FILTHY KIND.
NOT ALL OF BEASTKIND WISHES FOR SUCH THINGS.
SOME OF THEM ARE KIND...OTHERS ARE EASILY FRIGHTENED.
THEY'RE ALL DIFFERENT...

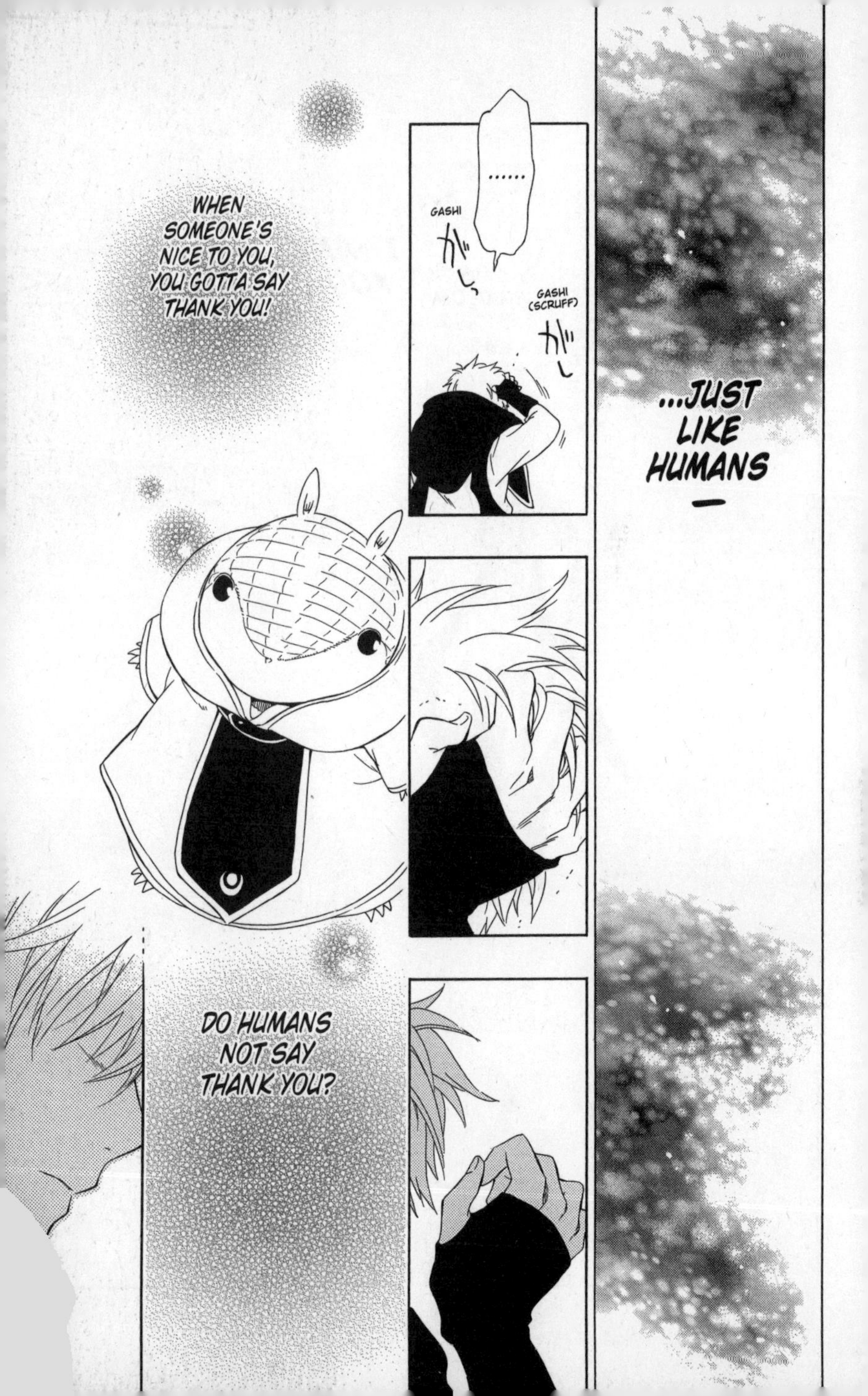

...JUST LIKE HUMANS —
......
GASHI
GASHI (SCRUFF)
WHEN SOMEONE'S NICE TO YOU, YOU GOTTA SAY THANK YOU!
DO HUMANS NOT SAY THANK YOU?

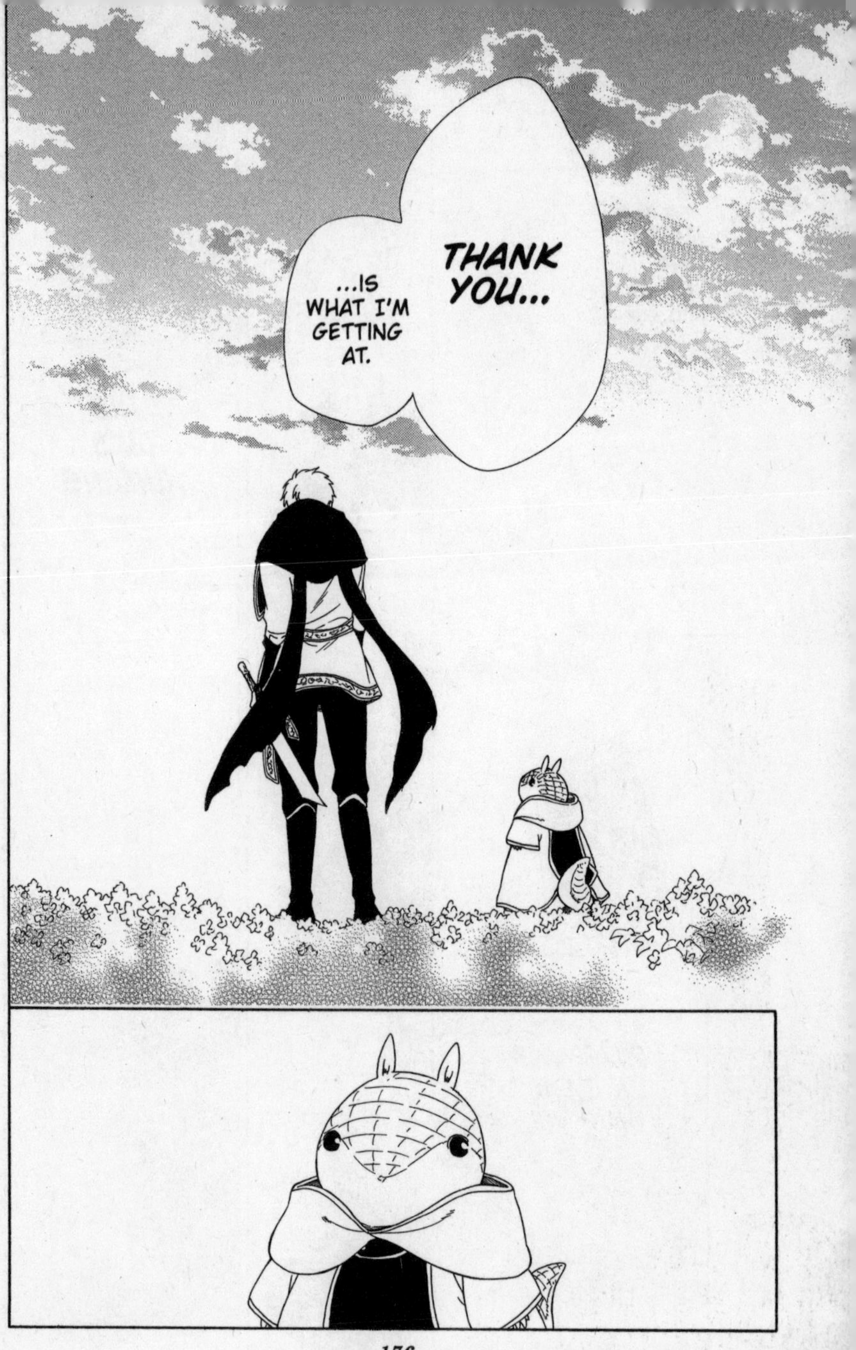
THANK YOU...
...IS WHAT I'M GETTING AT.

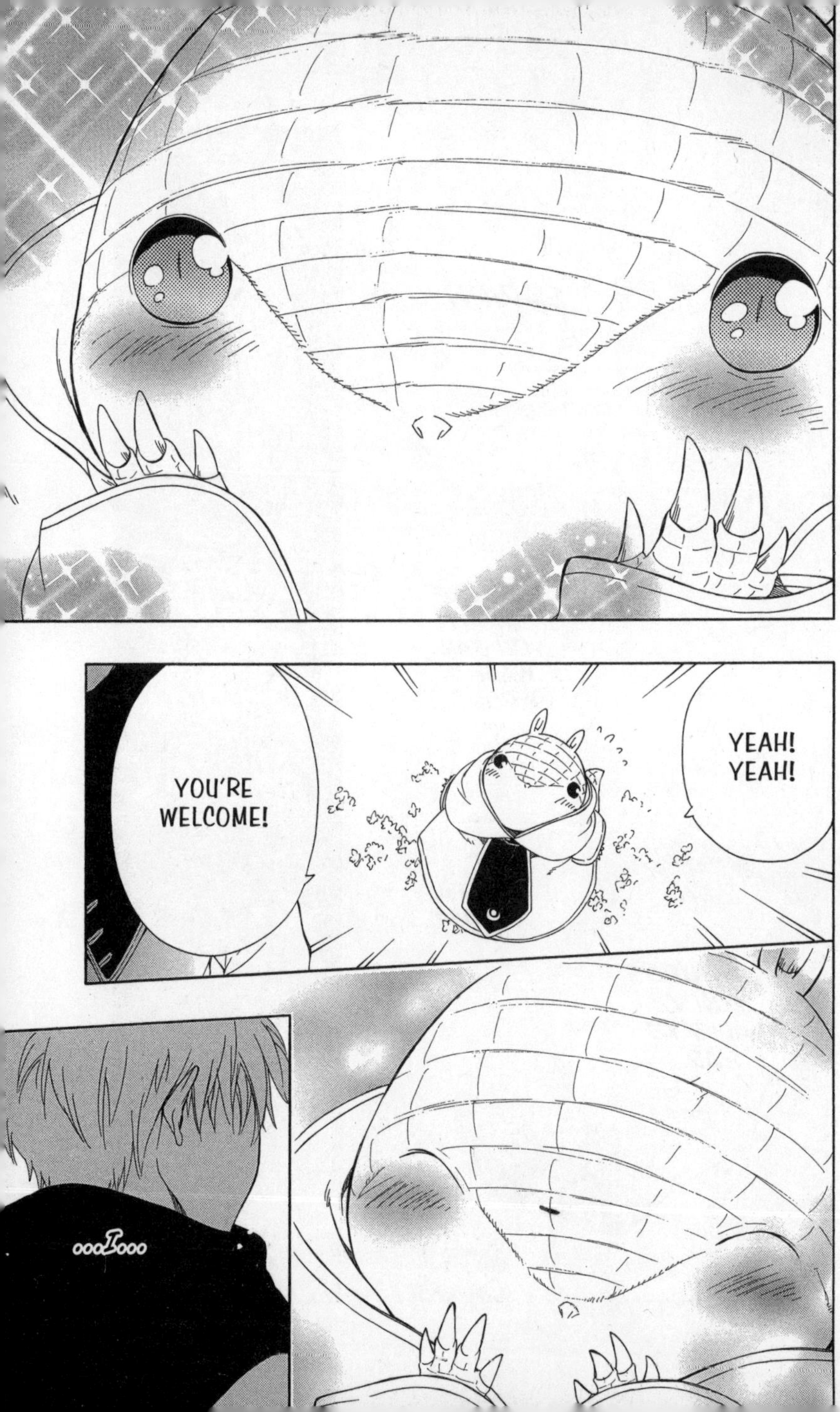
YEAH! YEAH!
YOU'RE WELCOME!
oooIooo

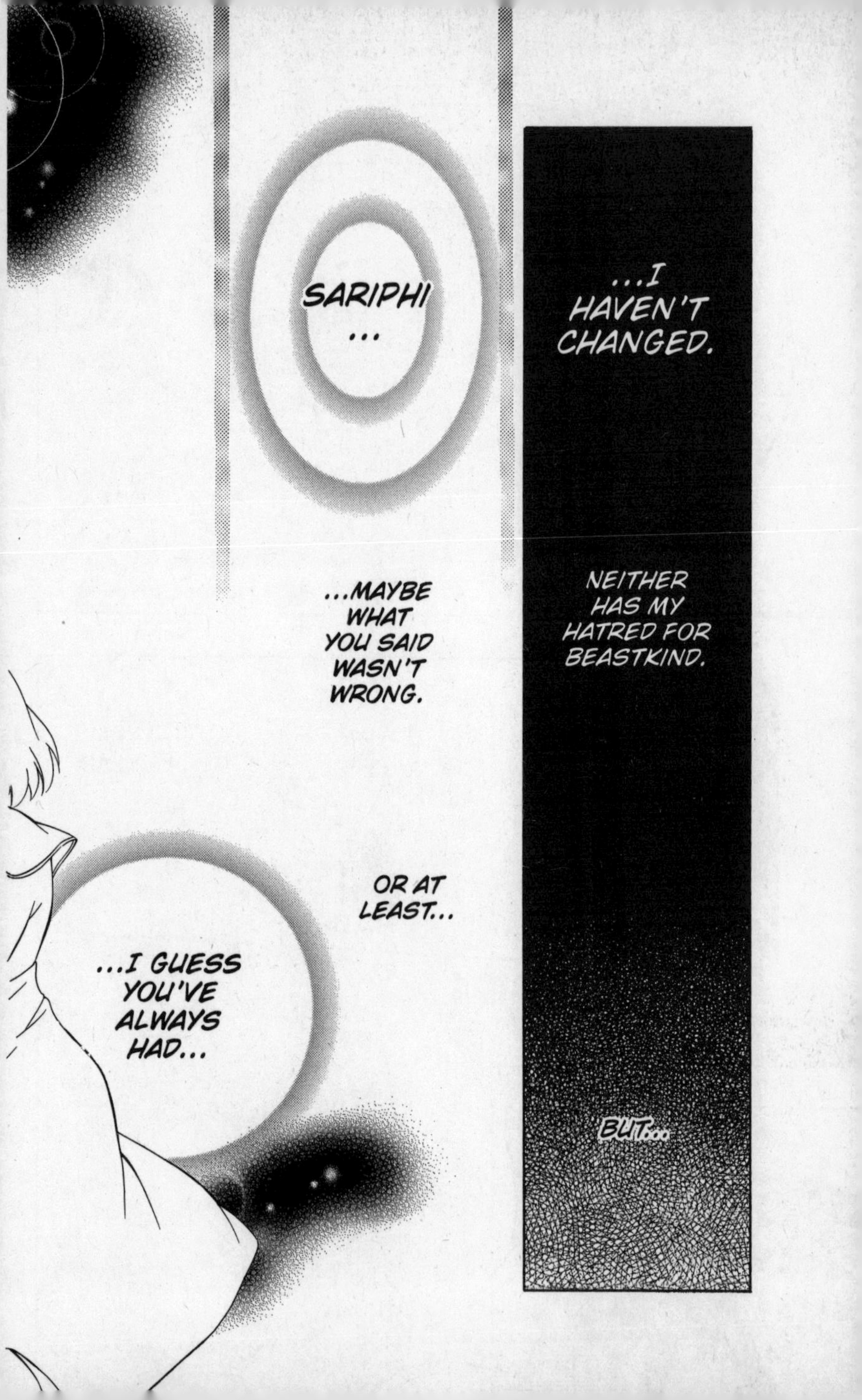
...I HAVEN'T CHANGED.
NEITHER HAS MY HATRED FOR BEASTKIND.
BUT...
SARIPHI...
...MAYBE WHAT YOU SAID WASN'T WRONG.
OR AT LEAST...
...I GUESS YOU'VE ALWAYS HAD...

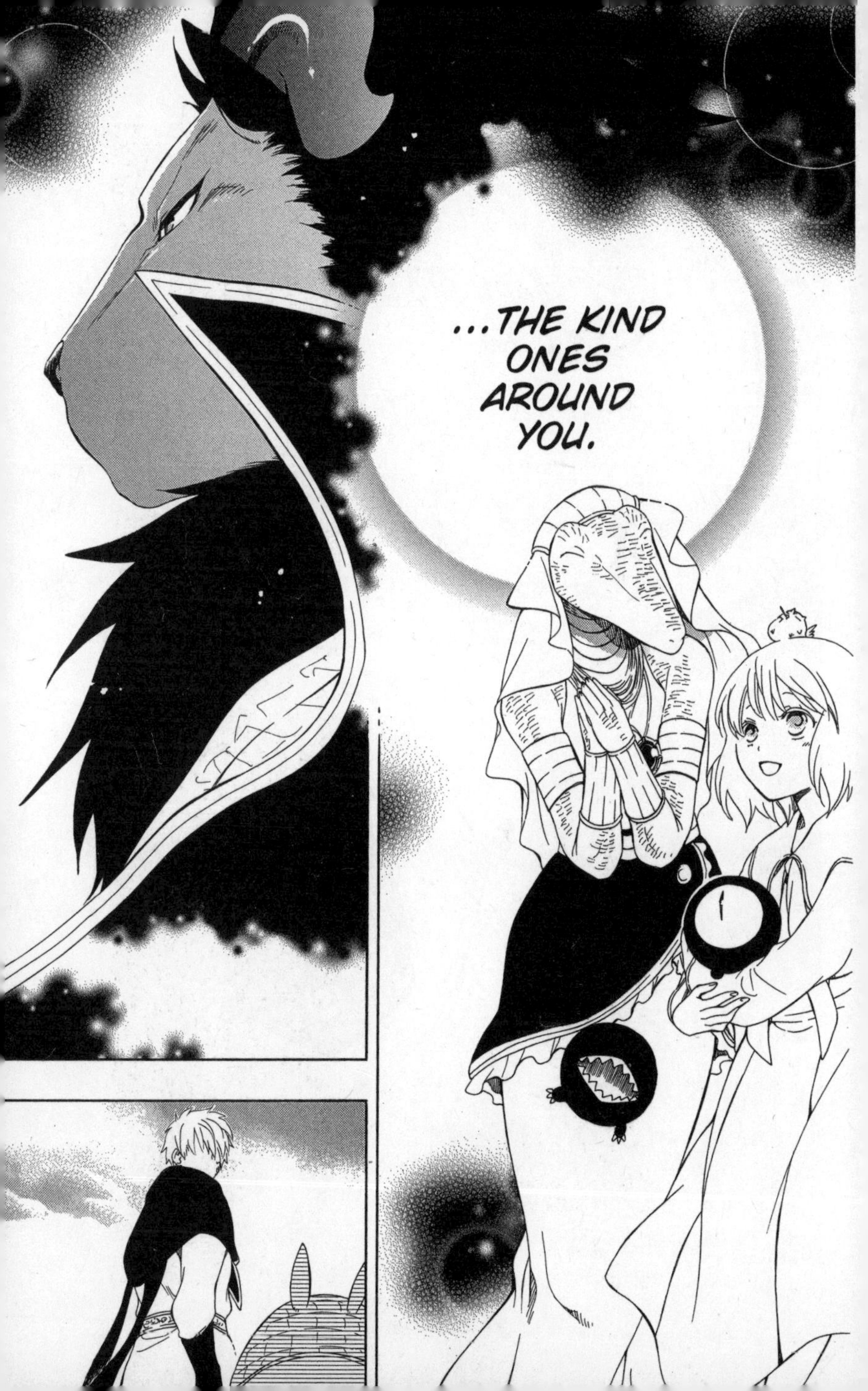
...THE KIND ONES AROUND YOU.

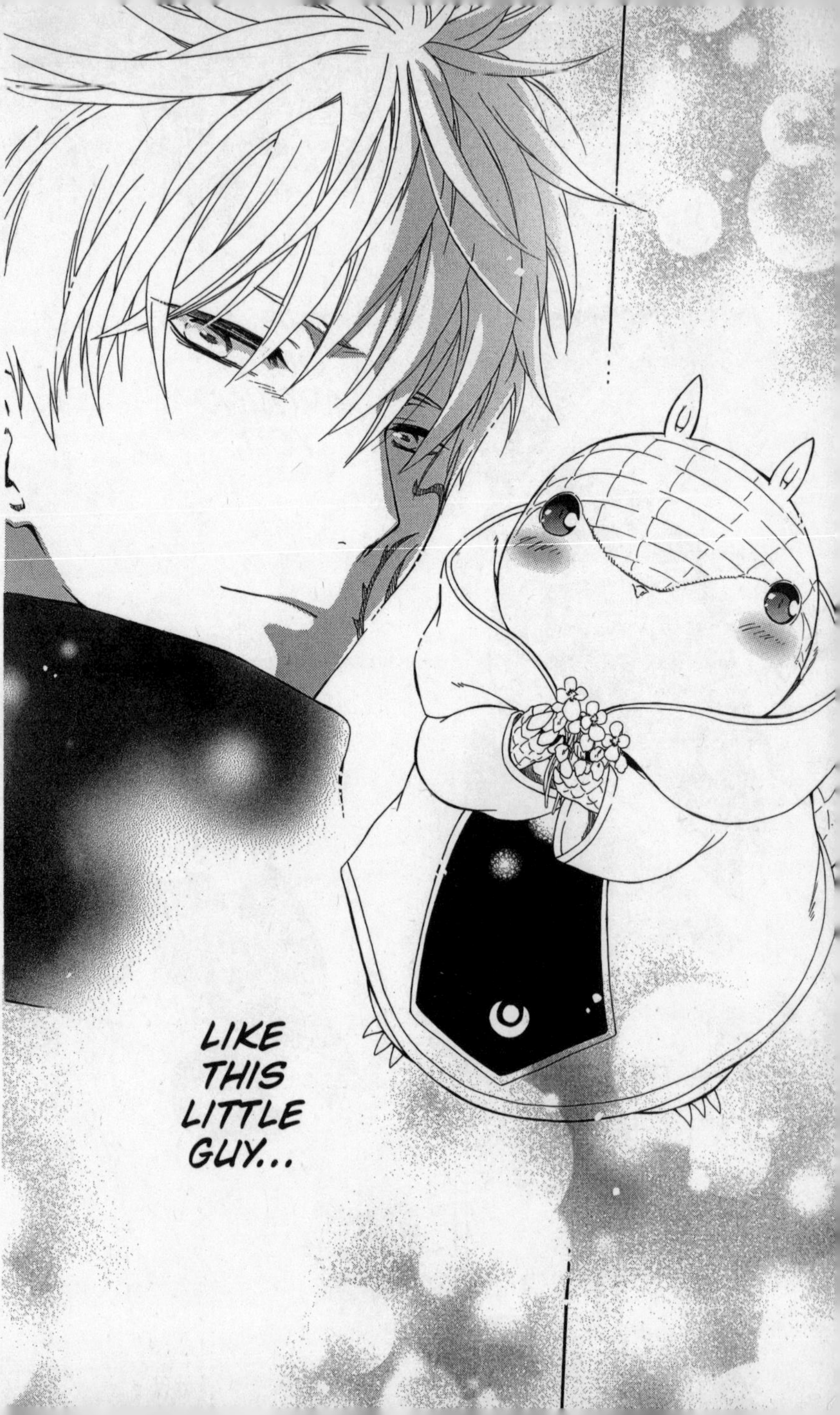
LIKE THIS LITTLE GUY...

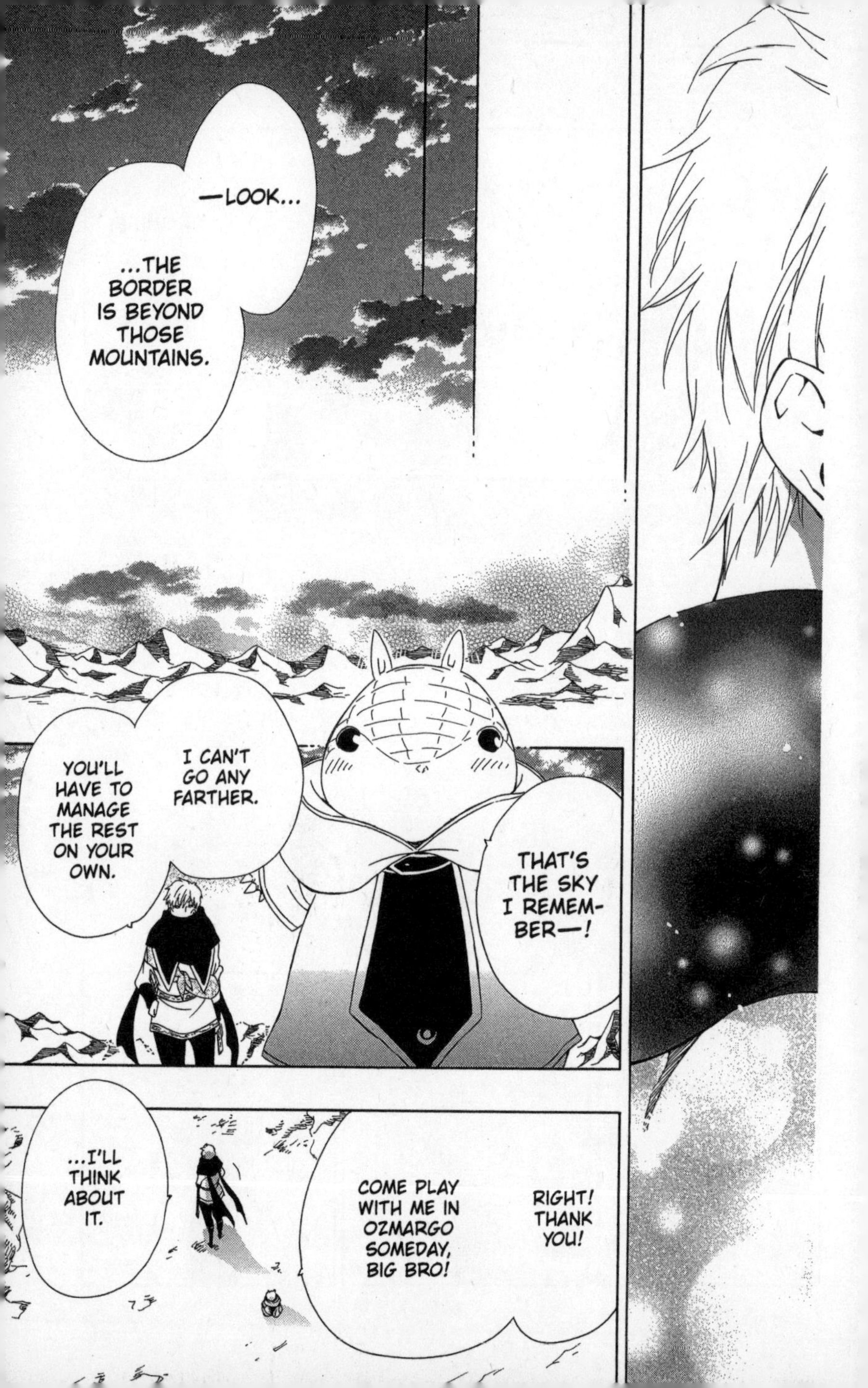

—LOOK...
...THE BORDER IS BEYOND THOSE MOUNTAINS.
THAT'S THE SKY I REMEM-BER—!
I CAN'T GO ANY FARTHER.
YOU'LL HAVE TO MANAGE THE REST ON YOUR OWN.
RIGHT! THANK YOU!
COME PLAY WITH ME IN OZMARGO SOMEDAY, BIG BRO!
...I'LL THINK ABOUT IT.

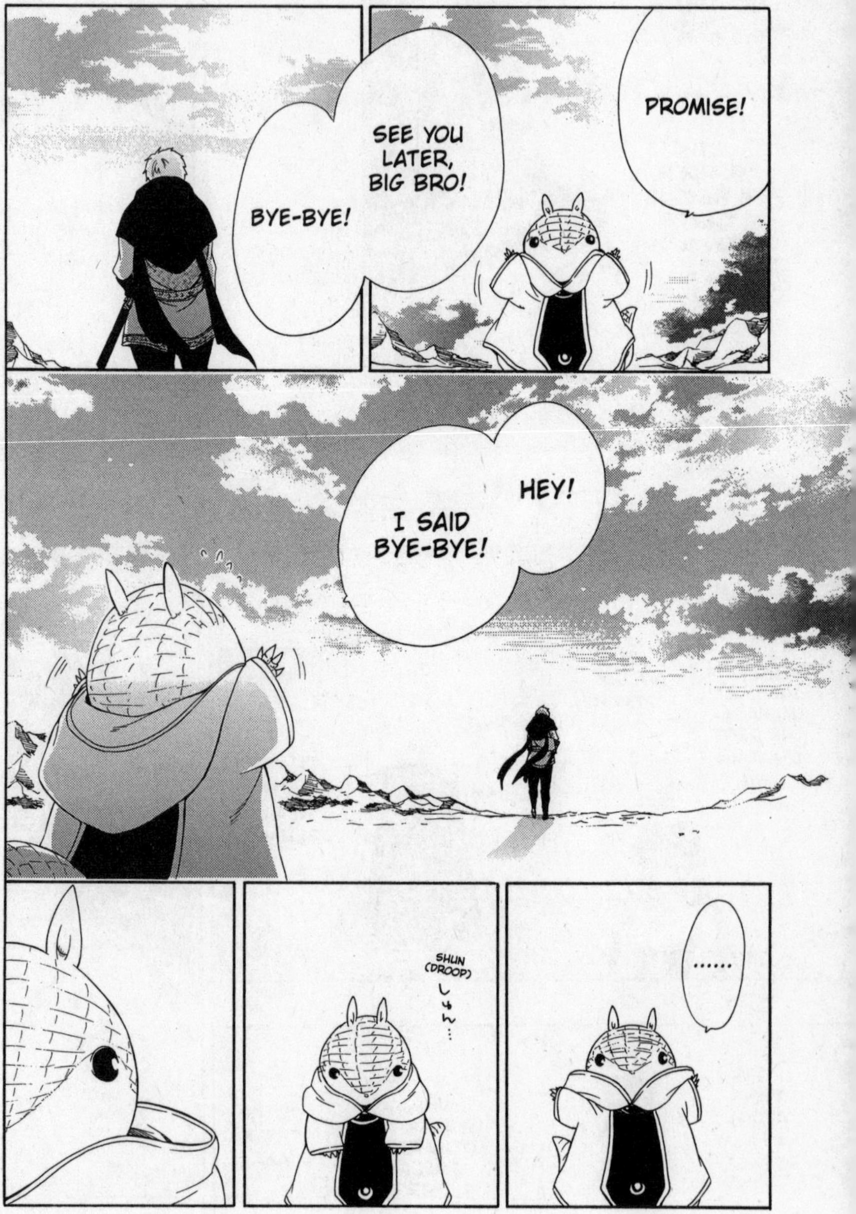

PROMISE!
SEE YOU LATER, BIG BRO!
BYE-BYE!
HEY!
I SAID BYE-BYE!
......
SHUN (DROOP)
しゅん…

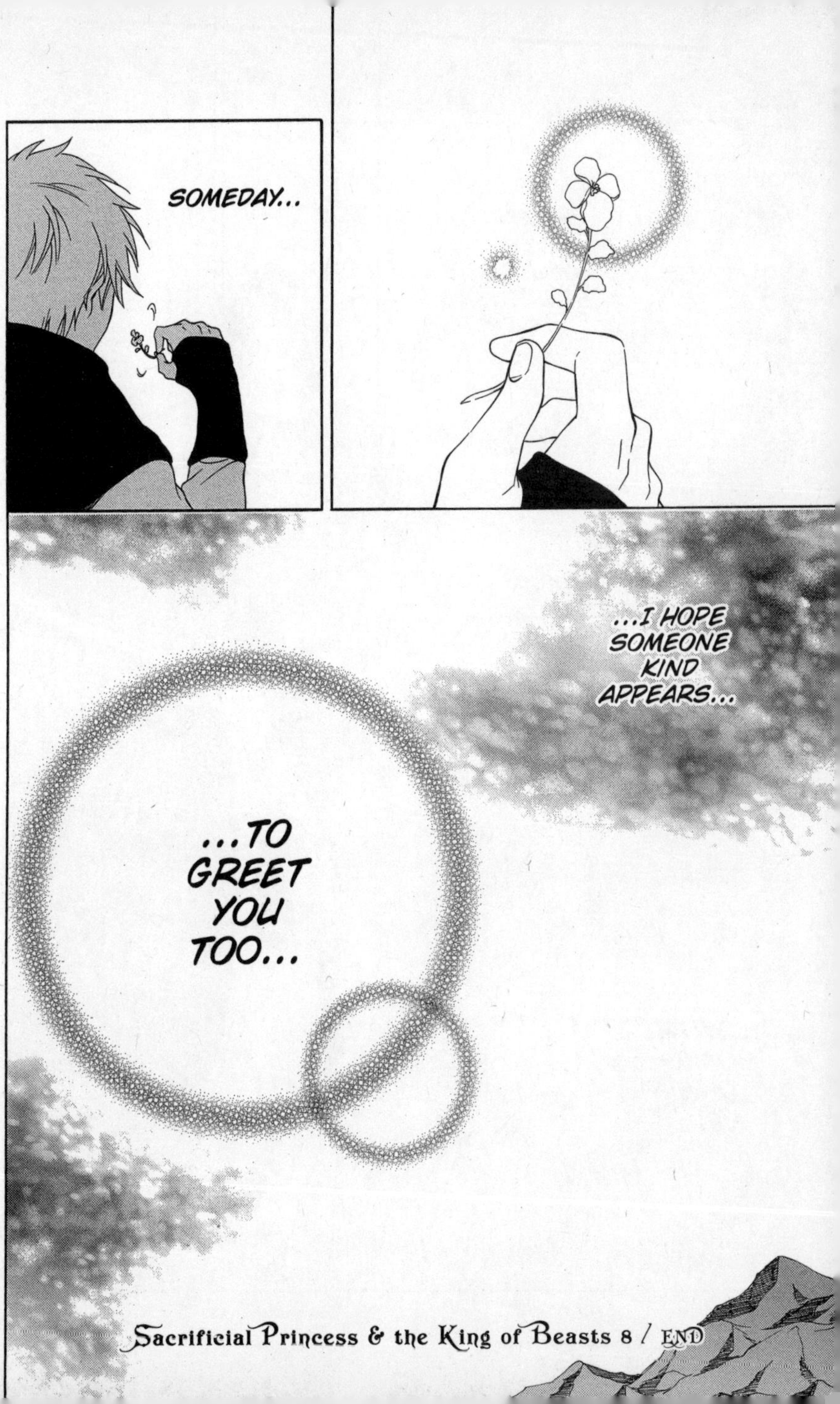
SOMEDAY...
...I HOPE SOMEONE KIND APPEARS...
...TO GREET YOU TOO...
Sacrificial Princess & the King of Beasts 8 / END

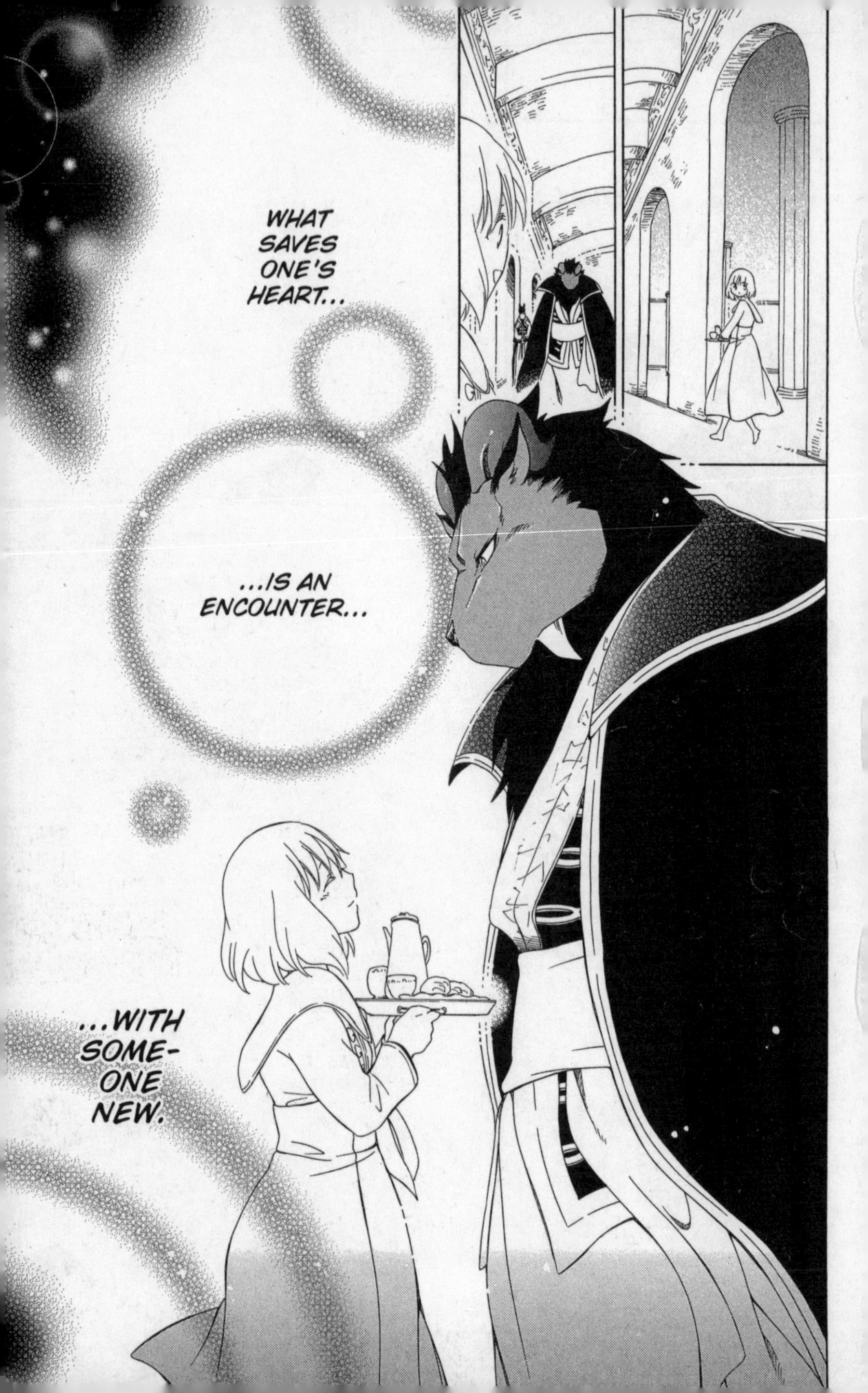
WHAT SAVES ONE'S HEART...
...IS AN ENCOUNTER...
...WITH SOME-ONE NEW.

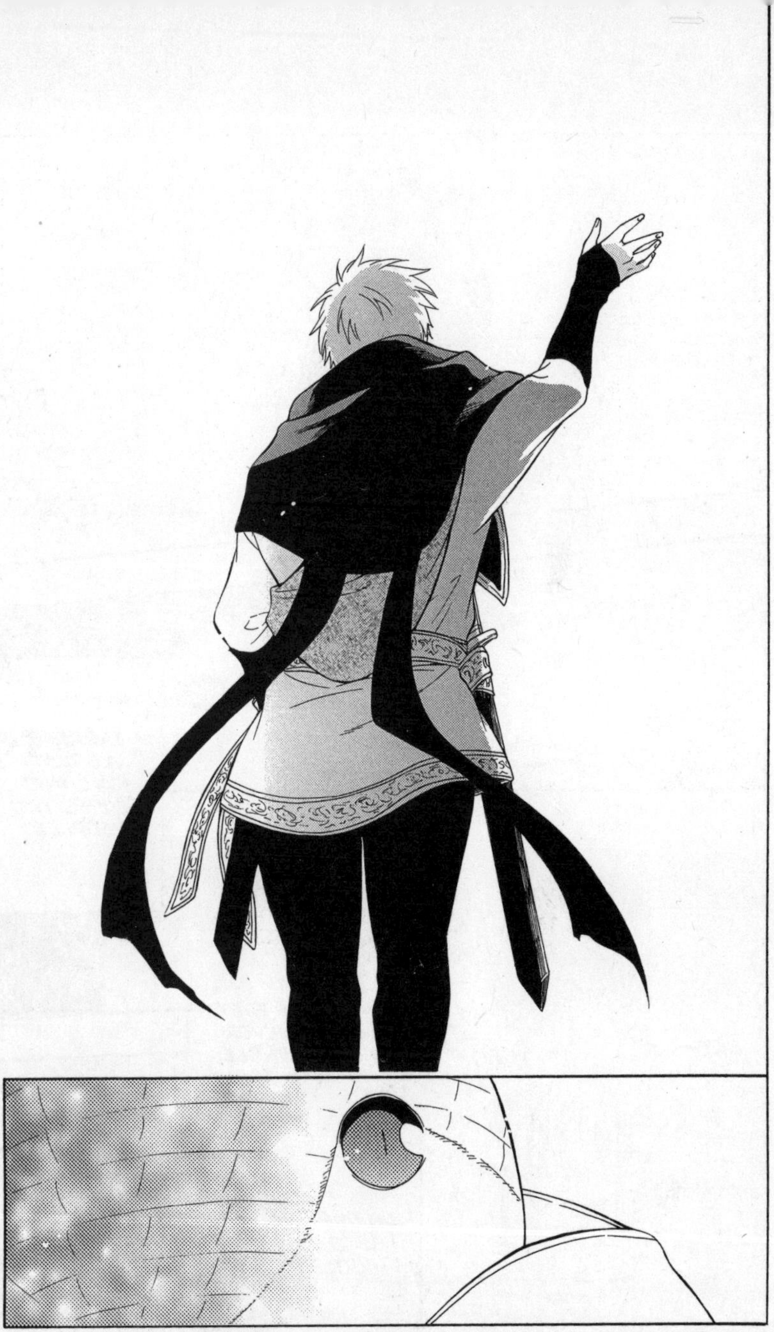

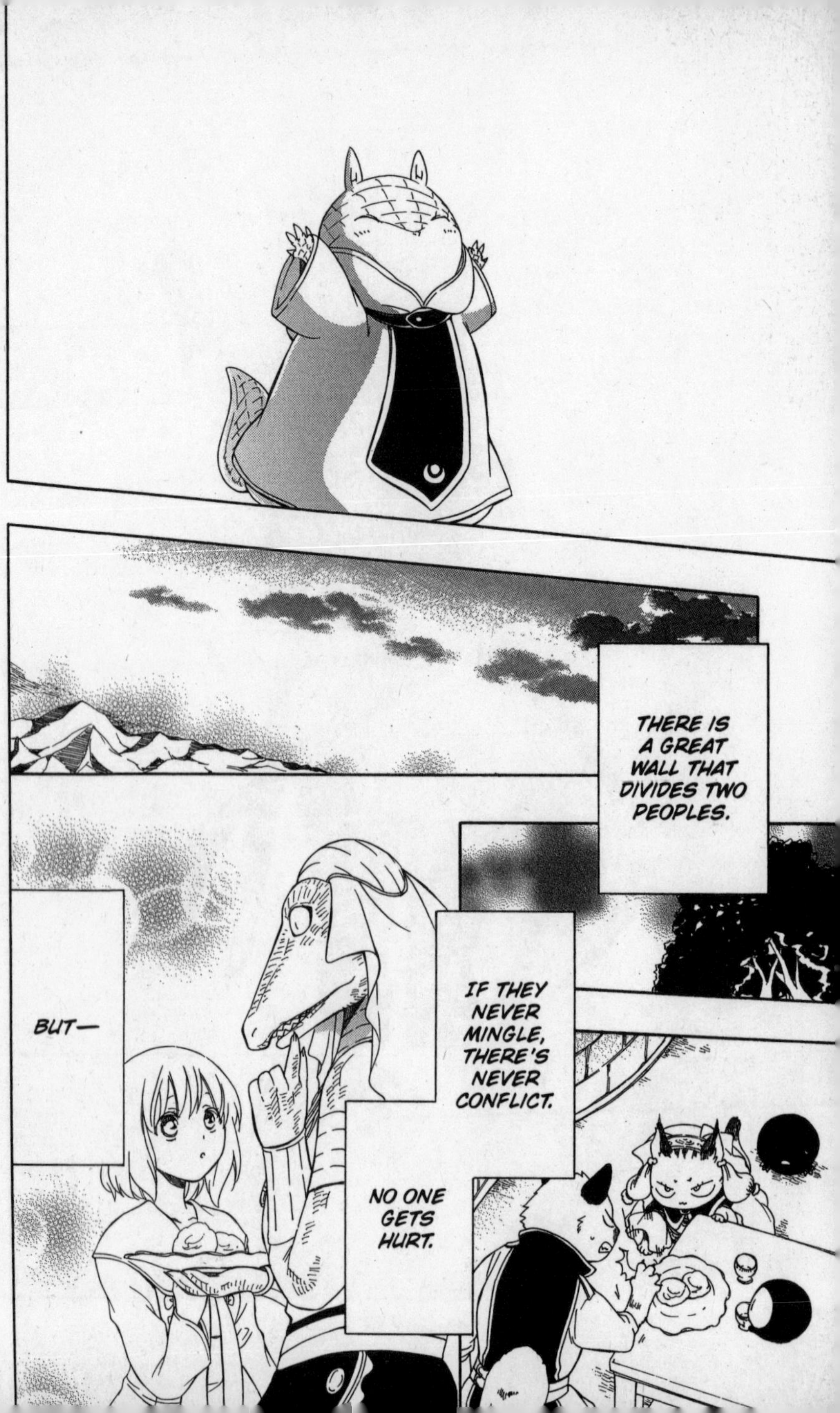
THERE IS A GREAT WALL THAT DIVIDES TWO PEOPLES.
IF THEY NEVER MINGLE, THERE'S NEVER CONFLICT.
NO ONE GETS HURT.
BUT—

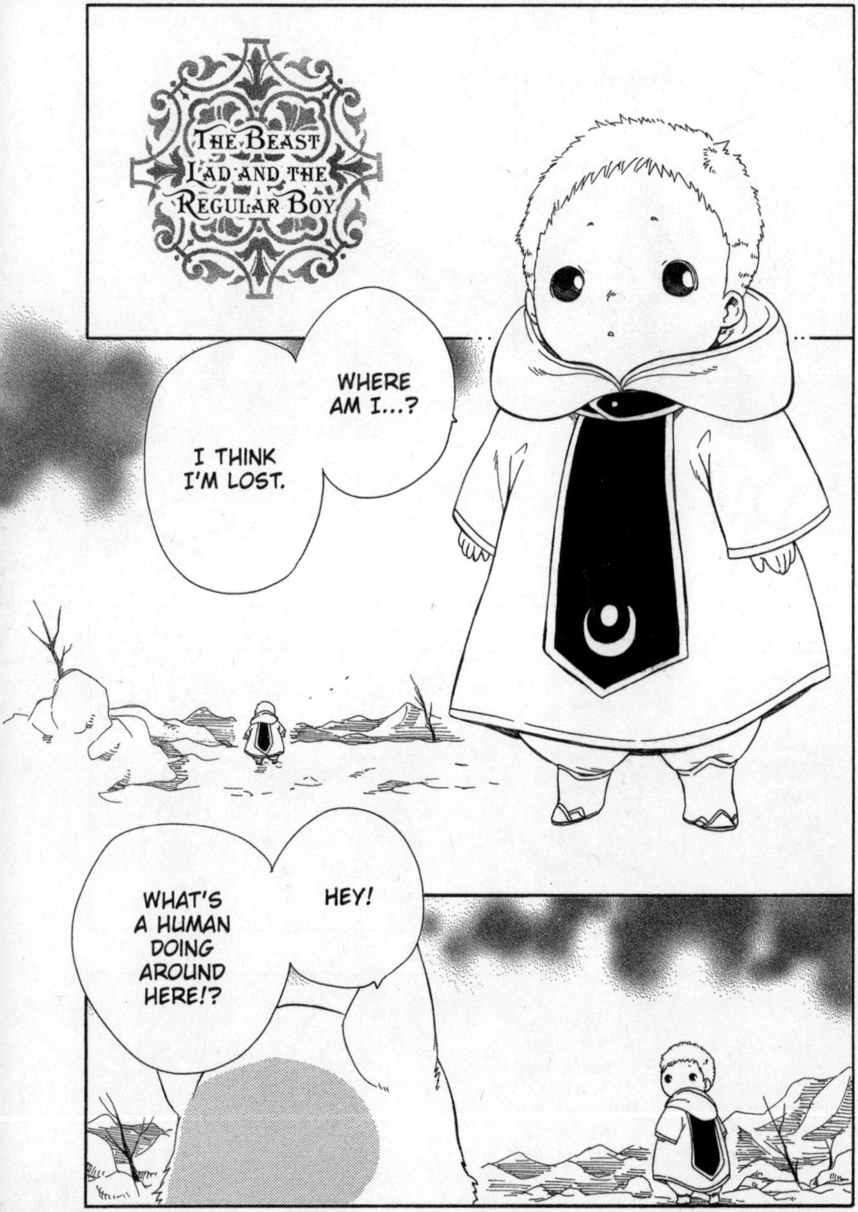
THE BEAST LAD AND THE REGULAR BOY
WHERE AM I...?
I THINK I'M LOST.
HEY!
WHAT'S A HUMAN DOING AROUND HERE!?

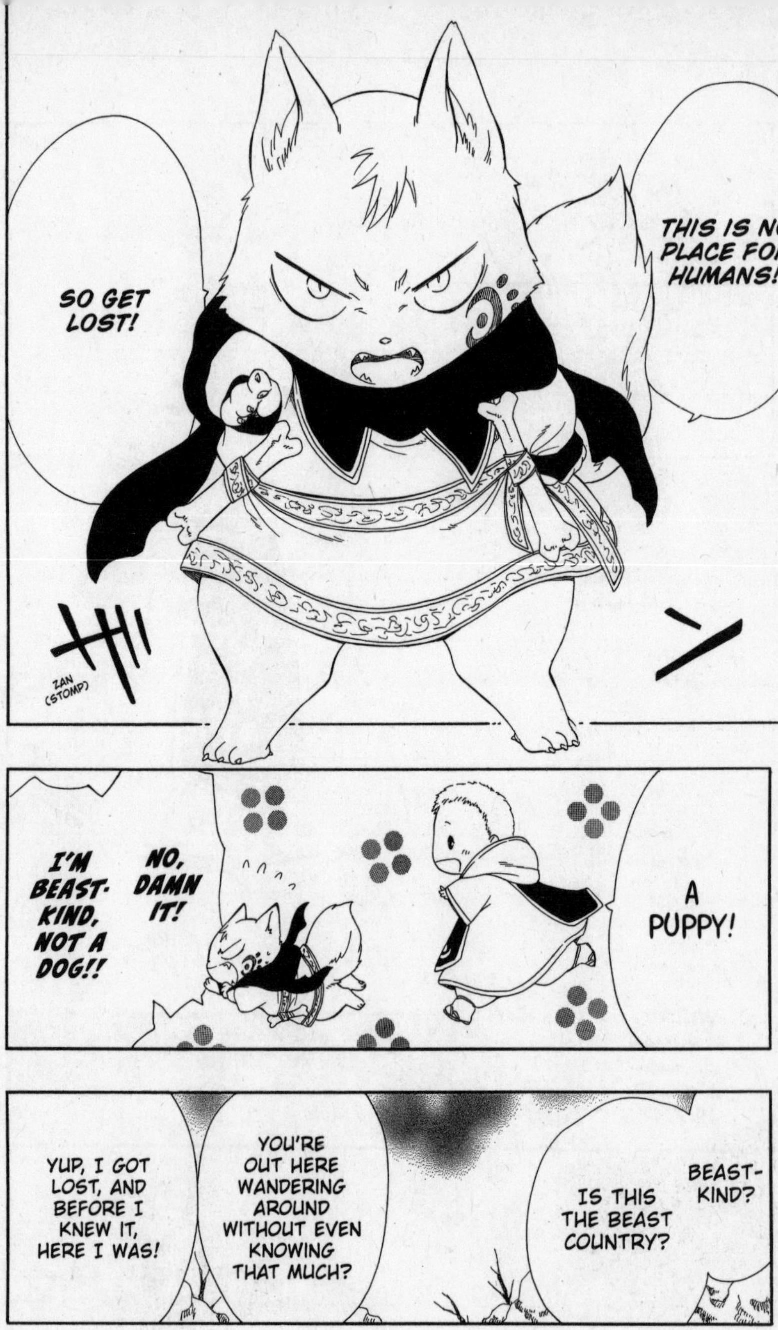
THIS IS NO PLACE FOR HUMANS!
SO GET LOST!
ZAN (STOMP)
A PUPPY!
NO, DAMN IT!
I'M BEAST-KIND, NOT A DOG!!
BEAST-KIND?
IS THIS THE BEAST COUNTRY?
YOU'RE OUT HERE WANDERING AROUND WITHOUT EVEN KNOWING THAT MUCH?
YUP, I GOT LOST, AND BEFORE I KNEW IT, HERE I WAS!

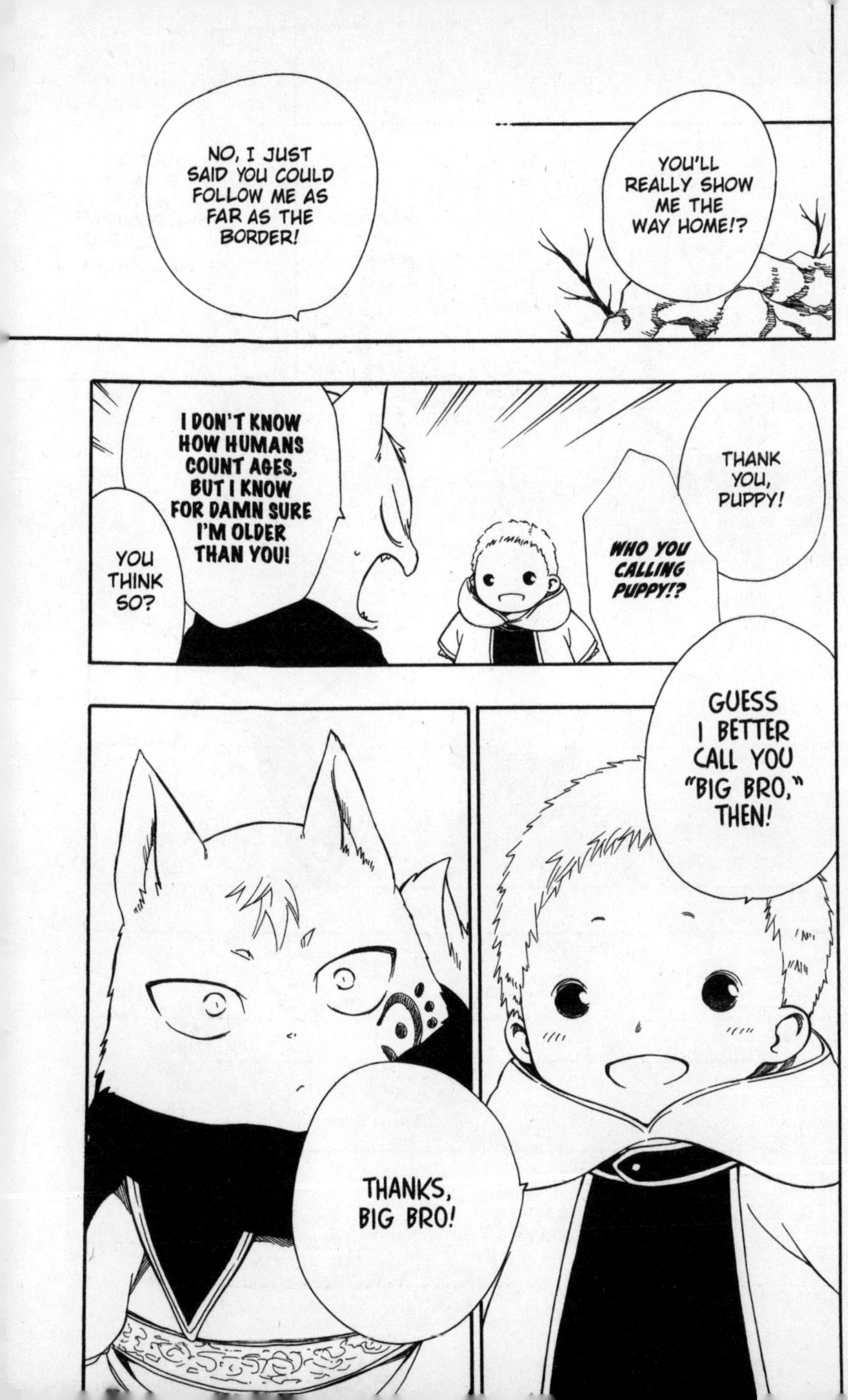
YOU'LL REALLY SHOW ME THE WAY HOME!?
NO, I JUST SAID YOU COULD FOLLOW ME AS FAR AS THE BORDER!
THANK YOU, PUPPY!
WHO YOU CALLING PUPPY!?
I DON'T KNOW HOW HUMANS COUNT AGES, BUT I KNOW FOR DAMN SURE I'M OLDER THAN YOU!
YOU THINK SO?
GUESS I BETTER CALL YOU "BIG BRO," THEN!
THANKS, BIG BRO!

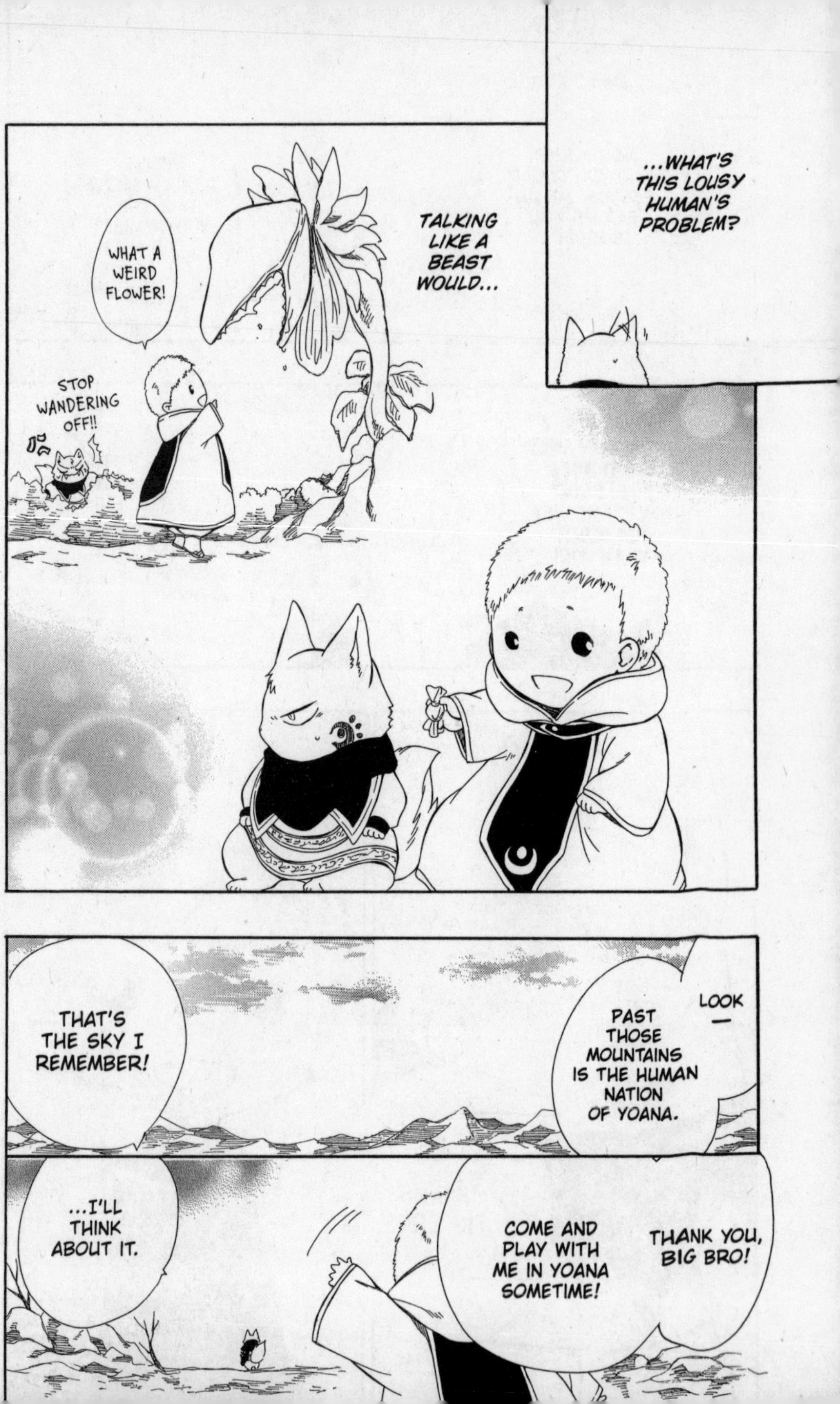
...WHAT'S THIS LOUSY HUMAN'S PROBLEM?
TALKING LIKE A BEAST WOULD...
WHAT A WEIRD FLOWER!
STOP WANDERING OFF!!
LOOK—
PAST THOSE MOUNTAINS IS THE HUMAN NATION OF YOANA.
THAT'S THE SKY I REMEMBER!
THANK YOU, BIG BRO!
COME AND PLAY WITH ME IN YOANA SOMETIME!
...I'LL THINK ABOUT IT.

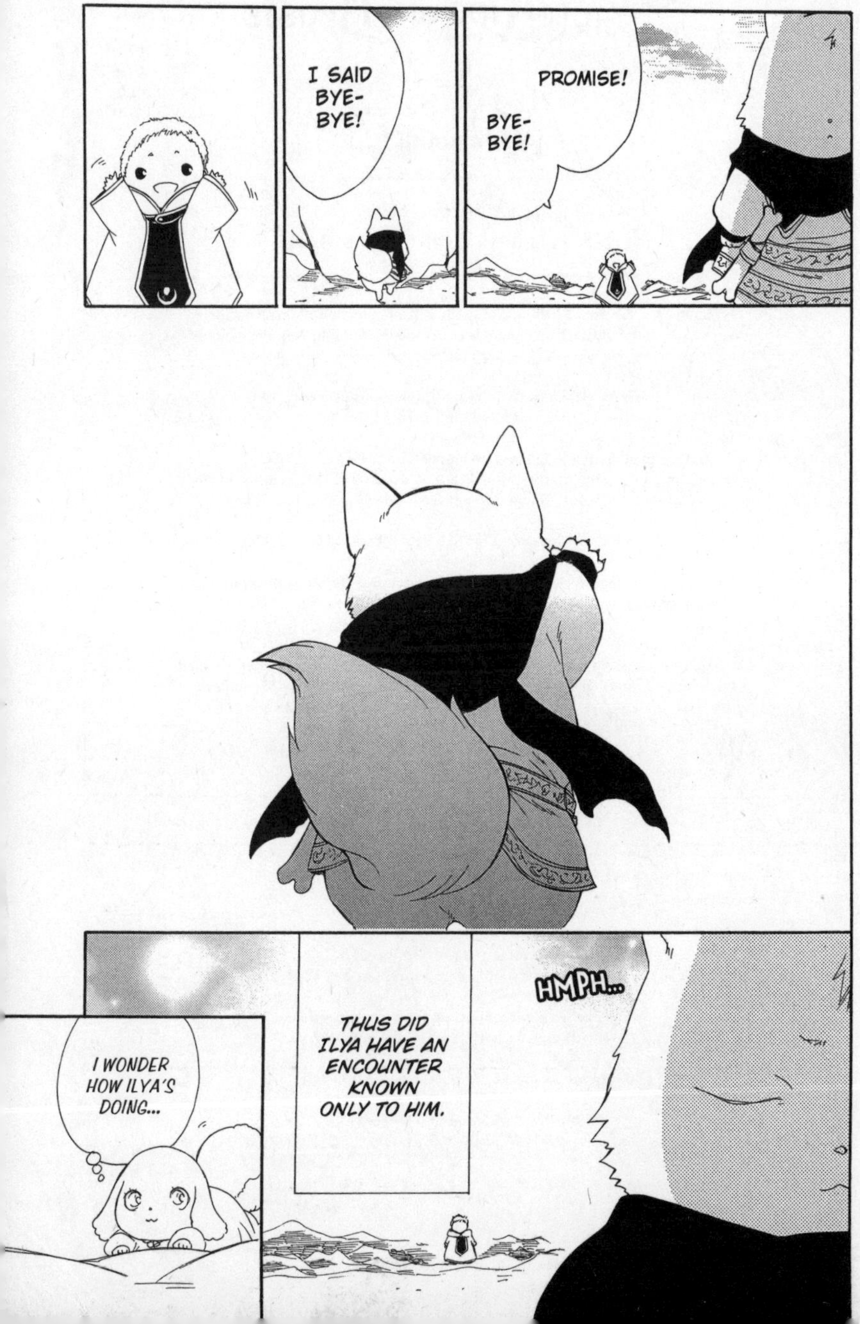
PROMISE!
BYE-BYE!
I SAID BYE-BYE!
HMPH...
THUS DID ILYA HAVE AN ENCOUNTER KNOWN ONLY TO HIM.
I WONDER HOW ILYA'S DOING...

SACRIFICIAL PRINCESS AND THE King of Beasts

Yu Tomofuji

TRANSLATION: Paul Starr

LETTERING: Lys Blakeslee and Katie Blakeslee

This book is a work of fiction. Names, characters, places, and incidents are the product of the author's imagination or are used fictitiously. Any resemblance to actual events, locales, or persons, living or dead, is coincidental.

NIEHIME TO KEMONO NO OH by Yu Tomofuji
© Yu Tomofuji 2018
All rights reserved.
First published in Japan in 2018 by HAKUSENSHA, Inc., Tokyo.
English language translation rights in U.S.A., Canada and U.K. arranged with HAKUSENSHA, Inc., Tokyo through Tuttle-Mori Agency, Inc., Tokyo.

English translation © 2019 by Yen Press, LLC

Yen Press, LLC supports the right to free expression and the value of copyright. The purpose of copyright is to encourage writers and artists to produce the creative works that enrich our culture.

The scanning, uploading, and distribution of this book without permission is a theft of the author's intellectual property. If you would like permission to use material from the book (other than for review purposes), please contact the publisher. Thank you for your support of the author's rights.

Yen Press
150 West 30th Street, 19th Floor
New York, NY 10001

Visit us at yenpress.com ✦ facebook.com/yenpress ✦ twitter.com/yenpress
yenpress.tumblr.com ✦ instagram.com/yenpress

First Yen Press Edition: December 2019

Yen Press is an imprint of Yen Press, LLC.
The Yen Press name and logo are trademarks of Yen Press, LLC.

The publisher is not responsible for websites (or their content) that are not owned by the publisher.

Library of Congress Control Number: 2018930817

ISBNs: 978-1-9753-0443-0 (paperback)
978-1-9753-0444-7 (ebook)

10 9 8 7 6 5 4 3 2 1

BVG

Printed in the United States of America